JAKE WALK

WHITE LIGHTNING, BOOK 4

DEBRA DUNBAR

J.P. SLOAN

debra dunbar
FIENDISHLY FUN FICTION

CHAPTER 1

FEBRUARY 1927

*H*attie jolted awake as the front tires of the Studebaker hammered a pothole uncovered by the early thaw. Rubbing her eyes, she blinked at the faint predawn light outlining the hills surrounding Cumberland, Maryland.

"Good morning," Sadie muttered.

Hattie stretched and turned to check the two girls in the back seat. They were awake, but only just barely.

"We're here?" Hattie asked.

Sadie lifted a hand off the wheel to point to a rail station tucked alongside the North Branch of the Potomac. "That's the one."

"Morning already, though," Hattie said. "Weren't we supposed to arrive in the cover of night?"

"That was the plan," Sadie replied through tight lips.

Hattie turned again to spy the two cars behind them. "Slow going?"

"If you'd stayed awake, you'd know."

Hattie winced. "Aye, sorry 'bout that. I've been sleeping for shite, lately."

"We'll both sleep better once we get these children moving west." Sadie set the brake and climbed out of the sedan.

This caravan of Charge refugees had weighed heavily on the woman, that much was clear to Hattie. They'd lost contact with the last two groups moving over rail to the promised land in Utah, a patch of unspoiled American West they'd come to refer to as Eden. The money they'd nicked from the gangsters at the Ithaca facility was supposed to change everything. Make it easier to ferret these free pinchers to the safety of Eden. And it had, in fact, helped. This brand-new Studebaker was a big part of that.

But greasing palms and paying for transport didn't mean someone wasn't selling them out somewhere along the line. It didn't ease the fact that once these people, most of them children, got on the train, they were out of her and Sadie's hands, vulnerable to being snatched up for a profit.

Although it wasn't just the trials and travails of the Charge that had robbed Hattie of sleep as of late. It was the parade of harrowing dreams that had plagued her mind each night. Dreams of fire and demons. Of hooded-eyed Saracens wielding evil magics.

Of the day they'd finally face the Hell pincher.

The two cars behind them parked next to a B&O boxcar. Hattie stepped into the crisp morning air, her breath misting around her face as the dusting of snow on the nearby hills began to reflect the morning light into the rail yard. She reached inside the car for Sadie's thermos. A cup of coffee was what she needed to shake off the cobwebs.

Two girls stepped out of the back seat. They were thin and quiet, long ponytails of braided red hair dropping from the sides of their heads. Hattie held up the thermos.

"You girls need something warm?"

They shook their heads almost in unison, saying nothing. They were a quiet pair, these two. Much like their father.

Hattie searched the rear car as its occupants emerged. Charley wove through the free pinchers to trot up to his girls, scooping them in his gangly arms.

"You two been good?" he whispered.

Again, they nodded in unison.

Charley offered Hattie a demure smile. "Thank you."

Hattie patted Charley's arm. She'd wanted more than anything to at least get the girls to smile. But that was perhaps asking too much. After all, they'd lost their mother in birthing the youngest, and then their father to Ithaca. Hattie had returned their father to them, but he was a ghost of the man he once was thanks to the ministrations of those beasts in Ithaca. And he'd been gone for over a year of their young lives. Who was this haggard, bearded fellow suddenly uprooting them to move west? Alas, there was little choice. Charley's sister-in-law had been their caretaker in his absence, but she'd needed to move to a care facility for consumption. Fate had not been kind to this family, to be sure.

Sadie rounded the Studebaker and began barking marching orders, hustling her Charge into action. She kept eyeing the line of morning light on the hills as it crept lower and lower toward the rail yard.

"Alright, everyone has their partners?" She began counting the free pinchers into pairs, or a trio in Charley's case.

Hattie helped Charley open the boxcar. They jumped backward as a pair of smelly hoboes eyed them from inside, fists lifted.

"Oy!" Hattie bellowed. "You lot! Out!"

The vagrants refused to move. One of them reached for a walking stick, slowly lifting it to brandish as a weapon.

Sadie marched up, face twisted in frustration. "What's the hubbub?" She looked inside the car, then sighed. "This is perfect."

Hattie ran several illusions through her head to chase off the men, but Sadie hopped up into the car with a deft jump and thrust her hands onto her hips.

"Okay, listen up fellas. We bought this boxcar last month. I have some people gonna travel with you. These people are more than capable of shellacking your asses if you give them so much as a curly eyebrow. So. We gonna play nice here? Or do I need to get physical?"

The hobo with the stick set it onto the floor beside him, and replied with a thick thick accent, "Listen, lady. Don't want no fight here. As long as you ain't got no bulls we ain't got no beef."

Sadie lifted a hand. "Fine. Let's get moving. We're running way too late as it is."

Hattie helped the children onto the boxcar with Charley and Sadie, as well as the newest helping hand who'd arrived just last week—a skinny blonde man barely out of his teens. Blake was a blink pincher from the Nags Head safehouse who decided he'd rather stick around and lend a hand than take a train to Utah. He stepped up to the boxcar, and with a quick pinch he was standing instantly on the deck alongside those already loaded.

"Blake. Not in front of the gents," she hissed, nodding at the hoboes, who had either failed to notice Blake's use of powers or knew better than to make a situation out of it.

Blake tucked his chin with a wince. "Sorry, Miss Malloy."

Hattie grinned. She'd never get used to him treating her like a respectable adult woman, as someone with authority, someone who had influence, was in charge, ran things.

Was this what she'd become in the last month? Not a bootlegger always two seconds from running for her life, but someone who took a stand and worked to make the world a safer place for others, even at the risk of her own freedom?

She'd never thought a life like this could feel so…right.

As soon as the last of the children and adult escorts were loaded onto the boxcar, Sadie called Charley to the edge of the deck, lifting a book for him to take.

"Now, you know what to do with this. Right?"

Charley nodded. "Yeah. I give this to Orson."

"Until you get to Utah, you keep this safe. Guard it with your life."

Hattie asked, "What is that?"

"Chapterbook," Sadie replied. "A list of all the names we've sent to Eden."

"That's a dangerous thing to be sending out on its own, don't you think?"

Sadie nodded. "It's all coded, but yes, if this lands in the wrong hands, and if there's any chance they could crack Jonas's code, then it'll be a nightmare."

"Why send it at all?" Hattie pressed.

"Orson needs the information. Last chapterbook I sent west was a year ago. Without this info, it's too easy for spies to infiltrate Eden. No way for Orson to know who we've sent and who might be working for the goons."

Hattie nodded. "Right. Well, you've left it in good hands I think."

Charley reached down to shake Hattie's hand. "Thank you. For everything."

Hattie smiled at his daughters. "You just take proper care of these girls. And live a life. That's all I ask."

Sadie made a whipping motion with her finger. "Okay, let's button her up."

She and Blake pulled the boxcar door closed as a clutch of railway workers wandered into the yard from a corrugated metal building across the way.

Sadie waved the pair of them back to their vehicles. "Okay, let's head back. You awake, Malloy? Good to drive?"

Hattie nodded. "I'm awake."

"Blake?"

Blake nodded.

"Then let's get the hell out of here. And pray that train makes it to Eden."

They made it back to Baltimore and the Charge headquarters in time for a quick bite of lunch. The warehouse they'd occupied had undergone a dramatic transformation. Old furniture was either replaced or repaired. Floors had been swept. Blackout curtains had been strung up over the filmy and shattered windows on all levels. The building was almost like a home, even if temporary.

The day's business now managed, Hattie had her own nerves to quell. Tonight was a big night, and she had a dress to pick up, so after settling things at the Charge headquarters, Hattie headed over to Locust Point.

The warehouse was lit, and Lizzie sat in her office. No sign of Raymond, who was probably out on the Bay with a quick delivery. Hattie knocked on the open office door, pulling Lizzie out of the books spread across her desk.

"Did you get't?" she asked.

Lizzie dropped her pencil and pulled her reading glasses off her face. "Of course, I got it."

Lizzie stood and crossed the office, reaching for a white linen dress cover hung on a hanger from the hat rack. She pulled the cover away to reveal a dazzling sleeveless gold dress covered with tiny crystal prisms. The hem, Hattie noted, would fall just shy of her knee. It was gorgeous, a breathtaking extravagance, even if she had bought it from a consignment shop—reduced, the shopkeeper said, because not that many women were short and slim enough to wear it.

Indeed. If it barely touched Hattie's knee, the dress would have been indecently short on a taller woman.

Still, so much money for a dress she'd probably only wear a handful of times in her life. Her stomach churned at the thought as she wondered if she was doing the right thing here. It's not like she could show up tonight in the day-dress she'd stolen from Richmond, or the two other dresses she'd splurged on this year. And she certainly couldn't wear her hand-me-down yellow that was starting to show some serious wear around the arms.

And this dress had been so beautiful, like one of the dresses of her fantasies as she'd looked through shop windows. Once in her life a girl deserved something this fancy. Just once.

"That'll do," she whispered, reaching out to touch the crystal embellishments.

"It better. If this don't lift your man's eyebrows, then you need to check his pulse."

Hattie lifted a hand to her hair, pulling it back over her ears. It had been years since she felt like impressing anyone. And here, suddenly, and without warning, she cared again.

"Do you think…do you have an iron to do my hair?" She'd brought some makeup in her purse. Nothing excessive, just a compact with powder, something to darken her brows and lashes a bit, and lipstick.

Lizzie grinned at Hattie. "Do I look like I own an iron? You'll be fine. I got you a silver band to match. We'll do something with your fringe. Maybe dampen it down and crimp it with some pins."

A silver band for her hair. Hattie grimaced, adding that cost to the expensive dress in her head. "I'll pay you back."

"Listen, you bought the dress. Let me bother over you a little. Never had a girl of my own, so maybe you owe me."

She smiled. "Well, thank you then."

A date. *The* date. It seemed odd. She and Vincent saw each other regularly, sharing coffee, walking along in the market, or grabbing a sandwich. They sometimes met in shadowy speakeasies with sultry jazz in the background, sipping whisky as they talked. It had been so easy, so comfortable. They'd fallen right back into that comradery she valued, walking hand-in-hand. Vincent would wrap his arm around her waist and pull her close, clearly affectionate with a brush of his hand, or of his lips on hers.

Gah, she was about to explode with the pace of it all. When was that dratted man going to go on with getting on? After that kiss they'd shared up in Pennsylvania, she'd assumed... Well, she'd assumed they'd be doing more a month later than holding hands.

This dress better get more than a peck on the lips from him, or she was going to kick that man in the backside.

"Relax," Lizzie drawled. "It's a date, not your execution."

"A date in some fancy restaurant." She wiped her hands on her pants, eyeing the dress once more. "A really fancy restaurant. I think Gloria Swanson ate there once. I think Calvin Coolidge ate there once."

"They serve food. You go. You dazzle this man with your beauty. You eat. What's there to be worried about?"

Hattie shrugged. "I honestly don't know what to do on an actual date. I mean, what's there to talk about? We already know everything about each other."

Lizzie laughed. "Now that's a lot of bushwa. You don't know anything about that drink of water."

"I know as much about him as he does, I think."

"But that's the past. What about the here and now? And the future? What're his plans? His passions? Men adore talking about themselves. You just get that boulder rolling, and he'll do the rest. Trust me."

"Perhaps, but Vincent's different. I have to use pliers to pull full sentences out of him when he's in a mood."

Lizzie snickered. "That's what the gin's for." Her smile faded, and she gripped Hattie's hand to guide her to the chair in front of her desk. "Speaking of the future, I want to talk to you about something important."

"Uh oh."

Lizzie took a seat behind the desk and rested her palms atop the ledgers. "I've been at this for a while, now. Ever since Jake…"

Hattie nodded as Lizzie failed to finish her sentence.

"This business is strong. We're busy. For now."

"What, the boat-legging?"

"How long do you think we'll be in the hooch business, though?"

Hattie thought on it. "As long as there's a demand, right?"

"And when the good people of this nation come to their senses and repeal the Eighteenth?"

"You think that's likely, then?"

Lizzie leaned back in her chair, knitting her fingers behind her head. "Inevitable. We'll look back on all of this one day and shake our heads for shame. I'm sure of it."

"We'll find something when that happens. We'll adapt."

Lizzie squinted. "That's the idea. Only, I'm not about to sit here and wait for it to happen. That's a good way for the money to leave you behind." She sat forward and opened a new book. "I've been talking to one of Jake's cousins down in Texas. He's started an enterprise that sounds promising, and…well, I've found my angle."

"What is it?" Hattie prodded, leaning forward to scan the ledger's meaningless numbers.

"I'll tell you this. America's thirsty for booze. But it's even thirstier for oil. It takes work transporting oil from field to refinery." She ran a finger down a column of figures. "They're drilling for oil now in the Gulf waters. That's right on the coast, and nowhere near the railways."

"You want to transport oil over the water?"

Lizzie smiled. "You're a clever girl. It's the future, I'm sure of it. No prohibition. Only growth. But it won't take long before every Johnny-Come-Lately has a tanker on the water and this window will close."

"It's a long way from the Chesapeake to the Gulf, though."

"It is. And I need new vessels. Tankers. I figure I'm not solvent enough to buy more than one. But with Jake's cousin in Galveston ready to put me together with Esso, I think I can float a loan long enough to start turning a profit."

Hattie nodded with enthusiasm. "That's amazing. I'd never think about anything but liquor. Okay, I'm in."

Lizzie squinted. The look seemed almost pained, and it sent a wave a dread through Hattie's chest.

"What's wrong?"

"I have a tanker I've scouted out. Just outside Charleston."

Hattie shook her head. "Charleston? You can't be serious."

"The mob down there has a line of credit they're willing to extend for a reasonable rate. Plus protection fees."

"You're allowing the mob to thumb you under before you even begin? And...I can't believe you'd consider doing business with that lot in Charleston. After they—"

Lizzie's face hardened. "You think I've forgotten? I haven't."

"Then how in the name of Mary are you doing business with Jake's killers?"

Lizzie took a moment to find her words. "Because, it's business, Hattie. It's the business we're in. And it's the business I'm trying to exit. Once I pay off those goons for the tanker, I'm done with them. Done."

Hattie rubbed the sides of her arms with nervous energy. "I didn't mean anything by't. I'm just surprised, is all."

"I know you are. Which is why I wanted to talk to you first."

"Well, I suppose it'll take getting used to. But the Charleston mob? I'll have to be on my highest guard around them." As Hattie said the words, Lizzie's face tightened even more.

And that's when it hit her.

"You have no intention of my working on these tankers."

"It's an enormous risk both for you and for me, Hattie. I can't put you in that situation."

"So, I'm still running hooch on the Bay?"

Lizzie nodded.

"And when they repeal?"

"We'll see."

Hattie stood up to pace, her stomach twisting. "This…this is my only income. You know that."

"I do."

"What about Raymond, then? At least you'll have a place for him?"

With a heavy breath, Lizzie replied, "These boys in Texas aren't keen on doing business with Raymond's type. The oil is coming from the South. Those are the people I have to deal with."

"So, both Raymond and I are out then? That's what you're telling me."

Lizzie stood and lifted both hands. "That's not what I'm saying. I'm putting together a plan. That's all."

Hattie gestured at the books on her desk. "That's more than a little planning. You have a bloody ship ready to purchase, already."

"Maybe I can run both enterprises for a while. If I need to sell, I'll find a buyer for the boat-legging business that will keep both you and Raymond on. This isn't the end, Hattie," Lizzie stated with a clipped tone. "This is just the future."

"And when is this future supposed to be arriving?"

"Who knows? How can any of us know? This could be years from now. By then, you may be elsewhere. Married, perhaps. Kids."

Hattie stood silent.

Lizzie sniffled, then pointed to the dress. "If that dress looks as good on you as I suspect it will, maybe that'll be sooner than later?"

Hattie couldn't help but smile. "Now you sound like my Ma."

Lizzie rounded the desk and put her hands on Hattie's shoulders. "I didn't want to blindside you when the time came. I know it's hard to discuss this sort of thing. But better you hear it now, so you're ready for it if, or when, it happens."

Hattie fought back a tear, clearing her throat. "Will you be moving away, then?"

Lizzie turned away. "Probably Charleston, at first. Then closer to the Gulf once I can. Not sure yet."

"Is this really just business?" Hattie asked. "What about you and Tony?"

"It is business. I mean, mostly. Okay, I confess a need to be just…somewhere else. Most of the memories in this place are painful, now. The bright moments have faded." She chuckled. "I like Tony. He's fun, and he's smart. But he's no Jake, and I'm worrying that maybe he's getting ideas in his head that don't need to be there. It's time for me to move on, to put my memories behind me and make a new life in a place without all these ghosts."

Hattie nodded. "I know what you mean."

After the two stood in silence for a minute, Lizzie sniffled, rubbed her face, then declared, "Alright. Enough of this. We have work to do. Now, get out of those clothes and let's see how this dress looks on you."

Hattie nodded, welcoming the change in subject. She forced a smile as she shimmied out of her overalls, a smile which became more earnest as she tried on the dress. And though the tension had lifted as Lizzie ran a brush through Hattie's hair, her mind was already elsewhere. Looking ahead, planning for the day when Lizzie closed the doors to this warehouse for good.

CHAPTER 2

"*L*isten, you gotta pull your head outta the oven, Tony," Vincent said. "You're managing more than just the bootleggers and your water distribution right now. There's no time to be mooning around."

And he was a total hypocrite for saying this when he'd been using every spare second he'd had the last month to spend with Hattie. Still, he hadn't taken his eye off the ball as far as the Crew activities went. There was a lot at stake here, and he was playing both ends of the game.

Tony cracked his neck and tried to smile. "Yeah, yeah. It's just hard, you know? Trying to spend time with someone when you're up to your cuffs in all this work."

Vincent slapped him on the shoulder, nodding to the broad, square table at the center of the Philadelphia cannery's speakeasy. "So embrace it, huh? Put your meat in the freezer and get to work. We got an opportunity here. New routes. New business. No bushwa from our new friends here in Philly." Vincent eased him back to the war table. "Although when it comes to women, I'm no expert."

Tony laughed. "Ain't that for sure. Lizzie's a professional.

I know she's as busy as I am. I got enough smarts to know when to back off and give a gal some space."

Vincent ran a finger along the map, tracing a line between Philadelphia and Baltimore. "Good, because those smarts? We need them right here."

Footsteps clacked in the passageway, and soon their two hosts entered the lounge. Arnoud dropped a bundle of books on top of the map with an impatient huff as DeBarre brandished a bottle of light amber liquid, holding it up to the light.

"Found the damn thing," DeBarre declared at full volume. "Nineteen nineteen. Genuine Kentucky whisky. Been saving this for an occasion, you know."

Tony asked, "What's the occasion?"

With a jab of his finger into Vincent's ribs, DeBarre replied, "Today's the day I give this palooka a swift kick in the shorts for drawing me into a war with New York. Might as well enjoy it now before they come for the lot of us and we're all pushing up daisies."

Tony stood with a stiff grin, unsure if DeBarre was joking.

Arnoud cleared his throat. "Yes, yes. So, here's the situation in our fair city. We have a few concerns. The first is Sabella's people. They're loyal and trained, but few in number. Then we have the brewers, who are increasingly reluctant to take orders from Sabella and may not be quick to hop in to fight. So let me show you where we'll need some assistance from Baltimore to shore up the holes in our defenses."

Tony nodded as Arnoud indicated the spots on the map. DeBarre nudged at Vincent's arm, urging him to follow to the bar near the rear of the speakeasy. Once they were clear of the business conversation. DeBarre uncorked the bottle of whisky and poured Vincent a modest portion, and himself several fingers.

With a lift of his glass, DeBarre said, "Here's to getting our asses handed to us by New York in the near future."

"Sorry we dragged you into this. If it counts for anything, I was barely involved in the entire scheme."

"Yes, I'm well aware that Hattie is both the brains and the brawn in your relationship." DeBarre said with a wave of his glass, "Honestly, I'm shocked you made it out of that hell hole with your noggin unscrambled. These past few years, I've seen the sort of pinchers who came outta that joint. They're more machine than human, if you ask me."

They both turned and regarded Arnoud, standing cross-armed as Tony asked a bevy of questions. His scarecrow frame barely held up his suit, which was showing signs of overuse around the cuffs and elbows. Vincent speculated whether that was the only suit he owned.

"Still though," Vincent mused, "an alliance between our two cities can't be too much of a burden on you."

"Oh, no," DeBarre said with a sweep of his hand. "There's money to be made. What Sabella lacks in muscle, Vito makes up for. Which will come in handy when the old New York guard inevitably decide to break up this little party we've got going on here."

"They're too busy trading licks with each other to worry about us."

"Nice fantasy."

"You children done playin'?" Lefty grumbled as he came into the room. "I gotta borrow Vincent, boys. Last minute business in Baltimore."

Tony turned with a concerned look, but Lefty eased him down with a flat palm.

"Nothin' you gotta get worked up over, Tony. The Capo wants you here soaking it in."

Vincent finished his whisky and offered DeBarre a handshake. "So, we're good?"

DeBarre nodded. "As long as you're willing to throw in up our ways when we need a hand."

"You can count on it."

Vincent turned to bid Tony farewell, offering Arnoud a hand. The man simply stared at it with a lift of his brow, then reached out to shake Vincent's hand with a clammy palm. "Yes, goodbye."

Lefty led the way as they withdrew down the passage and up the ladder to the main floor. They cleared the cannery and reached Lefty's car. Once inside, Vincent released a long breath. "Thanks for getting me outta there on time."

"Hey, anything for young love. Now what?"

"Now we beat feet back to Baltimore before I'm late."

Lefty steered the car onto the highway with a smug grin.

"What?" Vincent grumbled after glaring at Lefty for a minute.

"It's about time, is all."

"Please don't start."

"Listen, Vincent. I'm dead solid for certain this girl means something to you. The stakes are high with this one."

"You think too much about my love life, you know that?"

Lefty gestured, pulling his one hand off the wheel with regularity. "You have my wisdom at your disposal, is all I'm saying. Might as well use it."

Vincent leaned back, closed his eyes, then nodded. What he knew about women would fit in a thimble. Not that he was completely sure Lefty knew any more, but it was worth a shot. "Right, yeah. Okay. What've you got for me?"

"So, first of all you always hold the door for the girl. No exceptions. Unless she's gone to powder her nose, then it's a bad idea."

"Believe it or not, I've figured that part out already."

"Next—conversation. Dames love talking about themselves. So, all you gotta do is prime that pump and she'll take over from there. Just nod and smile and repeat, like, every third thing she says back at her."

"Or I could actually listen."

"Sure," Lefty chuckled. "Then when you're on hour two of her complaining about servants, and inheritances, and some flatware a cousin stole two years ago, you'll think twice."

Vincent fought back a laugh. "Fine. What's next?"

"Next is shoes."

"Shoes."

"Yeah. Comment on her shoes."

Vincent cocked his head. "Who gives a flat flip over shoes?"

Actually *he* gave a flat flip over shoes, but that was *his* shoes. He'd never seen Hattie in anything but work boots and some nondescript, thick Oxfords. Nothing he could actually comment on about those without seeming a total fool.

"Women care about shoes, you mook. So, take a moment and notice her shoes. And her hair."

Vincent nodded in earnest. "The hair, I notice."

"Good. So, anyways," Lefty added with a clearing of his throat, "we're getting to the important stuff."

"Oh, Christ."

"When a dame orders a drink, you have to be the one to hand it to her. As in, the barkeep or the waiter brings the drink, be sure you grab that glass before he sets it down. It's all about power with women, and you have to demonstrate a degree of initiative. And you have to order a new drink if you don't get your mitts on the glass first. Make the waiter take it away and bring another."

Vincent squinted. "Order a new drink? Send it back and order a new one?"

"Absolutely. Oh, and don't let her order beef. Or pork. I'm serious. Get her to order the fish, because if there's any meat tougher than perch on the table, you have to cut it for her."

Vincent blinked, imagining for a moment what would happen if he attempted to cut Hattie's steak for her. Lefty couldn't be serious. That, or he'd never courted a woman as independent and feisty as Hattie. "You're blowing smoke up my ass, aren't you?" he finally asked.

Lefty managed a deadpan for nearly a full second before smiling.

"You're a piece of work," Vincent grumbled.

"You asked for it."

"I almost believed you for a second."

Lefty's chest bobbed in silent laughter. "Seriously, son. If you try to snatch a drink from that girl's hand, you'll pull back a bloody stump. And I should know."

Vincent laughed out loud. "No way I'm gonna try to cut her dinner either. She's got a hell of a slap."

"But do comment on the shoes," Lefty said with a wave of his hand. "I can tell you that from experience. Compliment her shoes."

* * *

VINCENT STRAIGHTENED his tie as he stood nearly paralyzed in front of Boulevard Provence restaurant. He was supposed to pick Hattie up at her house, enjoy her father's hearty approval and endure her mother's frosty glares until Hattie was ready to go. Then he'd drive her here in Lefty's car with plenty of opportunity to open doors and pull out chairs. Instead he'd arrived home to a note that she was held up at Lizzie's and would meet him at the restaurant.

So here he was. Feeling like a total jackass outside of an

overpriced, snooty restaurant, worried that all his plans to court her the right way were falling apart.

The windows flickered with yellow candlelight, a few couples visible through the glass, conferring over haute cuisine. Vincent didn't know haute cuisine from flapjacks, but it was a bit late to be thinking that now.

What the hell was he doing? This was a bad idea. A terrible, terrible idea. He was a kept pincher, brought up by a bunch of priests and nuns then promptly delivered into servitude. Hattie was the daughter of a seamstress and a steelworker, a river girl by trade who had gone out of her way to prove she was all grit and no frills. So how did a jumped-up French joint like this make sense for their first official dinner date? Although a formal date *had* been a long time coming. Lefty was right—this did matter. It mattered a lot. He'd known how he felt about Hattie for months now—long before she'd sprung him from Ithaca.

Nothing had been quite the same since Ithaca. They'd met several times a week, for sure. They'd joked, laughed, flirted. But he wanted to show her she meant more to him than just a woman to laugh and flirt with. He needed this date to prove to her that she was more than a friend, more than a casual romance. So much more.

So, Vincent had made a reservation at the Boulevard Provence. It seemed proper. It might have been proper for a girl living in a rich neighborhood, but Hattie Malloy?

Too late now.

Vincent crossed himself and stepped inside, handing his outerwear to the girl at the coat check and striding into the dining room with the sort of bravado he reserved for when he had no idea what the hell he was doing.

He found Hattie already inside, seated at their table. Damn. He'd arrived early specifically to hold the door for her, to pull out her chair for her. But that ship had sailed.

She stood to greet him. A gold dress hugged curves on her body that he'd never truly seen before. The crystal embellishments caught the light, nearly blinding him as she twisted at the waist and thrust an impatient hand onto her hip.

"You're late, Mister Calendo!"

He took a moment to drink in the sight of her. She was gorgeous. Still with that Mary Pickford gamine charm, but all wrapped up in a dress meant for sin. Just beautiful. And just as saucy and bold as ever.

After taking a moment to catch his breath, he replied, "I most certainly am not late."

She grinned. "Well, I'm here and you aren't. Hence, you're late boy-o."

He nodded to the table and the half-empty cordial glass. "I see you've started without me."

"Oh, that's my third. You'll have to catch up."

"You're a lush."

"And you're gullible." She gestured to the glass. "I've got no idea what this is. Sherry, maybe?"

"Probably." He wound around her to grab her chair. Because that's what he was supposed to do, right? Hold her chair? Or was that only when they first arrived? No, he clearly remembered that not only did men stand when women rose, or returned from the lady's room, but they also pulled out the woman's chair. And maybe did something with the napkin? Or was that what the waiter did? He scooted the chair out, and looked on the table for a napkin.

"What're you doing, then?" She glanced up at him, clearly perplexed.

"Holding your chair."

"Why?"

"For you to sit."

She bit back some comment, then nodded. "Oh. I suppose so."

Hattie took a seat, and Vincent returned to his, unbuttoning his jacket before lowering himself into his own chair.

"Well, here we are," he declared.

"Aye, here we are."

He searched her face, which seemed to be searching his.

"I, uh… I like your hair," he said.

She lifted a flat hand to the silver band holding aloft crimped red locks.

"Thank you."

His eyes grew wide, and he blurted, "And your shoes!"

She sat stiff. "What, now?"

"Your shoes. I, uh…I noticed. Them."

Damn it. He hadn't looked. Did she even have shoes on? Well, of course she had shoes on, but he had no idea what sort of shoes they were. Hopefully she wouldn't quiz him on exactly what he found admirable about her footwear.

Hattie nodded slowly. "Fine, then. I…I like your shoes as well."

Vincent balled fists in his lap, vowing to find a way to punish Lefty for this later. Still, though. What did he say? Get her talking? Wasn't that what he was supposed to do?

"How are your parents?"

Hattie rolled her eyes, then she nodded. "They're fine."

"Oh. That's nice."

"Yes."

They stared at each other for a yawning minute of tension until the server arrived to take Vincent's drink order.

His stomach twisted. Shit. What did he order? What was a man supposed to drink in the presence of a woman on a dinner date? Was that sherry she had? But wasn't that supposed to be a woman's drink? Whisky? No, too coarse. Gin? This was a fine restaurant. Even in Baltimore where

Prohibition hadn't been enforced, there were few options available, and he was pretty sure ordering a glass of gin would get him branded as a drunk or a hayseed.

"Red," he finally said.

The server lifted a chin. "Sir?"

Vincent rifled through his memories for the times he'd waited at Vito's vineyard, whiling away the hours thumbing through the bottles lying around the estate. Finally, he pulled an answer from the chaos of his mind.

"Barbera."

The server nodded with an approving tuck of his lips before trotting off to fetch a wine Vincent was worried he might hate.

"You know your wines, then?" Hattie asked as she took a sip of her sherry.

"I…" He grimaced, not wanting to lie to her and make himself out to be someone he wasn't. "Not much beyond the basics."

"I'm assuming Barbera is a red?"

"God, I hope so," he blurted out.

She laughed and nearly sprayed him with sherry from the top of her glass. The laugh was infectious. As was her smile. And finally, for the first time since he'd walked into this joint, Vincent began to relax.

Well, relax just a bit. He released an audible sigh, and shifted in his seat, drumming his fingers on the tablecloth.

"So…" Hattie offered.

"So…"

"How was your week?"

"Complicated."

She nodded.

He nodded in return. It occurred to Vincent that perhaps he could have expounded on that, but Lefty had told him to let her do the talking.

"In what way was your week complicated?" she nudged.

Vincent eyed the surrounding tables, then leaned in to whisper, "Probably shouldn't. Not in public like this."

He eyes went wide and she nodded. "Right. Business. Well, then. If we're not talking about our business, then it looks like we're stuck. Unless you want to discuss the weather or the potholes on Light Street, that is."

Oh, God. Not this again.

Before he could come up with something else, the server returned with a wine bottle holding it at chest height. Vincent eyed him with suspicion, wondering why he was just standing there. Finally, it occurred to him that the server was expecting some sort of answer. Before Vincent could review the bottle, the server set it onto the table to uncork it and pour him a glass.

The server only poured a splash, then stood with that same anticipatory glare.

This was hell, but at least he'd figured this part of the whole fine-dining wine ritual out. Vincent lifted the glass to his nose and inhaled, swirling it in the glass and nodding. The server waited for him to set the glass down, filled it, then took his leave.

Hattie smirked. "At least it's red. Although it would have been funny if he'd shown up with something blue or green."

"True." Vincent laughed. "Would you like to hear some gossip?"

Her face lit up as she leaned forward. "Is the Pope Catholic?"

"So, I saw Tony today. Seems affairs between him and your employer have gone a bit...how do I say it? Cool? Infrequent?"

Hattie's face dimmed, her smile dropping.

Hell's bells, how was this going so wrong? She wasn't even making eye contact. "Sorry," he mumbled. "I thought—"

"It's fine," she said. "There's just a reason to it. One I'm not at liberty to gossip on."

"I see."

She took a long sip of her sherry, and he followed suit with his wine.

They'd nearly polished off their drinks, and Vincent was wondering if it would be proper etiquette for him to pour some of the wine for her when Hattie set the glass onto the table and reached for the menu.

"Well, then. Let's see what sort of dinner we're in for, shall we?"

"Sounds good."

Vincent picked his up to review, then froze. Of course, it would be in French. Of course. And he didn't understand the first word on this page.

He took a moment, then ventured a look over the top of his menu to Hattie.

Her face was twisted in disbelieving humor. It drew a smile to his lips.

Hattie dropped the menu onto the table with a sigh. "Well, then. Seems we're eating frog legs."

Vincent shook his head. "Is that what *Potage du Soir* means?"

Hattie leaned forward to whisper, "Actually, I do believe that's French for Crock o' Shite."

Vincent held back a laugh that threatened to choke him.

He looked for another menu item. "*Moules frites?*"

"Fried moles," she offered before searching for her own offering. "Oh, what about this one? *Côte de Veau?*"

Vincent went with his gut. "Oh, that's a fine navy-blue jacket folded several times then topped with a heavy cream sauce."

She snickered loud enough for the tables nearby to offer a harsh glare.

Vincent joined her, not giving the first concern about those around them. *"Pochouse?"*

"A fish soup cooked exclusively by pockmarked chefs in their own homes. *Fuseau lorrain?"*

"A rare, exotic, fussy bird boiled in rainwater. *Confit de canard?"*

"Oh, that's a popular hobo dish—fish chopped up and cooked inside a tin can." She pointed at her menu. *"Choucroute garnie?"*

"Over-ripe model trains sautéed in pickled cabbage."

By this point they were nearly in tears, the entire restaurant turning to watch with disapproving eyes as they laughed.

Finally, Hattie looked across the table, wiping her eyes with her napkin. "Vincent, this isn't us. This place isn't us at all. I appreciate the effort that went into you getting this reservation, but let's go somewhere else."

"Before they kick us out, you mean?" He eyed the approaching waiter.

"Aye."

He pulled some money from his wallet and slapped it on the table, hoping it was enough to cover the wine and her drink. "Okay, let's go somewhere else. You pick."

An absolutely adorable lopsided smile creased her cheeks. "You sure about that boy-o? We might be a bit overdressed."

He got up to assist with her chair. "You pick. Just please make it someplace with a menu in English."

* * *

AFTER AN HOUR AT A RIVERSIDE SHACK, huddled up against a steel drum fire alongside a rickety wooden service bar, eating raw oysters and sipping dark beer, Vincent found himself walking Hattie arm-in-arm back to her home. They lingered by the stoop to her parents' row house, and he pulled her close, his arms wrapped around her.

"Promise me you'll never do that again," Hattie insisted.

"What, the thing with the cracker and the horseradish? That's how I eat oysters. And you said it wasn't half bad."

"No, no, not the horseradish, the French place. You don't need to do that for me. I like you the way you are boy-o. Don't try to be something you're not."

He nodded. "Agreed. As long as you do the same."

"Well, I'll have to figure out what I am first."

"Oh, I know exactly what you are."

She tilted her head. "Do you, now?"

"Yes. You're a huge pain in my ass."

She smiled at him, then reached up to slide her fingers along his jawline. He dropped his face to meet her mouth with his—a tiny kiss that was meant to be the proper sort of kiss a man would give a woman right outside of her parents' house. She responded, leaning against him, her arms wrapping tightly around his neck.

Fire roared through him. Maybe it was the beer, the oysters, the heady excitement he felt whenever they were together, maybe it was the feel of her body against him, the crystal beads of her dress pressed rather sharply against his suit jacket, maybe it was the promise of an early spring in the air, but all his gentlemanly intentions of giving her a proper chaste kiss went right out the damned window.

By the time they eased apart, Vincent knew he didn't want to contemplate a future without this woman by his side. And he was going to do everything in his power to make sure that future wasn't one of them hiding and running from the mob—or hiding and running from anybody.

Hattie sucked in a jagged breath, reaching up to touch his cheek. "Worth every penny. I guess the dress really did do the job."

"What job? Impaling me? Because it's kinda like hugging the chandelier at the Old Moravia here," he teased.

"I don't see you bleeding and running away," she countered, pulling him in for another kiss.

"I need to escort you upstairs," he murmured once they came up for air. "It's getting late."

"You do realize I'm a boat-legger? There are times when I don't get home until morning, or even lunchtime?"

"Yes, but those times you're out on business, not a date with me." He glanced up at the window, wondering if they'd had an audience. "I'm trying to get your mother to like me. Dragging you off to my apartment and returning you in the morning is only gonna make her hate me more."

Hattie rolled her eyes. "Newsflash boy-o, I don't really care what my mother thinks."

"But you do," he insisted. "And I do, too."

Something that looked an awful lot like frustration swept across her face. He recognized the emotion, feeling a bit frustrated himself.

"Come on then," she took a step back, sliding her hand down to hold his. "Let's go on up and face the dragon."

Vincent walked by her side up the stairs, still holding her hand. She opened the door to her home, ushering him in.

Alton, Hattie's father, lingered near the door by the kitchen, nearly bouncing on his heels. "Vincent, my boy!"

"Good evening, Mister Malloy."

"Please, lad. Call me Alton."

"Whatever you prefer, Mister Malloy."

Alton chuckled, slapped his arm, then nodded for the kitchen. "Time for a quick nip?"

Branna Malloy stood in the sitting room, arms crossed while Hattie did her best to stand between her mother and Vincent. "It's a bit late, Alton," Branna declared.

"Nonsense, woman. This boy's a gentleman. Brought her home at a polite hour. Come! I'll pour us both a hitch."

Vincent entertained Alton for a good fifteen minutes as Branna looked on at the entry to the kitchen. He twisted a little, wondering how he'd stumbled so effortlessly into Alton's graces, while still struggling with Hattie's mother. How could he make her like him? Or even tolerate him? Because in spite of what Hattie said, a future with her would have some difficulties if he couldn't get her mother on board.

"Mrs. Malloy," he finally ventured, "I understand you work in textiles?"

She scowled. "I don't work in textiles, I work in a factory. I have a job like an honest person. Not shooting guns and double-dealing like some hooligan."

"Ma!" Hattie squealed.

Vincent focused on his whisky, regretting he'd even tried. That had been a terrible mistake. Maybe flowers again? She'd seemed to like the flowers.

Alton shook his head at his wife. "Now, you don't go waxing inhospitable like that, Branna. The man's our guest!"

"I don't recall inviting him," Branna replied, turning away.

Hattie sucked in a breath to retort, then surrendered the entire sentence in a histrionic sigh.

Flowers. Next time he'd try flowers. And maybe some of those chocolate candies with the sweet cherries in the middle. And if that didn't work...hell, he had no idea what to do if that didn't work.

Vincent finished his whisky and stood "Best I be on my way. Thank you for the drink, sir."

"You'll come back soon, eh?" the old man urged.

"I intend to, sir."

Hattie reached with both hands, easing Vincent toward the door. "Let's go, boy-o."

In the hall, Vincent shuffled aside. "Sorry about that."

"No, don't you go apologizing. It's her fault she's full of piss and vinegar. You did nothing but try to make conversation."

"She's got reason to not trust me. I just need to figure out how to get through that, to make her not hate me at the very least."

"Oh, she doesn't hate you, she just abhors the thought of you." With a smirk, Hattie added, "Which makes you even more tempting."

She pulled him close, only to jump back as her mother cleared her throat behind them.

So much for a good night kiss. He glanced over at Branna then back down to Hattie. "I might be up in Philadelphia tomorrow, or possibly out west to escort some product across state lines. If I'm not back too late, I'll swing by."

Hattie rubbed Vincent's arm. "Okay. I'll probably be either at Sadie's or Lizzie's warehouse."

He nodded and watched as she headed back into the apartment, turning as she passed her mother to give him a smile.

Vincent waited until the door closed, then descended the stairwell and headed out onto the street, whistling to himself as he walked. The future. A future with Hattie. That's definitely what he was working toward. He just needed to step up the timeline a bit, because he wasn't sure how much longer he could wait for that future to happen.

CHAPTER 3

*H*attie bolted out of her bed, her nightclothes soaked in sweat. Reaching to open her window, she gasped for air. The cold breeze flowed over her chest and forehead, sending chills across her body as the dreams faded from her mind—dreams of loved ones perishing in flames as the Hell pincher looked on.

The sounds of night greeted her ears as her breathing calmed. A cat wailed a few houses over. A beat cop whistled as he made his way up the street in a lazy, winding line. Far in the distance, a train whistle sounded. Hattie focused on the mundane sounds and took a seat on the window sill, steadying herself as the nightmare eased into shadow.

They were getting worse. Each night now, she was plagued with these dreams. She'd watched her own family incinerated before her eyes by a demon in the dressing of a woman. She'd seen Vincent burned to bones and ash. And tonight, it was Raymond's turn.

But it was always about the demons. And in every dream the Hell pincher was there, somewhere, watching. She could never see his face, but she could feel his presence closing in.

What were these dreams, anyway? Were they some sort of warning? Or had she simply grown paranoid after her brief hunt for the Hell pincher in Pennsylvania?

Hattie reached for her working clothes, and pulled the tiny black marble from the pocket to examine it in the moonlight.

The soul trap.

The tiny red veins seemed even more brilliant in the low light, crisscrossing the obsidian surface like blood vessels. They pulsed with life, and she was certain there was a soul inside. But what sort? Human? Demon?

Regardless, Hattie felt sure this tiny orb was the source of these nightmares. And if that were the case, she wouldn't find answers in her bedroom. Putting the marble back in her pants pocket, she shed the nightdress and put on her work clothes.

Creeping out of her home, Hattie latched the door quietly so as not to wake her parents, and walked into the moonlight.

The outside of the Charge was its typical dark, derelict self. Hattie waited for a slow-driving car to pass the warehouse, then pinched light to cross the street unseen. Caution was everything when harboring free pinchers.

The interior of the building was silent, save for some light snoring from a nearby room. Hattie poked a head into one of the makeshift bunk rooms to find Blake sprawled half-off his bed, his snores sounding like a leaking bellows.

Continuing on to Sadie's office, Hattie made her way to the desk, unlocking the drawer to pull the codex from inside. The leather-bound book itself had a tiny lock, one additional key required to access the secrets within. With a click of the lock and a careful tug, she pulled open the hasp and thumbed through the book. It held several hundred pages written in three separate languages, its ink illustrations painting curious scenes of long-forgotten history.

She turned to a familiar section, one she'd pored over several times already. The time had come to lay into the matter with her full attention.

Hell pinchers.

Most of the language in this section was in Polish, and as Hattie's eyes skimmed over the foreign words, she did her best to attempt to divine their meaning. But ultimately, the illustrations were her best guide for what was the content of the codex. Sadie, for her part, only knew a little Polish. It was just enough to give Hattie the basics she'd already known. Hell pinchers were a sort of practitioner, men who mastered secret knowledge of the magical arts without possessing the natural abilities of pinchers. By and large, practitioners of these esoteric arts were harmless enough, their charms and enchantments limited in power, pale and puny when compared to a pincher's intrinsic magics.

But from time to time, a practitioner would dig too deeply into these secrets. The thirst for power would drive them to pierce the veil between Earth and Hell itself, a transaction of absolute power.

And in the process, they created the pinchers.

"Hmm…'nother sleepless night?" a voice rolled from the door to the office.

Hattie started, then squinted at the frame of Sadie O'Donnell, holding herself up against the jamb. "Aye. Thought I'd come over and give this book another go. How about you?"

Sadie took a halting step into the room, steadying herself with each step before reaching one of the chairs to drop into it with a sigh. "No sleep for me either.

"Worried about the westward train?"

"I am. But no more'n usual."

Hattie shrugged. "It's been four days, now. No news is good news. Maybe you should try and sleep?"

A single tear ran down Sadie's cheek, and Hattie realized there was more to this bout of insomnia than the pressures of her office.

Hattie stood up and rounded the desk to face Sadie. "Eh, what's the matter?"

Sadie shook her head, as a second tear joined the first. She gasped, then wiped her cheek with the heel of her palm.

"Today…would've been ten years."

"Ten years since what?" Hattie whispered.

"Our anniversary," Sadie replied, straightening in her chair. "Me and Jonas."

"Oh, I'm so sorry." Hattie reached for Sadie's hand. "I had no idea."

"Well, I don't exactly advertise it. Don't mind me. I'm just indulging. Was supposed to be alone."

"Well, maybe you shouldn't be. I'll stay with you the rest of the night."

"No need. I should try to get some sleep." The other woman stood, pausing as she reached the door. "I miss him. He was like a part of me, my best friend. Things were different with him by my side—better, easier. The grief, the loss never really goes away, you know. It's always there, like a bruise that never heals. I work. I try to make our vison of the future a reality. But sometimes it all feels hollow without Jonas."

Hattie thought of Vincent. What would it be like to lose him like this? What if like Sadie's husband, he'd not come back from Ithaca? Been broken and sold to some family? What if he left one day to do business for the Crew and took a bullet to the head like Lizzie's husband, Jake? How would she go forward, keep a sense of purpose in her life without Vincent to share it all with?

It wasn't something she wanted to contemplate. In some way, that would be just as horrible as the nightmares of fiery demons she'd been having each night.

Sadie headed back to her room, leaving Hattie to the codex. Eventually, the eastern sky adopted a light blue and the stars began to fade. Hattie pulled aside one of the blackout curtains near the top floor to look out over the warehouse district and the harbor just beyond. A few marshes across the inlet sat in inky black silhouette against the sunrise.

One of the silhouettes near the street slipped into Hattie's view. Someone was watching the building.

Pulling away from the window, Hattie held her breath. The same dread flooded her chest. That feeling of being watched from the shadows.

She balled a fist and set her jaw. No. She wasn't about to just stand there in a nearly empty building waiting for some shadow man to attack. Rushing down the stairs, she stopped at the first-floor bunk room to shake Blake's shoulder.

He snorted as he jerked awake. "Hmm, whah?"

Hattie lifted a finger to her lips, then whispered, "Someone's outside."

Blake's eyes shot open. "Who?"

"Someone who doesn't want to be seen. Which means trouble."

Blake jumped out of bed and searched for the hunting rifle he'd stowed behind the door. Hattie eyed the weapon with uncertainty. If this was the Hell pincher, what good would a rifle do?

Edging aside one of the curtains, Blake looked out.

"Do you see him?" Hattie whispered.

He nodded. "I think so. Just standing there across the street."

Hattie joined Blake to cast a quick glance. Indeed, the

silhouette of a man loomed across the yard of scrap steel, swaying a little, pacing up and down as if making a decision.

"Wait," Hattie muttered. "Is that—?"

Blake groaned, then rushed for the door, jerking it open.

Hattie sprinted after him, the two traversing the littered scrap yard to cross the street. There, they found Charley, a swath of dried blood painting the side of his face all the way to his beard.

Hattie swept underneath his arm, propping him up just as he was about to fall. Blake slung the rifle over his shoulder and took the other side. Together they helped Charley into the warehouse and sat him down. Hattie searched the room for water but found nothing. With the children gone, the daily chores and washing up had fallen away. Instead, she spotted a clear, uncorked bottle on a table near the office. Hattie gave it a sniff. White lightning.

Snatching a roughly clean cloth from a cupboard, Hattie doused it with the liquor. Charley hissed and groaned as she wiped clean the dried blood. The injury itself wasn't so bad once she's gotten it clear. While she worked, Blake opened two of the curtains to let in the morning sunlight as Charley sat bleary-eyed, rocking to himself.

"Charley," she finally asked. "What happened?"

He stared blankly until Hattie urged him again. Even then, his eyes searched empty space for words to convey the thoughts colliding in his head.

"They…were waiting."

"Who?" Hattie pressed.

"Them. They…they were at the first stop."

Hattie exchanged impatient glances with Blake, then crouched in front of Charley so that he was forced to look her in the eye. "What happened to the children, Charley?"

His eyes welled up. "They took them all."

A wave of nausea swept through Hattie as she gripped Charley's arms. "Who took the children?"

"Were they gangsters?" Blake asked.

Charley glanced up to Blake, then nodded a few times.

Hattie stood up with sharp breath, swearing under her breath.

"What's going on?" Sadie marched down the steps, hand on her forehead. When she spotted Charley sitting in the chair, she stiffened.

"Looks like the last train west got hit by the gangsters," Blake told her.

Sadie plodded forward, eyes narrow and focused on Charley. "Is this true?"

Charley nodded once, then stared at his knees.

"Which waystation got hit?" Sadie demanded.

Charley didn't answer.

Hattie pressed, "Did you make it as far as Ohio?"

He shook his head.

Hattie looked up to Sadie. "Must have been Parkersburg. It's the only waystation on the back side of the Appalachians."

"I'll go," Blake offered.

"No," Hattie said. "If there's gangsters waiting for us, they'll just take you."

"I can get outta their grip easy enough," he said. "Done it before."

"Aye, but if we have children being carted off..." She glanced down to Charley, remembering his two daughters. They weren't pinchers, as it turned out. They were simply in transit to a better life. But would that really matter to the gangsters? Were they on their way to Ithaca even as they stood there?

"We need information before we go haring out there into

what could be a trap," Hattie said. "And I know where to get this information."

Sadie shook her head. "No. Not him."

Hattie glared at the other woman. "I know you don't trust him, but we do not have the luxury of playing ideals, here. If Vincent can help us find those children, then he's our first stop. Besides, you helped save him from Ithaca. Do you really think he wouldn't do the same for us?"

Sadie stood stone-faced and didn't answer.

Blake offered, "Need me to help?"

"No, I've got this. I'll be back. Take care of Charley." She reached down for the man's shoulder. "I'll find your girls, Charley."

In a sudden motion, he grabbed her arm. His eyes were wild, heavy with immeasurable emotion. "I'm sorry...for this. I'm sorry. I'm so sorry."

"No, don't you apologize to us. It's the goons who will answer for this." Hattie pulled free of Charley's grip, then nodded to the others before rushing out the door under a light pinch, to head for Vincent's home.

CHAPTER 4

*V*incent peered over a tableau of rolling farmland reaching out from the foothills of the Alleghenies, stretching out like bunched brown velvet as it rolled east. Red-painted barn houses sat nestled between cow pastures, quiet in the late winter as a line of trucks sat ready to roll behind them.

"That's a view, huh?" Tony mumbled, leaning against their car.

Vincent nodded. "It ain't bad. Could do without the ruckus, though." He squinted back at the trucks of beer as they belched diesel exhaust into the sky. "Where's this specialist DeBarre called in?"

Tony pointed west. "Meeting him in Morgantown."

DeBarre had quickly called in a favor for the first official act of Baltimore-Philadelphia cooperation. Philly had a shipment of beer barrels meant for Michigan, but had difficulty steering them clear of the Pittsburgh mob. Those boys were still beholden to Masseria and the rest of the New York Italians. Hence, they'd shut down overland shipping through Harrisburg to all points west. The next easiest solution was to route the entire pipeline through Maryland, where Vito had managed to assert hegemony against Pittsburgh, then skirt Pennsylvania entirely by way of West Virginia and Ohio.

But while Vito held some sway over West Virginia, Ohio was totally out of their control. Thus the need for DeBarre's "specialist."

Tony looked over at some signal from one of the truck drivers. "Alright. Let's roll."

Vincent returned to the car, waiting for Tony to get behind the wheel. When he did, Tony eyed him with a smirk.

"What now?" Vincent grumbled.

"Just wondering if you're enjoying your yard pass from Lefty. It's not often I see you out and about without him."

"Wasn't my idea," Vincent replied. "Vito's got him working on something else today. Guess he trusts me enough to cut me loose for these dreary road trips."

Tony chuckled as he pulled the car onto the highway behind the convoy. "This is some straight bushwa, isn't it? Sending you out to accompany a bunch of beer on delivery?"

"I understand it," Vincent admitted. "Remember Dryfork?"

"I remember."

"Can't have that monkey business in front of our new friends."

Tony sighed. "Do you really think all of this caution is worth it? What are the chances Pittsburgh would try to hit us this far south?"

"Won't know until it's too late, I suppose." Vincent glanced behind them to check the highway. No vehicles. Nothing following them. Nothing for miles but their own trucks as far as he could see.

They continued west over the hump of the Alleghenies and on into Crew-controlled West Virginia. Before long, the quiet town of Morgantown popped into view hugging the curve of the Monongahela River.

"That's it?" Vincent asked.

"Yeah. This specialist is taking the load up river right under Pittsburgh's nose. But that's his problem."

"Whoever this mook is, he'd better know his way around a riverboat."

They descended into the township, trucks belching through the main street without a concern for discretion. Tony pulled their car up to a loading dock hosting a bevy of dull-coated diesel boats. A small army of workers emerged before the trucks killed their engines, rushing to pull open the tarps concealing the beer barrels.

Vincent hopped out of the car, surveying the activity. These men moved with practiced precision, almost silently. "Feeling a little outclassed here, Tony."

"Can we poach this specialist fella from DeBarre, you think?" he joked.

A voice boomed from the wharf, "Not unless Corbi wants a known felon on the payroll!"

Vincent and Tony squinted at the lean, kind-faced man in a fedora and white linen shirt trotting along the ground toward the convoy. His skin was ruddy and sun-leathered, the look of a man who'd just traveled from the tropics.

Vincent took his hand, wincing at his vise grip. "Afternoon. Vincent Calendo."

The man nodded with self-effacing mirth. "Name's Bill."

Tony squinted at the man. "No. Can't be."

He chuckled, then waved at Tony to relax. "DeBarre didn't tell you? Sounds like him."

Vincent shook his head. "What am I missing, here?"

Tony grumbled, "Jesus Mary, Vincent! This is Bill McCoy!"

Vincent blinked a few times before it dawned on him. "The...the Real McCoy?"

McCoy snickered and shook his head. "Call me Bill, for the love of God."

Vincent shook his hand again. "Figures DeBarre would keep that under his hat. Damn it all, it's a pleasure to meet you, sir!"

McCoy raised his hand and stepped away. "Honestly, fellas. I'm just an old fart on retirement. Courtesy of the Feds."

Tony said, "Yeah, I thought you got nicked out at sea a few years ago."

"And you heard right."

Vincent squinted. "And you turned state's evidence, if I heard right."

He nodded. "You both heard right. And I see where you're going with this, but you can relax. I rolled on the Atlantic City boys, who sailed me out to begin with. Not Philly. Never Philly."

Vincent nodded. "Well, look. If DeBarre trusts you, then so do I."

"That's good to hear." He chuckled. "Because I'm all you got right now."

"I'm surprised you're willing to get involved," Tony said. "After everything."

McCoy grinned at Tony. "Me, too. But I heard my boys up here decided to give the whole New York apparatus a what-for, and they needed a hand."

"Won't the Feds get sore if they find out you're back in the game?" Vincent asked.

McCoy nodded. "I'm not back in the game. This is a one-time thing for DeBarre. But you're right about the Feds. I'm supposed to be in Havana right now. They find out I'm north of Key West, sticking my nose into beer barrels, it'll be a one-way trip to the Big House."

Vincent peered over his shoulder. "Then less talk and more barrel loading might be wise."

They observed as McCoy's men unloaded the product and rolled them up a gangplank to the riverboats.

"Kinda small, aren't they?" Vincent commented.

"Small enough not to attract too much attention. It's more work loading them down, but if one gets nicked, we still have most of the load chugging upstream."

Tony nodded. "I pitched that idea to Vito last summer. He said it was too much money."

McCoy winced. "Every time I've heard that come outta someone's mouth, they ended up bankrupt or in the poke by the end of the month. If you don't spend money in this business, you'll end up on the end of the branch when the pruning comes."

Vincent squinted past the truck at the highway leading to the river. A line of three cars were driving up the access road, slowing enough to catch his attention.

"Gents," Vincent muttered with a snap of his fingers. "I think we have company."

"These your boys, Bill?" Tony asked.

McCoy shook his head. "All my boys are behind me."

"Feds?" Vincent asked.

"Maybe," McCoy replied.

"Best you get on the boat and get things moving, Bill," Vincent said. "I can help a bit, but if these are the Gee, then you'll want to be outta sight."

McCoy slapped his shoulder and made a winding motion with his finger at the rest of his crew, urging them to button up the riverboats.

The cars sped up, rounding the access road onto the riverfront and barreling straight for them.

"Can you pinch these mooks?" Tony asked. "Buy us some time?"

Vincent surveyed the area. "That's a lot of space. I might give you ten seconds, out here."

"We'll wait until they're closer then." Tony reached into the car to pull out a tommy gun.

Vincent scowled. "You're gonna start a dust-up with the Feds?"

Tony shook his head. "It's not the Feds. I'm thinking someone sold us out to Pittsburgh. Front car, passenger seat."

Vincent peered at the first vehicle, already sliding to a halt. A man with muttonchops spilling from the sides of a squat bowler hat sat beside the driver. His face was ruddy and amused. As the car slid to a stop, he cracked his fingers and stepped out.

Tony checked his magazine, and Vincent calculated the distance and eyed the boats. If it was Feds or Pittsburgh, either one would spray lead and grab the shipment.

Figures poured out of the three vehicles, most wearing dark suits and trench coats. One or two from the back carried choppers, keeping them low but at the ready. Vincent tested the flow of time rushing around his skin. Too many people. Too spread out. He'd have to save his energy for the right moment when a time pinch would be useful.

Three of the interlopers, including Muttonchops, continued forward as the rest fanned out behind them. The drivers stayed behind the wheels, engines running. Whatever this was, it was meant to be fast.

Which pointed more toward Pittsburgh than the Feds.

"Afternoon, folks! "Tony shouted. "How about we keep things friendly?"

Muttonchops stepped up to one of the emptied liquor trucks. He reached underneath the carriage and nudged it with a flick of his finger. The entire truck spun into the air, hurtling overhead like a toy tossed by a petulant child. The hunk of steel reached the apex of its arc, angling down for Tony and Vincent.

Vincent pinched time. Grabbing Tony by the collar, he dragged him closer to the river and released the time pinch before he'd spent too much of his energy.

The truck smashed onto their car in a roar of metal and shattering glass. Tony jumped, popping off two shots from his chopper before getting his bearings.

Vincent muttered, "That'll be a no, I think."

"They've got a pincher, so it's gotta be Pittsburg," Tony said.

Vincent checked the riverboats, each of which had fired up their engines. "Gotta hold these goons off. Ready for a scrap?"

Before Tony could respond, Vincent pinched time again, pulling him to a vantage point off to the side past the convoy, setting him up to aim at the intruders. He then swept around the back of the group just as the pull of magic began to eat away at his insides.

He released the time pinch and ducked behind one of the goons' cars. Tony sputtered for a second, then opened fire. A pale man with stringy black hair dodged behind one of the cars, lifting his hands at Tony. A plume of black smoke billowed from his fingertips, rushing through the air as it blossomed into a cloud of darkness.

Vincent crept up behind the line of gunmen as the cloud of shadow spread in a circle around the scene. He clocked one of the gunmen across the back of his head, grabbed his gun and pinched time.

Moving fast, he sent the butt of the gun against the temple of another gunman, then swept the feet out from underneath a third before a wave of nausea racked his frame. As he released time his two victims went to the ground.

Tony's gunfire relented as he became enshrouded in the black plume spreading its tendrils throughout the riverfront.

Vincent moved back several steps, aiming the gun he'd snatched at the backs of the besuited thugs and fired. They shouted, the ones who weren't shot dropping to their hands and knees and scrambling for cover.

All three of the pinchers turned their heads. The third pincher, a lean woman with short-cropped black hair, pounded a fist into her open palm.

The ground beneath Vincent lurched. He sailed into the air as a column of granite thrust from the ground where he had been standing. Tumbling, Vincent dropped his gun as he hit the ground several yards away.

Catching his breath, Vincent scrambled to his feet, and checked the river. Two of McCoy's boats had already disembarked.

Before he could reach the gun, the ground rumbled again, shaking until he couldn't stand. Vincent leapt for a nearby car, pinching time as he slid midair into the turbidity of his time bubble. Gripping a fender, Vincent pulled himself through the thickened air away from the rippling ground.

He crouched behind the car and returned the flow of time. The rumbling continued for a second before abating. Groans sounded nearby from the goons he'd shot, as well as voices.

"Any idea?" the woman shouted.

"Blink pincher, maybe?" a man replied.

"Pittsburgh don't got no blink pinchers," a third said.

Vincent scowled. These weren't the Pittsburgh crew, after all. So, who the hell were they?

Gunfire sounded from the riverfront. Vincent peered over the car's hood as the pinchers returned their focus to Tony. The shadow pincher pulled the cloud of darkness back into his fingers, clearing the air for the earth pincher, who sent a wall of granite slicing out of the ground in front of Tony. His bullets sprayed against stone.

Vincent made a quick mental calculation of his opponents. This was a lot of work for that earth pincher. She might be tapped out soon. The shadow pincher, on the other hand, could have a lot of juice left. It depended on how difficult it was for him to spread that weird cloud of ink in broad daylight over such a large area.

Muttonchops, however…what was the limit of his exertions?

Just as he pondered the subject, the car Vincent had crouched behind lifted into the air. Vincent pedaled away on hands and knees to spot the heave pincher holding the car over his head with three fingers, hoisting it like a dinner platter. He smirked at him.

"Look here," the earth pincher shouted with a polished London accent, "I do believe I've found our little rabbit."

Vincent gambled with his energy and pinched time once again. He crawled along the ground until his feet could find purchase. With just enough momentum through the time bubble, he shoulder-checked the heave pincher, pulling his fingers out from underneath the car suspended overhead.

And he didn't stop there. Vincent pressed on as his intestines throbbed and his chest began to heave. When he reached the other pinchers, he crouched and swept his leg against both of their knees, cartwheeling them just a few inches into the time-suspended air.

And that was all he had.

The time pinch dropped as a trickle of blood slipped from Vincent's nostril.

The heave pincher grunted as the car crashed down just inches in front of him. Vincent sprinted for the riverfront as the upended pinchers wheeled to the ground, shouting a string of vulgarities. He rounded the bulwark the earth pincher had raised in front of Tony who turned on Vincent, gun ready to fire.

Vincent ducked, holding up his hands. "It's me!"

Tony exhaled and lowered the chopper. His face sported a wide, dark blotch running from nose to ear. "You okay?"

Vincent ran a finger under his nose to wipe the blood. "Getting low."

"Who are these mooks?"

"Not Pittsburgh."

The ground rattled again, and Vincent gripped Tony to pull him clear of the wall.

The granite pulverized into a wide pile of gravel. The trio of pinchers stood in the center of the space glaring at them. The fierce-eyed earth pincher held herself up at her knees, gasping for air. There it was…she was tapped out.

Not that it mattered. He was pretty close to tapped out himself. They'd go down fighting, but it was pretty clear that he and Tony weren't going to prevail against these three with what firepower backup they still had remaining.

Muttonchops stared at Vincent, then nodded at the others. "Right, then. Time pincher. Must be."

Tony lifted his gun. The shadow pincher lifted both hands into the air. A ball of inky smoke shot toward them, encircling them both. Tony pulled the trigger, shooting blind into the black smoke until his magazine clicked empty.

After a few seconds, cars doors slammed shut and the vehicles that hadn't been ruined slipped out of the smoke on their way back to the highway.

They braced for the death that was surely about to come, only to see the dark plume dissipate. When it cleared, all that was left was the wreckage of the encounter, and their opponents' cars speeding off into the distance.

Tony took a few tenuous steps for the truck that had smashed their car. "Jesus and Mary. What was that all about?"

Vincent shook his head, lifting a hand for Tony to hold off as he held back a stab of nausea. Wiping the cold sweat from his forehead, he replied, "Search me. But we should probably head to Philadelphia. DeBarre needs to know."

* * *

"SON OF A BITCH!" DeBarre shouted as he paced around the table in his headquarters below the cannery. "Three of them?"

Vincent nodded, sipping some water from a glass.

Arnoud peered at Tony's face, standing just a little too close for Tony's comfort.

DeBarre continued, "They were there, huh? Right there? At the right time?"

Vincent said, "They could have followed us. Didn't attack until we'd had all the barrels loaded."

Tony swatted Arnoud's hand away. "You mind getting your mitts outta my face, fella?"

Arnoud pointed. "The mark. That mark on your face."

"Yeah," Tony grumbled. "I walked into some of that black smoke." He ran a hand over his cheek. "Won't come off."

DeBarre nodded with a scowl. "Shadow pincher. Ran into one once out west."

"Same one?" Vincent asked. "Skinny, tall goon with pale skin?"

"Not likely," DeBarre replied. "I dropped that one out of a train car."

"So?"

"We were crossing a gorge at the time."

Vincent winced. "Ah. Okay, so we got a whole new crew here."

DeBarre grumbled, "Yeah, but whose crew?"

Arnoud turned to Vincent. "The woman. You said she manipulated the ground underneath you?"

"Yeah."

"Earth pincher," Arnoud stated as he stepped toward the chairs to take a seat. "I've met one before. And she was a woman."

"Where?" asked Vincent.

"Ithaca."

Vincent shook his head. "I met her. It's not the same woman. This is someone else."

DeBarre broke the silence with a sigh. "It's got to be the New Yorkers. Damn."

Tony asked, "How can you be sure?"

"Makes sense," answered DeBarre. "They know about the Philly-Baltimore alliance. They have pinchers to spare. I figured it would take them longer to come down and do something about it. I guess there's a break in the turf battle up in the City."

Tony shook his head. "Well, ain't that just spiffy?"

Vincent frowned. "You think this is Masseria? Or Maranzano? Or maybe them both working together for once in their damned lives?"

DeBarre nodded. "Could be. It fits."

"But they didn't go after the hooch," Tony said. "They practically let it sail right up the river."

DeBarre shrugged. "So, they were a day late and a dollar short."

Vincent shook his head. "No. They didn't even try. They were more focused on engaging the two of us. And when they figured out what I was, they left. They could have easily killed us at that point, but they left."

DeBarre squinted. "So you think they might have been there for you?"

"Well, not for me exactly, because by that point they

probably could have killed me or grabbed me and hauled me off. It was like they were trying to figure out my powers, and once they did, they left."

Arnoud tented his fingers. "It was a feeler raid. Testing your strength. Probably waiting to see how many pinchers were there, what we had available in terms of magical ability. I can see New York doing that."

Vincent shook his head. "I don't know. They thought we were the Pittsburgh crew when they first got there. New York would've been better informed, I think."

Tony said, "But they were packing heat. Looked a lot like gangsters to me."

"Could it be Luciano?" asked DeBarre. "You said that Sparks Floresta had his eye on you. He's a schemer, that one. We might be looking at the first play in a bigger plan."

The meeting wrapped up with more questions than answers, and Tony and Vincent hit the road well after sunset. The drive back to Baltimore was quiet. In spite of the loss of a car and a few of DeBarre's men, the mission was a success. The beer was on its way to the Great Lakes, and they'd even met a living legend in the process. But the possibility that either Masseria or Maranzano had decided to get involved with Mid-Atlantic affairs wouldn't be welcome news for Vito.

Tony dropped Vincent off at his house just before sunrise. Vincent hauled himself up the stairs vowing to get at least a couple hours shut-eye before Vito inevitably summoned him for a report on the day's business.

As he reached his floor he froze as he spotted Hattie Malloy standing at his door.

CHAPTER 5

*V*incent put on a kettle as Hattie took a seat at his dinner table. A lean black kitten hopped onto the table, marching up to Hattie with wide amber eyes.

"Off the table, Roscoe," Vincent chided.

Roscoe blinked at Hattie, then lay down to expose his belly.

As she reached for the kitten, Vincent shook his head. "That's a trap, right there. Fine way to get a hand full of claws," he warned her.

"I can't believe how big he's gotten already," she said, choosing to scratch the cat's chin instead of venturing near his belly. "What a pretty boy he is. Aren't you a pretty boy?"

"A pretty boy who knows he's not supposed to be on the table." Vincent scooped Roscoe up and settled him on a pillow directly beside the stove. The cat immediately stepped off the pillow and lay down on the floor beside it.

"Brat," Vincent grumbled, turning back to the coffee.

"Thought I was the brat," Hattie teased, standing up to walk over to him.

"You're both brats." He shot her a quick smile and pulled two mugs from the cabinet.

"So you've been on a job today?" Hattie asked, taking in the dirt and smudges on his clothing.

"I have, escorting some beer as a favor to our friends up north. You?"

She shook her head. "I'm supposed to do a quick run with Raymond tonight, but I might need to put it off. Something came up."

"Something to do with official Crew boat-legging, or with your own personal hush-hush bootlegging on the side? Or something to do with the Charge?"

She grimaced, reluctant to involve him when he clearly was up to his ears in his own business. "The latter. Listen, boy-o. I'm afraid I need to ask for your help."

He poured hot water over coffee grounds, then leaned against the counter to face her. "Whatever you need."

She stared at him a moment, fighting the familiar tug of attraction that urged her to step into his arms and bury her face against his chest. She hadn't slept. He'd clearly had a rough day. The last thing she wanted to do was ask him to put his neck on the line once more, but these were children who had been taken—children who had trusted Hattie and Sadie to provide safe passage.

"It's a big ask, I'll warn you."

"Doesn't matter," he stated matter-of-factly. "I'm in."

Hattie blinked at Vincent, a warmth spreading through her chest. Didn't matter, he was in. Just like that. Without even knowing what it was she wanted, he was in because she'd asked him. How amazing was it to have someone in her life, to care about someone, who would drop everything for her? She trusted him like she'd trusted no one before, not even her parents. He'd always be there for her. He'd always help her no matter what the problem. And if she needed him, no matter what, he'd come. No questions asked.

She loved him. And as the realization roared through her, she pushed it all back. Now wasn't the time for that—not when he was still owned by the mob and she was in danger of being found out and hauled off to Ithaca. Now wasn't the time for love. Sorrow gripped her heart as she realized that there might never be a right time for them, for love.

"So what do you need me to do?" He reached out a hand and pulled her closer.

"A group of our kiddos was laid into yesterday." She wrapped her arms around his waist and relaxed against him. "I suppose it was day before yesterday, at this point."

"When you say 'laid into,' what does that mean exactly?"

"It means they were waylaid, taken on their way out west. All of them save for Charley."

He pulled back to look down into her face. "The fur pincher? Didn't he have a couple—?"

"Aye. His girls were taken, as well."

"It wasn't Vito's men. I can tell you that much."

Hattie nodded. "I know."

"Any idea who's behind this?"

"Well, boy-o. That's the favor. I need to go to the scene. Pick up the trail. And I don't want to do it alone." She stepped back and reached for his hand. "You and I are stronger together, you know."

He chuckled wearily. "Yeah, I coulda used you today."

She cocked her head. "That so? What happened on your beer run?"

"Never mind. One thing at a time. How far do we need to drive? Because I'm pretty sure Vito's gonna want an accounting from me sometime soon."

"Down the B&O line. First waystation's in Parkersburg. That's where Charley said they were grabbed."

"West Virginia? Hell's bells, I can't seem to escape West Virginia, today." He sighed. "I don't have a car right now, but I can—"

"I have one waiting downstairs."

"What," he asked with a lift of a brow. "That shiny new Studebaker?"

Hattie nodded. "Right. Feed your cat, grab a thermos for the coffee, then we'll leave. I'll drive and let you catch up on sleep."

Within fifteen minutes, Roscoe had a bowl of mackerel and Vincent had settled into the shotgun seat of the Studebaker. As Hattie drove west out of Baltimore, Vincent dozed, his head resting at a backward angle against the bench seat.

The quiet of the road once they'd cleared the city gave Hattie time to think. Children in chains being shipped off to Ithaca. It was a nightmare—one worse than she'd been plagued with recently. Rescuing Vincent from there had practically taken a miracle. How the heck was she going to rescue a dozen children? It made her sick to think of what they might be going through right now.

Those children had trusted the Charge—trusted her—and she'd let them down. She needed to find them, to make sure this didn't happen again. And then figure out a way to rescue the children who'd been taken, to give them their freedom once again.

They arrived in Parkersburg just after noon. Vincent's morning nap had seemed to bring his mind into focus. Hattie parked the car beneath an iron trellis bridge crossing the Ohio River. As they stepped out, breath puffing clouds in the still-cool air, Vincent gave her a cautious look.

"You feeling okay?" he asked.

"I'm fine. Just worried about these children, that's all."

"You sure? You look like you're coming down with something. Croup going around?"

"I haven't been sleeping," she told him.

He halted, holding her by both arms as his eyes searched her face. "I'm worried about you, Hattie. You need to take care of yourself."

"I'm trying. It's just…bad dreams. And I've got a lot going on right now."

He leaned in to kiss her forehead. "I know all about bad dreams."

Of course he did. Suddenly she felt like a complete heel, whining about lack of sleep and bad dreams when he was probably reliving the torture of Ithaca every night. If he was strong enough to keep himself together after that experience, then who was she to complain?

An image floated into her mind, of her and Vincent curled up in bed together, each of them keeping the night-mares at bay with the combined strength of…of whatever this was they had. Not just the soul twin thing, but *them*. Together.

They were stronger together.

"Waystation's this way." She pulled back with a smile and took his hand leading him to a patch of muddy turf shaded with scrub and short trees. A gravel path led to the slope beneath the trellis bridge's support post. A clutch of trees had been parted to reveal a wood-framed door leading into a hole dug into the hillside. Hattie continued along the path as Vincent paused to examine the trees.

"What is it?" she asked.

He crouched into the mud, running a hand along the top of the dead grass and dried leaves that rolled along with the ground to pull the trees apart.

"Not sure yet," he replied, looking at what seemed to be soot clinging to the tips of his fingers.

She squinted at him, then turned to examine the wood framing. "Looks like a mine."

"This is the safe house?"

"First stop westward," she said. "Caravans let out here to rest and get some food. Boxcars aren't high in luxury, and these are just children."

"I understand the concept, but you said this joint was attacked."

He was right. This didn't look like the scene of any violence. Hattie ran a hand over the unblemished wood planks of the door frame. "No busted door. No bullet holes," she noted.

"No shots fired. Hmm."

"What's in your head?"

He pursed his lips, then shook his head, "Still not sure."

The door to the waystation stood ajar, the iron latch unscratched. Hattie nudged it open, peering into the dark interior.

Vincent eased the door open farther, allowing more noonday light into a long but narrow hall of bunks. The air was dank, but the space was clean.

Hattie spotted an oil lamp hanging on a nail not far from the door.

"Do you have a match?"

"Don't smoke," Vincent reminded her.

She pawed over a shelf near the front door until she found a box of wooden matches. Lighting the lantern, she set the wick, holding it over her head to step deeper into the safe house.

Vincent joined her, running a hand over the blankets on the nearest bunk. "Beds are made," he said. "No one left in a hurry."

"Or they were hit in the middle of the day," Hattie offered.

"Still," Vincent mumbled. "This place is tidier than mine."

"Perhaps they never made it to the waystation? Could the *train* have been hijacked?"

Vincent squinted at the long wall behind the bunks.

Hattie leaned in. "Vincent?"

"Bring that lamp over."

She complied, lifting the lamp over their heads.

Vincent stepped cautiously toward the wall, dabbing it with his fingers then inspecting his fingertips.

"Ease back a step or two," he urged.

Hattie took a few steps back, the light of the lantern expanding in the space. A long shadow refused to widen along with the rest. Vincent traced the edge of the shadow. The dark mark ran diagonally along the wall, disappearing into the floor, where one of the bunk legs bore a blemish like a water stain.

"What is that?" Hattie asked.

"*Now* I'm sure," Vincent replied, turning for the front. "Let's get outta here."

Hattie stood frozen for a second, then double-timed it after Vincent.

Outside, he pointed to the rippled earth running in parallel dykes alongside the gravel path. "See that?"

"Aye."

"Those trees were peeled away."

"What could do that?"

"An earth pincher." He sighed. "Let me tell you about my day yesterday."

He filled her in, from his trip to Morgantown not far from where they stood, to meeting Bill McCoy, to the attack from three highly-trained pinchers.

Hattie shook her head as they got back into the car, Vincent taking the wheel this time. "The mark on Tony's face. That was permanent?"

"Time will tell, I guess. But whatever that shadow pincher does, it leaves a trace behind. He was here. As was the earth pincher."

"Then it's true. New York is on the attack. And they probably have the children now." She shuddered at the thought.

Vincent sat behind the wheel staring forward in thought.

"At least we have a trail," she commented. "First here, then Morgantown. That means they're moving west."

Vincent shook his head. "I'm not solid on this."

"Not solid on what? That they're moving west?"

He turned in the seat to face Hattie. "None of this makes any sense. How did they know, is the question no one's asking. How did they know where this place was? When the Charge would be here? For that matter, how did they know we'd re-route the barrel shipment through West Virginia instead of skirting north past Pittsburgh? Who the hell are these people?"

Hattie shook her head.

"And what's more," he continued, "why did they let the beer escape? It's like they didn't even care about the beer, like it was me they were after. Only, they could've nabbed me if they really wanted. It was like they were testing me. Testing us."

Hattie caught her breath. "They're not after the bootlegging business. They're after the pinchers."

"Both free and owned. Is it possible this is some new group that has nothing to do with the New York mob?"

"What else would there be? If it wasn't the New York mob, or Pittsburgh or Philadelphia."

"Or Baltimore."

"Which leaves maybe, what? Cleveland?"

Vincent shook his head. "They'd be more interested in the beer shipment, if it was Cleveland."

"And the Charge is the only organized group of free pinchers on this continent."

Vincent lifted a finger. "That you know of."

She held a breath. "You think these are independents?"

"I'm saying we can't rule that out." He turned back to the wheel and started down the road. "DeBarre's convinced it's Masseria, so let's not go sharing this theory willy-nilly."

"God in Heaven," she groaned. "What's next?"

"Food is what's next. I for one am starving. What say we make lunch?"

They found a cafe in town and ordered coffee, meat pastries with ramp chutney, and a thick slice of apple pie to share. As they ate, Vincent stared out the window deep in thought.

Hattie watched him as the line of his jaw clenched in and out, his dark, deep eyes searching tiny circles as his brain clicked. He was a handsome man, better looking than Valentino in her estimation, but it was more than his good looks and boyish charm that attracted her. He was smart, brave, thoughtful. Loyal. Her knight.

What other man would continue against such impossible odds to convince her mother to like him?

He caught her staring at him, and demurred. "What?"

"A radio."

He blinked at her, then shook his head.

"One of Ma's friends has a radio and they've come down a good bit in price, but she won't let us get one. Flies into a rage every time I suggest it, saying we need to be saving that money and not spending it on frivolous nonsense."

Vincent's eyebrows shot up. "You're telling me to buy her a radio? Sounds like a good way to get stabbed by those knitting needles."

Hattie grinned. "Da and I would get stabbed by those knitting needles. You, she'll grumble about, accusing you of buying it with ill-gotten gains. Then as soon as you're gone, she'll sneak over to that radio and start listening. The woman will never admit it, but you'll move up a notch in her affections."

"I can't get much lower in her affections," Vincent drawled. "But you know her better than I do. If you think a radio will help, then I'll get her a radio."

"Good." Hattie pointed. "And you have some chutney on your chin."

He grabbed a napkin and wiped his chin in alarm. He pulled it away clean, then squinted at her.

"You're a bigger brat than Roscoe."

She snickered. "If I can't give my own soul twin the business, then who can I?"

"Soul twin," he grumbled. "Not crazy about that word. Makes us sound…"

"Incestuous?" she suggested with a mischievous smirk.

"Pretentious, is what I was gonna say. But you go ahead with your perverted thoughts."

"Hey," she protested with a light slap to his arm. "You know you should've taken me with you yesterday on that beer run. The pair of us would have taken those rogue pinchers in a shake of a lamb's tail."

He nodded with a grin. "The thought had occurred to me."

"Well," she said, running her fingers up his sleeve. "You'll just have to keep me close, then. Won't you?"

"I'd like that. I'd actually like that a lot," Vincent said. "But I thought it was too dangerous for us to stay so close."

Her smile faded. "That's what the book suggests. A Bright Soul being so close together against all odds? It's like a Christmas present wrapped up and ready for any Hell pincher to scoop up."

"Well, I'm not about to let that happen. No Hell pincher's gonna grab you when I'm around."

Images of Hattie's recent nightmares flooded her mind. The dark, sinister figure just out of sight, always watching, always winning. And as Hattie sipped her coffee, she was very much aware of the marble in her pocket pressing against her leg.

CHAPTER 6

Tobacco smoke hung in a wispy blanket near the ceiling of the Havre de Grace vineyard parlor. No fewer than twenty men sat or stood in a ring around the mahogany-paneled room while a fire crackled in the hearth at the far end. A lean, young man gestured with a cigar as he outlined worries from the distribution network of a possible upcoming hit on Sabella.

Vincent and Lefty stepped through the ring as Vito beckoned from his writing desk opposite the hearth.

"Alonzo. Vincenzo," Vito called. "I trust you have some useful information from our new allies to the north?"

"We do," Lefty replied.

"Then, please. These rumors have become a distraction." Vito thumped his desk with the flat of his fist. "Do me a mercy and dispel them."

Vincent glanced to Lefty, who gave him a reassuring nod.

"I'm afraid, Capo, that these rumors are true."

A murmur spread through the onlookers.

Vincent continued, "I was there when it happened. In

Morgantown. Just as the shipment was nearly loaded, we were hit by a war party."

"Pittsburgh?" one of the men asked.

"No."

"Are you certain?" Vito grumbled.

"I am, Capo. I overheard…" He searched for a diplomatic way to put it. "There was some confusion on their end as to whether we were, in fact, the Pittsburgh crew."

"Then the attack was meant for them?" another of Vito's minions posited.

"Or the shipment?" a third asked.

"It wasn't the shipment they were after," Vincent said. "They barely noticed the barrels, which got off safe. No, they were feeling us out."

Lefty took over. "It's what the army refers to as a probing mission. Testing the enemy's defenses and capacity for waging war. A feint or measured attack meant to draw a response. They knew this was a Philadelphia shipment, and most likely were uncertain if Pittsburgh was involved or not. They hit fast and ran, trying to determine the players involved and their strength."

Vito asked, "Where is Antonio right now?"

Vincent answered, "He's still in Philly, helping DeBarre and Arnoud break the news to Sabella." He lifted a finger. "There's more. Among this probing raid were three pinchers."

Vito's face darkened. "*Stregone?*" He took a seat once again, eyes searching his desktop for the conclusion Vincent was sure he'd arrive at. "This…this is the work of Masseria."

More rumblings in the crowd.

Vito continued, "Masseria was most outspoken against any cooperation between our territory and Sabella's. This has to have been his doing."

Vincent held his tongue. This was the same supposition DeBarre had made. With the unilateral poaching of all pinchers from the Ithaca farm, the New York families had soured their relationships with all of the East Coast families. Which they could do, as they held the lion's share of pincher power.

And there they'd been—three pinchers versus one. It seemed so obvious to everyone in the room that this had been a hit from Masseria, testing the strength of Philadelphia and their new alliance with Baltimore.

Vito called for a map. In minutes, two men wheeled in a map of the immediate area on an easel as the furniture in the parlor was cleared. Vincent had seen this ballet of wordless reorganization before, when the Bratva had fired the first shot in their brief war with Corbi more than a year ago. This meant the Crew was shifting from the business of liquor to the business of war.

Lefty eased to the side of the room to keep out of the way of the eager young bucks ready for a place at the table. Vincent joined him, listening with a casual face for clues as to the Crew's next move.

"Well, this is a damn mess," Lefty mumbled.

Vincent nodded. "I figured Vito would kick his heels over this, but it's like someone rang a dinner bell."

Lefty shrugged. "He's frustrated. He feels he's not afforded proper respect from the other families."

"Philadelphia's been nothing but buttons and bows to Vito."

"Yeah," Lefty said with a smirk. "But at the end of the day, they got two pinchers. He only has one."

"Then it's not respect Vito wants."

"Doesn't matter what he wants. It'll never be enough."

An enormous wood-carved table was carried into the

room, with three leaves set into the center. The war table had arrived. A bizarre quiet settled over the room as Vito took a seat at the head of the table directly before the map of the Chesapeake Bay and surrounding region. Men stood stiff, waiting for Vito to name his council.

One by one, Vito nodded with the subtlest of motions to his veteran gangsters. Twelve men were chosen, with one seat left empty.

As the young bucks shuffled on nervous feet waiting for him to name the last of the war council, Vito announced, "This seat will be saved for Antonio when he returns."

A rush of disappointed breaths spread through the room. Vincent sighed in relief. Though it would've been a significant break from Vito's typical procedure, ever since Ithaca the Capo has held Vincent in higher regard. The notion of sitting at the war table set Vincent's nerves on edge. He'd need to move freely in the coming days, particularly with Vito focused on New York and not this nameless threat.

"Gentlemen," Vito declared, "we must prepare for open hostility from New York." He spun in his chair to glance at the map. "If they have come as far south as West Virginia, then they have been allowed passage through Pittsburgh's territory."

"Hardly a surprise," one of his war council said.

"Indeed. The happier news is that we now benefit from a relationship with Sabella in Philadelphia. And with Richmond vacant of interested parties, we have only a western front to maintain."

"And Philly's borders," another at the table added.

Vito scowled. "Bah. They have manpower of their own."

Vincent's eyebrows shot up. As much as DeBarre had committed to this mutual protection of the two cities, it was jarring to hear Vito abandon his end so quickly.

Vito continued, "We must redouble our presence in the

foothills from Baltimore to the mountains. Protect our land lines flowing from the distilleries."

"And the Bay?" one of the war council asked.

Another added, "With Richmond empty, we have an opportunity to open business to the southern coast."

Vito nodded. "We do need to secure our claim on the entire Bay, such is certain. These animals in white sheets will continue to threaten our shipments unless they are taught a lesson. That is for another day, however. Now we need to concentrate on defending against any attack from New York."

Several at the table nodded. The violence along the waterfront had doubled over the winter. Tony had made it quite clear this was an issue that needed to be addressed before a repeat of May's attempted piracy occurred. It seemed that Vito had listened for once, but liquor distribution would always take a back seat to any rumored attack from New York.

"So," Vito declared, "we will turn all of our attention to Masseria. Matters on the Bay will wait."

Vincent held a breath, rolling a thought around his brain. With a straightening of his spine, he took a step forward.

"Sir? Tony should be here to address matters of Bay security. This isn't just a matter of safeguarding our liquor distribution, but ensuring we aren't vulnerable to a water attack."

Vito nodded, then spread his palms over the table. "That is true. Would someone bother very kindly to fetch him for me?"

Before any of the sycophants left standing could cash in on the opportunity, Vincent said, "I know exactly where he is, Capo. I'll get him for you."

The young bucks nearby grumbled, but Vito was already done with this distraction. "Fine. Go. Hurry."

Vincent bowed, then rushed for the door.

As he stepped into the bleary midmorning sunlight, the door opened and closed behind him once again. Lefty trotted up to Vincent, pulling his coat over his right shoulder.

"You mind easing up?" he grumbled.

Vincent waited a second for Lefty to catch up. He turned to Lefty, ducking his head to whisper, "Listen. I need you to get Tony down here. I've got somewhere I need to be."

Lefty cocked a brow. "And while I'm running errand boy, where are you going exactly?"

"Somewhere. You just have to trust me on this one."

Lefty shook his head. "I don't like this, Vincent. I don't like being kept in the dark on these things."

"Trust me," Vincent urged.

"Okay." Lefty smacked Vincent's arm. "Go on then, before Vito needs you back here."

Vincent liberated one of the cars parked in the circular drive in front of the villa, stranding one of the gangsters at the vineyard while he drove for Locust Point. Lizzie Sadler's warehouse was their agreed-upon meeting point for the day. The last time Vincent arrived unannounced, Lizzie pulled a gun on him. As he pulled up to the warehouse, he hoped Hattie was there.

Or anyone. There were no cars parked in front of the warehouse door.

He strode up to the sliding door, pulling it open on its squeaky rail.

"Hello?"

A figure stepped from the dark interior, lit from behind by a single oil lamp. "You're early, boy-o."

Vincent sighed in relief. "Yeah, I scurried free of the meeting sooner than expected. Any news? Did you talk to Charlie and Sadie about what we found in West Virginia?"

Hattie pulled him to a cluster of moonshine barrels, hopping up to take a seat on one. "First I want to hear about your meeting. Is our dear Uncle Vito beating the war drums against New York yet?"

"He is. Philadelphia is in a panic, and Vito's ready to close ranks and hunker down. He's worried about Masseria probing the mountain supply lines and plans on doubling manpower toward West Virginia, and possibly on key inlets along the bay and the river."

"What about sending some of the Crew to help Philadelphia?"

Vincent shrugged. "Looks like this new alliance is a one-way street for Vito."

Hattie chewed her lip. "How I hate that man."

"I'm with you. What news do you have from Sadie?"

Hattie rubbed her face. "I haven't been back to the Charge yet. I was supposed to go on a run with Raymond tonight, but…"

Vincent reached out to touch her cheek. "You okay? What happened?"

"Raymond was supposed to be here loading up the Runabout. It's not like him to be this late."

"I'm sure he's fine. Probably something to do with the baby."

"Perhaps. Lizzie's gone to check on him."

"I'm surprised you didn't go, yourself," Vincent said.

"I knew you were coming by and didn't want it to be Lizzie here when you came knocking." She sighed, running her hands over her face once more. "But, anyway. We were discussing Vito the Tinpot Dictator."

Vincent took a seat on the barrel next to Hattie's. "This group that hit the Charge caravan and DeBarre's beer shipment. Vito and DeBarre are both convinced they're from New York. I'm convinced it's rogue pinchers, kind of another Charge."

"Either way they took those children. Charley barely escaped. Whoever they are they're no friends of ours."

"True, but if these rogues can be, I don't know. Channeled? Directed into Vito's blind side? That would weaken his position, perhaps fatally. And neither of us would be in the center of it."

She squinted at Vincent. "And how do you propose we channel these pincher snatchers without knowing who they are or what their agenda is?"

He shrugged. "That's as far as I've gotten. I mean, clearly we have a lot to learn before anything good can come from this. But how often do we have a force ready to aim at Vito without sticking our noses in the middle of it?"

"This is less of a plan, more wishful thinking."

"I never said it was a plan."

"Well, you're the brains of this outfit," she teased. "I'm the bloody muscle."

He smiled. "Guess I need to do better, then."

A motor outside captured their attention. They slid off their barrels, Vincent taking a position behind the door's opening. Hattie peered through the opening into the late morning sunlight. Her eyes tensed as Lizzie's car came to a screeching halt in front of the door.

"Something's wrong," she muttered.

Vincent moved to join her beside the door as Lizzie Sadler rushed into the warehouse. Hattie reached for Lizzie, pulling her to a halt as the woman glanced back and forth between them.

"You're both here," Lizzie gasped. "Good."

Hattie asked, "What's wrong? What's happened?"

"It's..." Lizzie closed her eyes to compose herself. "It's Raymond."

"Is he hurt? Where is he?" Hattie demanded.

"There's smoke...on Curtis Creek."

Vincent leaned in. "Smoke?"

"And men," she added. "With guns."

Vincent and Hattie exchanged glances and ran for the cars. Hattie jumped into the Runabout with Lizzie while Vincent took his borrowed Crew car, and they made best speed for Curtis Creek. Vincent spotted the smoke a good mile away, curling in a wicked twist into the air over the thick canopy overlooking the outlet of Curtis Creek. The boughs of white oaks sported winter-browned leaves, some drifting onto the dirt path leading to the line of modest shanties running in a line along the river bank.

Two of the shanties belched dark black smoke from their ruins as orange flames flickered from gaps burned open in the rafters. A line of dark-skinned residents rushed back and forth to the river with buckets, tossing meager handfuls of river water onto flames that didn't seem to notice.

Vincent jumped out of the car, rushing toward the commotion. Hattie sprinted alongside him shouting Raymond's name.

Sparks lifted into the overhanging trees, catching some of the dried oak leaves aflame as they rained down onto the remaining houses. Vincent paused to help a young girl off the ground. The terrified child screamed as tears ran down both cheeks. As he lifted the girl into his arms, searching the faces nearby for her parents, a lean woman rushed from a clutch of onlookers, face drawn in panic.

"Is everyone safe?" he asked her, handing the child over.

The woman replied in incoherent blubbering. A shirtless man raced from the bucket line, stepping between Vincent and the woman, his expression menacing.

Vincent lifted his hands. "Easy. How can I help?"

The man's expression shifted to one of relief. "Ya carry a bucket?"

Vincent nodded and began rolling up his sleeves. As he

ran behind the shirtless man to join the bailing brigade, shouts from a nearby shack pulled his attention away.

Flaming leaves had caught a new structure on fire. The bucket line split in two as they divided their attention.

A woman near the river flailed her arms. "They're inside!" she screamed as she ran for the door.

Vincent rushed to beat her to the building, pinching time with a snap of his fingers. He pulled himself up the rickety porch steps and threw a shoulder into the door. It thumped against his weight once, twice, and then on the third strike it eased open.

Inside the shack a rippling carpet of flames rose along the underside of the gables, frozen in time as its light throbbed in the time bubble. An elderly couple lay on the ground, a man covering his wife with his jacket. Vincent reached for the old man, pulling his time-frozen frame off the ground and hoisting him through the open door. He laid him on the ground several yards away before returning to the burning building. As he reached around the old woman's arms to pry her off the floor, the toll on his time pinch tugged at his guts. He paused, swallowing back a knot in his throat.

A shadow filled the doorway. Vincent glanced up in panic, relaxing as Hattie swam into the room. The pull of the magic eased as she joined him, reaching for the woman's legs. Together, they hauled her out of the building and settled her beside her husband.

Hattie nodded to Vincent, and he returned the flow of time.

Vincent caught his breath and waited for the nausea to subside. "Raymond?"

Hattie gave him a nod. "They're safe." She pointed to the river where Nadine cradled Dougie.

They both went to lend a hand with the buckets, taking

place in a line directly behind Raymond. In an hour, three houses stood in ruins, including the home of the elderly couple Vincent and Hattie had rescued. Sniffles and moans sounded from a clutch of displaced residents, while the rest stood or plodded around in silence.

Raymond reached for Hattie, gripping her in a tight hug as a tear fell from his face. "They hit us from the water."

"Who? Who did this?" she asked through tight lips.

"Those Bianco Fiore crazies. They came up the river firing guns. Didn't hit nobody, but they lit two houses on fire before they left."

Vincent crossed his arms thinking once more about Vito's disinterest in taking care of Bianco Fiore while New York was first in his mind. He wasn't even sure the theft of one of their shipments would shift the man's focus. The only thing that would get more security on the inlets and the Bay right now would be if New York hit them from the water.

And if these pinchers weren't New York as Vincent suspected, then Raymond and these people along the waterways were on their own.

Hattie went off to check on Nadine, then rejoined Vincent as they gave the Bowleses some space.

"This was too close to Baltimore. The Bianco Fiore are growing bolder," he told her.

"Reckless," Hattie said. "There's nothing keeping them on a leash."

Vincent rubbed his face with a sigh. "I'll take this to the Crew. Maybe between Tony and I we can convince Vito to send a party into the Bay to mop these animals up."

Hattie gripped Vincent's arm tight. "Even if you do, that's just a short-term solution. You said it yourself that these people are decentralized. The Crew might be able to get them to lay off the distribution, but I can't see Vito bothering to stop this sort of thing from happening." She huffed a breath in frustration. "Slavery was bloody-well abolished, but these people are still living like they can just decide a person don't have a right to live. How is this possible?"

"Some people love to hate. Some people *live* to hate. I don't know if we'll ever be rid of those. Best we can do is make them too afraid to act on it."

"Then we'll terrify them," she snapped. "We need to take care of this."

Vincent blinked. "Yeah, okay. First let me see if I can get some guns."

Her face was dark, not from smoke but from some shadow of anger that clung to her like a ghost.

He tried to pull her into his arms. "We'll take care of it. *I'll* take care of it. Hattie, look at me. I said I'd help, and I mean it. That's whether I can convince Vito to send support or not."

"And what about Raymond?" she huffed, pulling away. "Where are they supposed to live, now?"

Vincent surveyed the damage along the river front. "Their home didn't get burned, did it?"

"No, but they're not safe here. Not anymore. None of them are safe."

She hadn't been sleeping. She'd been afraid for her best friend and her family—was still afraid for them. She'd just had a group of children, children she felt responsible for, snatched from a train. He understood. He truly understood.

Once more he reached out to her. "I'll take care of it."

"No, it's not enough! Everything has to change. No one's safe anymore! Not Raymond. Not the pinchers we're trying to help. No one."

He pulled her into his arms as her face twisted and she began to cry. This wasn't just about Raymond and his family,

Vincent realized. The free pinchers weren't safe. Her friends weren't safe. She wasn't safe.

Vincent held her close as she unloaded her grief into his chest. "Everything will change," he whispered. "I swear it will."

CHAPTER 7

"**O**h, hold still you little inchworm!"

Hattie bounced Dougie on her knee as he squirmed to free himself from her grip, bending himself backward and shifting his weight over her knee. She pulled him back onto her lap, turning him around to face his mother, who had joined three women at an enormous cast iron kettle slung over a bonfire. The flames were fueled by charcoaled timbers from the ruined houses. With so many of the locals busying themselves with cleanup and tearing down the still smoldering ruins, no one had time to make dinner. It was Nadine's idea to pull out the old kettle they used to boil crabs at Easter and start up a large vat of soup for the whole creek. All she needed was for someone to watch Dougie, and Hattie was happy to volunteer.

Raymond trod up from the pile of unscorched timbers he and several others had collected from the victims' houses. His clothes were covered in soot, as was his face from wiping sweat off with a dark-dusted rag. He plopped down onto the ground beside Hattie, lying on his back to stare up at the trees which were now largely empty of leaves.

"How are you?" Hattie asked.

"Fit to be tied."

"I understand the feeling."

He sighed and closed his eyes. "Wish I'd known they were comin'," he grumbled. "Coulda gotten my gun from the boat. Maybe dropped three or four before they let in. Maybe they'd have turned around if they knew we had guns to fight back. Maybe—"

"You would have been killed," Hattie interrupted. "And this little bean right here wouldn't have a father."

He hammered the ground with his fist. "It just ain't fittin'. We got no one to go to. Police'll find some way to make this our fault. Damn governor don't give a shit about anything now he's back in office. Just roads and trains and bridges. Not us."

Raymond's words hit Hattie direct in the chest. She knew that feeling all too well. But when it all came down to it, she could walk down the street without anyone knowing she was a pincher. People like Raymond? There was no way he or the others here at Curtis Creek could pass for something they weren't.

As Hattie ruminated on the injustice of it all, her hands clenched into fists. "It just makes me so angry."

"Yeah, I know." He took Dougie from her lap. "You're looking like you need some sleep. Let us finish up here while you go on home."

"There's so much to do," she said, gesturing to the burned out buildings. "I can help with clean up, or give Nadine a hand with the food. I feel like I gotta do something."

"Baby girl." He patted her on the shoulder. "I appreciate it, but we're gonna be at this for some time here. And we still have a liquor run to make in the next day or so. Best you head home, and rest up."

Hattie stared at Raymond for a long moment before

nodding. "I suppose so." She reached over to rub Dougie's tummy before standing up. Giving Raymond a sideways hug, she went to say goodbye to Nadine.

The marble in her pocket felt heavier than it should as she joined Lizzie at the Runabout.

"Everyone okay?" she asked as they both climbed in.

"Physically? Yes."

Lizzie took the wheel, steering back into the city. "It's a hell of a thing," she finally said to break the silence.

"Seems it's only getting worse," Hattie replied with a shake of her head.

"Maybe your beau will drum up some muscle from his betters."

"I hope so."

Vincent had left several hours ago to report the events to his mobster brethren.

Brethren. That didn't really describe the Crew, anymore. Not for Vincent. Ithaca had opened his eyes to his situation. Ever since then, he'd been musing about a future where there was no Crew, no Vito. And now he was floating the idea about setting these rogue pinchers against his own boss. It was the first time he'd brought up open rebellion against the Crew. Whatever he'd endured at Ithaca had been some catalyst, transforming him into an independent man.

Hattie pursed her lips as she pondered her own transformation. She'd been assuming more of a leadership role with the Charge. She still made boat-legging runs with Raymond and weekly bootlegging trips on the sly, but both of those were taking a backseat to the Charge.

And then there were the nightmares, the lack of sleep. Anger was too easy to come by these days. Violence seemed to be an answer she was far more willing to accept than she had months ago. Was that her? Was she becoming jaded, numb to the idea of taking a life? Or did the marble in her pocket have something to do with her acceptance, embrace even, of a violent solution to all the world's problems?

Perhaps Absalom was right. Was it too dangerous carrying around this soul trap? Was hell itself slipping into her world through this tiny marble?

Lizzie dropped Hattie off at her home in Hampden where she climbed the stairs in an exhausted haze. When she stepped into her apartment, both of her parents jumped up from their seats.

"'Attie!" Alton called. "Where've you been, girl?"

Hattie just lifted hand and kept walking.

Branna stepped in front of her. "What happened? You reek of smoke, and your clothes are black with soot. Honey, are you okay?"

Hattie fought back sudden tears. "Raymond and his neighbors were attacked. They set fire to two houses."

"That's your colored friend down by the river?" Alton asked "What happened?"

Hattie shook her head. "Please, Da. I need to wash up."

"You do that," her mother said. "You wash up, but you come right back and tell us what happened."

With a weary shake of her head, Hattie retired to draw a bath. She soaked for a good while, trying to force the images of burning houses from her mind. At least no one had been shot, or burned, at least no one had died or been seriously injured beyond some minor burns. All was not lost.

Once she'd scrubbed the grime from her body and toweled off, she slipped on a dress and returned to the kitchen. Hattie took a seat as her mother set a cup of tea in front of her.

"Now then, is your friend hurt?" Branna asked. "Is his family okay?"

"They're all fine. Just frightened and angry."

"Who attacked them?" Alton asked.

"Some feeble-minded bigots from the Bay. Call themselves the Bianco Fiore."

Alton nodded and lifted his fork. "Aye, I've heard of them. Lynched a young man just last month over by Easton."

Branna said, "Thankfully that's a long way from here."

"Raymond's not so far," Hattie grumbled. "They're coming up the Bay and down the rivers and inlets. It was just burning some buildings this time, but I'm scared of what they might do next time."

Alton nodded and sliced another piece of meat. "It's the times we live in. Everyone's looking for their share, and they'll take it from anyone they can." He chewed his pork a while, then added, "I'm sorry for your friend and his neighbors. People should be able to live in peace without this sort of thing happen'en"

"Thanks, Da."

"Were you in danger?" Branna asked with a worried frown.

"No. I came after. Helped clean up the damage. They burned two houses and a third took some fire next door."

Branna let out a breath. "Well, perhaps it's best if you keep clear of there until all this blows over."

Hattie shook her head. "I need to help them. I won't slink away like some frightened rat."

Alton reached out to touch her arm. "Your mother is right. We worry enough over you. No sense in you getting shot over someone else's problems."

Someone else's problems. Hattie glared at her father. "No."

"Well, don't get riled up," he grumbled. "We're thinking on your safety, is all."

"Da, I run booze up and down the same waters every week. I deal with gangsters and crooks and hoboes and good people all the same. I'm not about to let these bastards frighten me off."

"We worry enough about you boat-legging. We worry about your safety," Alton repeated.

"What about Raymond's safety, then?" Hattie countered. "Where's he supposed to go? He can't move somewhere else. Who's going to solve all this? No one will if we just tuck our heads and look to ourselves."

Alton stood up and patted Hattie on the shoulder. "Aye, it's a terrible state he's in. And I feel for him, I do." He headed out of the kitchen, turning in the doorway to look at her. "I think you know that."

"Aye, Da," Hattie sighed. "I just want to help."

Branna stood up, turning to take her cup to the sink. "You should rest. I've been hearing you up all hours of the night, not sleeping. It's making you a fusspot."

Hattie rubbed her face. "Sorry. It just feels like everyone's turning on each other."

Her mother sat down beside her. "Things got better for us. And they'll get better for your friend. It'll take time, but it'll get better. You'll see."

"It'll take time and good people to make a stand," Hattie added.

"Perhaps." Her mother patted her hand. "And if you feel it's your place to take that stand, just know what it'll cost. I don't want you flying off into a rage and putting yourself in needless danger."

Hattie nodded, then reached for her mother's hand. "Aye, I know."

"It's for people with power to change things. Sometimes you have to step aside and let someone else do the work, Hattie."

"Vincent's looking into it," Hattie said, sniffling through her emotions. "Maybe he can talk the Crew into helping."

Branna scowled. "I don't see how his lot can improve anything."

"He was there today, Ma. Helping save lives on the river. I wish you could see what I see in him. He's a good man."

"He's a gangster."

Hattie sighed. "I'm not having this argument again. You've passed judgment on Vincent, and I can't change your mind. So, I won't try. Just know that I…I care very much for him. And it's hurtful that you can't find it in your heart to like him just a little, to maybe give him a chance."

"I'll judge a man by his deeds, by the way he treats you, the way he makes you feel."

"He treats me like I'm the most important person in his life, Ma. And he makes me feel…he makes me happy. Being with him makes me so happy."

Branna leaned forward. "And what happens when some night he doesn't come home? When he takes a bullet to the head out doing some gangster business? What happens if you're with child and they sell him to some other mob family, or ship him out of state for years? Or they find out you're a pincher and he has to turn you in?"

Hattie pulled away, her heart racing at her mother's words. How many nights had she worried about Vincent dying in a hail of gunfire? Or being sold? Life without him would be bleak.

But all she could counter was her mother's last question. "He wouldn't do that. Vincent would never turn me in. Never."

"Maybe not, but in the end you're going to be hurt. And if he hurts you on purpose, leaves you heartbroken and pregnant, then I'll hunt him down myself. I want to see you happy, Hattie. That dream of a strong man and a family for you? That's a dream I've held on to for a while, now. But he's married already, honey. He's married to his family of criminals. And even if he wants to leave it all behind, do you really think they'll let him?"

Hattie couldn't respond.

Branna shook her head and eased back in her chair to take several breaths. "You're an amazing woman, and I think you can do better than a charming, good looking gangster, Hattie. So much better."

Her mother stood up to gather Hattie's teacup, dumping it into the sink.

"Get some sleep," Branna concluded as she withdrew to the bedroom.

Hattie sat alone in the kitchen until the sun set, sending the entire apartment into shadow. Her chest heaved in silent sobs until she could barely sit upright any longer. Finally she retired to her bedroom and fell asleep to the sound of neighbors bickering in the next building.

CHAPTER 8

*V*incent stopped by his home to clean up after bailing water onto burning shacks at Curtis Creek. He parked his borrowed car on the street in front of his building, and nearly bowled over Lefty who was loitering on the stoop.

"Whoa," Vincent coughed as Lefty stepped aside. "Lefty?"

Lefty nodded.

"So," Vincent muttered as he shuffled on his feet, "what about Tony?"

"I gave DeBarre a call. He's sending Tony home with one of his men."

"Good. That's…that's good. So, are we supposed to go back to the vineyard?"

"Yes, so hustle up and put on something that doesn't look like you rolled around in a bonfire." Lefty told him. "You wanna tell me about what you were doing?"

Vincent shuffled from foot to foot. "No, I don't."

Lefty speared him with a steely glare. "Tracked you down, you know. I figured I'd head you off at Winnow's Slip, where Sadler's people keep their boat. But you never showed. Then

I saw the smoke up the shore. Got worried you and Miss Malloy found yourselves another one of those fire-faced sons of bitches."

"No," Vincent grumbled as he walked up the steps and held the entry door open for Lefty. "The sons of bitches behind that were our old friends, the Bianco Fiore."

"So close to the city?" Lefty scowled. "I'm not liking that."

"Me neither. This means Vito's pull isn't enough to hold the barbarians at the gate."

Lefty followed Vincent up the stairs and into the apartment. Once inside, Vincent pulled off his shirt and ran a washcloth under the sink faucet to scrub his arms and face clean while Lefty paced.

"Think we can spin this for Vito?" Vincent glanced over to the other man as he scrubbed the back of his neck. "Get a war party down the Bay to take out the trash?"

Lefty shrugged. "Possibly. Depends on how focused he is on Masseria. Even if these sheet-wearing goblins are a genuine threat to the Crew, it might not be enough to capture Vito's attention."

"Well, we gotta try."

Lefty smirked. "You doing this for the Crew? Or Miss Malloy?"

Vincent tossed the washcloth into the sink. "I'm doing it for the people on Curtis Creek."

He finished dressing and the two drove back to Havre de Grace, where most of the gathered cars had thinned out although the activity inside the parlor had not. The map was now covered in pencil marks showing primary and secondary land routes to and from West Virginia, known arteries that the Philadelphia mobsters employed up and down the coast, and a large black circle around Morgantown.

Vito loomed over the table, reading a handful of telegraph prints through a thick pair of reading glasses.

Lefty eased between Vito's attendants with Vincent close behind. They stood for a minute as Vito finished his reading. Then, as if he'd known they were there all along, he asked, "So, what news?"

Lefty spoke up. "There's trouble on the Bay."

"Masseria?"

"No," Lefty replied. "Remnants of the Upright Citizens."

Vito scowled. "It was my understanding that they were liquidated."

"They were, Capo," Vincent told him. "But Betty Sharp had employed some muscle just before we removed her from power. That muscle is running rampant now, burning communities on the waterfront."

Vito set aside his telegraph tickers and put his hands on his hips. "Have they hit our water traffic?"

"No, not yet," Vincent replied.

"Then how is this our problem?"

"It's only a matter of time," Lefty offered, "until they grow bold enough to hit our boats. They have before, and I believe that if we don't nip this in the bud, they will again."

Vito took a seat. "Are they organized? In other words, how quickly can they be taken care of?"

Vincent exchanged glances with Lefty, then answered, "They cluster around a fuel depot on the James River. Last time I was there, I counted five or six Fiore boats."

One of the war council members leaned forward across the table. "Fiore? You're talking about the Bianco Fiore?"

Vincent sucked in a breath, then nodded.

The man shrugged. "No worries then, Capo. They're some holdover from the old Confederates looking to..." He smirked at Vito. "Whiten up the Bay."

Vito squinted. "Lynch mobs?"

The man nodded. "They've been hitting colored communities up and down the Bay ever since the New Year. Nothing to do with us."

Vincent pulled in a breath to reply, but Lefty gripped his arm urging him to hold his tongue.

Vito nodded to himself. "Without leadership, they're not likely to pose a threat to our water traffic."

"They don't respect the Crew's authority," Vincent warned.

"And they shall be dealt with in good time," Vito declared. "Most assuredly. But at this very moment, we are facing an offensive from the New York families. Masseria has pinchers. These Confederates do not."

"It would only take three boats and about fifteen men. Good shots. It'll take a day at the most," Vincent told him. "It would be one less thing for us to worry about."

Vito made a slow slashing motion with his hand. "No, Vincenzo. If we allow these sorts of distractions to draw our focus away from the matter at hand, then we would be playing directly into Masseria's hands. End of discussion."

Lefty pulled Vincent away from the table. "Let's not poke the bear, huh?" he muttered.

Once they'd reached the hearth at the far end of the room, Vincent whispered, "He's going to let this happen?"

"He's choosing not to care, is what's happening," Lefty whispered back. "There hasn't been a single sighting of Masseria's advance scouts since your and Tony's run-in. But that hasn't swayed Vito in the least. He's preparing for total war. I'm sorry, Vincent, but if you want to deal with Bianco Fiore you'll have to go through more traditional means."

Vincent cocked a brow. "What does that mean?"

"Well, if the *famiglia* can't help, take it to the Gee."

"The Feds?"

"I'd try the State House first. I hear the governor has deputized a passel of sheriff's deputies into an organized state police. This sounds like the sort of thing he might want to use as a test case."

Vincent ran a hand through his hair. "Shit, Lefty. I don't know."

"It's worth a drive to Annapolis. If you really care about all of this, it might be your best bet."

"I'm not exactly the State House type, you know. You'd be better off making the case."

Lefty snickered, then laughed out loud. A few of the gangsters at the near end of the war table turned to scowl at him.

"Hell," Lefty said as he caught his breath. "Last time I was in a provincial governor's office, I decked a Duke's nephew across the jaw and spent Easter in a prison cell on the Mediterranean."

Vincent smiled. "One of these days, I'm gonna plug you with enough wine to start spilling these stories."

"Don't count on it." Lefty squinted at the ceiling. "Thinking on who has connections in the State House. Tony used to, but I think..." Lefty drifted off, a smile rising on his face.

Vincent shook his head. "What?"

"You know who has a cousin in Annapolis? Jake Sadler."

Vincent frowned. "No."

"Yes."

"I'm not doing it."

"The woman's shrewd. You'd do worse than Lizzie Sadler if you wanted to get an audience with Governor Ritchie."

"Hattie would murder me in my sleep. And that's if Lizzie didn't do it first."

Lefty shrugged. "Might be your best chance, you know?"

"I hate you."

"Look, it's your call. Find a way to convince the governor's office to commit forces on the Bay against these Bianco

Fiore bandits, or, take them on all by your lonesome. Speaking as your handler, I'd advise the former over the latter."

Vincent sighed, looking toward the ceiling. "Yeah. Thanks."

* * *

Lizzie Sadler glared at Vincent from across her desk.

Vincent shifted in his seat, re-crossing his legs for the second time in one minute. "I don't know who it is you know, but—"

"I'll do it," she said.

Vincent held his breath for a moment, then exhaled. "Oh."

"You think I don't want justice for Raymond and his neighbors?"

"I, uh—"

"Because I do. Even if it means cutting open old wounds and pouring salt right in there, I'll do it."

"I realize this is delicate, what with your husband—"

"Delicate?" She laughed and reached into her desk drawer to pull out a bottle of clear liquor. "Son, I'm drawing up a contract to buy a boat from the very people who put a bullet through Jake's brain. I loved my husband, but he's gone. If I let his memory keep me from doing what's right for me and my people, he'd be the first one to call me out on the carpet."

She uncorked the bottle and took three long slugs of what had to be pure white lightning. She gasped after pounding the hooch, sending a fumy waft across the desk into Vincent's face.

After shuddering for a second, she opened her eyes and said, "You're driving."

Vincent settled behind the wheel of the same Ford Model T Runabout that he'd taken with Hattie so many times. But with Lizzie Sadler riding shotgun, the vehicle had taken a decidedly formal air.

He glanced down at his suit. "I should stop and change my clothes, if we're going to the State House."

She laughed. "You kidding, son? You're better dressed than most of those worthless louts in Annapolis. If anything, you're sporting a professional air…if you take my meaning."

"A problem, you think?"

"Not if you keep your mouth shut and let me do the talking."

With a smirk, he nodded. "Yes, ma'am."

"Lord. You keep calling me ma'am, I'll start feeling old. I only have, what? Fifteen? Twenty years on you?"

Vincent glanced over to her with caution. "I'm not about to ask how old you are."

"Good man. But, what? You're in your late twenties at least. Right?"

He nodded.

"You know, I understand what the girl sees in you."

Vincent squinted. "I'd rather not discuss it."

Lizzie turned in her seat. "I *would* rather discuss it, if you don't mind."

"Is there any choice?"

"No. See, you're young and virile. Handsome as that Valentino, and probably a damned sight more charming. There's a confidence about you, a take-charge attitude. You carry yourself like a man of years when there's a need for action." She slapped his shoulder. "You're going to have to start looking at yourself. Take a long, good gander in the mirror. You're the sort of man every woman dreams about, wants to spend her life with."

Vincent squirmed, trying to concentrate on the road. "I'm not entirely sure what you mean."

She glared at him. "It means you're dangerous. You're like

a smooth pour of moonshine. You slip across the palate easy, but until you hit the gut a girl won't know how much she's gonna regret you. So, you be careful."

Vincent blinked rapidly, wishing he'd never gotten in a car with this woman. "Careful with what?"

"With Hattie, you horse's ass. She has no idea what sorta heartbreak you're packing."

"With respect, Mrs. Sadler, I have no intention of breaking her heart."

She turned forward. "Of course not. Which is the problem."

"I'm not in the habit of picking up dames and leading them on," he protested.

"Hattie ain't no dame! She's a survivor who's wound just as tight as you are. Add to that the fact the two of you are... well, what you are."

"Pinchers. You can say it out loud. I won't be offended."

Lizzie lifted her hands. "Oh, thank you most kindly. Well, you both being pinchers, there's this sense of destiny hanging on you."

Vincent squinted as he mused over the whole Bright Souls acorn their lives had thrown under their feet. "It's more like a curse," he replied.

"Well, you keep your curse inside your trousers, is all I'm saying."

Vincent shot her an incredulous glance. "Excuse me?"

"You heard me. And don't act fragile. You're a man. I know what men are like. I know what they want. You get her pregnant and run off, and I'm gonna hunt you down and make you sing soprano, you understand what I'm saying?"

Good grief. First Hattie's mom, and now her boss. "Ma'am, I have no interest in—"

"What'd I say about calling me ma'am?"

"I did it on purpose."

She stiffened, then laughed. "Okay, finally. Jesus."

"What?"

"You're finally taking off the kid gloves. Listen to me, son, I'm shooting straight with you."

"I wish you wouldn't."

Lizzie turned in her seat again, her face drawn and earnest. "Hattie's lonely. She's searching for a place in a world that by all rights wants nothing to do with her. And that's not her fault. Maybe it's not your fault, either. Maybe it seems right and proper that the two of you should fall in love. But I'm here to tell you that love only takes you so far. After that comes reality. And tiny mouths to feed."

"I'm not the kind of person to get a girl pregnant and leave, if that's what your heartburn is about."

"Then you admit you're thinking about it?"

Vincent sighed. "I'm not the type to get a girl pregnant without plans to put a ring on her finger, is what I mean." He frowned. "And I should probably start thinking more about that. I've been feeling my way through it, which is probably a good way to end up in a bad situation."

"Well, if you need advice…"

"No thank you. I've had enough bum advice from my betters."

She slapped his leg. "Trust in age, son. I've seen it all."

He smirked. "You're worse than Lefty, you know that?"

"Give me his number. I bet we'd make a hell of a pair."

"What about Tony?"

She groaned. "The man used to make me laugh. Now he's about as much fun as you are. No offense intended."

"None taken. But I have to say, he's still quite taken by you. You're giving him the chill-out, and it's gotten under his skin."

She nodded. "That a fact?"

"It is. He's basically useless."

A smirk spread over her face. "Well, then. That's…good to know."

They reached Annapolis just before sunset. Lizzie urged Vincent to park illegally in front of the State House. She bolted from the car, spurring him to sprint after her in confusion. Racing across the wide, winter-browned lawn in front of the squat red-bricked Maryland State House, she lifted a hand over her head as a clutch of men in dull gray tweed suits moved in a herd for the taverns along East Street.

One of the clutch scowled at them, then ducked his head in an attempt to disappear.

"Cyrus," Lizzie bellowed. "You worthless piece of monkey squat! You stop right there!"

The rest of the herd pressed forward with increased alacrity while Jake Sadler's cousin remained motionless, frozen in a posture of defeat. Lizzie and Vincent trotted up to the sidewalk where he stood as the man straightened his spine, removed his spectacles to give them a good cleaning, then turned to address them with a clearing of his throat.

"Why, Elisabeth. How good to see you."

"Stuff it, Cyrus. We have a problem on the Bay, and you know we do."

He pursed his lips as his eyes shifted to Vincent. "Is this your new…?"

Lizzie laughed. "Please. He's a citizen of the state of Maryland who needs an appointment with the governor."

"Well, that's not at all likely."

"Why is that?" Vincent asked.

"Look, folks." He paused to choose his words carefully. "Governor Ritchie has a full schedule, now that the election is over."

Lizzie said, "You'd think it'd be wide open."

"Well, it's not," Cyrus replied. "His new plan for the highways and byways has consumed all of his time."

Vincent stepped forward. "There is a band of armed thugs boating up and down the Chesapeake Bay. They are burning the homes of colored people in an attempt to terrorize them."

Cyrus winced. "They're doing much worse, I assure you."

"Then what are you doing about it?" Vincent snapped.

Lizzie held a hand up against his chest, pushing him away. "What my associate means to say is that we are concerned about the governor's disposition, vis a vis the lynching on the Eastern Shore. And the burning of houses at Curtis Creek, as the case appears to be." She added with a lean into her cousin, "A bit close to home for you lot here in Naptown, no?"

He sighed. "Listen, Elisabeth. I'll tell you what I told everyone else just after Easton. The governor is dedicated to justice for all Marylanders and asserts that the rule of law will be respected and enforced to the limits of his ability to do so."

"Limits?" Vincent blurted.

He glared at Vincent. "It's unfortunate that the rumors appear to be true, my cousin."

Lizzie asked, "What rumors?"

"That you're in the gangsters' pockets." Cyrus shook his head. "Jake had these moments too, you know."

"Don't," she whispered.

"Moments of weakness. The entire family knew he was dirty. Let's not put on airs, huh?"

"I'm trying to save lives," Lizzie replied.

"Black lives."

"*Human* lives," she snapped. "Jake could see through all this color bullshit. Why can't any of you? Here where it matters?"

"Elisabeth," he huffed. "The governor's on your side, but there are considerations."

"That's a lot of—"

He held up a hand. "You're not getting a meeting with Ritchie. He's not even in the state. He's on vacation with his family. If you're here to rattle the saber over this Bianco Fiore kerfuffle, I can add your name to a long, long list."

"But what will the governor do when he's through with his vacation?" Vincent asked.

Cyrus shrugged. "Maybe he'll work with the federal task force to root out organized crime in Baltimore."

Vincent balled a fist.

Lizzie stepped between them. "People are dying."

Cyrus rolled his eyes. "They're going to die, Elisabeth. If the governor saves one life, it'll have to matter in four years. I'm sorry, but that's the brass tacks."

He turned to walk away, and Lizzie looked ready to take a swing at him.

Vincent caught her arm and dragged her away. "Easy."

"I can't…he's…he's family, for Chrissakes!"

Vincent nodded. "In my experience, that don't mean much."

"It should. It really should."

They wandered back to the car in a funk, Vincent cranking the engine. He got in, taking the wheel as Lizzie got onto the bench next to him. They sat in silence for a moment.

Lizzie said, "This isn't over."

"I know it," Vincent replied.

"What do we do now?"

"What do we do? Well, you make sure Raymond's secure in his job. Hattie, too, for what that's worth."

Lizzie retreated into herself. Vincent pulled the car onto the highway headed back to Baltimore. So much for appealing to the governor, or anyone on the right side of the register.

What did Lefty say? Either convince the governor to solve the problem, or take them on himself?

Fine.

Lacking any option, Vincent braced himself for a private war with the Bianco Fiore. And he welcomed the opening salvo.

CHAPTER 9

A late morning shower had cleared the air by the harbor, washing the grime off the flagstones alongside the loading pier. Vincent glanced up the paved lane between the gray water of the harbor and the Baltimore Crew's holding house for inbound traffic. A Model T rumbled up the stones, parking in front of the store house. Vincent waved as the driver stepped out accompanied by four men with guns.

"Calendo," the driver called.

Vincent reached out a hand. "Heya, Curly."

Curly balanced his chopper in his left hand as he shook Vincent's. "Carmine's bring up another three palookas from the west side. You got anyone else?"

Vincent turned and gestured to the store house. Lefty emerged with six men in tow, leaning into the door to slide it open enough for the vehicles inside to reflect the bleary morning light.

Vincent said, "We're at about seventeen in all, if my math's any good."

Curly nodded to Lefty. "You signed on for this, too?"

Lefty frowned. "Not really, but I can't let this one go off half-cocked without landing myself in a world of hurt. So, here I am."

Carmine approached with his crew, and the crowd gathered in a half-circle around Vincent.

"Gentlemen, thank you for coming," Vincent announced. "If you haven't heard already, this is a war party. So, I hope you brought enough lead for the job."

One of the men released a whoop.

Vincent continued, "This is a clean-up job. Today we're hunting the Bianco Fiore. I realize this probably all feels very familiar to you."

A ripple of chuckles swept through the crowd, including Curly.

"We were right here last year, me beating the war drum over the Bianco Fiore and Upright Citizens. And we all got played the fool. Some of us paid for it in blood." He nodded to Curly, who rubbed his side where he'd taken a Bratva bullet. "But this time is no hoodwink. The Bianco Fiore have tread on Crew turf, and they show no signs of snapping out of it. It's time we ended it."

Lefty stepped forward. "This raid is not sanctioned by the Capo. You should all know this, as any hiccups this causes might come back to Vito, which turns into a whole handful of headaches for all of us."

"This isn't Crew business," Vincent added. "This is personal. This is us taking out the trash."

Nods greeted Vincent as he paced in front of the war party.

"If you're not up for the heat, that's okay. Head on out now, and we'll buy you a drink later. But if any of you have a beef with these lynch mobs, and you're sick of waiting for the police to do something about it, here's your shot."

Vincent nodded to Lefty, who took over. "We have four cars to carry us down to a quay along Curtis Creek just south of town. From there we intend on recruiting some of the locals to join us, making this a bona fide war party."

"Blacks?" one of the men asked.

Vincent nodded. "Yes. If anyone has a problem fighting alongside colored men, you let me know now."

No one spoke up.

"Good. Because they're the ones with the boats. Like I said, we don't have Vito's sanction on this, so we can't use Crew boats."

Lefty walked a circle. "Everyone clear on the mission? We're are hunting Bianco down and executing them. That's the deal. You boys ready to roll?"

A cheer rose from the crowd. Vincent regarded them as they disassembled and piled into the vehicles.

All four cars pulled out of the wharf and onto the highway, slipping around the south of Baltimore and into the muddied county roads leading to Curtis Creek. As the row of shanties pulled into view, a new wood frame already nailed together in the middle of the houses, Vincent urged Lefty to slow down. The convoy came to a halt a couple hundred feet from the creek.

As Vincent stepped out of the car, a commotion arose among Raymond's neighbors. Several men shouted one to another, about six of the locals approached wielding hunting rifles and bludgeons, Vincent waved for his men to remain calm.

One of the approaching locals shouted, "Y'all get on outta here!"

Vincent held up his hands, "We're friendly. We're here to help."

"Ain't need your help, so you get! Don't need no more trouble!"

"Is Raymond Bowles around? He'll vouch for us."

The men conferred with each other, and one rushed back to the neighborhood. A car door opened behind Vincent, and he spun around to urge everyone to stay put. Before long, the enormous figure of Raymond Bowles trotted alongside his neighbor to approach the convoy.

"Oh, it's you," the man said, gesturing for his neighbors to lower their weapons.

"It's me," Vincent replied, venturing a step forward. "I've come to make you a proposition."

He thrust his hands onto his hips. "What sorta proposition?"

"Payback," Vincent replied. "You all have an interest in making sure you're safe here. If we're gonna do this, we think you should have the opportunity to be involved."

Raymond eyed the convoy, then Vincent. "Those your gangster brothers?"

"A trusted few. I promised Hattie I'd see if the Crew could do something about Bianco Fiore. This is the best I could pull together." He took another step forward. "Which means we need more bodies. More hands. And boats."

"You want us to join up, is what you're saying?"

"Yes. Join me. Not the Crew, but me. No one has more at stake than you and your neighbors here. We have a chance to strike back, and speaking as a professional gangster, I can tell you the time is right."

Raymond squinted, rubbing his chin. "Hattie know about this?"

"She knows my intentions. I didn't come to her with this war party, though. I came to you." He extended a hand to Raymond. "Are you in?"

As Raymond stared at Vincent, several of his neighbors urged him to agree.

At last, Raymond gripped Vincent's hand and shook it. "Yeah, I'm in."

"Good," Vincent said before turning to give his men the all-clear.

Raymond gestured for Vincent to follow on into the village. "You know I got a boat up at Winnow's. Gonna need at least three more with this many."

Vincent nodded. "Best to spread us out, too. More mobile."

"Good thing you decided to show your face this time. Too many of these boys are getting itchy with white people rolling up on us."

Vincent shrugged. "I'm not hiding. And I know I'm not your favorite person in the world, but this is important. Important enough to…" He paused by the new construction, squinting at Raymond. "What do you mean?"

"Hmm?"

"You said 'show my face this time.'"

"Yeah."

"Last time I was here, I was bailing buckets with the rest of you."

Raymond frowned. "And this morning."

"I was in the city this morning."

Raymond lifted his chin, then stared back at the line of vehicles near the dirt road. "You didn't roll up about five hundred yards with three cars?"

Vincent's stomach knotted. "That…that wasn't me, Raymond."

"Looked like your cut, if you take my meaning."

"Gangsters?"

Raymond nodded.

Vincent turned back to the dirt road, eyes moving up and down the tree line. "Did any of them step out of the vehicle? Was there a woman with them?"

"No. They just came in, sat there long enough to put some of us off our feed. Then they left. Figured you was showin' your people what'd happened. Kept the boys from gettin' trigger happy on them, but it got us all on guard."

Vincent released a long breath. "Well, whatever that was about, looks like they're gone." He turned back to Raymond. "Pull together any able-bodied fighters you can. You have any vehicles?"

Raymond gestured at the river. "No cars, but we can run up the way to get old Bingham to ferry us down to the slip. We'll meet you there."

Vincent nodded and called his men back to the vehicles. Once he'd sat down behind the wheel and Lefty had taken a seat beside him, Vincent steered the convoy onto the road heading for Winnow's Slip.

"That was easy," Lefty muttered.

"They're ready to fight. I was counting on that." Vincent added as he leaned to Lefty, "Keep your eyes open. There's been cars poking around this morning."

"What, here?"

"Raymond thought it was us, so it could be our friends from Morgantown."

"What would Masseria be doing this far south?"

Vincent clenched his jaw as he chose his words carefully. Lefty was left with Vito's assumption that these pinchers were working for the New York families. Vincent remained unconvinced, but it was best to keep Lefty in the cold. For now.

"Probably probing our water traffic, looking for outlets and inlets."

"That's a stretch," Lefty grumbled. "Still, if Masseria's looking for a fight, he'll want as much intelligence as he can get. We should take his example."

"That'll be peachy."

Vincent guided his convoy the few minutes south to Winnow's Slip. His war party unloaded and loitered around the gravel-topped parking area just behind the row of rickety loading docks and boathouses. Several of the boys lit up cigarettes and checked and rechecked their weapons as they waited for the Curtis Creek locals to arrive via boat.

After an hour's wait, Vincent trotted down to the piers to glance up the shore at a wide, squat ferry chugging south with at least seven armed men in overalls and jackets.

"They're here," Vincent shouted, turning to Lefty then freezing as he spotted movement along the tree line behind their vehicles. A tendril of black smoke snaked its way in an arc around the gravel pad.

"Heads up!" Vincent yelled.

Lefty peered at the smoke as it split in two, easing through the midday sunlight to encircle the vehicles.

Shouts erupted from the war party. The boys separated, turning in circles as the smoke curled around them. Lefty rushed for the wharf, trying to close the gap between him and Vincent before the smoke connected with itself to wall him off.

Vincent shouted, "Don't touch it! I don't know what it'll do to you."

Lefty skidded to a halt just as the smoke fully encased the gravel pad. "Can you hear me?" Lefty called.

"Yeah," Vincent replied. "It's like fog."

"This the same shadow pincher you told me about?"

Vincent nodded grimly. "Yeah. They must be here."

But why were they here? And who the heck were they?

The ferry's engine grew louder as it sidled up to the pier behind Vincent. He turned to wave off Raymond and his compatriots. "Stay on the boat!"

Raymond cupped his ear, shaking his head in confusion as the diesel motor chugged behind him.

Vincent eased away from the smoke ring. "Hostiles!" he shouted.

Raymond hopped off the ferry, his eyes wide as they took in the writhing tentacle of living shadow looming over Winnow's Slip.

A loud crack filled the air, followed by a loud sucking noise. Mud spattered the side of Vincent's face as a slab of loamy earth hurtled out of the ground between him and Raymond. Tiny rivulets of muddy water spread along the ground as the river rushed in to fill the hole it had left behind. The shouts inside the smoke ring intensified along with the sound of gunshots.

Vincent hit the deck as the air sizzled around him with flying bullets. The monolith of muck raised behind him popped and splattered as the bullets smacked into the earth. Reaching into his jacket to pull his gun, he peered into the smoke but couldn't make out any figures or targets through it.

A grunt atop the muddy bulwark behind him caught his attention. Raymond clambered to the top of the slab of stone and mud, arm and face covered in slick gray clay. "The hell?" he sputtered, eyes wide in amazement.

"Get down, Raymond!" Vincent shouted.

Raymond scowled, then shouted over his shoulder. A rifle flew into the air behind him. Snatching it out of the air, he racked the bolt, then took aim to fire. As the man shot down over top the inky fog from his perch on top of the earth monolith, Vincent heard several alarmed shouts. The gunshots inside the smoke circle ceased for a second before resuming, this time the bullets were smacking into the dirt near Raymond's feet.

The shadows beside Vincent billowed. He braced as a figure emerged. Lefty stumbled forward, a handkerchief held over his mouth. He pulled it away once he was clear of the shadow pinch, a line of dark skin running at an angle over where his kerchief had been. Vincent reached for him, pulling him to the ground as Raymond popped off another shot.

"There's twenty, at least," Lefty grunted. "Came right in from all sides. Through the smoke, so I figured it was safe to cross. Our boys are huddled up between cars, but there's no real cover."

Raymond lowered the rifle, wide eyes tracking something in the air. Vincent glanced up to find one of the Crew cars hurtling in a high lob over the smoke ring.

He pinched time, reaching for the mud earthwork, pulling himself against the mutable gravity in the time bubble to reach Raymond. The car remained suspended in the air, halted in its trajectory directly for Raymond.

Vincent took a quick look over the ring of smoke. Three of their cars remained, his boys back-to-back between the vehicles, firing at the march of gunmen closing the circle around them. At the rear where the fourth car had been, Vincent spotted the heave pincher cracking his knuckles.

Jerking on Raymond's arm, Vincent pulled him off the wall, then lugged him lower through the time-frozen air until he was clear of the earth pincher's embankment. When the flow of time resumed, the car smashed into the mud with a tumbling crash. It plowed a gap through the mud wall, throwing grit and rocks against Vincent, Lefty and Raymond, before it cartwheeled over the pier and into the river.

Raymond coughed, jerking as he regained his bearings. "What...that was..."

"Don't mention it," Vincent said, getting to his feet. "Lefty, you got your piece?"

Lefty lifted his weapon with a nod.

Vincent made slicing motions with the flat of his palm toward the smoke ring. "Fire at shallow angles. Our boys are dead center. Theirs are on the outside."

Lefty pivoted and trained his gun to fire at a tangent into the smoke circle. Vincent followed suit, squeezing off several rounds through the smoke. Shouts from inside the ring indicated he'd plugged at least one of the attackers.

Advancing, Vincent winded his way around the smoke, angling his blind shots to where the gunmen had been. A tendril of smoke slipped from the ring, slashing against Vincent's face. For a second, he could see nothing but darkness. He pawed at his eyes, wiping them clear of the shadows. When his sight returned, he found a gap had opened in the smoke barrier, setting him up as a target to the assailants inside.

Vincent rolled away from the gap. His gun dry-clicked, and he reached into his jacket pocket to pull out a speed loader, feeding a fresh bevy of bullets into his revolver just as the gap widened to deprive him of cover once again.

Three gunmen turned to take aim in his direction.

Vincent pinched time and lurched forward into the field of engagement. He took aim at one of the attackers, then dropped the time pinch to pull the trigger. He managed to bring up another time pinch as three muzzles flared. A trio of bullets hung in the air perilously close to Vincent's face.

He side-stepped, slipping into his rhythm of combat pinching he'd developed when the Crew first went to war with the Russians. A pinch, displace, then drop the bubble to fire again. Repeat in short bursts and pray no one gets off a lucky shot.

Vincent dropped one gunman and moved three feet. Just

enough to dodge bullets. He fired again. New gunmen took notice as the heave pincher shouted and pointed in his direction. With a curse, Vincent kept shooting until the revolver clicked empty, turning in surprise as two approaching attackers fell from gunshots. Lefty emerged from the smoke ring, his arm held stiff as he approached sideways.

The ground beneath Vincent rumbled again. A divot formed in the center of the gravel pad and gravel began to slide as the entire circle of land at the center of the shadow ring sank inch by inch. Vincent slid along with the gravel, reaching to gain a handhold on something as an enormous funnel formed. Cars tilted and fishtailed toward the center of the funnel. The Crew war party staggered, waving their tommy guns as they tumbled down the slide.

Vincent pinched time and spent more magical reserve than he wanted attempting to race clear of the funnel.

He pulled himself over to Lefty, and with tremendous effort pulled him to level ground. When time was restored, Vincent felt a sharp pain in his midsection. He was running low on energy.

The ground ceased shaking, and the last of the gravel slipped into the center of the funnel to form a sort of floor inside. The Crew gunmen gathered themselves, aiming up at the attackers lining the rim. Gunfire erupted as Vincent's men found themselves playing the part of fish in a barrel.

Shots rang out behind Vincent. He looked over his shoulder to find Raymond's people rushing into the smoke ring, some firing at the attackers, some rushing forward to clobber them with lengths of lumber.

Lefty nodded to Vincent. "Hallelujah."

"Earth pincher's probably out of juice."

"Is that your Muttonchop Muscles?" Lefty asked with a nod to the heave pincher.

One of Raymond's neighbors rushed a gunman just in

front of the heave pincher. He reached out to stop the club which shattered in his hand.

Muttonchops clamped a hand onto his arm, jerking him off his feet. The man bent at the waist, flinging his poor victim in a circle over his head like a ragdoll. He clobbered two of Raymond's men with his human bludgeon before tossing him into the middle of the gunfire down the funnel.

"That's the one," Vincent grumbled.

"Well, he's a problem."

"Agreed."

Lefty lifted his hand to fire a shot at the heave pincher, when the smoke ring reached out with more tendrils to block his view.

Vincent dropped to a crouch, blinking away the smoke. "That son of a bitch shadow pincher's the real problem."

"Got eyes on him?" Lefty asked.

Vincent peered along the ground, counting feet. "He has to be outside the ring. But at a vantage point where he can see…"

He looked about, pivoting toward the boathouses. There, just beneath the denuded bow of an old ash tree, he spotted the lean, black-haired shadow pincher crouched on its gently sloping roof.

Raymond stumbled as he lost his footing, nearly slipping into the gravel cone. Vincent reached for him, steadying his massive weight just as a hand reached through the smoke, sliding beneath Vincent's chin. Fingers clamped over his windpipe, jerking him through the smoke and back into the stripe of land between the kill zone and the river.

Vincent thrust an elbow backward, landing into the chest of his attacker.

A grunt.

The grip on Vincent's throat eased.

Vincent pinched time with what he had left, pulling apart

the fingers around his throat. He turned to stare into the auburn-tinged muttonchops of the heave pincher.

Vincent lifted his fingers in a V, jabbing them into his eye sockets, then released his time pinch.

The heave pincher staggered backward, hand clamped to his face.

Just as Vincent prepared his next move, he heard a noise behind him. He spun on his heels to find Raymond looming overtop a gunman he'd just brought low with rabbit punch.

"Don't mention it," Raymond said with a nod.

Vincent turned and threw a punch into the face of the heave pincher, sending him sprawling over the remains of the mud wall. This man seemed just as weak to a jab in the eye and a solid right-cross as anyone else. His heave pinching powers must reside in the hands only.

Raymond lifted his rifle to the heave pincher and racked the bolt.

Vincent reached out a hand. "No!" He turned to point to the top of the boathouse. "That one!"

Raymond peered into the distance, then nodded. "Suits me."

He lifted the rifle and squeezed off a shot. The shadow pincher twisted at the shoulder, tumbling over the far side of the boathouse. The ring of shadows dissipated almost instantly.

Lefty peered at Vincent in confusion. "The hell?"

"Nicked the shadow pincher," Vincent shouted. "Got the heave pincher on his ass."

Lefty nodded.

Raymond bellowed, "Down!"

Enormous arms brought Vincent close to the ground as air rushed over their heads. A crashing racket exploded behind them. Looking over his back he saw a massive slab of granite sinking into the river in the midst of the ruined pier.

At the far side of the kill zone, the earth pincher lifted her hands in an ominous gesture. Blood ran from her nose, covering her lips like carnival makeup. Her gunmen marched across level terrain she was lifting from the cone in the center of the gravel pit. The gunmen turned to Vincent, rifles and tommy guns lifted.

Raymond grumbled, "Well, shee-it. Guess this is it."

"It's been an honor, gents," Vincent sighed.

Lefty reached for Vincent, trying to move in front of him to shield him from the onslaught about to arrive. Vincent closed his eyes, hunkered between Lefty and Raymond as the gunmen lifted their weapons to fire.

But there were no shots. There were only shouts of alarm.

"The hell, now?" Raymond grunted.

Vincent peered up to find the attackers in a near panic, turning tail and rushing for the tree line.

Lefty sighed, then began laughing. "Well boys? It won't be the long sleep but looks like it'll be the Big House."

Vincent scrambled to his knees, taking in the scene before him. Most of the opponent gunmen had made it more than halfway to the trees. The earth pincher glared at the road, trotting backward with a mix of confusion and frustration.

Raymond dropped his rifle and knitted his fingers behind his head.

Lefty shrugged at Vincent, then followed suit.

Vincent got to his feet, shaking his head. "What in God's green—?"

Lefty jerked his head at Vincent, urging him to drop to his knees and follow suit.

Vincent surveyed the scene one more time. There was almost no one left in the field of engagement. The earth pincher had disappeared into the woods behind her gunmen. He turned around to check on the heave pincher. He, too, had vanished. A wide rut led through the mud toward the trees near the river.

"Shit," Vincent grumbled.

"Vincent!" Lefty whispered. "Don't be stupid!"

"What are you talking about?" Vincent grumbled. He moved for the funnel sunken into the gravel pad, bracing for what he'd find. The scene within was a horror.

The wounded crawled from underneath the dead, their faces covered in blood. They were indistinct, writhing in a maw of gore as they struggled to free themselves from a tomb of flesh.

Vincent gasped and took a step away.

A figure trod onto the gravel pad from the road. "You owe me big for this, boy-o," Hattie told him as she approached the pit.

Vincent waved her away from the pit. "Don't."

Hattie proceeded to the edge of the funnel, where she stopped with a raspy wheeze. "God!"

The two descended into the pit, reaching for outstretched arms, pulling men clear of the mass of corpses. They were joined by Lefty and Raymond, now no longer victim to whatever light pinch Hattie had produced. Between the four of them, they spent a good half-hour pulling the survivors clear and tending to wounds. The casualties were horrifying.

Vincent sat on the ground after a while to catch his breath. The day started with the promise of reprisal against the Bianco Fiore and was about to end with nearly half of his gunmen dead or injured. There would be hell to pay when Vito found out.

Hattie reached for Vincent's shoulders, giving them a vigorous massage as she sighed.

"What?" he grumbled.

"Didn't we just say we needed to stick together?"

He glanced up at her, then back down to his hands. "I told you I'd take care of it."

"I heard that as 'we' not 'I.' As in 'we'll take care of it.'"

"I didn't want you involved in gangster business."

She slapped the back of his head. "You're daft, aren't you? You'd have died if I hadn't caught the lot of you skulking away from Curtis Creek."

He reached for her hand and pressed it hard against his cheek. She rested her free hand on his other shoulder. They remained there for a long moment, until Hattie pulled away.

"These the ones who hit the Charge?"

He nodded.

"Well, then. Looks like they're interested in more than just free pinchers. Did they mean to nab you and drag you off, or just kill the lot of you?"

"I'm not sure. They were certainly eager to kill the Crew gunmen. I'm thinking I might have been a dead-or-alive part of this scheme."

Vincent got to his feet. Lefty and Raymond were still tending to the wounded near the two remaining vehicles. Most of Raymond's neighbors had gathered by the boathouse, keeping a distance from the carnage. "How did they even know we'd be here?" he grumbled.

Hattie shook her head. "Maybe they followed you?"

"No, this was an ambush. They were here. Ready." He glanced back and forth between the faces nearby. "It's like they know where I'll be."

"But why you?" Hattie asked. "What's the angle?"

"No idea." He gestured at the ground where the heave pincher had lain. "Damn near had one of them, too. Could've pried him for information. But now..."

Hattie stepped toward the boathouses. "We might yet."

She trotted toward the river as Vincent followed. They arrived to see the Curtis Creek crowd gathered in a circle around something slumped in the reeds behind the pier posts. Vincent shouldered his way through the throng, crouching to pull aside a length of reeds.

"Well, what do you think about that?" he muttered as the foliage revealed the unconscious but breathing body of the shadow pincher.

CHAPTER 10

*C*urly sat with his face in his hands, most of his head matted down with dried blood that wasn't his. At the final tally, the Crew had lost six men. Another four had taken shots to the midsection or were otherwise incapacitated. Vincent and Lefty paused to take a breath as the last of the wounded was guided onto the ferry to ship back up to the city.

Curly wiped his hands on the ground then struggled to his feet.

Vincent held out a hand. "You sure you're not hit?"

"I'm sure. Just took a butt of a gun to the head when we fell into that pit." He paused to stare at the lifeless form of Carmine lying on the ground, his jacket removed and draped over his face. "We never even got to the Bianco guys."

"I know," Vincent grumbled.

"Who were these people?" Curly asked.

Vincent glanced at Lefty, who was conspicuously eavesdropping only a few steps away. "We think they work for Masseria," he replied. "It's the same party that hit the Philadelphia shipment."

"We really are at war, aren't we?" Curly groaned.

Vincent patted him on the shoulder. "Get on back to the city. There's gonna be some hell to pay here."

Curly drifted off as Lefty joined Vincent.

"At least we have one of them," Lefty muttered. "Give me some time, and I'll pry some info loose."

Vincent nodded. "I definitely want some answers."

"Is this shadow pincher dangerous, you think?" Lefty asked. "He took a bullet to the shoulder. Still knocked out. But when he comes to?"

"Of the three, he's the easiest to handle," Vincent said. "He can pinch all the shadows he wants, it won't untie him from a chair."

Hattie trotted up to Vincent from the river. "Last of the wounded are on board."

"How's Raymond?" Vincent asked.

"He's just fine. Rattled." She added with a smirk, "I hear tell you saved him from falling cars?"

"And he saved me from a gunman who got the drop on me. We're evened up. And I gotta say he's is a hell of a shot with that rifle."

"Be careful, or the two of you will end up friends," she teased

Vincent winced. "I promised him some payback. Still haven't delivered."

Hattie gestured to the dead. "I think he'll understand."

Lefty walked away in the direction of the shadow pincher they'd tended to on the pier before tying him up with rope.

Hattie reached for Vincent's arm once Lefty was safely out of earshot. "We can't let your gang question that pincher."

"Don't see how we can avoid that."

"Then you'd better get creative. He was there at the Parkersburg safehouse. He knows about the Charge. If that comes out in front of Corbi…"

Vincent rubbed his face. "Too many of the Crew have died today. I'm going to catch hell for this as it is. All I have going for me is that this hit just validates Vito's paranoia about Masseria."

"He'll spill about the Charge," she urged. "Then Vito will come hunting us once this false war of his flies apart."

"Maybe it's not so false," Vincent mused.

"You think these are actually Masseria's pinchers?"

"I don't know what to think. But this hit right here? This had nothing to do with the Charge." He nodded to the boathouses. "Just like at Morgantown, they're hitting the Mid-Atlantic supply routes. You and Raymond funnel most of the Bay traffic through Winnow's. They must have put that together."

"Raymond says they were spying on Curtis Creek, though. Why? What do the Curtis Creek folk have to do with the Crew?"

Vincent turned to glance at Raymond. "Him."

"Raymond? These pinchers were after him?"

"I'm thinking they've got two goals here—grab free pinchers and either kill or nab owned pinchers, and hit the area *famiglias* where they move their booze. Raymond is a known boat-legger. They waited for the business to come to Raymond and prepared an ambush. Only it wasn't liquor business this time around. And they weren't expecting a second pincher to ride in at the last moment like the cavalry." He smiled at Hattie. "What was that illusion, anyway? Feds?"

"Always effective with you gangster goons." Hattie nodded over toward the shadow pincher. "What are we going to do about this hostage?"

"Lefty's going to want to take the lead. He's the most experienced with wet work."

"Think you can talk him into handing him over?"

Vincent held a breath, turning it over in his head. "This pincher might have info that'll help us with my little project."

"The sort of project that unseats Vito Corbi? Hell, I'm all in. But we're still stuck with the problem of prying that info loose. And ditching your Crew mates."

"Well, I have an idea on that." He put an arm around her shoulders and kissed the top of her head. "Thanks for pulling my bacon out of the fire, by the by."

"Just stop trotting off without me, boy-o, and this sort of rescue won't be necessary." She reached up to run a thumb over a slash of shadow on Vincent's forehead. "You got a little evil on your face."

"I hope that shit doesn't give me the black lung."

She gave Vincent a jab in the ribs. "Come on. Let's see if we can pry this hostage out of Lefty's hands."

Vincent and Hattie joined the others at the pier. As he caught Raymond's eye, the enormous boat-legger gave Vincent a long, meaningful nod. Vincent returned the gesture. Perhaps not friends, but there was respect now. That was enough.

Lefty loomed over the shadow pincher. The man squirmed against his bonds weakly. His shirt had been stripped off and his wound bandaged.

"What's the next move?" Vincent asked Lefty.

"Waterfront. Vito will probably want me on this personally."

Vincent leaned in to whisper, "You told me once to always shoot straight with you."

Lefty squinted at Vincent. "What now?"

Vincent led him away from the others. "I have an idea, but I need to keep this pincher away from the Crew."

"Like hell," Lefty snapped.

"Listen, I'm being straight with you. I'm not blowing

smoke up your…" He eyed the shadow pincher. "Okay, bad choice of words."

Lefty glared at him. "You want to drive off with our only hostage, so you can interrogate him by yourself? Do I have to count the ways this is a bad idea?"

"I won't be alone," Vincent urged. "I got a ringer I want to call in…which is why the Crew can't participate. Vito's on edge as it is and bringing in outside talent to interrogate this pincher will probably get us all floating face-down in the Bay."

Lefty cocked his head. "What outsider?"

Vincent hesitated, then decided he needed to let the other man know. "Arnoud."

"That creep from Philly?"

"He knows his stuff when it comes to interrogation. And we were hit the first time guarding their beer shipment, so Philly has an interest in this, too. I need you to trust me on this one."

Lefty sighed. "You're not going to back off on this, are you? I can tell. You have your heel-digging face on."

"It'll save all of us time, but I have to move now. If I hustle, by the time the dead and wounded are tended to and Vito's been briefed I could already have the inside scoop on what Masseria's up to."

Lefty stared at the pier for a long moment before his shoulders wilted. "We're in the deepest shit already. I suppose one more bad idea won't get me any deader."

Vincent smiled and shook Lefty's hand. "Thanks."

"No. Thank *you*."

Vincent lifted a questioning brow.

Lefty added, "For shooting straight."

Raymond helped Hattie and Vincent load the shadow pincher into the back of the Runabout. Hattie slipped behind the wheel, giving Vincent some time to rest and clean himself up a bit while Raymond kept an eye on the shadow pincher in the back. He groaned against his gag once or twice but was otherwise dormant.

Hattie pulled up to the Locust Point warehouse, hopping out to slide open the door while the men lugged the hostage inside. Lizzie emerged from her office as Hattie snatched a chair to settle the man upon.

"Hey!" Lizzie shouted, "what in hell is this all about?"

"He's an enemy pincher," Hattie answered.

"A what?"

"A band hit Winnow's Slip. Nearly got your boat driver killed," Vincent told her.

Lizzie turned to Raymond. "You alright?"

"Yeah…thanks to this one." He nodded to Vincent.

Lizzie crouched to inspect the shadow pincher. "He took a bullet, huh?" She straightened back up. "Who's he work for?"

"We don't know," Vincent said. "Which is why we're here."

Lizzie squinted, then shook her head. "If you're getting into some gritty business, then I'm taking the afternoon off." She turned for her office.

"There a phone in that office?" Vincent asked Hattie.

Hattie nodded and led him to Lizzie's office just as the other woman snatched a coat and took her leave. As she passed Vincent she lifted a finger.

"Remember what I told you, moonshine boy."

Hattie paused to shoot Vincent a quizzical grimace. He just shook his head and stepped into the office to pick up the phone.

Vincent, Hattie and Raymond gathered around one of the drums set out by the side of the warehouse, warming their hands by a fire made of driftwood and scrap lumber while they waited.

A fine car sat in front of the closed warehouse door. It was an elegant four-seater. Looked to Vincent to be one of the new Chrysler Imperial, but he wasn't sure. In either case, business had been good in Philadelphia to afford a car like that.

"How long do you think this will take?" Hattie muttered.

A fresh spate of howls erupted inside the warehouse, the blood-chilling screams muffled only a little by the tin walls of the building.

"Can't be much longer," Raymond grumbled. "Sounds like your spook in there's about to kill him."

"He won't kill him," Vincent said. "Just make him hurt in a way nothing else can."

Hattie shivered. "All that screaming sets my teeth on edge."

"Me too, but he'll get the info quicker than anyone in the Crew. Plus, we'll be in control of whatever gets back to Vito."

"And if Arnoud feels like being generous and going straight to Corbi with this?"

Vincent squinted through the flames. "He won't. That would be…I don't know. Gauche? He'll definitely tell DeBarre, but that's it. Arnoud's a product of Ithaca. He's all about the job, the chain of command, and answering to his own masters. Vito is not his master."

After a long silence, the front door slid open with a loud squeal of its rusted rail. The three trotted around the corner of the building to greet Arnoud. He was pulling on his jacket, and adjusting his cuffs.

"This has been fun." Arnoud grinned.

"What'd you get?" Vincent asked.

"Well, he's not from New York. Though he knows a lot about the families and who's who in each of the major cities."

"Who does he work for?" Vincent pressed.

Arnoud frowned. "That was tricky. He kept saying that he only works for honor but wouldn't drop a name."

"Honor?" Hattie repeated. "What kind of an answer is that?"

"The man seems to be some sort of zealot," Arnoud replied. "Spouted off some nonsense about freedom and how they were targeting free pinchers."

Vincent and Hattie exchanged glances.

Vincent asked, "What do free pinchers have to do with beer barrels and boat-leggers?"

Arnoud shrugged. "He doesn't know what the strategy is behind what happened here and in Morgantown. His higher-ups tell him where to go and what to do, and he does it without getting the details. The man's effectively a foot soldier. He doesn't write the marching orders, he's simply following them."

"Any idea where we can find these higher-ups?"

"I was hoping you'd ask, because that was the single most useful bit of information I drew out of him. Waynesboro, Pennsylvania. Not far from Hagerstown. There's a shack they're holed up in deep in the woods outside of town." He lifted a slip of paper. "I jotted down the specifics along with a crude map."

Vincent took the paper, then nodded. "What do I owe you?"

"Owe me?" Arnoud's eyebrows shot up. "Calendo, this has been a pleasure." He pivoted to offer Hattie a deep bow. "And any opportunity to see Miss Malloy is well worth the trip." He straightened and turned to face Vincent. "But with regards to this group of zealots, I'm fairly convinced they are no real threat to Philadelphia. Thus, in the future should you require such services, I might not be as…available."

"That a fact?" Vincent asked.

"Philadelphia comes first," he said.

"Not very much in tune with our alliance," Vincent grumbled.

"Neither is Vito Corbi," Arnoud replied with a sharp tone. "We have eyes and ears in lots of places, Calendo. Loren and I will offer aid for any legitimate threat to our business, but this is an arrangement of mutual security. And we have doubts that Corbi is on board with the mutual part of that equation."

Arnoud gave Vincent a quick nod before turning to his car.

Raymond shook his head as the vehicle spun its wheels over the gravel on its way onto the road. "That is one off-putting man."

"Tell me about it," Vincent mumbled as they went to enter the warehouse.

The air around the shadow pincher was acrid with the smell of sweat and urine. A puddle had formed around his chair where he'd lost continence under Arnoud's touch pinching torture. The nearby barrels and walls were marred by shadow dust.

Hattie stood in front of the man who was still tied but ungagged. "Do you have a name?"

"B…Bolton."

"So, tell me, Bolton. What have you done with those children you kidnapped four days ago?"

He shook his head. "We set them free."

"They were free already," she snapped. "Where are they now?"

"They're…they're with…Honor."

Hattie huffed, "Enough. I don't want to hear about honor or dignity or freedom. I want the children back."

Bolton shook his head, his black hair swaying and heavy

with sweat. "You don't…understand. Galloway. Honor Galloway."

"Honor is his name?"

"He has them. All of them."

"And this Galloway is in Waynesboro, then?"

Bolton nodded.

Hattie turned away, marching for Lizzie's office. Vincent trotted after her.

"What now?" he asked.

"Simple. We go get them."

"And if they have more pinchers like that Earthquake Woman? Or Muttonchops, who can toss cars around?" Vincent shook his head. "We need a war party if we're going to take these guys."

She grabbed a jacket and a scarf. "Maybe not. It's like Richmond last year. You and I together. Just the two of us. We'd be hard to spot, especially with my powers. It'll be us taking them by surprise, for once."

Vincent nodded. "Yeah, okay, but if it's too much for us to handle on our own, we need to head back here for reinforcements. Think of this as reconnaissance, and if we get a chance we take it. Agreed?"

"Agreed."

"Who do you think this Galloway is?" he mused.

"I'll ask Sadie about it when we return…with the children." She pulled on the jacket and stepped around Vincent, the pair heading out of the office. "Can you watch him for a few hours?" she asked Raymond.

Vincent lifted a hand, feeling like he was losing control of the situation. "At this point, we should turn him over to Lefty."

"No. We need to keep him," Hattie said.

"Why not?"

"We might need him when we meet this Galloway."

Vincent scowled at Hattie. "Hostage exchange?"

"Insurance. If these people are zealots, then they might not be in it for the money. Best to have something they care about."

Raymond shrugged. "I can stay until you come back."

Hattie planted a peck on Raymond's cheek. "Thank you. We really need you right now."

Vincent clapped Raymond's arm with a nod, then followed Hattie out to the Runabout. This was crazy, but he understood her motivation. These people might be readying to move out, and if they didn't act fast, they'd miss their one opportunity to find out who the hell they were.

"You know the way to Waynesboro?" he asked as he went to start the engine.

"Well enough," she replied. "Made a trip or two west lately. Shouldn't be difficult with Arnoud's map."

"Are you okay with what we did?" He gestured for the warehouse. "What Arnoud did?"

She climbed into the driver's seat and waited for him to settle in beside her before answering. "You mean torture? No, I'm not okay with that. But there's children out there in the hands of people who are willing to kill. I'm not sure what's right or wrong anymore," she declared as she steered onto the street, plunging westward into the night bound for this mysterious Honor Galloway.

CHAPTER 11

A tiny hunting cabin sat in the dense tangle of a winter-stripped forest outside of Waynesboro. Vincent pressed against a hillock of dried leaves, eyeing the building from a safe position.

Hattie stole a glance, her eyes sweeping back and forth before she ducked down again.

"I see four," she whispered.

"Me, too."

"Did you see any guns?"

Vincent shook his head.

"Shite."

Hattie's reservations were valid. No visible weapons meant that all four guards were pinchers of some sort. All along the drive to this remote cabin, Vincent had mulled what Bolton had told Arnoud. They were looking for free pinchers. No, that wasn't right. They were looking *to* free pinchers. Arnoud had described the shadow pincher as some sort of zealot. Whether that was due to the gaffe of confusing Honor Galloway's name with his virtue, Vincent couldn't say. But these guards outside the cabin had maintained a sharp lookout for an hour now. They moved in a full two-by-two cover spread, much the way the Crew would post a guard. If these were zealots, then they were highly trained zealots.

A noise penetrated the moonlit night. A motor.

Vincent rolled to his side and peered around the trunk of a tree to spot headlights weaving along the drive to the cabin.

"Now what?" Hattie grumbled.

"Maybe it's Galloway?"

The car rolled up to the cabin, and two of the four lookouts marched over to greet it. Voices raised as the driver jumped from the vehicle. That driver and the two lookouts rushed into the cabin in a flurry. After a short minute, they all emerged, the driver and two of the others returning to the car, which spun its tires as it whipped a turn to exit again, leaving only two lookouts behind.

"If that was Galloway, then he's in a lather," Hattie muttered.

Vincent shook his head. "I don't think so. They went inside for marching orders. He's in the cabin."

"And there's only two guards, now," she commented.

He nodded to her. "Think you can scare up an illusion and draw them away?"

"You know I could. For how long, is the question."

"True. I'll need as much time as I can get, assuming Galloway's inside and he's inhospitable."

Hattie sat up to take in the dark forest surrounding them. Moonlight streamed through bare branches, illuminating scattered spots of ground all around the cabin. "It's like a bloody funhouse out here."

"How's that?"

"The quality of light. I bet I could pinch illusions in bursts. The right image, and I could have these stooges chasing shadows all night."

"Yeah, and the wrong image will send them inside to fetch their boss."

Hattie rolled onto her back, staring into the sky as a smile rolled across her face. "Don't worry about me, boy-o. Just find those children for me and I'll take care of the illusions."

She sat up and tucked into a crouch, winding her way around the trees in a circle back toward the road.

Vincent pushed himself onto hands and knees, watching over the hill line as the branches overhead clacked with a gust of night breeze, and waiting for a sign that Hattie had begun her light pinch.

Finally, one of the lookouts raised a fist, holding it out over her head. A flicker of light emerged from between her fingers, coalescing into a ray that shot into the forest like a spotlight. She waved it back and forth, scouring the path leading into the woods.

Her companion eased around the cabin. "What's wrong?"

She replied as she dimmed the light emanating from her hand, "Thought I saw something."

"Probably a deer."

He swiveled to return to the rear of the cabin when the woman popped her light again.

"There," she shouted.

He pulled two batons from his waistline. They crackled as they grew in length, large axe heads emerging as the batons blossomed.

The girl with a fistful of light shook her head. "I thought…"

"Let's check it out," the man grumbled.

He led the way into the forest as the spotlight swept the terrain. Before long, the pair had caught sight of another one of Hattie's illusions, rushing just over another hillock and behind a clutch of tree trunks. Vincent held his ground until he couldn't hear their footfalls any longer, then rose up from his position.

The ground was littered with dried leaves, making a quiet approach next to impossible. He was tempted to pinch time, but he had no idea what he'd find inside this cabin. It would be wiser to conserve as much of his energy as possible.

Vincent eased along the slope leading to the cabin, taking careful steps and pausing to listen for signs he'd been spotted. Reaching the cabin, he put a hand out to steady himself as he eased along the perimeter toward the door. He'd just seen members of this gang rush in and out of the cabin, but that didn't mean Galloway hadn't set some sort of booby trap.

With a nod to himself, he pinched time. He gave the latch a push and eased the door open. If there were any explosives or guns trained at the door, he'd have plenty of time to avoid the fallout. But the door swung open without resistance, and he found no booby traps waiting for him.

The interior of the cabin was bathed in warm orange light from an oil lamp slung on a nail in the center of a crossbeam. Animal skins ran along the floorboards, leading to a modest clutch of chairs. Deer heads were mounted on the far wall overlooking a writing desk.

At the desk sat a young man with dark auburn hair combed straight back. Spectacles sat over his forehead, pulled high as he busied himself with a pen and a sheet of paper. A revolver sat on the desktop within easy reach.

Vincent took in the rest of the room. A shotgun leaned against the corner behind the entry door. He picked it up and emptied it of shells, stashing it beneath a sofa along the near wall. Then he pushed his way across the cabin to take the revolver from the desktop.

He paused a second to view the document this man was writing. It was, indeed, a letter. His looping cursive was difficult to read, and all Vincent could make out was a long-winded salutation addressed to someone named Enid.

With a flip of the revolver barrel, Vincent checked the bullets. Six rounds, ready to fire. In a moment of inspired caution, he reached for the desk drawers, pulling each one out enough to check for more weapons. He found a sawed-off shotgun strapped to the underside of the desk drawer, aimed straight out. Vincent wrestled with it, freeing it from the metal clamps holding it against the drawer deck. As the weight of the time pinch began to press on him, Vincent emptied that shotgun and tossed it aside.

Satisfied the room was empty of threats, Vincent moved to stand directly in front of the desk, revolver in-hand, and released his time pinch.

The light in the room danced from the modest flicker of the oil lamp.

The man continued his scribbling unaware of Vincent's presence.

Vincent pulled back the hammer of the revolver with a loud click.

The pen froze in this man's hand.

He glanced up slowly to find Vincent holding the weapon on him.

"Good evening," Vincent said. "You must be Galloway."

Galloway's hand moved instinctively to the side where the gun had been. His fingers pawed at empty desk, and his eyes grew narrow.

"I am," he replied in a tone completely devoid of panic. Dropping his chin with a tiny snap, Galloway sent his spectacles back to the bridge of his nose. He examined Vincent thoroughly, sizing him up like a clerk at a bank.

"Your lookouts are otherwise occupied, so don't worry about calling them in," Vincent told him.

Galloway nodded slowly, spreading his hands out on the

desk. "I see. That appears to be my gun you're holding. I take it, therefore, that you're a pincher?"

"Are *you?*" Vincent asked.

"If you don't know whether or not I'm a pincher, then you barely know me. Which means I haven't likely offended you myself."

"Just answer the question," Vincent snapped.

"You're wearing city finery. Pinstripes, fedora, waistcoat. Which means you're either one of the kept pinchers, or you want me to think you are. Are you from Pittsburgh?"

Vincent scowled. "In case you missed the fact, I've got a gun on you. Allow me to also remind you that I'm the one asking the questions."

Galloway eased his hands off the desktop to his lap.

"Keep your mitts on the deck, Galloway," Vincent said with a smirk. "I took care of that boomer you had strapped to the underside. You got no leverage here."

"Impressive." He lifted his hands back to the desktop. "I'm asking if you're from Pittsburgh, because you're not a blink pincher. You couldn't police both of my weapons without me noticing. Which makes you…" He snapped his fingers. "A time pincher. And I hear Pittsburgh's got a time pincher in their passel."

"You heard wrong." Clearly this man's information network wasn't as reliable as Vincent had thought.

Galloway leaned forward, lacing his fingers to cradle his chin. "You're not one of mine, obviously. And you're not one of Sadie's. I'd know."

Vincent frowned at that. The man knew about Sadie O'Donnell and seemed familiar with the pinchers in her charge. But he didn't know who Vincent was.

Which meant he wasn't part of New York.

"You people kidnapped a train load of children headed

west," Vincent told him, holding the revolver steady. "Where are they?"

Galloway cocked a brow. "Why do you care? Are you looking to haul them back to whichever mobster's holding your leash?" He added with a squint, "Is it Cleveland?"

"Where are the children?" Vincent repeated with fraying patience, lifting the revolver to Galloway's face.

"They're not here, if that's what you're asking."

"It wasn't, and you know it wasn't. Why are you stalling? Waiting for some split-second to pull out your powers on me?"

"Why would I do that?" Galloway asked, folding his hands together casually. "You're the one with the gun, as you were so eager to remind me. One wrong move, and it's curtains for old Honor Galloway."

"One last time. Where are the children?"

Galloway's eyes grew wide. He drew in a breath, leaning back in his chair. "Wait one second! You're...you're from Baltimore."

Vincent scowled.

Galloway's practiced nonchalance melted into a beaming smile. "My God in Heaven, you're Vincent Calendo!"

Vincent took a step away from the desk as Galloway stood up.

"Hey, ease it back down into the chair," Vincent told him.

Galloway ignored him, stepping around the desk, almost vibrating with excitement. "I can't believe it! No one told me you were a time pincher. You'd think they'd have mentioned that. How did you find me?"

"Uh..."

Galloway stepped up to Vincent with an outstretched hand, his chest bumping the muzzle of the revolver. "I apologize, I had no idea. Let's start again. I'm Honor Galloway, and it's a pleasure to meet you."

Vincent pulled back another step, glaring at the outstretched hand. "What's your angle?"

"No angle. I'm just thrilled to meet the man who fetched ten grand out of Ithaca, who had mobsters up and down the East Coast in a bidding frenzy over him."

"Pal, you're pushing me to the edge here. Not smart."

With a snicker, Galloway pushed Vincent's hand down. "Oh, don't worry about that. Come, have a seat."

Vincent pulled back his hand to find the gun missing.

Galloway set the revolver back onto the desk as he gestured to the sofa. "I...I might have a little something squirreled away here. Liquor's harder to come by here in Pennsylvania, as opposed to you lucky bugs down in Maryland."

Vincent stood stiff, looking back and forth between Galloway and the gun. The man had turned his back to Vincent, reaching into a cabinet beside one of the chairs to fish out a bottle of amber liquid. Vincent tried to speak, but his thoughts collided into each other at such a pace that words failed him.

Galloway poured a bit of whisky into a couple shot glasses, then handed one over to Vincent as he plopped down onto the sofa. As the time pincher remained standing, gripping the shot glass like a statue, Galloway patted the sofa beside him.

"I'm on your side," he said. "And I'm thrilled to finally meet you. Come on. Let's toast chance encounters."

Vincent took a seat, scowling at Galloway.

The other man pounded his whisky, then grinned. "It's not poisoned. Like I said, I'm on your side."

Vincent set the whisky down without drinking it. "I don't think you recognize—"

Galloway waved his hand. "The children are safe. They're in a boarding home down by Zanesville. That's in Ohio.

They all have soft beds and warm meals. We actually have a full-time cook. A woman from Arkansas. You wouldn't believe what she can do with turnip greens and a slab of salt pork."

"You kidnapped those children," Vincent snapped. "Don't matter how good the food is."

Galloway held up a finger. "Correction, we *liberated* those children."

"They were already liberated. They were on their way to live their lives as free pinchers in Utah."

"You have to be joking," Galloway said through a scowl. "Utah? I know Sadie thinks it's the Promised Land, but what would she know? She's never been there. I mean, she literally calls the place Eden, doesn't she?"

Vincent shook his head. "I—"

"You know what's in Utah? Mormons, Mister Calendo. And they are not excited about coexisting with magic-wielding pinchers. You know what they call us out there? Witches. So, no. Those children weren't traveling to any sort of free life. Quite the opposite."

"How do you know so much about the Charge?" Vincent asked.

Galloway peered at the door, then straightened in his seat. "My lookouts…you didn't hurt them, did you?"

Vincent shook his head. "They're out chasing ghosts. I'll ask again, how do you—?"

"Oh, that's a relief. They're good people, really. Did you see them? My sun pincher and the fellow with sticks?"

"Yeah. I saw."

"Amazing what he can do with wood. I understand there was an entire wood pincher school of fighting perfected during the early Crusades. Gave the European invaders just armfuls of hell."

"I met one in Ithaca," Vincent grumbled.

"Right. Yes. Can't believe you're here. How did you find me?" Galloway snapped his fingers. "It was Bolton, wasn't it? Word just arrived about a half hour ago that there was some unpleasantness down by the Chesapeake Bay. We lost Bolton in the melee."

"He's alive," Vincent replied.

"That's good. So, he gave me up? That's very surprising. He's usually in greater command of his faculties. You must have plied him particularly hard."

Vincent shrugged. "Extreme measures for extreme times."

"He is a dour one, to be sure. Almost morbid. But I suppose that comes with the powers. I mean, spending so much time obsessed with darkness, I don't suppose—"

"Do you always talk this much?" Vincent shook his head, realizing that he'd once again been derailed from his line of questions.

Galloway grinned. "I'm sorry. I do this. I forget we just met, and I start going on and leave you behind. So. We both have questions. I asked mine, now you ask yours."

Vincent stood up, pacing a line to gather his thoughts while Galloway looked on with eagerness. "You say you're on my side," Vincent began. "So, why did you attack me twice?"

"Twice?"

"Once in Morgantown. And now, this unpleasantness."

Galloway thought it over. "Well, Morgantown was a fluke. Our intelligence said there was a shipment from Philadelphia headed to Michigan, so we assumed the handoff was to the Pittsburgh crew. We meant to hit *them*. See what they had to offer, if they had any pinchers under their thumb. What were you doing in Morgantown, anyway?"

Vincent clammed up.

"Hey, a question for a question. Fair enough?" Galloway grinned.

"We were skirting a shipment under Pittsburgh's nose," Vincent told him.

Galloway nodded. "Gangster intrigue. Well, I apologize. If my people had known it was Vincent Calendo, and not some random—"

"How do you know so much about me?"

"Ah. Your question. Well, I have people in various places including Baltimore who tell me what I need to know. The line of communication isn't perfect, and there are holes that develop. Especially lately. But I know you are a time pincher whose time to assert himself has arrived. To stand apart. To shrug off these invisible chains Vito Corbi has shackled you with."

Vincent leaned forward, an odd warmth spreading through his chest. "You're out to take down Vito?"

Galloway wagged a finger. "Uh, uh…it's my turn. You said my lookouts are chasing ghosts. Which means you didn't come alone. So, here's my question. Who came with you?"

Vincent closed his mouth and looked away.

"Reluctant to give me any vital information. I can understand that. I hear there is a second pincher working the Baltimore territory. One who isn't exactly under Corbi's control, but who has acted on their behalf in the past. A light pincher, if I recall correctly. I'll assume that's who's drawing away my scouts into the night. Can you at least tell me his name?"

"*Her* name is Hattie Malloy," a voice called from the doorway.

Vincent turned to find Hattie entering the cabin, her face resolute.

Galloway stood up. "Ah! Magnificent!"

Hattie walked up to Vincent and touched his arm. "You okay?" she whispered.

He nodded.

Galloway turned a quick circle. "I apologize, I didn't expect so much company today." He reached for Vincent's untouched shot glass of whisky. "Mister Calendo doesn't seem to trust my liquor, but perhaps I might offer—"

As he reached the shot glass over to Hattie, she swatted it from his hand. The glass fell with a *thunk* to the ground as whisky sprinkled Galloway's spectacles. He pulled them off to wipe them on his shirt.

"Who the hell are you?" she grunted.

"Well," Galloway muttered, "we're already playing the question game. If you want in, you'll have to wait your turn."

"Enough games," Vincent declared. "You know all about the Crew. You know about me and Hattie. You know about the Charge and all the free pinchers on their way to Utah. And you haven't used any powers against us, so I'm not entirely convinced you're a pincher yourself."

"Oh, I never use my abilities against other pinchers," he replied.

Hattie asked, "The children?"

Vincent answered, "They're in some boarding house in Ohio. He says they're safe." Vincent added, "He knows all about Eden. Says it's a load of bushwa."

Hattie shook her head. "Who the hell are you, Galloway? How do you know all this?"

"Has no one told you?" He slipped his spectacles back onto his nose. "I suppose that doesn't surprise me. Well, if you're in touch with the Charge, then you'll know Sadie O'Donnell."

Hattie nodded.

"And what has she told you? Who started the Charge in the first place?"

"She did," Hattie replied. "She and her husband."

"Then I regret to inform you that she lied. Perhaps 'lie' is too strong a word for it. She's never been one to accept the reality of the situation."

Vincent pressed, "So, if Sadie and Jonas O'Donnell didn't create the Charge, then who did?"

With a warm grin, Galloway lifted his palms in the air. "I did."

CHAPTER 12

"Is it true?" Hattie snarled as she stood cross-armed in front of Sadie's desk.

Sadie had her back turned to Hattie, staring at a spot on the wall where a window would be, if they hadn't blacked them out.

"The thing you have to understand about Galloway is—"

"It's a simple yes or no question, Sadie. He's telling me that he founded the Charge, and it was you and your husband who took it from him."

"Honor's always been prone to exaggeration. He thrives on it."

Hattie threw her hands up. "Then educate me."

Sadie spun in her chair to face Hattie. "What's the point? The Charge is what Jonas and I made of it. It's a means to save lives, to free pinchers from the grip of the mob."

"Galloways says it was his plan all along, and that you and Jonas ditched him outside of Chicago. Left him to fall back into the hands of the oppressors, I think was how he put it."

Sadie smirked. "That's classic Galloway, right there. Look…please sit. You're making my hair itch."

Sadie gestured for a chair, and Hattie took it with a huff.

"You want my side of this? Fine. I served under Johnny Torrio, and managed to get away. I told you all about that already."

Hattie nodded.

"Met Jonas, then Honor and the three of us worked in the Chicago area, even after Capone took over from Torrio in twenty-five. Jonas and I...well our powers are pretty obvious. Galloway? His are subtle."

"What are his powers?" Hattie asked.

"He's what Jonas and I called a sway pincher. He's oddly convincing. You'll go in mad as all hell at him, and five minutes later, you're not mad anymore. Another five and you're thinking he's a decent fellow with some pretty damn good ideas. Another five and he's your best friend. Galloway turns your heart more than your mind. But when he needs you to be loyal, he can turn it on full blast, and you're loyal."

Hattie shivered. She'd walked in on Galloway casually having a drink, a revolver on his desk behind him, with Vincent just standing there. Had the sway pincher worked his subtle magic on Vincent?

Had he worked it on her? She'd believed him when he said he'd founded the Charge, that the children were safe in Ohio, and that Utah was hardly an Eden.

With a nod, Sadie said, "Now you see the problem? You came in here with a head of steam, ready to burn me at the stake just because of what he told you. How much of that is you? How much is him?"

"He told us he never uses his powers against pinchers." Hattie scowled, thinking a man who would twist his words to bring people to his side would hardly bat an eye about lying.

"Why wouldn't he, though? If you were pulling the wool over some sucker's eyes, a subtle sway pinch might make the odds a bit more in your favor. We were based in Fort Wayne. None of us could have lived with ourselves if we did nothing to help others. That was the birth of the Charge. We took it as a holy charge to save pinchers from our fates."

Hattie nodded. "So what *did* happen in Chicago? He says you two abandoned him."

"It's not that simple. Jonas and I thought of the Charge as an underground railroad for free pinchers. Save them in groups and move them somewhere the mob couldn't get them. Honor had other ideas."

"What ideas?"

Sadie's eyes darkened and stared into space. "He wanted an army."

"An army of free pinchers?"

"It was insane. He was planning to pull together a handful of resistance fighters to aim them at Capone. Jonas and I knew it was insanity. All that would do is get pinchers killed. But Galloway convinced every free pincher in Indiana and Illinois to band together. It was a bloodbath. And it was over before it began. Capone's no fool. His pinchers caught the conspiracy in the wind, and it all ended in a hail of gunfire. Jonas and I refused to participate. We…we thought Galloway had died with the rest."

Hattie watched Sadie pace the room. "Did he know you weren't joining his fight?"

"We told him we were not going up against Capone, that we wouldn't be there. He'll probably deny that. He'll twist clever words and make it sound like we deserted him in the middle of battle, leaving him to die. That's how he operates. He plays fast and loose with facts whenever it serves his agenda."

Hattie looked to her lap, pondering the account Sadie had offered.

"You satisfied?" Sadie asked. "I don't know what else to

tell you. Ultimately you'll have to decide whether you believe me or him."

She would. And knowing Galloway's power, she was more inclined to believe Sadie.

"He's asking for a meeting," Hattie told her. "Vincent's with him now. Galloway wants to meet with you and iron things out. And most of all to get his man back."

Sadie sneered. "Fat chance. He can't just come marching into my city and demanding the keys to the kingdom."

"Well, he's got himself a new army. And I think he's looking to recruit. He's already hit a shipment from Philadelphia, thinking it was the Pittsburgh mob. And he hit a group down by the river by accident, thinking they were the Baltimore Crew."

"What was the point in that?"

Hattie rubbed her temples. "He wants to take down the mob families. And he was also looking for me—to recruit me. He'd heard about a free pincher operating in and around the Bay—a pincher other than Vincent. He has eyes and ears that feed him information. That info led him to Raymond, which led him to Vincent."

"His people have standing orders to strike a mob party when they see one, I'm guessing?"

"That's their mandate. It was, according to Galloway, one huge misunderstanding. They were to bring in any pinchers they found alive. That's what he says."

Sadie leaned forward. "And what do you say? Do you believe him?"

"I did," Hattie replied, "until I knew what his powers were. Now, I'm not sure what to believe."

"Good girl. You're already miles ahead of Galloway." Sadie ran her hand over one of her books. "He says our people are in Zanesville?"

"Aye. Insists they're all safe."

"And Charley's girls?"

Hattie shrugged. "I assume so. We're taking it all on Galloway's word, here."

Sadie nodded. "Then I guess I don't have much choice. Where's this meeting supposed to take place?"

"He suggested Frederick. Far enough out of the city to be neutral ground."

"Fine. When?"

"Tomorrow." Hattie lingered, then reached forward to tap on the desk. "Sadie? You're asking me to trust you in the face of a man who can force me to trust him with his powers. If I'm going to back you up, then I need you to be honest with me. The full truth. No half-truths or omissions."

Sadie frowned. "You want to know why you can trust me over Galloway? Because I have no reason to lie to you. I never have. I don't intend on it now."

Hattie nodded.

Sadie continued, "This meeting? It's not to keep the peace. Galloway is coming to pitch war to all of us. He wants us all to fall into lock step behind him and march on the mafia. But that's not going to happen, even if he decides to pinch our loyalties. I'm going to this meeting to tell him to leave."

"And if he won't?"

"Then we're all in for it."

* * *

A PATCH of fallow farmland alongside the Monocacy River housed the summit between Honor Galloway and Sadie O'Donnell. Hattie and Charley headed off the road, bobbling over the old plow rows as they approached the meeting point where a line of cars and trucks had already assembled. Hattie parked the car at a comfortable distance that wasn't too inconvenient. Sadie's car followed, driven by Blake. Hattie waved Blake to park the vehicles side-by-side.

Across the field, Hattie spotted Vincent still sporting the same suit he'd worn during the fight will Galloway's people.

It was jarring, seeing him there in the midst of the same people who'd tried to kill him only two days ago.

Hattie headed across the field with Charley and Vincent trotted up to join them, bending down to kiss her forehead.

"How're we looking?" he asked. "You get the story from Sadie?"

"I did."

"And?"

She shrugged. "It all sounds like a handful of drama. I don't see a true right or wrong, here."

"That figures."

"And you?" Hattie asked. "You spent a day with these people. Anyone get punchy with you?"

Vincent turned to discreetly point to the earth pincher, decked in a long brown overcoat and boots, her short hair clinging to the sides of her face from under a brown wool cap. "Haven't seen much from our muttonchopped heave pincher. And Maria over there hasn't spoken word one to me. I think she's harboring some sort of grudge."

"Good. I don't need you speaking to strange women when I'm not around," she teased.

"You're stranger than any woman I've met, so I think you're safe."

Sadie brushed past them. "Enough pillow talk, you two."

Hattie rolled her eyes. "They got room on your side of the field for a light pincher?"

"Come on." Vincent took her arm. "I don't want these two facing off without chaperones."

They joined Sadie as she walked to a central spot in the field, then stopped. This was her line. Galloway would have to come meet her. Hattie peered through the gathering across the way but couldn't spot him.

"Where's Galloway?" she asked Vincent.

"He's on his way, apparently."

"What, he's not here?"

A car rumbled up a dirt path on the far side of the field, kicking up a modest plume of dust as it approached. Hattie watched as it swerved around the cars already present.

The muttonchopped heave pincher stepped out of the driver side, then Galloway emerged to the cheers of his compatriots. He'd pulled his collar high over his neck, his trench coat drooping past his knees. His auburn hair slicked back, his spectacles giving him the air of an academic. He wasn't a tall man by any means, and of a slight build, but every last person on that side of the field seemed to fall over themselves to greet him. The process took several minutes.

Sadie shook her head. "That's definitely him."

"Does he have this effect on everyone?"

"What effect?" Vincent muttered.

"Sway pincher. I'll tell you about it later," Hattie said as Galloway, his heave pincher, and the earth pincher marched across the field to greet Sadie.

They stopped about ten feet away, standing in a line.

Sadie's jaw set as she held her head high and said nothing.

It was Galloway who made the first move. "Hello, Sarah Jane."

Hattie blinked at Sadie. That was her name?

"Honor."

He nodded to Hattie. "Miss Malloy."

Hattie nodded in return, oddly compelled to be civil.

"So, Sadie..." Honor declared, now addressing her with less formality. "Here we are again."

"Here we are," Sadie repeated with taut pronunciation.

"I was sorry to hear about Jonas."

Sadie's mouth hardened. "I was sorry to hear about you."

"What, that I'd died? Or that I survived?"

"Take your pick."

He smiled. "Rumors of my demise were exaggerated but I *was* lucky to make it out alive."

"Well, I did tell you Capone wasn't someone you wanted to mess with."

His eyes narrowed. "Did you, though? Or did you and your husband creep out in the middle of the night like cowards?"

"What are we doing here, Honor?" Sadie asked. "Are you looking for an apology or something?"

"Oh, Jesus. No. I don't want any such thing. What happened in Fort Wayne was the cost of war. Everyone in that room had no illusions as to what taking the fight to Capone would mean."

"No one in that room had a choice in the matter," Sadie scoffed.

Galloway turned away, waving his hands in histrionic offense. "Now, that's too much. You know I never use my powers against our own kind. That's been my dogma ever since I knew I wasn't alone."

"Yes, so you've always claimed. Anyway," Sadie said with a wave of her hand, "you've got a new army, and you're bringing the fight into my backyard."

"At least we're fighting!" Galloway said, slapping a fist into the flat of his palm. "Not throwing lives away in the name of safety."

"I wouldn't call what I'm doing, throwing lives away."

"But you are. Eden? It's anything but. And I would know, because I was there last year. I went personally to investigate your little paradise."

Sadie took a step forward. "You...what?"

"Yeah. I've been there. I've spoken to...what was his

name? Orson? Yeah. I wonder if you fully realize how much of his reports are wildly inaccurate?"

"You shut your mouth. Orson is an honest man."

"Is he? Then how is it he never mentioned me, even a full year after I left Utah." Galloway took a step closer to Sadie. "Uinta Reservation, just outside Fort Duchesne? I'm saying this out loud so that you know I'm telling the truth."

Sadie took one step back.

Galloway nodded. "Eden, as you call it, is a shambles. It's been hit twice in the past year. Once by run-of-the-mill brigands. Second time by the Mormons, who think we're a bunch of devil worshippers." He added with a whisper, "People have died."

"Why would Orson lie to me?" Sadie spat. "I trust him before I trust you."

Galloway turned to the muttonchopped heave pincher. "Ernie?"

Ernie nodded. "It's true. We pulled them all out, brought them back east. The, uh...the survivors, at least."

Sadie shook her head in disbelief. "What?"

Galloway said, "Your wayward children were hungry, filthy, crawling with lice. I offered them safe passage back to Ohio."

"Then..." Sadie looked away with a puzzled frown.

"Orson's been feeding you lies for about a year, now. I didn't want him. He's...weak. Unwilling to make the hard decisions. Unwilling to put guns in the hands of people who need them for protection. Unwilling to negotiate with local governments so that the basics like food and water could be provided. I left him there, and he's taken your money every month since."

"What about the people we keep sending?" Hattie asked.

"Yes. Well, you caught us this time, but we know every safehouse between here and the Mississippi. We've intercepted them all and folded them into our group. You see, my Charge is in fact the *real* Charge. Everything your friend is doing here," he pointed to Sadie, "is an illusion."

"Why the deception? Why not come forward sooner?" Vincent asked.

"Because," Galloway said, "Sadie is a formidable opponent when there's snow on the ground." He gestured at the dried field around them. "Parlay with Sadie O'Donnell is best accomplished in warmer months."

Hattie rebutted, "That's not really an answer. It's been a year since you've started siphoning off the Charge. Why now? Why suddenly start making moves on the East Coast?"

"I finally have both the skilled pinchers and the firepower I need to make a move toward disabling this system of mafia owned pinchers, to fight for a world where we're not just hiding in Utah or Ohio, but where we can truly be free. I'd originally thought to hit the weaker cities like Pittsburgh and Baltimore, but with the right additions to my team, we can take on even the New York families. We can change the world."

Hattie winced. "Right additions to your team?"

Galloway pointed to Vincent. "Yes. Him."

Hattie glanced to Vincent, whose face was as puzzled as her own.

"Me?" Vincent blurted.

"You've got an incredibly valuable talent. Combine that with your smarts, and your ability to strategize…. You're a leader! I need leaders with the power to face down the New York families." Galloway's eyes scanned Vincent, as if he were searching for something. "Take down the families, then take down Ithaca."

"That's quite an ambitious goal there," Vincent drawled.

"I know. And I intend to see that goal to fruition. Ithaca is the very symbol of what we struggle against, the place that turns free pinchers into kept pinchers. We can smash that system, destroy the families that own us as if we're animals. We can finally be free."

A tiny frown creased Vincent's brow. Hattie reached out to take his hand, and looked around at the others.

Charley's face was calm, almost eager. Even Sadie looked as if she were considering the sway pincher's words.

Then Sadie shook her head. "You'll leave," she told Galloway.

"Will I?" he replied with a smirk.

"Yes. You will. Because you're putting lives in danger, here. I'm never going to sign on to your war, Honor. It's insane. You'll poke the bear enough until it decides to get off its ass and maul you to death. It's happened before, and it'll happen again."

"These people aren't Capone," Galloway replied with a glare.

"Baltimore? You're right. They lack organization, sure," Sadie said. "But the other families? There's a kind of chaos here on the East Coast that you're not ready for. And, all due respect to Al Capone, the families in New York make him look like an amateur."

Galloway shook his head. "Now you're being contrary."

"*My* Charge is about saving lives. Not throwing them against bullets. And this is my turf. You want to run your own Charge? Fine. You go back to Chicago and take on Capone all by yourself. But you leave this side of the Mississippi to me."

Galloway sneered. "You accuse me of throwing away lives, when you're the one shipping them off in rail cars to starve to death in Utah?"

Hattie lifted her hands to diffuse the tone. "People? Shall we take a moment to cool down?"

Sadie jabbed a finger at Hattie. "No. He's here to bring his private war. I won't have it. Either he leaves, or I'll take him out myself."

Galloway sucked in a breath, then lifted his hands. "I'm… sorry to hear that sort of language from you, Sarah Jane."

"Don't call me that," Sadie grumbled. "And drop this olive branch act. It's unbecoming. You're a war monger. Nothing about you is peaceful."

"This from the one holding one of my men hostage?"

Sadie scowled, then nodded. "We'll return him today."

"I want nothing but peace for pinchers," Galloway declared. "Free pinchers," Galloway concluded, "are not the threat. Their masters are."

"You are so naïve. These masters have you outmanned and outgunned. And they have kept pinchers. There's no world where you win, Honor." Sadie shook her head. "We're done. Go home, Honor."

"I'm sorry, Sadie, but I won't simply pack up and relocate on your decree. You are not the head of the Charge, as far as I'm concerned."

"Then you're asking for a fight."

He squinted at Sadie. "I've pledged not to engage my pinchers against yours. Now you won't follow suit? Now who's unseemly?"

Hattie turned away, baffled by the turn of the conversation. This was what she wanted, wasn't it? To fight the Crew? To teach Vito Corbi a lesson he'd never forget? To live free, here, in her home?

"Can you…at least pledge to stay out of Baltimore?" Sadie pleaded.

Galloway bowed at the waist. "I can, at that."

Sadie gave him a sharp nod, then spun about to march for the cars.

"I'm on your side, Sadie," Galloway shouted at her retreating form.

Hattie turned to Vincent, the two exchanging a wary glance. The day had gone to Galloway, and Hattie wasn't sure that was a bad thing.

Hattie joined Vincent as he withdrew to Sadie's motorcade, spotting Charley still standing in the field.

"Charley?"

Charley turned to follow, when Galloway gestured to Ernie. "Where's that thing?"

Ernie pulled an envelope from his jacket pocket, handing it over to Galloway, who called, "Oh, Charley?"

Charley stopped.

"Here, this is from your daughters."

Charley eyed the envelope with a sharp breath, then took it with trembling fingers.

Galloway nodded and patted his arm. "They're doing well."

With that, Galloway and his crew turned to leave.

Hattie waited for Charley to rejoin them. He already had the envelope open, pulling the letter clear. A clumsy charcoal sketch greeted his eyes. Two girls and a man, all holding hands. The note below said, "Us soon. Love you, Daddy!"

Hattie put her arm around Charley, easing him forward as he lost his composure. She walked with him to the car, Charley taking the back seat as Vincent slipped into the passenger side.

"What does all this mean, now?" Vincent muttered.

"Either it means we have a new enemy, or we have an ally."

"Where's your money?" Vincent asked.

As Hattie cranked the engine. "I haven't decided on that yet."

Vincent frowned, staring across at Galloway and his people climbing into their cars. "Yeah. Me either."

CHAPTER 13

*S*adie marched up the stairs of the Charge headquarters, slamming her bedroom door at the top. Hattie and Vincent exchanged cautious glances.

"Well, this has been lovely," Hattie muttered.

Charley and Blake entered the warehouse behind Vincent, lingering as they waited for instruction.

Vincent nudged Hattie. "So, you want to cut the shadow pincher loose? Or shall I?"

"Why don't you wait in this room, in case he gets violent?" She turned to the others. "Blake? Give me a hand. Charley? Stay with Vincent. If he decides to make a fuss, Vincent might need some tooth and nail support."

Charley nodded, and Blake followed Hattie into the cellar where they'd left the shadow pincher blindfolded and gagged, with only his wrists bound. The back side of the cellar door was solid black from their captive's shadow mist striking against it repeatedly, more from outbursts of anger than any hope he'd somehow escape.

Blake closed the door behind them, leaving Vincent alone with Charley. The pair stood in silence for a moment, listening for any commotion. After a while, Vincent stepped away from the door to face Charley.

"Your girls are okay?" Vincent asked.

Charley nodded. "A-yep. Fed and clothed." He held up the note to show florid handwriting on the back side. "They got themselves some sorta school marm who's taking care of them. Giving them lessons along with the pincher kids."

"I guess that's a best-case scenario," Vincent told him. "I'm glad they're included."

Charley folded the letter and slipped it back into its envelope. "They lost their mother a good while back. And now my sister. I don't know what that does to girls, losing two mother figures like that. So, I'm glad there's a woman there."

"At least they have a father."

"Yeah, well..." He stared into space. "Their father isn't with them now, is he?"

"Thinking about going to Ohio?"

Charley flinched, then shrugged. "I volunteered to help Sadie, here. Payment for helping me up by Ithaca."

Vincent crossed his arms. "She doesn't require any payment, Charley. There's no wheeling and dealing here, from what I understand."

He grinned. "That's what Hattie said. But, you know... There's an obligation to all this."

Vincent stepped toward Charley to lower his voice. "There's an obligation to your girls. Listen, if you trust this Galloway then you should consider taking a train to Zanesville."

"It isn't so simple." He rubbed the back of his head. "The girls will be fine. I need to stay here and help the Charge out."

Vincent squinted. "Do you think what Galloway says is true? About Eden? Zanesville? About what happened in Chicago between him and Sadie?"

"You think he's lying?"

"I think he's brash and a bit of a fast-talker, but I don't know about outright lying. And if he really has the army to take down the mob families, to take down Ithaca… That's a very tempting proposition if he's got any chance of success." Vincent eyed the cellar door. "Either way the Charge may have two leaders, now. And you folk will have to start making some decisions soon."

Footsteps shuffled up the stairs. Blake popped into the room with a muted thump, turning to open the door for the shadow pincher who was marching up the stairs in front of Hattie.

Bolton stepped into the murky daylight of the ground floor, his face paler and hair stringier than before. He paused at the sight of Vincent, arms drawing up as his hands balled into fists.

"Easy, fella," Vincent urged. "I'm taking you back to Galloway."

Bolton's hands and arms eased, but his face remained the very picture of hatred.

Blake motioned for the door. "Car's out front. We'll get you going right away."

Charley marched for the door. "I'll go."

Blake peered at Charley. "Oh. I thought I was—"

"I'd rather go," Charley stated, stepping through the door.

Hattie shot Vincent a quizzical glance, to which Vincent simply shrugged.

Bolton moved to a point of equal distance between all of them, an animal trapped in a circle of predators.

"You talk to him?" Bolton finally asked.

"Galloway?" Vincent replied. "Yes."

"What'd he say?" Bolton asked with an almost desperate timbre.

"He, uh…he seemed surprised that you spilled on him."

A flash of panic crossed Bolton's face.

Vincent quickly added, "What he meant by it, I think, was that you were a good soldier for him. He claims it was all a mistake. We're not gangsters."

"Well, *most* of us at any rate," Hattie corrected.

Vincent smirked at her. "Hey, you had your shot. But no, you had to go live your life all free and happy."

Bolton shook his head. "Who…who are you people?"

"We're the Charge," Hattie replied. "The real Charge."

Bolton scowled. "Not for long."

"Alright," Vincent said with a shove. "March. We have to get you to Galloway before he sends Maria after us."

"You sure you want to spend two hours in a car with him?" Hattie asked.

"I have Charley with me. If he gets cute, I'll have Charley turn into a polar bear and bite his head off."

Bolton stiffened, and Vincent shoved him through the door.

"Be careful," Hattie called as he stepped into the sunlight.

He stuffed Bolton into the back seat as Charley rode shotgun. "Now, you behave yourself," Vincent chided as he started the car. "We're taking you to your people. No reason for shenanigans."

"Or what? You'll resort to torture?" he snapped.

Vincent pursed his lips as he steered onto the highway. "That was business."

"*Gangster* business," Bolton grumbled.

"Yeah, well…you people hit me twice, nearly shot me in the back. Tried to drop a car on me. We had no idea who you were, and I wasn't about to spin my wheels waiting for you to wax all cooperative."

"You're the mob," Bolton said, staring out his window. "We have standing orders to attack."

"Yeah, well, you were wrong."

"Was I?" Bolton asked, turning to glare at the back of

Vincent's head. "You're still at the beck and call of your masters. You're a kept pincher, whether you want to admit it or not."

Vincent took a deep breath. "I stand on my own, friend."

"But what have you done about it?" Bolton asked. "You're not a free pincher just by saying you are."

"You ever been to Ithaca?" Vincent asked.

Bolton eased back in his seat. "No."

"Then maybe you can shut up and let me drive in peace."

The rest of the drive to Waynesboro was silent. It took significantly less time to reach Galloway's hunting cabin, as Vincent didn't have to park a good mile away and hike through the woods in the middle of the night then wait an hour to surveil their guard patterns.

Charley hopped out and opened the door for Bolton, who swept past the two guards beside the cabin door. Vincent assumed these were the two whom Hattie had led away with her midnight illusions. The woman with a handful of sunlight gave him a smile as she tucked some of her jaw-length hair behind an ear. The other guard, the wood pincher, seemed preoccupied with the car. His eyes ran up and down the fenders and running boards like the damn thing was a dancing girl.

"I guess we wait out here, then," Vincent grumbled to Charley. "So much for a formal exchange."

"He sure is devoted to this Galloway guy," Charley whispered.

"They all are. Kinda makes you wonder."

After a couple minutes, a figure appeared in the doorway. Vincent raised his chin as Maria took two steps out into the fresh air, arms stiff at her side. This woman could open the ground underneath Vincent's feet. That made her a sort of dangerous Vincent wasn't used to. She simply stood staring for a moment before turning to the side, a vague gesture Vincent concluded was an invitation to enter.

"You gonna play nice?" Vincent asked.

Her eyes narrowed just a little. "That's up to Honor."

"Fine by me," Vincent said as he stepped past her into the cabin.

Galloway stood behind his desk, his spectacles clinging to his forehead. Bolton stood just behind him, face drawn tight like a bear trap.

"Ah, there he is," Galloway declared, gesturing with a flap of his arms for Vincent to approach.

Vincent turned to check on Charley, who remained just outside the door with his back to the entrance, before returning his attention to the others.

"Galloway," he said as he strode across the single room cabin.

Muttonchops sat at one of the sofas with a book in his lap, acknowledging Vincent with a chummy salutation. He swiveled his crossed legs to allow Vincent room to pass. Galloway stretched a hand over the desk for Vincent to shake. "Thank you for returning Bolton personally. I was rather hoping you'd come."

Bolton whispered something into Galloway's ear before retreating a step behind him.

Galloway shook his head slightly. "Bolton tells me about the means by which he was interrogated. Meaty stuff, Mister Calendo. In addition, Bolton has asked for certain considerations. One might even call them reprisals."

Vincent held a breath.

"A request which I have denied."

Bolton's eyes jerked to the back of Galloway's head.

Galloway swiveled to face Bolton. "The man's a fellow pincher, and we need to respect that."

"A kept pincher," Bolton grumbled.

Galloway lifted a hand to wag it in reproach. "Tsk tsk. He's beyond that, now."

"They tortured me," Bolton whined.

"It was justified," Galloway replied. "We attacked him. He responded by securing our location to launch his counterattack. You have to understand, friend, one can't be so circumspect in times of war."

Galloway gestured for Vincent to take a seat, and Vincent did so, pausing to check on Maria who was still looming in the far corner cross-armed.

"The tension in this room is positively suffocating," Galloway complained. "I don't want that, Vincent. In fact, I'm prepared to offer you a gesture of reconciliation in light of the inadvertent assaults on your person."

Vincent blinked in surprise. "You're saying want to make it up to me? To offer me something in return for twice trying to kill me?"

"In a nutshell, although in my defense, us trying to kill you was completely unintentional. A terrible misunderstanding." Galloway leaned forward, pulling his spectacles onto his nose to review some notes scratched onto a sheet of paper. "This Bianco Fiore."

Vincent scowled. "What about them?"

"Strange name, that. White Flower?"

"You speak Italian?" Vincent asked.

"As well as Portuguese. All to impress a Brazilian woman. Long story. Never mind. These Bianco brutes appear to have launched a campaign of terror against the dark-skinned residents of the Chesapeake region."

"Yeah. They're a gang of self-appointed strongmen with a hatred for anyone not lily-white."

Galloway sighed. "It's sad that such times are upon us. Alas, I wish this type of sentiment was confined by geography. No, there are too many Americans who feel threatened by others on these shores who don't share their history, background, or language." He gestured to Vincent. "Even those of Mediterranean descent are still frowned on, even in New York City."

Vincent scowled. "Yeah, well. That's all very interesting, but I was about to go deal with these mooks before your marauders rolled over my war party."

Galloway nodded with a wince. "Yes, yes. I realize that. Which is why I'm offering to help."

"Help? How?"

"I'm offering to send my specialists, here, to help cleanse the waters of this Bianco Fiore blight."

Vincent straightened in his seat. He eyed Bolton looming behind Galloway, almost bent in half by this pronouncement. Then he took a glance over his shoulder at the other two pinchers. Muttonchops had closed his book, balancing it on his knee as he offered a genial nod. Maria had uncrossed her arms and strode several steps to the center of the room. She remained silent, but her face was less nakedly hostile.

Vincent turned back to Galloway. "What's your beef with the Bianco?"

"My beef?" Galloway chuckled. "They're monsters. They sweep in and terrorize villages. They burn down homes and businesses. They abduct and execute people strictly by virtue of the color of their skin. In my mind, they've surrendered any right to a trial or jury. They must be dealt with." He leaned farther forward. "And it seems apparent that the Law has no interest in getting involved. Time for good men to act."

"And women," Maria chimed from behind Vincent.

Vincent asked, "So, you come after me twice in a week, and now you want to fight alongside me? You'll excuse me if I find this to be a bad idea."

"If we do this little errand for you and make nice, then we

can get back to the real reason we're here," Galloway said with a nod. "As I said earlier, I plan to unseat Vito Corbi and the Baltimore Crew."

Vincent drew in a long breath but said nothing.

Galloway continued, "Richmond is already bereft of organized crime. Corbi is the next weakest link. Removing him from power would create a vacuum, unsettling the balance among the East Coast families."

Vincent shook his head. "You're just taking out pawns. Nickel-and-diming your way through Baltimore won't accomplish much."

"I'm not blind. There is a long-term plan that involves New York. I want you to be a part of it. And I suspect you're of the same mind."

Vincent mulled over Galloway's words. The man wasn't wrong. Ever since Ithaca, Vincent's eyes had been opened to the cruelty and sheer injustice of the system he'd been born into. The indoctrinated loyalties they'd cultivated. The way his very humanity had been stripped from him. But he wasn't a fool. Vincent knew that confronting the Crew would be suicide, even with his powers. He'd already taken the first steps toward a long play that would end with villains like the Capo in ruin, and friends like Lefty left standing.

But this? Everything about Galloway screamed "long play." He was clearly a brilliant tactician. His pinchers were loyal. This might work. And for the first time, Vincent had some hope that his vision of the future might come to fruition.

Arnoud was wrong. These weren't zealots. They were soldiers.

Vincent nodded to Bolton. "And what about that one? If I take you up on your offer, how do I know he won't pull a gun and shoot me in the back the first chance he gets?"

"Because he knows I don't want that." Galloway turned in

his chair to give Bolton a sympathetic nod. "I know you were subjected to intense pain. You are a trustworthy companion, one who has earned my admiration. That they'd pried loose from your lips our secret location? I don't hold that against you."

Bolton paled a shade, eyes widening.

With a nod, Galloway turned back to Vincent. "I believe you'll be safe."

Vincent cleared his throat, then nodded.

"Alright. I accept. Bianco Fiore is our target."

CHAPTER 14

Hattie huddled behind Sadie's desk, a blanket wrapped around her shoulders. It wasn't a terribly cold day, but the lack of sleep had sapped the warmth from her body. She sat with the codex opened on the desk, but the words didn't even register. Her eyes unfocused, sending the words into bland images that floated in and out of her field of vision. She sat numb, simply staring at a desktop.

"You okay?" a voice called from over her shoulder.

Blake had popped into the room without bothering to walk.

Hattie jerked in her seat, sending the chair rolling on its casters. "Sweet Jesus, Blake!" she gasped. "Would't kill you to walk into a room on your own two feet?"

He ducked his head. "Sorry. When we're here, I kinda lose sight of stuff."

Hattie nodded. "I know the feeling."

"Don't you ever, you know…do one of your illusions just for you?"

"What?"

He waved a hand over the walls. "Make this a beach somewhere in the South. With those fruity drinks with fruit?"

She smirked. "Fruity drinks with fruit?"

A blush raced across his cheeks. "I mean, like, hanging off the edge."

She thought of the illusion she'd done with Raymond in the field, the one she'd gotten so lost in that she'd almost killed herself. "I know what you mean. And no, I don't."

"Never?"

"Blake," she said as she stood up, folding the blanket into a neat rectangle, "your powers are sudden. You blink, and you're over here. Doesn't really cost you a lot of energy."

He shrugged. "Well, I mean, if I blink to somewhere far away. Or somewhere I can't see at all? Yeah. I get sick."

"Well, my sort of powers aren't instant. I have to spend a lot of my guts just to keep up a simple illusion. Add to it the smell of the sea or the taste of those fruity drinks, and I can't do it for long. And when this bleak world comes crashing back, I'll have a hell of a hangover to go with't."

He frowned. "I guess I never thought of it that way. I hate that we can't just do what we want."

"Aye, well. Perhaps nature has a way of balancing the books?"

Blake nodded, then stepped around the desk. "Hey, lookit me. I'm walking out the room on my own two feet, here."

"I'm proud of you."

She returned her attention to the codex, then closed it with a thump. This was useless. She'd already missed her chance at a decent night's sleep, and there wasn't much left inside her head for studying. Not to mention she'd milked that codex about as far as it could give when it came to the blasted soul trap in her pocket.

And the Hell pincher.

Perhaps a trip to visit Miles Absalom would have to happen sooner than later? He was neutral ground. Surely all of his enchantments could defend him against the Hell pincher.

Then again, Absalom seemed wary enough just to deal with Assam al Ghasawi, the man she thought was the Hell pincher. No. The soul trap would stay with her. There was no way in Heaven or Hell she'd trust it to anyone else.

Hattie pulled herself out of the office and down the flight of stairs to exit the Charge. Sadie was keeping to herself ever since they'd met with Galloway. Hattie suspected there was more to the O'Donnell's split with Galloway than either party had admitted to. As Hattie walked the long trek to her home in Hampden, she pondered several possibilities. Had the O'Donnells actually warned Galloway, or had they indeed slipped out in the night to let him fall into Capone's trap? Or worse, had they tipped off Capone's people in the first place? Hattie couldn't imagine Sadie being so insidious, but she'd never met Jonas O'Donnell. The man was rather sacrosanct among the Charge. He was a fallen hero. A martyr. He was dead as far as they were concerned, and Sadie had done her best to lionize the man.

But a man is just a man. In extreme circumstances, anyone might be inclined to cross the line between what is right and what needs to be done. And Hattie had seen first-hand how easy it was to rationalize horrific actions after the fact.

As she ruminated on the fleeting morality of good people, Hattie's sense of danger prickled. She paused on the street, turning back to glance down the lane between the innocuous three-story row houses.

"Blake?" she called, wondering if he wasn't following her home. He'd done it before, just once. It was an act of bullish youth, a gesture of gallantry that was horridly misplaced, and Hattie ha called him out on it.

But this time, it wasn't Blake.

She scanned the road, searching each alleyway. No movement. Just that odd sense that she was being followed.

Hattie shook her head and rubbed her face. The lack of sleep was doing this to her. Paranoia. Irritability. She couldn't go running down ghosts in the street. Not when she had a meeting with Vincent to make.

Vincent. Everything inside her came alive at the thought of him.

But where was this thing between them going? They'd kissed…many times, and it was clear that they both wanted more. She knew she trusted him not to rat her out to the Crew. He'd pledged not only to help Raymond rebuild, but to exact vengeance on his behalf. And he did it without question. He'd even thrown himself into investigating the Charge safehouse without a protest. Which was fine, but that was all…professional.

He was an ally.

But weren't they more than that? She thought for a moment about a future with Vincent—marriage and children. But he was owned by the mob, both of them haunted by the shadow of powerful families that could smash whatever life they wanted to build together. What she wanted might be impossible. And she wasn't even sure marriage and children were in Vincent's long term plans either.

If that were the case, then they really needed to do more than just kiss in stairwells and alleyways. The man really needed to get on with getting on, because if the years had taught Hattie anything, it was that life was a fleeting thing. People needed to take advantage of opportunities lest they vanish in the wind, or with the speed of a bullet, the very next day. They both lived dangerous lives, and it would forever haunt her if she never got the chance to do more than just kiss the man she'd grown to love.

Love. Did she even have the luxury of that sort of thing?

Hattie felt that watched sensation once more and turned again, sure she'd spotted some movement out of the corner of her eye.

No. Nothing.

Just in case, she stepped up her pace, heading home as quickly as she could. Once there, Hattie changed quickly, splashing water on her face and pinching her cheeks to bring some color back into her visage. Alton was at work, and Branna was busy knitting. She was in and out within an hour, and well on her way to her luncheon with Vincent. They'd agreed to meet at the Fontainebleau for a light lunch and some heavy conversation. She was eager to hear how things went with this Galloway fellow and the return of their hostage.

And she needed to let Vincent know to be wary around Galloway. Sway pinching. Bending people's loyalties in the direction he chose. Compared to her illusions, or Vincent's time twisting, or even Capstein and his ability to use air as a weapon, this sort of power seemed mild, but in the hands of a man who'd mastered oration and shifting winds of allegiance, such a power could be unstoppable. What's worse, how could anyone close to the man know for certain that they believed in him, or that he was making them believe? In a way, that could be a hellish prison from which Galloway could never escape—never knowing if anyone truly loved you.

A natural flush reached her cheeks as she trotted along the street for the Fontainebleu. The ghosts of her paranoia evaporated with her resolve to spend some time with the one person who made her feel better about life.

The interior of the Fontainebleu was nearly empty. One

elderly couple sat in the corner window table slowly finishing their brunch. Hattie eyed the bar at the far end of the room. She'd spent many hours bellied up to that bar, idly chit-chatting with Leon. But now he was gone, fleeing the press of the mob for the fabled water pincher. Gone off to Chicagoland, ironically, where the mob held yet greater power. But if anyone was flexible enough to slip between the cracks of gangland, and these rival pinchers, it was Leon.

Placing an order for tomato juice, Hattie waited for Vincent. Minutes passed, and she re-crossed her legs. More minutes, and she drummed her fingers on the table top. This wasn't necessarily unusual for Vincent. Sudden Crew affairs had often interrupted their rendezvous, especially in the few weeks after Vincent had returned from Ithaca. But he'd always sent someone along with a handwritten apology.

And so, when someone arrived, Hattie was anything but surprised. What did surprise her, on the other hand, was that it wasn't his usual street boy.

It was Nadine.

Hattie stood up wide-eyed. "Nadine? Is everything all right?"

Nadine gripped Dougie against her chest as she walked through the dining room. Hattie gestured for a chair, but the woman eyed her surroundings and shook her head. "Oh, it's all fine. I'm just here lookin' for you."

"How'd you find me?" Hattie asked, already piecing together the answer in her head.

"Your man…that Vincent."

Hattie grinned at the way Nadine referred to Vincent as "her man."

"Aye?"

"He said that he's very sorry he can't make it."

Hattie sighed. "Right, right. He's off doing some mischief, and he'll meet me tomorrow for breakfast?"

Nadine nodded. "That's…yes. That's what he said."

"Why'd he send you? Was he at Curtis Creek this morning, then?"

"Ummm." Nadine looked for anything else in the room to stare at other than Hattie.

"Where's he gone?" Hattie asked, a suspicion settling in her middle.

"He didn't say."

"Right. I suppose he wouldn't." Hattie reached for Nadine, patting her shoulder. "It's alright. He does this all the time."

"Don't seem fittin'."

"It's usually just fine. But today? I think I know where he's gone."

Nadine's eyes widened. "I didn't say nothin'."

"No, you didn't. But I know Vincent. And I know your husband." Hattie shook her head. "One or both of those boys will be the death of me. Come on."

"Where are we goin'?" Nadine asked.

"I'm getting us a car, and we're bringing you back home. Then, I'm going to skin a man alive."

* * *

MEN AND WOMEN buzzed about Winnow's Slip like a cloud of bees. The pier was mostly repaired. A lithe young man stepped along a few trunks of felled pines, scraping the bark to make clean planks of lumber. He handed them off to a few of Raymond's neighbors who settled them onto a series of conical stone posts rising from the riverbed while Hattie observed the goings-on from a shaded patch of forest not far from the boathouses.

Vincent stood on a stretch of finished pier alongside the fellow with the bowler hat and muttonchops. They conversed casually as four boats lined up along the quay.

Men of light and dark skin hopped in and out, loading boxes of ammunition.

Galloway approached Vincent from inside one of the boathouses, nodding as Raymond thrust a finger into the air, indicating some targets farther to the south.

By everyone's posture, it appeared that Raymond had a hand in running this show. How deep had his anger over the Bianco Fiore run? How would he feel once he'd spilled blood in reprisal? Though she was pleased to see that Galloway and company had given Raymond a seat at the table, she worried that this bloody business would change her friend forever.

After a while, Vincent withdrew from the gathering to slip closer to the woods. Hattie slapped a hand over her mouth to stifle a laugh as she realized he was answering nature's call. Once he'd finished, she pinched light around herself to emerge from the forest, an illusion of some name-less and unmemorable dock worker.

She trotted up behind Vincent, clearing her throat. "Don't react," she said. "I'm using an illusion."

Vincent stiffened for a half-step, then continued his slow amble toward the boathouses. "Hi."

"Hi, yourself. We had a lunch date."

"I know. I'm sorry I had to cancel. Did Nadine find you?"

She elbowed him in the ribs. "Yes. And that's for getting Nadine involved. She's got a wee child, and her husband's out here putting his life in danger."

Vincent dipped his head. "If you don't want to draw attention, you might want to lower your voice."

"What's all this? Your war party?"

Vincent nodded. "Galloway's offered to throw in. His way of making amends for accidentally attacking me twice."

"You sure it was an accident?" Hattie muttered.

"No, but I'm not going to refuse his offer. Why? Do you know otherwise?"

She pointed for one of the boathouses, easing its door open to step inside. Once out of the view of the others, she released the illusion. "It just seems to me they went well out of their way to attack you, right here. On this soil. And then it's suddenly a massive cock-up and a terrible misunderstanding, and he's eager to make it right? Does a man like that look to be the sort who makes mistakes?"

"It *was* technically a mistake on the part of his people. They saw gang activity and decided to interfere."

"Then why were they spying on Raymond?"

Vincent shrugged. "He says they were looking for you. Following a trail of crumbs. This man knows a lot about Sadie's people. And about me."

Hattie put a hand on Vincent's arm. "I want you to be careful. These eyes and ears of his must be silent and invisible."

"Pinchers?"

"More like insiders," she said. "Which concerns me, because it means he's been planning a move into this area for longer than he's let on."

"Oh, I don't trust Galloway any farther than I can throw him." He added with a grin, "But I trust you. And if you tell me to keep my eyes open, I will."

"Good. I think I was followed this morning. And Galloway…he's up to something, and I don't like you being on a boat with his people so far away."

"You're just sore I didn't invite you," he teased, reaching out to pinch her chin.

She cocked a brow. "Well, aye. That, I am. But I've learned that giving you a scolding accomplishes toss all."

"I didn't want you in danger," he said. "This is gangster business. And honestly, I knew you wouldn't approve of me using Galloway's people for this, that you'd see it as a betrayal of Sadie."

She thrust a finger into his chest. "You know, this goes against our agreement of sticking together. We're stronger, remember?"

Vincent pursed his lips.

"You're sure you don't want me in on this bloodletting?"

He reached out and drew her into his arms. "I'm stunned you're not threatening my life and demanding to go."

She shrugged as she pressed her face into his chest.

"There's another reason I don't want you to go," he said.

She eased out of his arms. "And that is?"

"You're tired." He stroked the side of her face with the back of his fingers. "I'm worried about you."

Hattie frowned, then nodded. "I've not been sleeping."

"Then go home. Drink some hot tea, preferably with a helping of that whisky I bought your father. Sleep." He kissed the top of her head. "I'll let you know as soon as I'm back. We'll get lunch, or dinner somewhere that you can wear that sexy chandelier dress again. Maybe take in a picture show or walk through the market. I'll buy you some chips from those Utz people."

She smiled up at him. "I'd like that."

Vincent hesitated for a second, then nodded to the door. "Well, I better get back out there before Galloway starts wondering where I went."

Hattie held herself for a moment, waiting for Vincent to take his exit. Before he made it to the doorway, she unfolded her arms and rushed him from behind, clamping onto him with eyes shut.

She whispered, "Please come back from this."

He put a hand over hers. "Oh, I will. I plan to throw Galloway's people at the Biancos then beat feet back to Baltimore before they know I'm gone."

She chuckled. "Good plan."

He turned and kissed her, running his thumb across her lip as they parted. "We should talk when I get back."

Hattie nodded.

"I mean…about us."

Us. There were a million obstacles to any "us," but suddenly Hattie didn't care.

She glanced up at him. "I'd like that."

Vincent stroked her hair, then turned to leave.

Hattie took several minutes to compose herself, then pinched light to exit unseen.

As she plodded her way into the east side of Baltimore, that familiar feeling of someone breathing down her neck crept in. Twice in one day, both times in the city. This wasn't simple paranoia. Someone was watching her.

She maintained her pace, not pausing to look over her shoulder or betray the first sign of suspicion. As she turned a corner into an alley beside a bottling plant, she pinched light to camouflage herself against the brick wall behind her and waited.

Before the weight of her magic began to pull on her chest, footsteps clopped up the lane.

She braced, squinting at the corner of the building.

A figure took one step into view.

It was a man, that much she could tell. He wore a heavy coat and a charcoal gray Homburg hat. The man was peering away from Hattie, his face concealed.

She held her breath, steadying herself against the wall as the man froze. His shoulders tensed. His hand pulled into a fist.

A spike of pain from Hattie's illusion shot through her stomach, and she released her held breath. It was just a tiny puff, but loud enough for her pursuer to hear.

The man reached for his chest and stroked his necktie. And with that motion, his figure rippled into a muddle of shadows and a mind-fuzzing blur. When he turned to peer into the alley, she couldn't discern any features. He'd become a bizarre vision of confusing images. The only thing Hattie's eyes could latch onto was an ornate tie pin stabbed through the knot of his neck tie.

Hattie scowled, then released her light pinch to square her shoulders against this interloper.

"Alright, you. Whoever you are. Drop the enchantment and face me."

As she marched forward, he retreated several steps into the street. An oncoming car locked its brakes, tires slipping along the dirt of the street. The man turned on a heel and sprinted across the street to dodge the car.

Hattie hopped aside to catch a glimpse of the man as he bolted up the street. She tried to pursue him but lost her breath quickly. As she came to a halt, holding herself up on a wrought iron gate along the street, she chided herself for letting her exhaustion rob her of the ability to hound down this spy.

A spy using enchantments.

Fantastic. With Galloway in town, this new player would be an unwelcome distraction. And one thing was certain, now.

Hattie needed sleep, if she were to survive any of this.

CHAPTER 15

No one spoke as Vincent's vigilante flotilla chugged south on the Chesapeake Bay. The sun had set an hour ago, affording them some degree of cover though the group of four boats loaded with pinchers and dark-skinned foot soldiers weren't exactly keeping a low profile. This wasn't some probing mission, or a small band slipping behind enemy lines for recon. This was a full-bore strike aiming for the throat of the Bianco Fiore.

Raymond tapped Vincent on the shoulder, pointing to the southeast. A red glow loomed over the tree line.

Vincent grabbed a signal lamp and flashed three strobes to Galloway's boat, which chugged forward to come alongside Raymond's.

Galloway steadied himself on the rail as he leaned toward Vincent. "What's the word?"

"Fire on the horizon."

"Inland?"

Vincent checked with Raymond, who shook his head.

"There's a bend," Raymond said. "An inlet leading into a bog. Some folk set up there."

"Then we investigate," Vincent said.

The boats made for southeast, and in a few minutes the flames slipped into view beyond a marshy estuary. A handful of wood cabins on high piers stood in fiery repose, spilling light over the murky water spread before them. Raymond steered closer, spotting a clutch of survivors as Galloway's sun pincher shone her magical light over the mud flats. Vincent offered a hand as they rescued four people, all shivering from fear more than from the cold of the night air.

Raymond and a couple of his men conferred with them, offering blankets and a few slices of jerky. After a while, Raymond returned to Vincent.

"Was it the Bianco Fiore?" Vincent asked.

"Yeah, of course it was."

"How long?"

Raymond nodded to the west. "Not long. About an hour. They came in with six boats and hit them with kerosene and torches. Said they pulled outta the estuary and went south."

"Back to Richmond," Vincent stated. "You good?"

Raymond nodded with tight lips.

Vincent filled in Galloway, and they turned back into the Bay with the survivors, whom they deposited near Heathsville.

The boats collected at the mouth of the York River as Vincent called them together. Galloway, Maria, and Ernie climbed aboard Raymond's boat.

Vincent nodded to each of them. "Last time I was here, the Bianco Fiore had taken over a fueling depot up the James River. They'd run out most of the river traffic by then, but that was when Richmond had a kingpin in place. She's gone now, so I'm not sure what we're going to run into."

Maria asked, "How solid is your instinct on this?"

"Pretty solid. These men aren't organized, but they're also not very creative. My guess is they hit and run, all coming together again to pick a new target. They just made their hit for the night, so they'll probably be in a mood to drink and celebrate."

"That fuel depot is just upriver from the Chickahominy. They got diesel and kerosene there, so when the shootin' starts, it's gonna lick fire," Raymond warned.

"Suits me," Maria grumbled. "As long as it's them doing the burning."

"Your plan of attack?" Galloway asked.

"Go hard, go fast," Vincent replied. "Don't give them time to respond."

"And if no one's home?" Galloway prodded.

"Then we roll up to Richmond and knock on the damn door."

Galloway laughed. "I like that plan."

"Then let's go," Vincent instructed as they split up to their respective boats.

The flotilla rounded the mouth of the James River and throttled up. There was no river traffic to speak of. The sun pincher double-checked the shoreline with discreet bursts of light from her palms. Before long, the confluence of the Chickahominy appeared to their right. And just beyond, a glow of yellow light across the river.

As their vessels swept around the final bend, Vincent spotted twelve boats clustered around the depot. A dozen men stood on the pier, bottles in hand, bellowing and singing underneath kerosene lanterns. More than twice that number remained aboard their craft, some dozing, some keeping a sober eye on the water.

Vincent released a low whistle.

Raymond sucked in a breath. "That's double what we were expectin'."

"Won't matter. We still got them outmatched," Vincent

said, eyeing the second boat, and Galloways wood pincher who appeared to be limbering up.

"Better get your shots in while you can," Vincent said with a slap on Raymond's back. "I have a feeling this is going to be over quick."

The front boat eased up on the throttle until all four craft had lined up. Then, they hammered down for the depot.

The roar of four diesel engines caught the attention of the Bianco Fiore men on lookout. They raised an alarm with shouts and a few pot shots taken in the air.

Raymond lifted a rifle along with most of his posse. He squeezed off a shot, followed by a peppering report from the remainder of the rifles. Vincent didn't expect them to find many targets, but he knew once the pinchers got involved this might be their last chance for personal vengeance.

Muzzle flares from the Bianco boats flashed in response. Vincent ducked down as bullets whizzed overhead, one striking the side of the boat.

A shout from the third boat bellowed, "Eyes!"

Vincent clamped his eyes shut before the night burst into light so brilliant it was almost unbearable through his closed eyelids. When the sun pincher's blinding flash subsided, Vincent opened his eyes and blinked until they adjusted to the darkness once again.

Groans from the pier and enemy vessels indicated that her flash had either temporarily or permanently blinded several of the gunmen.

Their boats closed the gap between quickly, chugging for the pier. Raymond's men fired another salvo of rifle fire. A few shouts and splashes into the river indicated they were within range and finding targets.

A loud rushing sound spilled through the air as the boats slowed their speed on final approach. A titanic spike of stone shot up from the river floor, smashing through the engine house of one of the Bianco boats. The water poured away in waves, rocking Vincent's boat as it sidled up to the depot.

He pinched time and pushed his way onto the pier, shoulder-checking two of the blinded Bianco thugs into midair over the side of the pier planks. He cleared the landing for his boat and pulled his handgun before restoring the flow of time. Several splashes later, Raymond and most of his men were on the planks of the pier following Vincent, dropping two more Bianco men who'd managed to avoid the sunburst.

Another stone spike ruined a second boat. At this rate, Maria would burn through her energy. But that might not matter.

"Watch out!" Raymond shouted.

A line of six men rushed out of the pump house, eyes unmarred by the sun flash. They lifted tommy guns in Vincent's direction.

Before he could pinch time and do his best to clear Raymond's men, a crackling sound flared from the direction of the pump house. The six Bianco men cried out in unison as the planks beneath their feet erupted into a series of six-inch wooden thorns that pierced their shoes and legs. Each dropped their guns, gripping their legs which were now impaled onto the planks.

Raymond's men lifted rifles to pop them one at a time as the wood pincher sauntered up the landing with a grin.

One of the boats lifted from the water, hoisting into the air with a casual flip of Ernie's wrist. It careened end over end, smashing into two more vessels in a burst of timbers and popping steam pipes.

The wood pincher gestured for a nearby Bianco boat, ripping its hull in half, sending it underwater in a matter of seconds. The sun pincher illuminated several Bianco men swimming away, allowing Raymond's riflemen opportunity to pepper them from the pier.

Ernie picked up one of the blinded thugs and swung him several times overhead before flinging him into the engine house of one of the last remaining vessels. The thug's body smashed into the engine, bones pulverizing as blood sprayed into the diesel-fueled fire spreading across its deck.

Vincent stood silent, a disquieting feeling churning his guts. These pinchers weren't simply completing a mission. They were enjoying this. And it was…disturbing. He'd been very aware that this mission wasn't just a way for Galloway to make amends, this was an opportunity to not only test Vincent's potential loyalty but to show him the power and possibilities of Galloway's army, to convince Vincent to join them in their operation.

An army of pinchers like this most definitely could unseat Corbi, and possibly the other East Coast families. They were skilled. They were powerful.

They were also a bit too gleeful about what was quickly turning into a murder fest.

As the last of the Bianco Fiore men perished, Vincent wondered at the ease of it all. He'd survived gang wars with the Russians. Those were hard-fought battles waged with gunpowder and lead. Lives were lost on both sides, and Vincent's time pinching had made the difference. There were always casualties on both sides.

But tonight? It was so one-sided it baffled Vincent. He'd never fought alongside so many pinchers before. And there was no real strategy, here, they simply strolled right up and pounded these men into oblivion.

Vincent cast a glance to the fourth boat, and Galloway. The man stood on the deck, arms crossed, flames flickering on the spectacles over his forehead. He hadn't participated. He simply observed at a safe distance, like some field marshal. Nothing about this seemed to be a surprise to the man. If anything, it appeared to be a chore to Galloway.

With all of Sadie O'Donnell's protests that Galloway's mission to take on the mob was foolhardy, Vincent had never really considered that Galloway could ever succeed. In the wake of the violence that had come and gone with such ease, Vincent reconsidered. There was unspeakable power in a group of pinchers working together for one goal. Maybe Galloway had been right all along. Perhaps it *was* possible to take on the mob. All they needed was enough pincher talent to work together.

Could he accept the excessive bloodshed that these people seemed to revel in to achieve the sort of freedom he'd only dreamed about?

The rest of their boats finally arrived at the pier and the pinchers climbed on board.

Clearing his throat, Galloway turned to address them all. "My friends, this was a magnificent showing. Well done, all of you!"

Several applauded, releasing shouts of victory.

Galloway continued, "This isn't simply a victory for our cause. It's a victory for justice." He turned to Raymond's boat and the black men gathered along the rail with rifles slung over their shoulders. "Word will spread, my friends. The Bianco Fiore was routed. Any of their sympathizers left behind will think twice about acting on their hatred. Now they know that good people won't simply stand by. They will act. So, rebuild with ease of mind."

A few of Raymond's men cheered, though most simply nodded quietly. Vincent frowned, wondering if Galloway hadn't pressed an issue he didn't fully understand. Sure, the Bianco Fiore had been decapitated. And perhaps for now the threat of violence had been staved off. But as long as so many people believed that blacks were not equals, their problems wouldn't be solved with a wave of pincher magic.

It made him wonder if any of their problems could be

solved with only a wave of pincher magic. Maybe in the short term, yes, but even if they managed to unseat Corbi and the other families, how long would it be before others banded together and moved against them?

Vincent glanced around, a knot of worry forming in his stomach.

Galloway stepped in front of him and clapped him on the shoulder. "Well, Mister Calendo. How did we do?"

Vincent looked around at the burning buildings, the ruined boats, the bodies floating in the water. "This was impressive."

"I see you were the first one off the boat. I'm heartened you were so committed to this."

"Well, it's my friend we were helping."

Galloway nodded. "And now he has nothing to worry about."

Vincent winced. "So, listen. Maybe ease up on the whole speechmaking. These people aren't going to be all lollipops and cotton candy, now that we've done this. Their lives will continue to be a struggle."

Galloway lifted a finger. "Yes, but we did solve one problem. And it was a major problem. We can't fix all of the world's ills with one strike. But if that strike is followed by another, and another. If we turn the hearts and minds of those out there who would take up guns in violence, convincing them that people like your friend…" He tapped Vincent in the chest. "Or you and me…are worthy of equal standing? That's how you win the war."

"Hearts and minds, huh?"

"Do you believe me now?" Galloway asked. "We are not simple, blithe idealists. Every city we hit is a step toward pincher freedom. Hiding from the masters is no sort of plan."

Vincent nodded somberly. "Yeah, I guess I see your point."

"And I didn't even bring my own gunmen," Galloway

added. "I have two bands of mercenaries whom I've... coerced. Foot soldiers, if you will. For when our powers reach their limit."

"But you never coerce pinchers, right?" Vincent asked.

"Never once."

Vincent stared at Galloway. What if he sway pinched unconsciously? Or what if he was lying, binding everyone's loyalty with skillful oration and a subtle sway pinch to ensure everyone fell in line with his plans?

Galloway clapped his hands together and looked around him with a satisfied air. "We can win this, Vincent. We can win."

Vincent turned away. "I'm going to check on Raymond. We should pack up and get back on the Bay before the Feds catch wind."

He marched back to Raymond's boat, taking his hand as Raymond helped him aboard. They stood side-by-side as their war party packed up and loaded the boats with some spoils of war, mostly guns and ammunition, and a few dozen gallons of fuel liberated from the depot.

"Think there's ever gonna be a world where either one of us can go anywhere we want? Be anything we want?" Raymond asked.

Vincent replied, "Yes. I honestly do, but I think it has to be us that makes that happen. You, me and the others in the places we call home." He turned to Raymond. "And *I* intend to start with Baltimore."

CHAPTER 16

The sun hung just below the eastern horizon, spilling pink light across a wispy blanket of clouds. A brisk springtime chill had settled over the city, a dusting of frost clinging to the stones and slate shingles of Baltimore. Hattie adjusted her hat as she took a glimpse at the colorful dawn sky, then trod casually down the market street. None of the tables had been brought out yet, and all of the doors remained closed. It was that quiet hour before the business of the day resumed. These were moments Hattie had grown accustomed to in the city. In another life, she'd only ever watched the sun rise out on the water. But the long shadows of buildings slicing across the street as the smells of breakfast foods filled the air carried its own beauty. A city rising from slumber, huddled in on itself, preparing to erupt in activity.

Hattie buttoned another button on her coat as she passed the grocer, taking care not to look over her shoulder. She couldn't stifle a yawn as she paused to allow a street sweeper to cross the walkway in front of her. Despite her resolution to get some sleep, it remained elusive. She'd managed perhaps three hours of real rest before the dreams rattled her awake again. It wasn't the nightmares that prevented her from returning to her slumber. Rather, the cascading thoughts and plans that wouldn't calm enough for her to rest. So, she decided to make use of the early hours, marching with deliberate nonchalance through the city.

As she stopped to pet a cat that had trotted off a stoop to greet her, Hattie felt that familiar sense of unease. Her shadow man was on the hunt again.

Just what she wanted.

She fidgeted with her gloves, affording this practitioner enough time to close the distance before crossing the street. An oyster truck putted around the corner, basketfuls of shells loaded in its bed. Hattie paused a half-step to let the vehicle pass, then pinched light with as much art as she could conjure. An illusion of herself continued across the street to stare into a window while she rushed to crouch beside a concrete stoop.

She braced herself for what could be a costly illusion. The sunlight was only growing brighter, and she had to maintain this illusion for an undetermined amount of time while concealing herself. Just long enough to draw out this shadow man.

Hattie sent her illusion ambling down the lane.

The tug on her powers spiked as two men emerged from a door just behind the false Hattie. They tipped their hats to the image before walking the opposite direction. This ruse had better work quickly. The more people emerged to begin their day, the more difficult it would be to maintain the light pinch.

Peering up and down the street, she watched for that Homburg hat. Nothing. Hattie nudged the illusion down the street, the strain of the magic growing the farther it stepped away from her. She'd have to give the illusion something to do, or it wouldn't look convincing. And so, she had the false Hattie step onto a crack in the walk, pantomiming damage to the heel of her shoe. The illusion steadied herself against the corner of the building to inspect the shoe, ambling into an alley to adjust it.

As it slipped out of view, the illusion dissipated. It was too much effort maintaining a light pinch that she couldn't even see. Hopefully the bait would be enough. She waited beside the steps, watching the street. Still no sign of the shadow man.

Shaking her head, Hattie dropped her concealment pinch, and glanced to the rooftops across the street with a shrug. And just as she was about to straighten herself up and surrender the ruse, a man rushed past the stoop toward the alley. A man wearing a Homburg hat and charcoal cloak.

Hattie held a breath and froze. He was moving too fast to spot her in her hiding place. Indeed, he appeared almost reckless in his pursuit, as if he had been keeping too much distance and was close to letting her slip away.

With a low, loping trot, Hattie slipped onto the street, lifting a finger to signal the rooftops.

The shadow man paused briefly at the corner to peek around, then bolted into the alley. Hattie followed him, bracing for any surprise he might throw at her. But as she peered around the corner she found him rushing down the alley.

Digging deep, she pinched her illusion back to life, standing cross-armed in the middle of the shadow man's path. The man drew up, feet slipping on the stones and nearly falling backward.

As he turned to retreat he found the real Hattie staring at him from the street. His eyes grew wide, dark irises set into deep sockets above a streamlined nose, olive skin, and a neatly trimmed beard.

These were eyes she'd seen before.

Assam al Ghasawi.

A rush of air behind Ghasawi sent his collar into a flutter. He spun around to find Blake reaching for his necktie.

"I'll take that," Blake said as he snatched the tie pin from the knot before blinking back to the rooftops over the alleyway.

Ghasawi reached for his throat in reflex, but Blake was already gone by the time his hand touched the knot.

Hattie marched forward. "So, it's you again."

Ghasawi glanced left, then right, his face wary. "Miss Malloy. It seems the jig, as it were, is up."

She scowled. "Why are you following me?"

He glanced to the rooftop and Blake, who was examining the talisman he'd just pilfered from Ghasawi. "Clever ploy. I was following an illusion. Silly of me, to be honest."

"Well, I didn't have time to set bear traps."

He nodded. "I see you remember our last encounter."

"Can't bloody well forget it!" She stepped closer. "I'll ask again—why are you following me?"

He lifted his hands and took a step away. "This may seem unbelievable, but I mean you no harm."

"So you say."

"And I mean it. Truly."

She wagged a finger at him. "You nearly took my head off, last time we met."

"That was not intended for you. Not specifically. A man in my position must take precautions against horrors the likes of which you've seen personally."

Hattie shook her head. "What are you bleating on about?"

"The Hell pincher," Ghasawi replied. "This man you seemed so eager to find."

"Aye, well…I was desperate."

"Then you no longer seek him out?"

Hattie bobbed her head. "I'd rather he just jump off a cliff. But I get the feeling that's not likely to happen."

"Indeed not. This particular Hell pincher has been clever enough to elude my pursuits, even to the point of ensnaring and murdering my partner."

"Partner?" she repeated.

"If I may?" Ghasawi gestured to a crate nestled up to the gray stone building beside them, then took a seat. "I am not as young as I once was. This sort of pursuit leaves me with empty lungs and sore feet."

"I feel so sorry for you."

He nodded. "I haven't made my intentions clear, I see."

"I wish you'd do that."

"I am a representative of the Beylik of the Reformed Janissaries."

She shook her head. "And what's that supposed to mean, exactly?"

"It means I'm on your side, Miss Malloy." He sighed and stared down the alley. "Forgive my impertinence, but might we continue this conversation in more civilized environs? Do you drink coffee?"

* * *

HATTIE AND BLAKE sat across a deli table from Ghasawi, who sipped his coffee with a downcast expression.

"Hmm, it is difficult to find proper coffee on this continent."

Blake shrugged. "Seems okay to me."

Ghasawi wrinkled his nose. "Ah, but you see my friend, it is my people who brought *qahwah* to Europe in the first place. And none of the care the goes into preserving the flavor is given any consideration. The beans are not meant to be boiled and re-boiled. It's a shame, truly."

Blake shrugged again. "Seems okay to me."

Hattie lifted a hand. "Can we stop discussing the coffee and get back to what you were telling me in the alley?"

"Yes. In their day, the Janissaries were an elite guard of the Ottoman sultans. As their status improved over the centuries, so too did their sense of entitlement. Which led them to periodic revolts."

Hattie rolled her eyes. "Arriving at your point…when?"

"The Janissaries were eradicated in the early Nineteenth Century, owing to the threat they posed to the powers that be. The leaders were executed. The rest died or were imprisoned or exiled. Many who fled settled to live private, discreet lives. Others chose to take up the more noble charges of the Janissaries, now that they lacked wealth and status. A private reformation. They recruited from Europe and the Arab world." He placed a hand on his chest. "Such as myself."

Blake peered at Hattie. "Any of this make sense to you?"

Hattie shook her head. "No, and it's annoying me."

"One of the purposes of the Janissary corps was to police the use of forbidden magics."

A silence fell over the table.

Hattie nodded. "Alright, then. Now we're getting to it."

Ghasawi continued, "The Reformed Janissaries recognized that native-born magic users such as yourself continued to serve the Sultan, the sheiks, the moghuls, kings and princes. The spread of the ones you refer to as *pinchers* was impossible to contain. But it was not these pinchers the Janissaries sought to police, but the viziers. Holy men. Spiritualists who trace their secret knowledge back to King Solomon, himself."

Hattie nodded. "Practitioners."

"Men who were born with no abilities greater than a drive to learn, and an obsession with esoteric power that bordered on blasphemy. Viziers were useful to the Sultan, and so they were tolerated, and became an office of political importance. When the Janissaries were first formed as a private army loyal to the Sultan, part of their duties was to keep an eye on such practitioners of forbidden arts, so that their power may never threaten the throne."

"So, you hunt practitioners then?" Hattie asked.

"Not all. In time, the Reformed Janissaries adopted many of the talents and skills of the practitioners we observed."

Blake brandished the tie pin. "Like this little trinket?"

"The same. We have no vendetta against practitioners at large. No, it is those who cross the line of blasphemy, those who treat with infernal magics in defiance of Allah, those who ensnare souls and unleash demons—those are the ones we hunt."

"Hell pinchers," Hattie whispered.

Ghasawi sipped his coffee with a scowl. "When you came to me last year, Miss Malloy, I had just lost my partner, a fellow Janissary on the hunt for the Hell pincher you were so concerned with."

"The burned-out inn. He followed the Hell pincher's trail and fell victim to the trap," Hattie mused.

"Indeed. A terrible loss. He was an accomplished investigator and a good friend. And then, not a week later, you arrive at my doorstep brandishing a soul trap, asking me about Hell pinchers." He set down his cup and leaned forward. "You see, I wasn't entirely certain this Hell pincher was even a man at all. You could have been the one behind it all, luring me into some twisted game for your amusement."

Blake lifted a brow. "Yeah, that sounds like Hattie alright."

Hattie kicked Blake under the table, then said, "And I thought *you* were the Hell pincher."

"I can understand that. Two minds hunting the Hell pincher, revolving around one another. We were destined to collide."

"This wasn't destiny," Hattie chided. "You've been following me for a week, at least."

"I confess. When I fled from you, I took time to learn the truth of who you were. Happily, you'd given me your name and not some alias. I tracked you to Baltimore, where I watched and waited. Satisfied that you were no Hell pincher, my mission transformed from confrontation to protection."

"Protection?" Hattie laughed. "How do you figure that?"

"Do you still possess the soul trap?"

She set her jaw and remained silent.

He nodded. "I see that you do. And I believe you are now aware not only of what is imprisoned within, but what its significance is to you…and the time pincher."

She leaned back in her seat. "How do you—"

"I have advantages, Miss Malloy. Scrying implements. A lifetime of study and knowledge of such matters. Whereas you're grasping at straws, wandering in the dark, this whole time the Solomon's Crown walks the streets of Baltimore, ready for the Hell pincher to scoop it up in his hands and use it to dominate the entirety of Mankind."

Blake whistled. "Sounds bad."

Hattie shook her head. "We don't know if it's *our* demon inside this trap."

Ghasawi reached out to lay a palm on the table. "But you do. It calls to you. The certainty of it may feel nebulous, but is there truly any part of your waking mind that doesn't accept the fact that your dark twin resides in your pocket?"

A shiver ran through Hattie's shoulders. To hear it spoken so plainly rattled her.

"I suppose not," she muttered.

"Tell me," Ghasawi said, "are you plagued with night terrors as of late?"

She nodded.

"The connection you share with your dark twin transcends the bonds of the soul trap. Its mind reaches out to you. And though Allah has chosen to create both it and you in accordance with His will, do not be mistaken. It is a creature of evil and destruction."

"I don't agree," Hattie said. "It seems more like an animal in a cage, to me. Not evil. Just wronged."

"Such thinking will progress the longer you hold that soul trap so close to you. Sympathy with this demon will increase until you no longer recognize the goodness that once dwelt inside your soul."

Blake mumbled, "That sounds bad."

Ghasawi prodded, "Have you become irritable? More accepting of violence? Are you questioning your friendships and loyalties?"

Hattie stood up. "I've had enough of these fairy tales."

Ghasawi shook his head. "I haven't even begun this tale, Miss Malloy."

He gestured to the chair.

Hattie clenched her jaw then took her seat again.

"As long as the Hell pincher is aware of your existence," Ghasawi concluded, "there will be no peace for you. The elements of your complete soul are assembled in one place. It's the sort of opportunity a Hell pincher dreams of."

"You're saying that Vincent and I must part ways?"

He shook his head. "On the contrary, I'm counting on you staying together."

"But, won't that be giving the Hell pincher what he wants?"

"Yes."

Hattie frowned. "I don't follow."

"My purpose is to find and eliminate this blasphemer, Miss Malloy. If he's out there..." he waved his hand to the windows, "...I'll never find him. But if I know where he will go, then all I have to do is wait."

"So, we're bait is what you're saying?"

"You are a soul in jeopardy," Ghasawi said with soft eyes. "I wish to help. But you will never be safe as long as he's out there. I pledge my service to you, Hattie Malloy. In the name of the Beylik of Reformed Janissaries, the Prophet, and Allah. I will not let you fall into this Hell pincher's clutches."

Hattie smiled. "I guess we've come a long way from trick steps and bear traps."

"Then you accept?"

Hattie sighed. "Aye, I suppose you can come out of hiding now."

Ghasawi smiled, his ivory teeth painting a stripe through his beard. "A relief, to be sure."

She stood up, Blake joining her. "Well, if you're to be any use to me at all, we'll have to introduce you to Sadie."

Ghasawi finished his coffee and stood up, collecting his hat. "I've been eager to meet her. I understand she's encountered my order before."

"She has?" Hattie blurted.

"I believe he was a Polish Christian by the name of Nowak?"

"The codex," she said. "Must have been his."

Ghasawi straightened, eyes wide. "You have a codex?"

Hattie nodded slowly.

"We must make haste, my friends."

"Why?" Hattie asked. "What's wrong?"

"There are spells in such texts. Words that carry power. The simple act of reading a Codex could fire spells without your realizing it."

Hattie winced. "Oh, lovely. Well, let's go make sure Sadie isn't about to blow the Charge off the face of the Earth, then."

Vincent drove up to the Charge headquarters alone, having spent most of the early hours delivering Raymond to his home and settling affairs with Galloway, whose pinchers had returned to Waynesboro with him. He took care to park well away from the actual building, respecting Sadie O'Donnell's attention to secrecy. Winding his way behind two adjacent buildings, he scampered over the nearly ruined stone fencing between the Charge and the factory next door.

The yard was quiet, and there were no signs of activity within, though that was no surprise. Vincent had never visited the Charge without Hattie escorting him inside, which gave him pause for a second, but he'd done enough, in his mind, to earn his place here.

Vincent paused at the front entrance deciding whether to knock or just walk in. He elected to knock, giving the door five good raps. The interior was enormous, but hollow. With luck, he'd be heard before someone spotted him from the street.

Just as he was about to knock a second time, the bolt slid

inside and the door eased open. Sadie glared at him from the doorway.

"What do you want?" she grumbled.

"I have news." He paused, waiting for her to step aside.

"What news?" Sadie asked, refusing to budge.

"Well, first of all…is Hattie here?"

"No."

Vincent lingered. Again, Sadie stood like a monolith.

"May I come in?" he finally asked with a huff.

"You don't belong here."

"Are you serious?"

She stepped outside and closed the door behind her, crossing her arms as she faced off with Vincent. "You're a gangster. You're a part of the machine I'm trying to hide my kids from."

"I figured by now you'd see past that," he replied.

"See past what? You still answer to Corbi. You're still their errand boy, even though you've convinced yourself that you're better than they are. It doesn't mean anything from where I stand."

"You were there," he said with measured tone. "At Ithaca. You helped Hattie con my way out of the hands of the New Yorkers. I've kept her secret as well as yours. You've seen me actively working to help your people stay free. You know I'm not loyal to the system."

"I know your loyalties lie with Hattie Malloy. For now."

He bristled at the "for now." "Well, there you go." He shrugged. "She vouches for me. Isn't that enough?"

"What was this news you came barging in to tell me?"

Vincent gritted his teeth, took a breath, wishing Hattie was here. "We've eliminated the Bianco Fiore."

Sadie squinted. "And?"

"And what? That's enormous. We've struck a blow against injustice."

"Who is *we?*" Sadie asked, her arms tightening over her chest.

"Me, the folk from Curtis Creek. And Galloway's people."

"Uh huh." She sneered. "You're working with Honor now?"

"Just for this task. It was a gesture on his part."

"It was a *maneuver* on his part," she corrected, turning back for the door. "To sway yet another pincher to his side."

"There are no sides here, Sadie. I don't care about the personal history between the pair of you. You're both working for the free pinchers as I see it, and I want to help."

She pushed the door open before spinning on a heel to thrust a finger at Vincent. "We don't need help from the mob."

"I am not the mob," he snapped.

"Until you leave the Crew, Mister Calendo, I'm afraid I just can't trust you. And you're not welcome here, no matter who your paramour is."

Vincent scowled. "Paramour? Did you seriously just—"

She went inside and slammed the door behind her.

Vincent stepped away, glaring at the door. The naked antagonism Sadie had displayed was utterly unexpected. The woman was always wound tight, but this surprised Vincent. More than anything, her complete lack of interest in the strike against the Bianco Fiore dug under his skin. Didn't she care?

But then, it all came down to Galloway. If he'd done it on his own, she'd have shown some interest. But because Galloway was involved, she was compelled to disregard it even to the point of finding the whole gesture suspicious.

Vincent turned back to the stone fencing and he heard an engine on the street. One of the Charge cars rolled into the yard. A pop of energy released once it had parked away from the view of the street. It had to be one of Hattie's illusions.

He could never really tell until she dropped it, and that almost imperceptible release of power called his attention to what his eyes couldn't see.

Hattie rushed out of the car, barreling into Vincent.

He caught her as she nearly knocked the wind out of him, hugging him tight.

"You're alive," she whispered.

"Well I was until you broke all my ribs."

She released him and rubbed his arms. "In one piece, boy-o?"

"Remarkably so. You wouldn't believe it. I regret not taking you."

Her eyes shifted back and forth between him and the Studebaker. "Oh really, now?"

"Yeah," he replied as his words began to race. "We followed a fire in the distance. They'd hit some village not that different from Raymond's, and we—"

"Is he alright?"

Vincent nodded with an outstretched hand. "Yeah, he's fine. But let me tell you—we made our way to the James and that old fueling depot. You remember that one?"

She nodded as she checked the car again. "Aye."

"So, there we were. Galloway's girl, the one with the light in her hands? She hit them with this burst of light. Damn near blinded me with my eyes closed. Then—"

"Did you do it, though?"

"I'm getting to it," he grumbled.

"Because something's happened. I need you to meet someone."

"Okay but hold on. His wood pincher brought these spikes out of the planks. Actually physically nailed those poor bastards—"

"Vincent!" she urged. "Please."

"What?"

"There's something we need to do. Tell me all about it later, but for now…you won? Right? You won and both you and Raymond are unhurt?"

He sucked in a breath, then nodded, irritation cascading through him. He wanted to tell her all about the attack, to lay out the chance that Galloway and his army might just be able to achieve the impossible and win against the mobs. He wanted to tell her that the future he'd dreamed about—a future with her by his side—was within reach. But in typical Hattie fashion, she was off like a lightning bolt in a different direction.

Then she kissed his cheek, and the frustration eased.

"I have someone you must meet," she said.

He glanced to the car where Blake was holding the rear door open. A man emerged, a dapper fellow sporting European finery. He lifted a stiff hand to Vincent in greeting.

"Hmm," Vincent's eyebrows shot up. "And you're giving me the business for hanging around strange women?"

"Oh stop," she muttered as she led him to the car.

"Vincent Calendo, meet Assam al Ghasawi."

Vincent shook Ghasawi's hand. "Hi."

"A pleasure, Mister Calendo."

Vincent glanced back and forth between Hattie and Ghasawi. "So, what's your story?"

"My story is one of pursuit and protection. You are in danger, Mister Calendo."

Vincent smirked. "So what's new?"

Hattie urged, "Vincent, this is important. This is the man I told you about. The one up in Scranton."

"Oh." He scowled. "The one with the steel traps in his yard?"

Ghasawi smiled. "My methods may seem unconventional, but I assure you I am an ally."

Vincent glanced over his shoulder at the Charge building. "Well, there's a switch."

As if on cue, Sadie threw open the door and stormed into the scrap yard.

"Are you idiots going to keep shouting out here until all of Baltimore knows where we are? What is this?" She glared from face to face. "Malloy? Who is this?"

"Sadie, this is Assam al—"

"I don't care. Everyone lower your voice and get inside."

Vincent put his hands on his hips. "Oh, you'll deign to let me in now?"

She glared at him. "Everyone except you."

Hattie turned to Sadie. "What's going on?"

Vincent said, "Hot off the press, it turns out I'm the enemy and can't be trusted."

"Sadie!" Hattie scolded.

"Oh…" Sadie waved a hand, "…just get inside for Christ's sake!"

They filed into the warehouse, Ghasawi pausing to bow to Sadie before entering, a gesture that produced an eyeroll from the woman.

Inside, Hattie stepped between Vincent and Sadie. "Alright, now. You two tell me what this is all about."

They both spoke at the same time, to which Hattie lifted a finger to Vincent's lips to shush him and looked to Sadie.

"You. Spill it."

Sadie scowled. "I don't want him here."

"Well that's not happening, so what's the next subject then?"

"You are not the one who dictates terms inside this building!" Sadie replied.

"Oh, and you are? I think not."

Sadie threw her hands into the air. "Fine. You're both on Galloway's side at this point. You can *both* leave."

Hattie regarded the other woman for a moment. "I am on no one's side, here. If anything, I'm trying to keep you from turning yourself into a cabbage or something."

Sadie shot her a puzzled frown. "You think that's something I'm likely to do?"

"You're not in full possession of the facts," Hattie replied.

Vincent took a step away, watching as Hattie reintroduced Ghasawi to Sadie. They conferred in hushed tones for a moment, after which all three rushed off to an upstairs room, leaving Vincent behind with Blake. Yep. Typical Hattie. Off like a lightning bolt.

Blake nodded to Vincent. "Long night?"

Vincent sighed. "It was a pretty cherry night, actually. But no one seems to give a wet shake about me anymore."

Blake shrugged. "It's Sadie's world, fella. Us men gotta get in line and wait to be noticed."

Vincent turned to regard Blake. "Hey. Where do you stand on Galloway?"

"I don't know. Seems like a friendly guy, but he's got this weird, wormy quality. Know what I mean?"

Vincent shook his head. "I think he's a bookworm, if that's your drift."

"No, wormy like...wiggly. Talks too much. Talks his way around people and out of things. Like a politician only worse. Actually like those guys that show up at your house and convince your mother to buy an electric toaster she can't afford and doesn't really need anyway."

Vincent chuckled. "Well, okay. But I've just seen...never mind."

"What?" Blake asked.

"Oh. Well, I went on a raid with his pinchers. We hit the Bianco Fiore where they live."

Blake took a seat and nodded. "Those sheet-wearing shits? Outstanding!"

Vincent smiled and took a seat next to Blake. "They got this heave pincher."

"What's that?"

"He can lift anything. Some magic he uses with his hands. Anyways, he picked up a boat. An entire boat, you read me? And he threw it into another boat."

Blake laughed. "That'd be a sight."

"And then there's what their earth pincher did."

Hattie trod down the stairs rubbing her face.

Vincent broke off his tale, standing to greet her. "Everything alright?"

She nodded wearily. "I spent all morning catching this Arab, and now he's upstairs translating the codex. I swear to Mary, the way a day can turn on a girl."

Vincent nodded. "Who *is* that guy?"

"He's a Janissary."

Vincent shook his head.

"Aye, made no sense to me either. Still doesn't, but I'm almost convinced he's on our side." She shook off the cobwebs and forced a grin. "So. Tell me about this battle."

He eyed the stairs. "You need to get a hold of Sadie. She's falling to pieces."

Hattie shook her head. "I'm not her nanny. And I don't want to talk about her. I want to talk about the Bianco."

"Oh, *now* you do?" he gibed.

She folded her arms across her chest. "Aye. That's what I said, didn't I?"

He eased away. "Sorry. I just…"

She shook her head. "No, *I'm* sorry. It's me. I'm still not sleeping well."

"Should I go?" Blake asked.

Vincent and Hattie both replied, "Yes."

Blake popped away, and they were alone.

"She thinks I'm a gangster," Vincent began.

"You are," Hattie replied with a smirk.

"You *really* think that?"

She sighed. "I don't know what you are. I don't know what I am. Everyone's decided to draw tiny lines in the sand and it's annoying me."

"My point is that the Charge can trust me."

Hattie nodded. "I know that. I trust you. But just demanding that it be so doesn't make it so. Trust has to be earned, and you're still new to the Charge."

"So are you," he protested. "Why am I so different?"

She ran her fingers along the lapels of his suit. "The pinstripes and tommy guns, for a start."

"That again?" He turned away from Hattie. "Look, I just participated in the most one-sided fight I've ever seen."

"And I want to hear all about it," she insisted.

Vincent shook his head, a knot of frustration twisting inside his chest. "And here I come, ready to share the news. Immediately I get hammered down by Sadie O'Donnell. Having my intentions questioned. And then…"

Hattie reached for his shoulder and turned him around. "And then what?"

"Then you show up and I can't get a word in edgewise, because there's some strange Arab ready to read a book. And for some reason that's more important—"

"Strange Arab? This from the Great Damir?" she teased.

Vincent pushed her hands away and took a step back. "Don't."

"As it turns out, boy-o, it *was* more important," she said softly. "That book up there has actual magical spells in it, which if read out loud can cause all sorts of mischief. If there's a fire in the building, you put it out before you ask how your day was."

Vincent scowled. "Who is this fella, anyway? And don't say Janissary."

"Well, with an attitude like that, I don't think I'm inclined to explain anything to you."

"Oh, that's how it is?"

They stood in silence for a long moment, jaws tensed.

Hattie finally asked, "The Bianco Fiore's gone?"

Vincent nodded.

"That's good, then."

"Agreed."

She sighed and ran a hand through her hair. "I should..." She turned to the stairs. "I should probably check on the others."

"And I'm sure Lefty's expecting me to deliver a shadow pincher back to the Crew."

They lingered for another silent moment until Vincent turned for the door.

"I'll let you get back to your Charge."

"When will I see you again?" she asked, a worried frown creasing her brow.

"I'll be in touch."

He stepped through the door and out across the scrap yard, regretting the harsh words before he even reached the car.

CHAPTER 18

*H*attie rushed into one of the bunk rooms, slamming the door behind her. The room had been empty of children for a week now, so it was a private place to sit and cry. And fume.

How could he not understand?

Their mission was always the Hell pincher. Jeopardizing their Bright Soul could lead to the enslavement of humanity. Vincent knew this. And now they had a practitioner from the Levant who was willing to help capture and eliminate the Hell pincher. How could he not see how important this was?

It hadn't been just that. The way he turned away from her, like he'd dismissed her. As if he could just shut off the conversation and walk away.

And she'd let him do it, when she should have insisted he stay and air out their argument. She hadn't, and he'd left, and now there was this anger between them.

Hattie slumped onto one of the bunks as tears streamed from her eyes. The way he left…hurt. She didn't want him to leave. She wanted him to tell her about the Bianco fight. It was just…she had to get

Ghasawi to the codex first. Was that so difficult to understand? Couldn't he wait a bloody minute so that she could take care of business, and *then* share the moment with him?

She thought about his face when she'd arrived. He'd been positively beaming. Hattie hadn't seen that sort of energy in his face…ever. It made him look young and carefree. Vincent always carried that storm cloud with him wherever he went. It added to his mystique most times, but lately Hattie was haunted by her own thunderheads. She could use a ray of sunlight. And here she was, dousing it with her obsession with the Hell pincher.

Maybe he was he right.

The door opened. Hattie wiped her face and looked up to find Sadie looming in the doorway.

"Go away," Hattie choked out.

"Okay," Sadie said as she stepped into the room and took a seat on the bunk across from Hattie.

Hattie took several breaths, trying to collect herself. "I just need a minute."

Sadie nodded. "Okay."

"Will you say something other than 'okay'?"

"You should dump that bum."

Hattie blinked at Sadie. "What, now?"

"He's no good for you. There. I said my peace."

Sadie stood up and moved for the door.

Hattie stood up as well. "Hang back a second. What are you doing?"

"I'm trying to help."

"Right. I'm a mess, and you choose this moment to come in here and tell me to give Vincent the shove off? What kind of friend are you?"

"The pragmatic kind of friend." Sadie regarded her a moment. "Listen, I don't know what you see in him. Yeah he's good-looking, charming, a snappy dresser, but he's caused you nothing but trouble and heartache."

"That's not true." Hattie reached for a blanket and mopped her face with a sniffle. "I've caused him more trouble and heartache then he's caused me. And he's *not* a bum."

"That so? Tell me how he's helped you at all?"

"He saved me from the mob, for a start."

Sadie shook her head. "After he nearly handed you over to the mob. No good. What else you got?"

"He saved my Ma."

"After he put her in danger with the people his mobsters were waging war with."

"He helped you," Hattie blurted. "He found out who'd taken the children in Parkersburg."

Sadie stepped forward and lowered her voice. "And now he's joining those same people. Hattie, I understand what's going on. I've been there. People like us can't find love easily. Ordinary men just feel…flat somehow, and we can't trust them not to turn us over to the slave masters. So, we have to find a pincher to love. But our lives are so dangerous. We all live on a razor's edge, and it leads to one or both getting killed or captured." Sadie walked over and sat down beside her. "He'll die, Hattie. He'll get killed doing the Crew's business, or he'll get killed doing Honor's business, or he'll get on the wrong side of someone and they'll send him to Ithaca, and this time there will be no escaping. You'll come home one day and he'll either be gone or in a body bag."

Hattie's heart lurched, because that had always been her greatest fear. Yes, her nightmares were about demons burning her loved ones with their fire, but during the day, her terrors were that Vincent might die from a bullet to the head.

But she was too far gone to back away from this now.

"Vincent and I are different, though," Hattie protested, scrambling for something to counter Sadie's grim predictions. "He's my soul twin. That means something."

"Maybe so," Sadie said with a sigh. "Or maybe it just makes things more difficult. Perhaps when it's all said and done, the two of you are just people after all."

Hattie took a long breath, then nodded. "Aye. We're human beings. We're allowed our flaws. I just don't see why you can't accept his when you accept mine."

Sadie frowned. "Because he's a gangster. I keep saying this, and the two of you keep acting like I'm crazy. But it's the truth. He's owned, part of the system. I've spent years protecting children from his kind. You've got him confused, I'll admit that. He's thinking about things. But in my years, I've yet to see anything to convince me that an owned pincher can change."

Hattie shook her head. "You're a sunny damned woman, you know that?"

Sadie chuckled. "I'm just being realistic. And, you know. If I didn't care about you, I'd just shut up and let him walk all over your heart. But I hate watching you go through this, so I'm saying something. And that's all I can do."

Hattie nodded. "Thank you. For caring, I mean. I still think you're wrong, but at least you care."

"So," Sadie declared with a clap of her hands. "There's a stranger in my office reading my codex, and I'm about to jump out of my skin."

She led Hattie to the office, where Ghasawi loomed over the pages of the codex with an enormous magnifying glass in his hand.

"Anything interesting?" Hattie asked.

Ghasawi glanced up with a grin. "Happily, I've located several passages of magical weight and marked them. Two are in Polish, which I believe is safe enough. The third is in Turkish. Do either of you know Turkish?"

Sadie and Hattie shook their heads.

"Then you should be safe. I'm reviewing the bulk of the Polish passages. Most of this appears to be a sort of ledger of names."

Sadie nodded. "Nowak was attempting to record the names of the free pinchers in Chicago. I've begun adding the ones we've helped here."

"To what end?" Ghasawi asked.

"So that they wouldn't be forgotten," Sadie replied with a distant look.

Ghasawi nodded, then returned his attentions to the book.

"What were the spells?" Hattie asked. "Out of morbid curiosity."

"Hmm. Minor charms. A spell for clarifying water, and one to create a magical lock."

"What about the third?" Sadie asked.

Ghasawi waved her question off with a flutter of his fingers.

Hattie frowned. "That bad?"

He set down his magnifying glass and straightened his spine. "Such spells may prove more valuable to the enemy than to yourselves."

"What does that mean?" Sadie prodded.

"Not all hidden knowledge is meant to be uncovered. Some magics deal in matters of evil and blasphemy."

Hattie stepped toward Ghasawi. "If I'm going to trust you, then you'll have to do the same. What does this spell do that you think will help the Hell pincher?"

Ghasawi stared at Hattie for a moment, then replied, "It is a means to release a soul from a soul trap."

Hattie stepped back. "No shite?"

Ghasawi bowed his head. "Such a mechanism could prove…explosive."

"I've seen it before. Runes or glyphs…whatever you call them. They were in each of the booby traps."

"That would be one of the methods used. It requires a great deal more artifice then just releasing the dark soul."

Hattie nodded. "Trip wire. Aye. So, what is this spell, then?"

"An incantation to release the traps contents without conditions. An immediate release."

"What are the odds the Hell pincher already knows this incantation?"

Ghasawi frowned. "Above average."

"Then I want you to teach it to me."

"That would be inadvisable."

Hattie shook her head. "Why? If the Hell pincher is the only one who knows how to use these bloody things, then we're at the disadvantage."

"All it will accomplish is to release the dark soul. Without limits. It would be like releasing a wild animal amongst innocent children."

Sadie shook her head. "What are the two of you talking about?"

"Nothing," Hattie said, slipping through the doorway and out of the office.

Sadie pursued. "Malloy?"

Hattie paused at the top of the stairs. "Right, fine. You remember what you told me about the Solomon's Crown? The Bright Soul and dark soul coming together? The whole reason the Hell pincher's on the prowl to begin with?"

Sadie nodded.

"We already know we have a complete Bright Soul here. Vincent and myself." She reached into her pocket to produce the soul trap. "Here's the last piece."

Sadie squinted at the tiny orb in Hattie's fingers. "A marble?"

"It's a soul trap. And our dark soul is inside."

"How?"

"The Hell pincher found the Deltaville Demon at some point last year and trapped it."

"For what?"

"A weapon," Hattie told her.

"Then, all three of you are together in one place? God in heaven."

"Aye. It's a dangerous situation. But that's what Ghasawi's here for. He knows the Hell pincher's coming for us. And he'll be here waiting for him."

Sadie's eyes widened. "He's…a Janissary?"

Hattie rolled her eyes. "Why am I always the last one to hear about these things?"

Voices sounded downstairs.

Blake popped into the landing below them, a rifle in his hands.

Sadie lifted her palms. "It's alright. Should be Charley returning from Nag's Head."

The door opened to reveal Charley and his scraggly red beard. He held the door for a clutch of refugees, four in total. Two children, a man and a woman. They paused at the sight of Blake brandishing a rifle. He slung it over his shoulder with an apologetic shrug.

Sadie declared, "Welcome to the Charge."

The group huddled together, the man and woman lacing their arms around the children. The sight sent a thrill through Hattie's chest.

"Are they—?" Hattie whispered.

"A family, yes," Sadie answered. "We spirited them away from Charleston last month. Finally had a chance to get them up to Baltimore." She walked down the stairs to greet them.

The parents seemed weary but cheerful. The children could barely contain themselves, and as their parents felt more at ease they were released to bustle about the warehouse.

Hattie watched the children rush past her, exploring the rooms and claiming bunks.

Sadie conferred with the parents before she and Blake went to gather some linens. Hattie descended the stairs with a smile.

"Long drive, then?"

The father sighed. "Long, and bumpy. But we're grateful!"

The mother agreed, "Very."

"Well, you're in good hands now. All of the windows have been blacked out, so there's no worry about lights late at night."

The mother said, "Yes, Mrs. O'Donnell told us."

Hattie laughed. "If you keep calling her that, you're going to make her feel old. None of us need that."

The father asked, "Is, uh…is Mr. Galloway in?"

Hattie's smile dropped. "What?"

The mother said, "We heard Honor Galloway was in the city. Is he here? We wanted to speak with him about Zanesville."

Hattie shook her head slowly. "No. He's not here."

"Oh. Is he expected?"

Hattie looked to Charley, who shrugged.

"Galloway isn't with our group," Hattie replied.

Both parents paled.

"However," Hattie added, "we have a location in Utah we're sending people to. Lovely frontier land."

The father scowled. "Yeah, I hear it's a bust."

"From whom?" she blurted.

The parents exchanged glances. "I'm sorry. I think I've spoken out of turn. If you'll excuse us."

They swept past her up the stairs to join their children.

Hattie looked over to Charley. "Did you tell them about Galloway?"

He shook his head with vigor. "They've been talking about him since I picked them up. First thing they asked. Didn't know what to tell them, so I just clammed up."

"That's good," she muttered. "But this is a problem."

"What's the problem?" Charley asked.

Hattie took a look around the warehouse. "Too many of our people are catching wind of Galloway's rhetoric. And he knows far too much about what goes on inside these walls."

Charley whispered, "What's that mean?"

"It means he has someone on the inside."

"Inside of what?"

Hattie replied with tight lips. "The Charge."

CHAPTER 19

*V*incent sat at his table, a glass still half-filled with whisky idle in his fingers. He stared at the wood-grain of the tabletop—through it, really. His stomach churned with regret and frustration. Even as he'd driven away from the Charge warehouse, he knew he'd blown it with Hattie. All the indignation he felt at getting his trousers chewed off by Sadie O'Donnell, and then in having his victory stifled by the commotion of this arriving Arab, melted into sadness at having parted company with this lingering malice. Ultimately he was being a child. It was his expectations that were insulted, not him.

A tiny furry black face stared at him from across the table.

"I was a total ass," he told the kitten, who didn't seem eager to refute that assertion. "Wasn't really her fault," he continued. "She was fighting her own fight, one just as important as mine. Still, though," he added with a swirl of his whisky. "I'm tired of it."

The kitten hopped onto the table top from its chair, marching toward Vincent with tiny steps.

"I'm tired of having my entire life thrown in my face like this. I'm a gangster. Sure. But I'm not Capstein. Or Sebastian. There's a difference."

Roscoe gave Vincent a languid blink, then sat in front of him and cleaned a paw.

"I want to marry her, you know," Vincent told him. "I want to marry her, to wake up next to her in the mornings, go to bed with her at night. I want her with me. I want a future with her by my side. And that can't happen with things as they are. What could I offer her? In spite of what I said, I *am* a gangster. I'm worse than a gangster, I'm an owned man. Being my wife would put her at risk. Hell, even courting her puts her at risk."

The cat ended his cleaning to regard him with amber eyes.

"What if Galloway's right?" He waved the whisky glass at the cat. "What if he and his army can change the world? Then maybe I'd have something to offer Hattie in the way of a life. If she'll even speak to me anymore."

He took a sip of the whisky while Roscoe rolled over onto his side, his amber eyes glued to Vincent's.

"Being adorable isn't going to make me feel any better, you know."

Roscoe lifted a paw, planting it gently onto Vincent's knuckle.

With a sigh, Vincent grunted, "Damn it," before scooping Roscoe off the table and settling him into his lap. The kitten's chest rumbled with a purr as Vincent scratched the bottom of his chin.

"Guess I need to make up my mind, huh? Guess I need to grab this future I want by the horns and make it happen."

He sat with Roscoe for a half hour before the cat decided it had better things to do elsewhere. Finishing his whisky, Vincent got up and changed his clothes. As he looked himself in the eye, running a comb through his hair, he thought hard about the plans he and Hattie had mentioned but failed to pull together.

"Yeah," he told himself. "Time to make things happen."

Vincent gathered his hat and coat and stepped out of his apartment. He drew up as he found Lefty waiting for him. "Oh! Damn it, you're going to give me a heart attack!"

Lefty stuffed his hand into his pockets. "Where have you been?"

"Here. There."

"Richmond?"

"You heard?"

Lefty's face was tighter than usual. "Everyone's heard. Where's the hostage?"

Vincent cleared his throat and stared at the floor. "Are we still shooting straight with each other?"

"I'll save you the trouble. You don't have him. Either you killed him or he pulled some hoodwink on you and escaped."

Vincent smirked. "Holy God, you're actually wrong for once!"

"Where is he?"

"I traded him."

Lefty closed his eyes and groaned. "Why?"

"The firepower I brought against the Bianco Fiore? I bought their cooperation with him."

Lefty opened his eyes, suddenly full of exhaustion. "You think Vito's gonna hear that well?"

"Probably not, but the Bianco needed to be taken care of. I'm hoping we can find out some way to spin this to our advantage. Like how we only have one front to watch now."

Lefty rubbed the back of his neck. "It'll be a tough sell. Vito's so wrapped up calling in markers to draw up against Masseria, he hasn't even noticed the casualties from Winnow's. That'll help if I can roll this together into one fight and link Masseria with those Bianco goons. Will this 'firepower' you brought in pitch a fit if we steal credit for taking out the Bianco?"

"No. Definitely won't."

"And you're sure of that?"

Vincent nodded. "As sure as anything in my life right now."

Lefty smirked. "That's not saying much. Come on. If I'm going to put my ass out there with this story, I want you there to back me up."

Vincent grimaced. "Can't. I got somewhere I gotta be."

"I know you do. Havre de Grace. With me."

"This is important, Lefty."

Lefty's face lost every ounce of its familiar crotchety charm. In its place was the face of the man he'd met when he'd arrived at Baltimore and was handed over to the one who would tell him where he could sleep, eat, and show his face.

"Get your head," Lefty growled, "out of your ass."

Something shivered deep inside Vincent, but he steeled himself, betraying not a single whiff of weakness. It was a skill he'd perfected in Ithaca.

"My head is where it needs to be. This is important. Cover for me. Let me deal with this and I'll be at the vineyard tomorrow."

Lefty shook his head in disbelief. "You just came back from Ithaca, Vincent. Are you gunning for a repeat?"

"When I'm back in front of the Capo, he'll know that I've done my job. There's a war coming, Lefty. I don't have time to stand in a corner, waiting for Vito to make a move. Good men get killed that way."

Lefty replied, "Good men got killed following you down the Bay. Do I really need to remind you of that?"

"Good men died fighting. It was a worthy fight. Can you

look me in the eye and tell me you think this crap with Masseria is worthy?"

"It's not my place to decide," Lefty snapped. "And it's not yours, either."

Vincent took a steadying breath. "I'm looking past this fight with Masseria. There's a future when this all shakes out. I need to be sure that you and me are on the right side of things when the dust settles."

"That's dangerous."

"What is?" Vincent asked.

"Thinking ahead. That means you think you know what's gonna happen. And one thing all my years have told me is that you never know what's gonna happen. All you can do is keep your head down and wait for the shell to fall."

Vincent smiled and put a hand on Lefty's shoulder. "That's the way to think in the trenches, Lefty. But this is a new kind of war." He gave the other man's shoulder a shake. "Trust me, okay? I'll see you in a couple days."

"It's a couple days now?"

"Yeah. I'm feeling lucky."

Vincent walked past Lefty and down the stairs without looking back.

* * *

THE SUN pincher was waiting for Vincent outside the cabin. He approached with confidence as she gave him a smile.

"There he is!" she called.

Vincent buttoned his coat and adjusted his hat, kicking it at a little bit of an angle.

"Good afternoon." He cocked his head. "I never caught your name."

"Millie," she replied with a blush.

"Is Galloway in, Millie?"

"Yep. He's waiting for you."

Vincent paused a step. "How'd he know I was coming?"

She shrugged.

Vincent approached the door with guarded steps. Inside the cabin he found Ernie and Maria conspiring over a chess board, while Bolton huddled in a corner with a book.

Galloway sat at his desk, scratching away furiously at a piece of paper.

"Another letter for Enid?" Vincent called out.

Every face in the room snapped toward the door.

Maria glowered, returning her attention immediately to the chess board. Ernie's face erupted into a grin. Bolton latched a death glare onto Vincent and refused to release it.

Galloway, for his part, stared slack-jawed for a moment before launching out of his chair, pulling his spectacles back atop his head.

"Vincent!"

Vincent stepped to the middle of the room, almost losing his balance as Galloway rushed around his desk to shake his hand.

"Let's pull out some of the mountain brandy!" Galloway gestured to Ernie who reached beneath the sofa cushions to slip out a bottle of orange-amber liquid.

Vincent shrugged. "Don't waste good brandy on my account."

Galloway guffawed. "Rest assured, we won't be."

Ernie poured three glasses of brandy. Maria cleared her throat without looking up, and Ernie reached for a fourth glass. He handed Maria her brandy, which she pounded without ceremony. The rest, however, stood in a circle lifting their glasses.

Vincent nodded to Bolton. "What about our shady friend?"

"Oh, he does not partake," Galloway informed him.

"And Millie outside?"

"She's a bit young for this sort of thing."

Vincent stiffened. "How young?"

"She's sixteen years old."

Ernie nudged Vincent in the ribs. "Best keep it in the pants, old bean."

Vincent nodded then lifted his glass.

Galloway toasted, "To a future without masters."

"Salute," Vincent replied.

They drank their brandy, which was as jagged as a hunk of flint. Galloway ushered Vincent to the desk as Ernie returned to his chess.

"Millie says you were expecting me."

"And so I was," Galloway replied.

"How'd you know I'd come?"

"I have some experience with people and the way they respond to the call of duty. You're a man waiting for direction. You've stood at a crossroads for far too long. Perhaps you've simply needed someone to come along and show you the way."

He'd already met that someone last May, and it sure as hell wasn't Galloway.

"I'm interested in what you proposed earlier," Vincent told him. "I think our goals are in alignment here. I'm hoping I can bring some inside knowledge as well as skill to the table.

"Excellent! You'll be an incredibly valuable addition to our team here." Galloway rubbed his hands together. "So, I'd like to begin by discussing Philadelphia."

Vincent frowned. "I thought we were looking to overthrow the Baltimore Crew?"

Galloway nodded. "In time. But first we require additional talent."

"From Philly? Good luck with that!"

"I understand there are two pinchers in Philadelphia who serve Sabella."

Vincent paused to consider whether his decision to turn against Vito Corbi should necessarily include airing DeBarre out to these free pinchers. He was too deep at this point to dabble. No, if he was to commit to this, he'd have to go all in.

"Yes. Loren DeBarre and Bradley Arnoud."

Galloway reached for his pen and paper, scratching notes as he spoke. "Tell me about these men."

Bolton watched from the corner.

Vincent leaned forward. "Perhaps this should be a private conversation?"

"Nonsense," Galloway replied with undue volume. "We hold no secrets in this circle."

The other pinchers looked up from their chess game.

Vincent pulled himself out of his chair and over the desk in order to whisper to Galloway. "One of these pinchers was the one who gave your shadow pincher the works."

Galloway nodded somberly, eyes shifting left and right.

Ernie cleared his throat as he toppled his king. "Well, Maria. You've thrashed me again. Come on. Let's give Millie some company."

Maria cocked a confused brow until Ernie gave her a meaningful nod. She seemed to put it together quick enough, gathering the chess pieces into their case.

The two moved for the door, as Ernie paused to call over his shoulder, "Bolton? Shall we?"

Bolton muttered, "Not interested."

"Then discover your interest...old boy."

Bolton reeled back in his seat, glancing around the room. All eyes were on him, and he finally recognized that he was the problem. He slapped his book closed and stormed out of the cabin. Maria was shortly behind him. Ernie lingered by the door as he grabbed his hat to settle it on his head with a salute.

Once they had vacated the cabin, Galloway said, "Which one?"

"Arnoud," Vincent replied. "He's a touch pincher. He can make you feel whatever he wants you to feel."

"I'm sure he's a hit with the ladies," Galloway chuckled. "As well as those looking to interrogate a hostage. I fear I've underestimated your network, Vincent."

"DeBarre is the one you need to worry about."

"What are his powers?"

"He's a down pincher. He can...how the hell am I supposed to put this? He can make down up, and up down."

"Gravity manipulation," Galloway mused.

"I suppose. But that's the point. He's the senior of the two. And believe you me, he's the one with the brain. Arnoud's a bit of a strange bird. Recently from Ithaca, if you take my meaning."

Galloway nodded to the door. "I fully understand. But if he is new to Sabella's mob, shouldn't we focus our interests on this Arnoud before approaching DeBarre?"

Vincent crossed his arms and thought it over. "I don't think so. I can't explain it, but Arnoud is just a little too raw."

Galloway nodded. "Then, DeBarre. How does he stand? He's been around for a long time. Seems to have the respect of Sabella and the family up there in Philadelphia. I'm thinking that this DeBarre is more likely to listen to our pitch than is his lesser?"

Vincent laughed. "Our pitch? What, of taking on the families? That's rich!"

"Is it?"

"Well, yeah. DeBarre is about as much a kept pincher as I am. But he has one thing going for him that I don't."

"What is that?"

"Money," Vincent replied. "He's kept the independents happy. The man's shrewd, take it from me. If you want to toss him your line, you'll have to dress it up in long tails and a bow tie."

Galloway nodded. "I think I understand your meaning. Still, though. I wonder if this Arnoud isn't the one whom we should approach?"

Vincent shook his head. "No. Definitely not. Take my lead on this, Galloway. Arnoud isn't right in the brain. He's… broken. And he's absolutely loyal to the family. Ithaca did its work on him. There's probably only one person in the world who could convince him to go against Sabella's interests, and it's not you."

"Then I'll ask you a wholly new question. If we take our case to DeBarre, is he more likely to agree with us? Or is he likely to sail us out to the masters?"

Vincent thought it over. "He's more likely to tell us we're idiots. Then he'd pour us a gin fizz."

Galloway nodded, muttering, "I can work with that."

* * *

VINCENT WAVED his gin fizz in Galloway's direction as DeBarre sat cross-legged, a mysterious smile etched onto his face.

"So, that's the long and short of it. Vito's ready to sail you out. It's time we planned for a future without the Crew."

Galloway sat on the sofa across from DeBarre, his face tight and eager.

DeBarre lifted a brow and nodded before sipping some straight gin. "That's a hell of a pitch, Calendo."

"We see nothing but mutual advantage," Galloway told him.

DeBarre waved a scolding finger at Galloway. "And yet,

I'm a little lost. You're some sort of revolutionary. A freedom fighter for free pinchers, looking to wage war on us ugly mobster types. Why wouldn't I take offense at this?"

"Because," Galloway replied, "you are not a kept pincher. Not like the others. If anything, you're keeping the mob in *your* pocket. You, my friend are a free agent. I think Sabella serves you more than you serve him."

DeBarre grinned. "That's quite a bit of flattery you're laying on there."

"Then there's the brewers," Galloway continued. "They pay you for your services. This is not the traditional master-slave relationship that the families have profited from." Galloway leaned forward on the sofa. "If anything, you and I are more alike than even Vincent here."

DeBarre's smile sharpened. "Careful, Galloway. You might be trodding on someone's loyalties."

Galloway waved him off. "Vincent's loyalties are his concern."

Vincent scowled. Being suddenly shunted from the conversation was jarring, particularly since Galloway demonstrated nothing but a desire for equal partnership on the drive to Philadelphia. But perhaps that was his method. This was theater, an approach he'd tailored specifically for DeBarre. This approach must entail marginalizing Vincent in DeBarre's eyes. It made sense, in a perverse way. Though DeBarre had always been friendly to Vincent, he'd never lost that air of superiority and smug aloofness. Galloway had identified that in the half hour they'd spent pitching this new arrangement to DeBarre and was already crafting the message to suit.

Wormy. Just like Blake had said. The man was everything to everybody if it suited his purpose. And Vincent realized he'd do well to keep that in mind.

Galloway stood up, pacing a slow arc back around his

sofa. "The Richmond market is already in freefall. A new figurehead could be installed, one that was sympathetic to our cause. It could even be done with the full sanction of the families, as long as it was done artfully."

DeBarre snickered. "Right."

"The line of power then contracts to Baltimore, and then to Philadelphia. If we can work together to unseat Vito Corbi and the Baltimore Crew, we'd create a territory that encompasses the entirety of the Chesapeake Bay and the Delaware River. The Mid-Atlantic from Atlantic City to the Outer Banks would become a free zone for pinchers—a free zone with four major metropolitan centers, including the nation's capital."

"A promised land," DeBarre drawled.

"More like a base of operations. Don't mistake me, Mister DeBarre. I know what comes next. War. War with New York and Atlantic City."

DeBarre shrugged then nodded.

Galloway took a breath, frustration at DeBarre's nonchalance flickering in his face. "At which point we would have already made gestures to Boston, who from what I understand are already half-willing to turn on both Masseria and Maranzano if given the opportunity."

Vincent blinked at this. Galloway hadn't mentioned Boston before. How far ahead had he planned this?

And was Vincent really a "partner" or just a stepping stone in what Galloway really wanted?

DeBarre drained his glass, then re-crossed his legs. "So, you'll do business with one mob to take out two? So much for your ideology."

"I never claimed to be an idealist, Mister DeBarre. We will not win our freedom without bloodshed. No one in the history of the world has ever been given their rights. They were only ever taken. We're ready to go to war. My people are trained for battle."

Vincent muttered, "I can vouch for that."

"I have guns," Galloway continued, "and hired muscle. The more pinchers we cultivate, the shorter will be the conflagration. The violence will burn bright, but it will burn fast."

DeBarre set aside his glass and stood up, buttoning his jacket. "I have had several businessmen approach me in this salon. Newcomers to the bootlegging business, brewers and moonshiners, even weapons peddlers looking to leverage stolen hardware before they end up with the Feds up their trousers. They all come to me with practiced speeches and appeals to my vanity. I've become practiced at sniffing out a polished shit when someone tries to sell it to me."

Galloway sucked in a breath. "Then tell me…am I selling you shit?"

"I think you believe that what you're selling is a good idea. I even think you believe you can actually succeed. None of that is what I'm worried about."

"Then what *are* you worried about?" Galloway prodded.

"Two things," DeBarre said with a lift of two fingers. "First, I'm worried about Calendo, here." DeBarre stepped past Galloway to stand in front of Vincent. "Where's this coming from? Wasn't it just last month you'd gotten out of Ithaca? Didn't you learn anything while you were there?"

Vincent caught his breath. "I did. I learned that the system is broken."

"Is it, though? These mob bosses hold all the cards. You go calling their bluff, and you'll end up losing your shirt. Or your life."

"And the second thing?" Galloway asked.

DeBarre turned back to Galloway. "You're coming to me, a successful self-made pincher who claims to be more than a servant to the powers that be. And what have you brought me? An appeal to justice."

"What would appeal to you, then?" Galloway asked.

"You're not giving me a reason to get involved," DeBarre said. "If Philly throws in against the Crew, and then against New York, all of the bootlegging business will dry up overnight. Arnoud will turn against me, and I'll have to deal with that. The families will turn against me. There's an economic impact of your war."

"Economic?" Galloway repeated, rolling the word around as he thought it over.

DeBarre shrugged. "I only stand to lose. There's no upside for me. So, while I appreciate the sentiment of giving Vito Corbi a good shellacking, I'm making far more money with him in my pocket."

Galloway lifted a finger. "Have you considered—"

DeBarre interrupted him. "Sorry. Not interested." He turned to Vincent. "This was fun, Vincent. But in the future, when some pork-pie evangelist comes to you with a lick and a promise, do me a favor and take him to Pittsburgh instead."

Vincent nodded and shook DeBarre's hand. "I had to try."

"Sure. And for what it's worth, I appreciate the warning about Corbi. To be honest I half-expected him to welsh on the deal." He leaned close to mutter, "Don't buy into this, Vincent. It's gonna get you and Hattie killed. And while I'd be a bit saddened by your demise, I'd be truly devastated over the loss of that red-haired spitfire."

Vincent swallowed back any smart remark about DeBarre's chances with Hattie and tried to concentrate on the topic at hand. "It's gotta end somewhere, Loren. I've seen these people in action. I'm not trying to convince you, here. I'm just saying I'm not nuts."

"I guess we'll see." He nodded to the corridor as Galloway gathered his coat. "I'll see you two out."

They climbed up the ladder and into the cannery. Outside, three cars stormed up the road, tires sliding as the drivers slammed on the brakes.

"The hell, now?" DeBarre grumbled.

The lead car swerved into the cannery lot. Vincent braced for action, but relaxed when he spotted Arnoud in the passenger seat.

Arnoud jumped out of the car and rushed for DeBarre.

"What's wrong?" DeBarre demanded.

Arnoud took a second to catch his breath, then replied, "Attack."

"What?"

"Attack. A war party. They hit us up in Harrisburg."

DeBarre shook his head. "What war party? What are you talking about? You mean the Feds?"

"No," Arnoud shouted. "Not the Feds. It's Masseria. They hit us at dawn."

DeBarre winced. "That's impossible."

Arnoud continued, "Lost four men and most of our hardware. They didn't even take the merchandise. Just opened up on the convoy heading through Harrisburg and left them bleeding on the street."

Vincent glared at Galloway and whispered, "Is this you?"

Galloway lifted his hands. "No. I swear it."

DeBarre eyed Vincent. "You know anything about this?"

"No," Vincent replied.

Arnoud looked over at Galloway. "This is the one I sent you after? The zealot?"

DeBarre stepped between them as he addressed Galloway. "So, is your ragged band of independents responsible for this?"

Galloway shook his head as he stepped away. "It's not. They are all at my headquarters well south of Harrisburg."

Arnoud added, "I know it's Masseria, Loren."

"How?"

"Their iron pincher. He was there."

DeBarre straightened a little. "Well, shit."

Vincent asked, "Iron pincher?"

With a nod, DeBarre said, "Yeah. Ithaca trained. Nasty piece of work. Alright, call everyone in. Masseria's men still in Harrisburg?"

Arnoud shrugged. "Could be on their way to Philadelphia. Could have been a hit and fade. It's impossible to tell without scouts."

"Get the gang together and as much hardware as you can muster. Borrow and steal if you have to. Talk to the brewers. They're packing more iron than they like to admit."

Arnoud muttered, "Iron may be the problem."

"Yeah," DeBarre admitted. "But I don't have any options."

Galloway stepped forward. "You might. If this is a pincher you're after, you'll want pinchers to push back with."

Vincent nodded. "Galloway's right. You'll need backup on this. I've seen his people in action. I can work with them. Which means you can, too."

"You brought this fight into my backyard," DeBarre grumbled. "I suppose the least you could do is clean up the mess. Fine." He turned to Arnoud. "Get moving."

Arnoud nodded and returned to his car.

DeBarre turned to Vincent and Galloway, "Alright, you two. Gather your troops. Looks like the fight's come to me." As Vincent nodded and moved for the car, DeBarre stopped him with a hand to his shoulder. "This iron pincher is serious business, Vincent. This won't be some dust-up. It's gonna get bloody."

"Galloway's people," Vincent said, "are serious, too."

"That good?"

"I've been on both sides of their crosshairs. I speak from experience."

DeBarre nodded, then clapped Vincent's back. "Go."

Vincent cranked up the car as Galloway huddled up in the seat beside him.

"You have any insight on this, Galloway?"

He didn't respond.

Vincent pressed as he sped onto the highway. "You got eyes and ears everywhere, right? What do you know about this iron pincher?"

"I know his name." Galloway turned to Vincent. "And so do you."

"Who is he?"

"Jonas O'Donnell."

CHAPTER 20

*H*attie crept into the bunk room as the family took an afternoon constitutional in the rear yard. The clouds had parted to give Baltimore its first day of warmth in several months, and Sadie decided some sunshine was what everyone needed. It was a good idea.

It also got everyone out of the building, affording Hattie an opportunity to snoop around.

The new arrivals' belongings were basic. Hairbrush. A very poor selection of clothing. A locket with an elderly couple's photographs housed within. A couple toys carved out of wood. A ragdoll. Nothing suspicious.

Hattie slipped out of the room, nosing around the empty bunk rooms. She knew they were empty—she'd helped clean them and change the beds herself. Ever since the last train went west, the building had sat in a state of repose, waiting for more free pinchers to send to freedom.

The downstairs rooms, however, were reserved for the full-timers. Hattie didn't have such a room, since she had a home in Hampden. Blake lived in the warehouse, however.

As did Charley, who had inherited a room from the last adult to go west.

And then, of course, there was Sadie.

Hattie couldn't spend much time ferreting around the office, as Ghasawi was still busy translating the Polish text in the codex. His devotion to the task was only matched by his stamina, a sort of mental endurance he'd likely honed over a lifetime of hunting down magical practitioners.

Sadie's bedroom was unattended, however she found the door was locked. And Hattie couldn't believe that Sadie was an insider for Galloway. No, Hattie was left with two real options: Blake and Charley.

Charley's own children had been waylaid by Galloway, and subsequently relocated to permanent housing. And Charley had returned the night of the attack with injuries. And when it all came down to it, Charley wasn't the sort to plot against those he was loyal to.

Which left Blake.

Hattie had her doubts even as she skulked through the ill-lit corridors of the Charge warehouse toward Blake's room. She didn't know all that much about Blake. He was a blink pincher born in South Carolina to otherwise mundane parents. He likely had a soul twin somewhere in the world, born out of the conjuring of a demon. He was barely eighteen years old. Affable. Smart but a tad naïve. He had a way of looking at things in a simple light, a virtue that tended to slice through the colliding thoughts that typically plagued Hattie's own mind.

She had difficulty believing that Blake would be willing, much less capable, of this sort of espionage. But Galloway was a convincing figure, even when he wasn't using his powers. And Hattie wasn't convinced by Galloway's assurance that he wouldn't use his magic against another pincher.

Hattie tested the door to Blake's room, finding it

unlocked. She'd have to be careful. He could blink into the room at any point. But this was important. She had to eliminate all possibilities of spies within the Charge. Otherwise, more newcomers like this family of four would arrive fully intent on traveling to Zanesville.

Blake's room was spartan, even by Charge standards. An unmade cot. A crate with clothes tossed inside without folding. And that was about it. Hattie nudged through the clothing. The only thing of interest she found was a folding knife small enough to fit into a trouser pocket.

Hattie ran her hand along the tousled bedclothes, finding nothing but fabric and the stench of unwashed man.

She shook her head and sat on the cot. What was she doing? This was an absolute violation of trust. Wouldn't the more virtuous approach be to confront Sadie and the others with her suspicions? Or would that simply serve to give any mole an opportunity to dig themselves deeper? Hattie gave her face a brisk massage then stood up.

The cot made a slapping noise as her weight lifted from the mattress. She paused, listening for the noise to repeat. It did not.

Hattie turned to stare at the cot. She tested it with her hand, finding that the harder she pressed, the louder the slap sounded. She crouched down to glance underneath the cot, but nothing seemed out of place save for an alarming amount of dust. Another pat, another sound.

As Hattie pulled away the wool blanket, she found a series of straps holding the mattress off the ground. A wide, square object lay sandwiched between the straps and the mattress. She slipped it free of the straps, pulling it into the light.

It was a book...a register with leather binding. Hattie flipped it open to scan the nonsensical jumble of words and letters arranged in neat columns.

"Oh, hey there," a voice called behind her.

Hattie spun on her knee to find Blake grinning at her. She stood, lifting the book for Blake to see.

"Would you mind telling me what this is?" she asked without mirth.

Blake shrugged and took a look at the open page. With a smile, he said, "Looks like a chapterbook."

"Aye, I can tell that for myself."

"Oh."

"My point is, what's it doing underneath that cot?"

Blake shrugged. "Not much, I'm guessing."

"This is no time to be funny. What're you doing with a chapterbook? There's no caravan set to head west."

Blake furrowed his brow, reaching out to take the book. "Can I take a look? I learned a little of Sadie's code. She had me add in a name or two last month."

Hattie surrendered the book.

Blake flipped the pages, his face furrowing in confusion.

"Uh, no. This isn't new. This is the same book." He pointed to a few lines in pencil, clearly scribbled in a distinct handwriting. "This is what I added right here. Those were for Charley's girls."

"That's all well and good," Hattie grumbled, "but what is it doing here?"

"It's not supposed to be," Blake answered. "Supposed to go with the group to Orson." He flipped the page. "What the? There's more."

Four lines had been added on the next page. Names…not in Sadie's code.

"Who're the Mullinses?" Blake asked.

"It's the new family."

"Oh."

Hattie scowled, hands on hips. "The bloody thing is in your room, isn't it?"

"No."

"What?"

He shook his head. "No, Charley and me switched rooms last week. Wait. You were snooping around my room?"

"You switched rooms?"

"Yeah. He didn't like being so far from the front door. What're you doing nosing around our things, anyways?"

"Where is Charley now?" she asked

"Downtown, I think. Said he had to buy some cough medicine."

Hattie took the book, slamming it shut and tucking it under her arm. "Listen, keep this under your hat until I get a chance to talk to Charley."

"What, don't rat you out for snooping?"

"This is important, Blake," she urged. "Sadie's got enough on her mind. I need to get to the truth of things before she jumps to conclusions."

"I don't even know what's happening," he stated.

"Well, keep what you know, and what you don't know, quiet. Please."

"Well, alright. But don't go snooping. It's rude."

"I had good reason to." She met his gaze. "I need you to trust me on this."

He pursed his lips. "Um, okay?"

Hattie raced from the room, heading out of the warehouse and dodging the others on her way to the street. Charley could be anywhere in the city, but when it came to cough medicine, she was aware of a certain stretch of county road on the east side where vagabonds huddled up. One or two sold opium tinctures along with some bathtub gin. Charley had been through enough hell in Ithaca, it took a bottle of opium each month to keep his nerves from jarring his teeth out of his head.

The vagrant camp wasn't far from Locust Point, which made for a quick walk. Hattie gripped the chapterbook the entire way, a million notions flooding her brain. Why would Charley bring back the chapterbook after getting jumped and having to flee for his life? The truth dawned on her halfway to opium lane. Hattie and Vincent had established that Galloway had taken the Charge refugees peacefully. There was no struggle. Hence, the wound on Charley's head would have been self-inflicted.

And the Mullinses, the family that had spent hours with Charley before arriving at the Charge? Those hours may well have been spent with Charley swaying them to Galloway's cause. And here he was, inside Sadie's operation, adding new names to the register for Galloway's records.

The only question she couldn't unravel was the simple matter of why?

Four canvas tents lay at ragged angles alongside the gravel-dust road leading from the county highway off toward White Marsh. Hoboes and vagrants sat or lay beneath, some wrapped in blankets, others shirtless and sweating in the unseasonably mild temperature. Their eyes blinked heavy-lidded, heads swaying in opiate fume.

The far tent sported the bulk of the merchandise, bottles of amber glass lined up along the tops of crates.

Hattie spotted Charley standing just outside the far tent, his red beard waggling as he conversed with someone inside. His posture was bent, face drawn in what could have been anger, desperation, or some combination thereof.

Hattie approached from the side, almost making it to Charley before he finally spotted her.

She held up the book with a glare. "Hello, Charley. Mind explaining this?"

"Ohh, no. No, no." Charley swayed on his feet.

Hattie reached to steady him. "Easy, now."

"Don't hurt me!"

"I'm not here to hurt you. But you've a lot to answer for."

Tears streamed from his eyes. "Please. I didn't mean no harm."

"What's this about, then? You're in league with Galloway?"

Charley dropped to his knees. "Please…"

"Oh, get up. Just explain yourself."

"They…they wouldn't take them."

"Who?" Hattie asked.

"My girls. He said they weren't pinchers. He didn't want to help them. I said they were my girls, but he said that didn't matter."

"Galloway said that?"

He nodded. "He said he'd spare them if I came back and gave him information. About the Charge. And about you and Mister Calendo."

Hattie caught her breath. "Then your girls aren't guests. They're hostages."

"Don't tell anyone! He'll find out. And then he'll hurt my girls!"

She reached out a hand to touch his arm. "Charley, I've only ever helped you. I won't throw you to the wolves like that."

"But, they'll tell him!"

Hattie frowned. "Who? Who will tell?"

Charley lifted a trembling finger to the tent. "Them."

She glanced up to see two figures emerging from beneath the canvas. A young woman with ponytails along with a young man in a leather coat.

Charley stumbled away, rolling onto the street as he blubbered in panic.

Hattie tucked the book under her arm and frowned at the two. "Who are you, then? Are you Galloway's people?"

The girl laughed. "Oh, well. He said we'd probably have to take care of you."

The man nodded. "She was always the wild card."

Hattie tensed. "I'll be more than that, if you don't explain yourselves."

The man shoved his hands into his pockets, stepping to the side of the road in a slow but steady arc. Hattie eased away, keeping the two of them from surrounding her.

The girl said, "We'll need that book, if you'll be so kind."

"You can go to hell."

"Oh, be nice. We're nice. Why can't you be?"

Hattie scowled. "Because you're terrorizing this poor man, is why."

The girl held her hands up in a peaceful gesture. "We're not armed. We can't hurt anyone."

The man crouched down by the side of the street, picking through the debris tossed aside by the vagrants. "She won't believe you."

"Oh," the girl said, her innocence melting into a keen sort of malice. "Well, shit. I suppose we'll have to deal with her."

Hattie took a quick stock of her surroundings, planning her next move. A light pinch…but what? Where?

As the possibilities ran through her brain, a tiny spark flickered in the girl's outstretched palm.

Hattie remembered where she'd seen this girl before. The cabin. Galloway's cabin, as she lured her away.

Sun pincher.

Hattie clamped her eyes shut just as the area erupted in bright light. The intensity of the shine pouring through her closed eyelids was almost unbearable. Hattie dropped the book and wrapped her arms over her face.

When she opened her eyes she saw in the road beside her, instead of Charley a large red-feathered hawk. It released a pained screech before flapping its wings, taking off into the sky and out of sight.

At least Charley was safe.

Hattie checked the man, who pulled a pine cone from the side of the road. He flipped it at Hattie with a slip of his wrist.

She reached for the book, lifting it in front of her face just before the pine cone shattered into several thousand splinters. More than half buried themselves into the leather bindings of the chapterbook. The rest sank into Hattie's arms and legs.

Hattie yelped as burning pain spread across her limbs. She tried standing, but the twisting of her clothes ground the wood splinters into her skin.

The man laughed and cracked his knuckles.

The sun pincher rolled her eyes. "Just be careful with that book."

"Oh, just blind her already."

The girl pulled her hands together, cupping them as if preparing to catch a ball. More light flickered between her fingertips, lashing together like a lace of brilliant white light.

Light.

Hattie hissed against the pain of the splinters jabbing into her arm. Could it work? Closing her eyes, she tried to calm herself, reaching out with her powers as a bolt of unbearable solar light slashed into her.

And with a twist of her guts, Hattie pinched that light back at the sun pincher.

The girl shrieked, staggering backward until she tripped over one of the crates inside the tent. Glass bottles smashed to the ground as she flailed, pawing at her eyes.

"Enough!" the man shouted, reaching for the upended crate. He snatched whole planks free, the wood prying loose as if it had volunteered itself. The wood stretched, lengthening into poles that splayed before her eyes into axe heads.

Hattie pedaled away from the wood pincher as he slashed

his weapons at her. As he pulled them away, he pinched the wood back into a razor's edge.

Hattie made of copy of herself, sending it rushing at him as he wound up for a second strike. It was just enough to confuse him for a half-second before the illusion dissipated. The load she'd born twisting the sun pincher's bolt back on her had nearly drained Hattie. If only Vincent were there she could do so much more.

The wood pincher shook his head, then grinned. "Nice try."

Hattie growled, "Go to hell!"

He twisted the axes sharpening them into wood blades that slashed through the air toward Hattie.

They came to a halt a few inches over her head, colliding against a long, curved steel blade.

Hattie gasped, looking up at the face of Assam al Ghasawi.

Ghasawi twisted his scimitar, kicking the wood pincher's axe aside before swinging a foot in a wide arc, smashing it against the wood pincher's jaw.

The man tumbled backward, dropping one of his weapons. With a growl, he gathered himself and took a swing at Ghasawi.

The Janissary parried the blow, the scimitar slicing the wooden axe cleanly in half. The wood pincher gaped at his ruined weapon, a trickle of blood flowing from his nostril.

To Hattie's left, the sun pincher had gotten to her feet, her eyes bloodshot but focused on Hattie. With a shriek, the girl lifted her hands.

"Watch out!" Hattie shouted.

Ghasawi reached inside his jacket, flinging something tiny through the air. It was a length of silver chain with two miniature spheres on the ends. The chain tumbled through the air until it caught the sun pincher by the finger, wrapping around her hand.

The girl jabbed with her open palms, attempting to send blinding light at Hattie and Ghasawi. But nothing came. She shook her hands, sending the tiny bolo to the ground, then tried again. Still nothing.

Ghasawi held a hand to his chest with a half-bow. "A null enchantment, my dear. I'm afraid your powers will be useless for quite some time." He lifted his scimitar at the wood pincher. "And you, my wood-bending friend. Your powers are remarkable, but your form is weak"

The wood pincher exchanged glances with his compatriot, then bolted for the forest. The sun pincher followed suit.

Ghasawi held his ground for a moment before sheathing his sword and offering Hattie a hand to stand.

She did so, hissing at the splinters. "Damn!"

"Take care. We should get you to a doctor."

"No," she grumbled. "It's only splinters. Pine cone. If he'd gotten hold of a proper length of wood, I might be dead." She squinted at Ghasawi. "You followed me."

"Clearly."

"How did you know?"

"I thought I was clear on the point. I will protect you until the Hell pincher arrives. You'll be of no use in that regard if some rank amateurs kill you first."

She sighed. "Bloody sentimental of you."

"I take it your new associations have soured?"

"Aye. Soured, they have." She reached out to shake Ghasawi's hand. "Thank you, though."

"It was my pleasure."

"Let's get back to the Charge, before Galloway's loons warn him that we're onto him." She swallowed hard. "God... we have to warn Vincent!"

CHAPTER 21

Vincent regarded the gilded statue atop the Pennsylvania Capitol building. The figure stood gleaming in the sunlight, brandishing a wreath atop a staff as she held a hand out over the city of Harrisburg. The marble façade of the long building similarly shone in the orange sunlight of early evening. Long shadows sliced along the terra cotta shingles of the cupola, signaling the end of the day. The statue seemed to face Vincent directly, her stern eyes offering him silent counsel.

Survive.

Succeed.

Run away.

He couldn't decide if it was his nerves, or whether some higher power was reaching out to him in this golden hour.

DeBarre walked up to stand beside Vincent. "Nice building, huh?"

"The green's a bit much," Vincent replied, nodding at the lime green shingles covering the cupola. Vincent peeled his eyes away from the statue. "Any word from Arnoud?"

DeBarre shook his head. "Any word from Galloway?"

Vincent shook his head.

The sun was about to set, and there was no sign of either Jonas O'Donnell's war party, or of Galloway and his reinforcements. The city of Harrisburg had been oddly quiet, despite the massacre of Arnoud's men that morning. Had O'Donnell's army moved back upstate? Or had they remained in the city, waiting for a reprisal?

At last, Arnoud's car swung up the road. The touch pincher jumped out red-faced. "We found them."

"Where?" DeBarre asked.

"Downriver, near Highspire. Look to be mobilizing soon."

DeBarre turned to Vincent. "Are those other pinchers in or out?"

Vincent lifted his hands. "I have no way of finding Galloway. We might have to rethink this."

He wasn't about to give DeBarre the location of Galloway's headquarters, just in case Philadelphia elected to eliminate a rogue threat when this business with O'Donnell was over. But the trip to and from Waynesboro shouldn't have taken this long. Something was wrong.

"We have them on the road, and they won't be expecting us," DeBarre mused. "There won't be a better time to strike than now."

"Three pinchers versus one," Arnoud added. "The odds are still in our favor."

"I guess that depends," Vincent replied, "on how tough Jonas really is."

"It's not how tough he is," DeBarre said. "It's in what he can do. Everything we'd use against his gunmen is something he can turn against us."

Vincent nodded. "All the more reason I'd rather have the other pinchers to back us up. Galloway has a fella who can do what Jonas can do, only with wood. It's worth a wait."

DeBarre asked Arnoud, "How much time do we have?"

"They're fueling up now. We may only have a matter of minutes."

"Damn. And then we don't know which way they're headed." DeBarre shook his head. "We have to strike now. We hit fast, we hit hard, and we watch our asses."

Arnoud nodded and returned to his vehicle.

Vincent turned to DeBarre. "Stick close to me, okay? We're in the open. You go down pinching out here, and you'll end up killing yourself."

DeBarre grinned. "I fully expect you to save my life at least three times before nightfall."

They got back into the car and steered onto Front Street, racing alongside the Susquehanna River toward the borough of Highspire. The river reflected the aging sunlight, flowing like a river of gold alongside the road.

Arnoud's car pulled to the side of the road just before Highspire, taking its place behind a line of roughly fifteen Fords crammed with men and guns.

DeBarre parked and leaned out of the window. "This it?"

Arnoud pointed to a pair of smokestacks jutting from a factory just past the town. "There's a Lutheran church past the factory. They're holed up there."

"Alright, then. Cut me loose two choppers."

Arnoud snapped his fingers and pointed to the rear car. Two men hopped out with Thompson repeaters and swept back to jump into the car with DeBarre and Vincent.

"Okay," DeBarre shouted as he slapped the side of the car door. "Hit 'em hard! Hit 'em fast! Let's roll!"

The motorcade chugged to life, slipping onto the street in a single file line. As they entered Highspire borough, the line split into two columns. The old factory and its double smokestacks loomed to the east. And just beyond it, a copse of trees spangled with tiny leaf buds. And beyond that the white steeple of the Good Shepherd Lutheran Church. A gravel pad surrounded the tiny building, offering plenty of space between the church and the surrounding neighborhood.

DeBarre's motorcade swerved off the street, careening two-by-two into an arc that rushed around the building, nearly encircling it.

And they all came to a stop.

The gunmen in the back seat rolled down their windows and leaned out enough to pull their guns onto the roof of the car.

DeBarre peered back and forth between the neighborhood houses beyond the back fence, and the church itself. The only cars were their own.

"Where are they?" he whispered.

"We might have missed them," Vincent replied.

DeBarre paused, then stepped out of the car to greet Arnoud, who had just finished a brisk conversation with one of his gunmen. Vincent remained in the car, eyes working the surroundings. The gravel pad had been disturbed recently. But they hadn't spotted any traffic coming out of the church parking lot. Nor had they passed any cars on the way in. They could all be hiding inside the church, perhaps... but where were the cars?

DeBarre continued his conversation with Arnoud with rapid hand gestures and shouts.

Vincent shook his head. Perhaps it was best that Galloway hadn't seen this. The man had been upset about his inability to win the Philadelphia pinchers over to his side, and it had been difficult to convince him that the Philly pinchers wouldn't turn into a threat.

Was that why Galloway wasn't here? Maybe he'd decided he'd be better off letting Masseria's men take out the Philadelphia family, as opposed to using his army to convince DeBarre and Arnoud to join him.

As he mulled it over, Vincent spotted some tin fencing separating the church from the factory property. Most of the fencing was tucked away inside the copse of trees, serving more of a barrier to vehicles than pedestrians. The tin appeared to be largely unmolested, but something about it seemed off to Vincent.

He got out of the car and wandered across the gravel toward the trees. Three horizontal planks of corrugated tin stretched between metal posts, not quite blocking the entire path. Vincent could easily slip between the fencing and the nearest tree trunk. Just beyond, he could see the side of the red-bricked factory.

Shaking his head, Vincent wrote off his unease as nerves, and reached for the fencing to steady himself as his shoe slipped into a tire rut.

A tire rut.

That ran directly beneath the fencing.

Vincent shook the tin. Two of the metal posts slipped off at the ground, as if cut by an impossibly fine saw and set back into place.

His eyes followed the tire ruts onto the paved lot surrounding the factory building. A thin line of gravel traced a path from the cut-through to the front structure of the factory, leading back to the road.

Vincent turned and shouted, "Heads up! It's a trap!"

DeBarre and Arnoud turned to Vincent just as the first cars slammed into the church parking lot. The front car smashed into the rear of DeBarre's vehicle. The two gunmen hanging out of the windows squeezed off a handful of shots before they jerked from the impact, dangling limp as the car lurched forward into the next like dominoes. More of O'Donnell's party swung around the wreck, tommy guns opening fire.

DeBarre cupped a hand and pounded a fist into it. The

second car sweeping into the parking lot tumbled abruptly on its side, sliding across the gravel until it hammered the side of the church in a spray of metal and glass. It was quickly replaced by another attacker.

Vincent sprinted toward the melee, pinching time once he'd closed half the distance. He pushed the remainder of the way, jerking DeBarre aside as gunmen trained their weapons on him. Releasing the time pinch, they both hurtled behind one of their own vehicles, bullets peppering the spot where DeBarre had stood.

As they landed on the ground, DeBarre sucked in a breath, then coughed. "Okay. That's one."

Screams sounded from the nearest attackers. Vincent peered over their cover to spot the two gunmen gripping their hands in pain, their weapons dropped at Arnoud's feet. Vincent rushed to scoop one up, turning onto a knee to hose the front of the fourth attacking car in lead. Steam erupted from the radiator, and the car fishtailed on the gravel. As it nearly righted itself, the tires burgeoned and blew out, rims bending under the doubled weight of the vehicle thanks to another one of DeBarre's down pinches.

Vincent rolled away from gunfire, now sizzling through the air from both sides. The remainder of Masseria's vehicles had formed a line across the pad, and a sort of trench warfare had emerged with repeating fire flashing over the tops of hoods and through car windows.

Vincent nodded to DeBarre. "Careful with those down pinches."

"I am. What about you? What've you got for me?"

Vincent squinted back at the opposite line. "Too far. I'll be tapped out by the time I get there." He turned to Arnoud. "What about you? Can you reach them from here?"

Arnoud shook his head. "They need to be closer, or it won't amount to much more than a tickle."

"Understood." Vincent spat some dust from his lips. Damn it, where was Galloway?

The gunfire continued, Vincent electing to use his trigger finger rather than his powers. As the sides of the opposite vehicles crated in bullet holes, the gunfire on their side slowly subsided. One by one, their tommy guns went quiet. Vincent glanced down their row of marksmen, several of whom held their guns up for inspection, attempting to clear magazines in frustration.

"What's going on?" Vincent shouted.

DeBarre muttered, "Must be O'Donnell."

"Where is he?" Vincent asked, peering over the hood of his cover car.

"Can't see him," DeBarre replied. "Bradley?"

Arnoud shook his head.

"He has to be here somewhere."

Vincent tested his gun, squeezing off a couple shots which spattered against the cars across the pad. As he took aim at a hat through one of the car windows, a creaking noise emerged from the end of his weapon. The muzzle vibrated, curling up into a U shape. He threw it aside just as the magazine crumpled, sending bullets bursting free of the canister.

"Toss 'em!" Vincent shouted, but it was too late.

Three of the gunmen jerked backward under backfires and exploding canisters, their faces and chests full of shrapnel.

DeBarre covered his head and ducked. "He's gotta be here somewhere!"

The car he and Vincent hid behind trembled, the door peeling open like a sardine can. Bolts snapped, the metal screamed from shearing strains. Vincent pinched time as the car ripped in half, dragging DeBarre several feet away from the blossoming shrapnel. When he released the time pinch, strips of jagged steel plunged into the ground where they had crouched.

"That's two," Vincent gasped, running a hand underneath his nostril to clear the trickle of blood.

Arnoud rolled away as his cover suffered the same fate, two of the gunmen next to him impaled on vicious blades of iron-pinched Ford chassis.

"Where the hell is he?" DeBarre growled.

Vincent swallowed hard against a wave of nausea, then glanced back at the church house.

His eyes widened.

"He's inside the church!" Vincent shouted, pointing to the shattered window just beyond the wreckage DeBarre had made of the side of the building.

DeBarre smacked his hands together, hurtling Arnoud's ruined car into the church house as if dropped from a height of ten feet. Timbers on the side of the building smashed, falling free from the hole he'd just created.

The wreckage of the car peeled away from the hole, squealing as the steel twisted and sheared, opening like a flower blossom as a tall man stepped through the gap. He was a head taller than Vincent, a neatly-trimmed beard hugging his jaw line. Deep set eyes gazed with cold intensity from behind dark lashes.

DeBarre's gunmen turned to open fire on Jonas O'Donnell. Bullets shredded the wood framing behind him, some sparking as they rattled against the twisted remains of the two cars he was unfurling. Several bullets smacked into his body, pounding his shoulders and chest as they smashed flat. Soon, a disc of lead the size of a dinner plate had pancaked out along his chest.

Jonas slipped his fingers underneath the sheet of lead, gazed at it as the last of the magazines ran empty, then gave it a flick of his wrist. The disc shot through the air, slicing one of the gunmen's heads clean from his shoulders.

Stepping clear of the iron wreckage, Jonas's eyes leveling hard on DeBarre. "Your name is Loren DeBarre?"

The down pincher stood upright from his crouched position. "I'm guessing you're O'Donnell?"

Jonas peered at Vincent. "Are you Bradley Arnoud?"

Vincent set his jaw. Before he could decide whether to correct the man or try to spare Arnoud some grief, Arnoud shouted, "I am."

Jonas nodded then returned his attention to Vincent. "Which leaves you."

Vincent pinched time, his stomach twisting with the distance and radius of the affected area. Shoving off his cover, he reached for a length of green stained glass smashed from a church window. Gripping it as tight as he dared, he muddled through the time-stiffened air, toward Jonas. As he reached the man he felt the trickle of blood from his nose.

Hold on. Just keep the time pinch up long enough to slash the man's throat.

Vincent extended the glass, realizing that Sadie would hate him even more for this.

She'd thought her husband was dead—or as good as dead. Ithaca had probably destroyed the man she'd known and loved. Or had it? He'd managed to keep a portion of himself safe from those torturers, his sanity kept intact with the hope of seeing Hattie again. Maybe Jonas had done the same.

Or maybe they'd told him Sadie was dead and he'd lost all of himself in the grief.

He had a split second to make a decision. He only hoped it was the right one.

Vincent slipped around Jonas, lacing his arm underneath the man's shoulder to angle the shard of glass across his throat.

Then he dropped the time pinch.

Jonas stiffened as Vincent pulled back with the glass and leaned a shoulder into the small of his back.

"Relax," Vincent whispered.

Jonas said nothing.

Muttering and gasps from the front line filled the air.

"Take it easy," Vincent added. "And don't get funny."

"Who are you?" Jonas asked, his chest rumbling with his deep voice.

"Name's Vincent."

"I see," Jonas rumbled. "You're the Baltimore pincher."

"Well, it's good to be recognized."

"Are you going to talk me to death, or are you going to cut my throat?"

"That depends." Vincent adjusted his grip on the glass.

"On?"

Vincent lowered his voice. "On whether or not I want to break Sadie's heart."

Jonas held a breath. Vincent could feel it from the stillness in his chest. And then, a long exhale.

"She's…alive?"

"Alive and well. She talks about you, you know. All the time. She thought you were dead."

Jonas's chin dipped, the short whiskers of his beard brushing against the glass in Vincent's hand. "I am dead. And you know what's in that piece of glass you're holding?"

Vincent caught his breath, eyeing the green glass. "What?"

"Lead."

The shard exploded in Vincent's hand. White-hot pain shot through his arm as blood splattered the side of his face. He gripped his hand, staggering away from the iron pincher.

With a dry chuckle, Jonas approached. Vincent's eyes shifted to DeBarre, who'd lifted his revolver to take aim at the iron pincher's back.

Jonas lifted a single finger, hooking it in the air. DeBarre released a blood-curdling shriek as a strip of steel shot from the side of his car, spearing him through the chest.

Jonas never once broke eye contact with Vincent.

"Tell me, Vincent of Baltimore. Where can I find him?"

"Who?" Vincent gasped, clutching his hand.

DeBarre glared at Jonas, lifted the revolver again and fired.

Jonas twisted as the bullet smashed into his face, spattering into pieces as it sent him hurtling into the wreckage of the church wall.

Vincent scrambled away from the iron pincher, who was picking the remains of the ruined bullet from his skin, leaving behind only a pink blotch on his cheek. He'd pinched the bullet just in time to keep it from killing him, but as a bright crimson trail of blood slipped from the man's nostril, Vincent realized his powers were reaching their limit.

Arnoud reached for Vincent, pulling him down as the opposition resumed their gunfire, their weapons now reloaded. Bullets sprayed their cover as Vincent inspected the damage to DeBarre. Bubbles emerged from his chest as he struggled for breath.

"Shit," Vincent muttered.

DeBarre nodded. "Gonna…take it easy."

"Anything you can do?" Arnoud nodded toward O'Donnell.

"Not much. I think we're all tapped out, including Mister O'Donnell up there."

"Why didn't you kill him when you had the chance?" Arnoud demanded.

He should have. Damn it, he should have. The one time he tried to be more than a gangster and that decision was most likely going to cost them all their lives.

I'm sorry Hattie. Please forgive me. This would be the time he didn't come home. And all their deaths would be on him.

As the car rattled with gunfire, Vincent steadied himself in his crouch. "Did you feel that?"

He rested his hand on the ground. Arnoud followed suit. The ground trembled beneath Vincent's fingers, and he let out a breath.

"What is this?" Arnoud asked.

"Earth pincher," Vincent replied, torn between relief that Galloway had finally arrived and anger that it had taken the man so long.

The tremors increased until a deafening crack filled the air. The gunfire ceased almost immediately to be replaced with shouts of confusion. Vincent ventured a glance up through the ruined car windows to find a forty foot long wall of granite had shot from the ground, completely cutting them off from the firing line.

He stood up, turning to the street to find two cars parked there. Maria stood with her arms in the air in a gesture of exertion. Ernie had hopped out of the car and was rushing for Vincent and the others. When he reached them, his face drew back in alarm at the sight of DeBarre impaled on the vehicle.

"Bloody hell!" Ernie shouted.

Vincent pointed to the church. "Get O'Donnell!"

Jonas hopped out of the church, eyes hard on the far car— on Galloway.

Ernie trotted up to Arnoud's car, slipping his fingers beneath the frame and hoisting it over his head. With a quick heave, he tossed the car in O'Donnell's direction. It landed short, somersaulting side-over-side as it careened across the gravel pit.

In a spray of ruined metal, the car cleaved in two, the halves tumbling on either side of O'Donnell. The iron pincher's face was pale, his nose bleeding profusely. He doubled over with a wince, grabbing his stomach.

"Another!" Vincent shouted. "He's empty!"

Ernie nodded. "Right!"

But before he could reach another vehicle to toss, O'Donnell rushed for the corner of the church.

Galloway's car chugged up and around the granite wall, spinning around the corner to pursue. Vincent caught his breath, turning again to inspect DeBarre.

"We have to get him to a surgeon," he urged.

Arnoud nodded. "State hospital. Just minutes away."

"Get a car!" Vincent shouted to Ernie,

Ernie rushed back to Maria, and the two brought their car up. Vincent and Arnoud eyed the metal spear, which had curled into place under Jonas' torture.

"Any clue how to get him off this?" Arnoud asked.

Vincent lifted a hand to Ernie. "Hey, can you give us a hand."

Ernie hopped over, inspecting the metal.

"Easy," Vincent urged as Ernie gripped the spike with two fingers.

With an easy tug, he straightened the metal as easily as if it were silk. DeBarre gasped, then went limp as Ernie scooped the down pincher in his arms, guiding him gingerly off the spike. Fresh blood poured from DeBarre's back, and Vincent clamped a hand over the hole, helping Ernie guide him to the car.

When Arnoud moved to join them, Vincent shouted, "There's an army of gunmen on the other side of that wall. I need you to clean them up."

"I'm not leaving Loren," Arnoud argued. "It's my duty."

"Look, these are your men. They won't listen to me."

Arnoud glanced to DeBarre, resting a hand on his leg for

a second, then nodded. "Fine. I'll mop up then meet you at the hospital."

* * *

VINCENT WINCED as a middle-aged woman slipped a needle into the flesh of his thumb, stitching up a laceration from Jonas' exploded glass. Several deep punctures had savaged Vincent's right hand, but it was the long cut that was the most dangerous. Happily, the glass had avoided tendons, but the damage was more to Vincent's resolve than anything.

He'd had the chance to eliminate Jonas, but he'd allowed his sentiment to cloud his judgment. DeBarre was grievously injured because of it. All because of Vincent.

Because he'd hesitated, thinking maybe the man had something there worth saving.

"Hold still, please," the nurse chided.

Maybe he needed to accept the fact that he was a gangster, that there would be no escaping this life, that the moment he hesitated or tried a solution other than violence, everything would go to hell.

Footsteps approached, and Vincent peered up to find Ernie returning with Maria and Galloway.

"Where were you?" Vincent snapped. "You were supposed to be there early and go in with us."

Galloway removed his spectacles to wipe them clean. "I had an unexpected entanglement. The question is why didn't you wait for us?"

"They were escaping."

"Apparently not. They were waiting for you."

"If you'd been there—"

"I would have if you hadn't gone off half-cocked—" Galloway shook his head and slipped the spectacles back onto his forehead. "Jonas escaped."

252

"Where's Arnoud?"

"He's in with your other friend."

Vincent swallowed hard. "How is he?"

Galloway shrugged.

The nurse finished up with Vincent's stitches, and as soon as the gauze had been taped, he snatched his jacket and hat, and rushed past Galloway's crew to find DeBarre.

Vincent found him in a room of beds mostly empty. Arnoud stood at the foot of the bed, arms crossed, face twisted in frustration.

A long swatch of thickly-packed gauze surrounded DeBarre's chest. His skin was ashen, almost cadaverous.

DeBarre opened his eyes, glancing up to Vincent. "It's you again."

Vincent crouched beside the bed. "They patch you up?"

"Not much..." he released a weak, wet cough, "...to patch."

Vincent looked to Arnoud, who simply shook his head.

He gripped DeBarre's hand. "I'm sorry. I could've..."

"You...have to...pick your fights." DeBarre's eyes fluttered, then he coughed again, this time bringing up blood. "Don't let them...pick for you."

"I'm going to find this rat bastard," Vincent grumbled. "I'll get him for you. I swear it. He'll pay for this."

DeBarre grinned just a little. "Yeah. I bet."

Arnoud uncrossed his arms, then re-crossed them, shaking his head as he tried to figure out what to do with his own emotions.

Vincent whispered, "What should I tell Sabella."

Arnoud muttered, "Let me handle that."

DeBarre's eyes lolled back and forth between Arnoud and Vincent. "You two...play nice. Okay?"

Vincent nodded to Arnoud. "We will."

Arnoud didn't meet Vincent's eyes.

Another coughing fit stampeded through DeBarre's chest. A fresh spot of crimson blossomed on his chest wrappings.

DeBarre struggled for breath, his chest heaving, then shifting to light rasping breaths.

He blinked hard, then turned to Vincent. "Hey."

"Yes?"

"Tell…tell Hattie…"

Vincent waited.

DeBarre stared at him.

And stopped breathing.

Vincent gripped DeBarre's hand tightly. It gave way without resistance, falling away as Vincent released it.

Arnoud shook his head, then turned to leave the room. "I'll get the doctor."

Vincent tucked DeBarre's hand to his side, then pulled up the blanket to his chin and reached out to close DeBarre's eyelids.

CHAPTER 22

Sadie just shook her head. "Charley, huh?"

"If it helps," Hattie offered, "he looks to be blackmailed into this. They have his daughters."

Sadie nodded. "What else would he have done? What would any of us do?"

"It's Galloway who's the problem," Hattie said. "His people wouldn't have stopped until I was dead." She turned to Ghasawi. "Thanks again."

Sadie leaned back in her chair to stare at the ceiling. "Is Galloway the problem, or am I?"

"What, now?"

"Where are we sending these people?" Sadie asked, gesturing to the bunk room. "If Galloway's right about Utah, then we're sending our people to suffer and die in the desert."

Hattie frowned. "He lied about Charley's girls. What else has he lied about? It could all be a load of horse apples."

"I sent a letter to Orson by US Post. If he responds—if— then I'll have to decide whether it's Galloway or Orson who's giving me the runaround. And now we're a man down with Charley taking wing."

"We have Blake," Hattie said. "And Vincent's offered to help several times, now."

Sadie closed her eyes. "Taking help from the gangsters because our own people are lying to us. What's the point of the Charge if that's what it's come to?"

Hattie considered offering more consolation, but Sadie was closing off. She probably wasn't even hearing Hattie, at this point. And she couldn't blame the woman. The Charge existed for a single purpose, and they couldn't follow through on it.

"I'll leave you alone." Hattie stepped away from the desk and nodded to Ghasawi, who followed her out of the office, closing the door behind him.

"If this man made an attempt on your life," Ghasawi said, "then is he not the enemy?"

"That's how I see it, at any rate," Hattie replied as they descended the stairs.

"What is the debate, then? He is not to be trusted. He is clearly willing to spill blood. There appears to be no room for conciliation."

Hattie sighed. "If only that were so. We have this family, though, with their heads filled with notions of Zanesville."

"But if it's more a prison than sanctuary—"

"I know," Hattie said with a lift of her hand. "It's just not a simple matter, is all I'm saying. Those people in Zanesville may or may not be hostages. But if we go after Galloway now, without knowing anything about what goes on in Ohio, then we'd be putting their lives at risk. No matter how much I'd love to go after the bastard, I can't risk him killing all those people he's got in Ohio."

"Then what is the plan?" Ghasawi asked.

"We keep Galloway at arm's length," Hattie said. "Until we know what the truth is."

"And if you discover this Galloway is nothing but a thug?"

"Then he'll pay."

Blake popped into the room, making Hattie jump.

"Sweet Jesus, Blake!"

Blake frowned. "Car's in the yard."

"Who is it?" Hattie asked.

"Your friend. The gangster."

Hattie ran for the front door, swinging it open to spot Vincent plodding across the scrap yard. He looked like hell. His sleeves were rolled up, stained pink from what she assumed was blood. His right hand was bandaged for something more than a simple flesh wound.

Hattie held a hand to Ghasawi and Blake. "Wait here."

They both nodded, remaining in the doorway as Hattie rushed out to Vincent.

"What's happened, then?" She reached for his bandaged hand. "Whose blood is this? Yours?"

He cleared his throat. "DeBarre's."

Hattie's throat tightened. "Is he…?"

Vincent shook his head. "He's dead. He's dead and it's my fault."

A knot formed in Hattie's stomach. Tears stinging her eyes. "How?" she whispered. "What happened?"

"For one hot second I decided not to be a gangster, that's what happened." Vincent looked her in the eye. "I won't make that mistake again."

She searched his eyes, trying to make sense of what he was saying. "Vincent, what happened?" she repeated.

"Where's Sadie?"

She gave him a puzzled frown. "Inside. Why?"

Vincent's face grew stern, and resolute as he eyed the two standing in the doorway. "Let's take a walk."

Hattie stood rigid. "What's this about? Is DeBarre really—?"

"Yes. But we can't discuss it here."

Hattie turned to the others, waving them off as she took Vincent's good hand and strolled with him back to the street. Once they were out of the line of sight of the warehouse, she prodded, "Alright, now spill it. What happened?"

He stopped, turned her with a tug of her arm, then wrapped his arms around her, holding her so tight she could barely breathe.

She relaxed into his arms, rubbing her hands along his back and pressing her cheek against his jacket.

"God, Hattie…I just can't. I can't change. I show the slightest bit of humanity, of mercy, I hesitate for just a moment, and people pay for it with their lives. I can't do that again. I'll always be the gangster, be the monster. I need to be that. I can't give someone the benefit of the doubt again and have people I care about die because of it."

She let out a breath. "You're more than just a gangster, Vincent."

"That's dangerous thinking, Hattie. Maybe I'm more than a gangster. Maybe I'm not. But at the end of the day, I'm still a gangster."

There was a bitter edge to his words and she realized that the best comfort she could give him right now was just her presence.

After a few minutes, Vincent sniffled. "I'm sorry."

"What're you sorry about?"

"Yelling at you. Acting stupid. Storming off in a huff. I thought for a moment out there that I was going to die, and the one thing I kept thinking about was how I wouldn't be coming home to you, how we'd left things the last time we spoke."

She pulled away to wipe a tear from her cheek with her thumb. "I'm sorry, too. Now, can you tell me what happened?"

"A war party came down from New York," Vincent said as

he turned to walk down the street with Hattie. "They hit DeBarre's people in Harrisburg. It was Masseria's lead pincher with a throng of gunmen. We were in Philly when we got the news."

"Who's we?" Hattie asked with a cock of her brow.

"Me and Galloway."

She halted a step. "There's something you should know…" She remembered the last time she'd cut Vincent off with her own problems and thought twice about it. Last time Vincent came with news, he was giddy over some success on the Bay. Now…someone they knew and considered to be a friend had died.

"I'm sorry," she muttered. "That can wait. Go on."

"Galloway went to collect his people and throw in against this war party. His idea was to make nice with DeBarre and maybe win them over to our side."

Hattie clenched her jaw at "our side" but held her tongue.

Vincent continued, "But he got held up. We went in without him. Things went sideways."

She stroked his forearm. "You got hurt."

"Could've been worse."

"And DeBarre?"

Vincent squared up against Hattie. "He was run through with a metal spike."

Hattie covered her mouth with her hand. "Jesus."

"He held on for a couple hours at the hospital, but it was just too much damage. Lost too much blood." Vincent took a deep breath and let it out. "We'd all be just as dead if it weren't for Galloway's people."

Hattie scowled. "That so?"

"He pulled our fat out of the fire. But there's more. This pincher from New York?"

"Yes?"

"It's Jonas O'Donnell."

Hattie gasped. "The hell you say."

"He's an iron pincher. He ruined our guns, our vehicles. The man's basically bulletproof. But I didn't want to say anything in front of Sadie."

Hattie nodded. "Aye. Are you certain it was him?"

"One hundred percent. I thought…I thought maybe he didn't know she was still alive, that Ithaca had claimed she'd died. I hesitated and told him, hoping it would make a difference. I had him. I could've taken him down." Vincent grimaced. "But I didn't do it. I thought…maybe…"

"You thought maybe you could pull him back from the brink?" She reached out to him, suddenly understanding his previous words. He might see his gesture as foolish, but knowing he'd given Jonas a chance made Hattie love him even more.

Vincent nodded. "I was stupid. I won't make that mistake again."

She skated her hand down his arm to hold his hand. "You were right not to say anything in front of Sadie. Things have gone badly here."

Vincent composed himself. "What happened?"

"I found one of our chapterbooks in Charley's bunk. I figured for a while now that Galloway had to have an insider here at the Charge. He just…he knows too much."

"Charley?"

"Found out Galloway isn't helping his girls. He's holding them hostage, forcing Charley to spy for him."

Vincent shook his head. "That don't sound right."

"It's true, though. Charley confessed to it. Right before two of Galloway's people tried to kill me."

Vincent scowled. "They what?"

"It happened. The wood pincher and the bitch with the handful of light."

"Millie?" Vincent snarled. "You sure about that?"

"Oh, aye. And she learned not to throw light at a light pincher."

Vincent held still, a hard expression on his face. "Why did they attack you? What happened?"

"I found Galloway's insider. Charley was evidently meeting them and giving them information when I confronted him. They jumped me. And they made it very clear that Galloway told them to eliminate me if I became an issue. I'd be dead if it weren't for Ghasawi."

"Pinchers that don't fall in line with his plan get eliminated," Vincent snarled. "That's what he's doing. Manipulating with his sway pinches and threats, then killing when that doesn't work."

"He's trying to take over the Charge, then use those free pinchers in his army," Hattie said. "It's like Chicago. It's just like Sadie said he'd tried to do before."

Vincent shook his head. "And if he'd killed you, he would have had some glib explanation about how it was all a misunderstanding. Just like at Winnow's Slip"

"If he'd killed me, you might not have even known. There would have only been three witnesses, and Charley would do anything to protect his girls. I would have just vanished. Disappeared. And Galloway could claim he had no idea what happened to me."

"Or claimed one of the families grabbed you." Vincent scowled. "Which would have given me even more motive to fight for him with everything I had, trying to find and free you."

Hattie lifted her hands. "We can't trust anything he says. His plans, his assurances, his promises—they could all be lies."

"And the people in Zanesville?" Vincent asked.

"We can't know for sure if they're unknowing captives or actual prisoners. Just like we can't know if Eden is as bad as he's led on. But I *can* tell you that Sadie is about to give it all up. This business with Charley really put her on her heels."

"Which would leave the Charge in Galloway's hands."

Hattie sighed. "I can't believe we might end up stuck with Galloway, with a man we can't trust."

Vincent snorted. "Welcome to my world."

"Hmm?"

"That's my entire life with the Crew. No trust. No options."

Hattie reached out and held on to Vincent, gripping him tight. "So, what do we do?"

Vincent was silent for a while, then replied, "We air it all out. Force Galloway's hand. I've seen him in action. He'll adapt and adjust when his plan hits an obstacle. His plan so far has been secrecy. If we bust it all wide open, he'll have to adapt. Might be enough to bring him around."

Hattie nodded and let go of Vincent. "The Charge won't survive like this, at any rate. We need Sadie and Galloway at the same table, even if it's not the same side."

"Especially with Jonas coming. And he *is* coming."

Hattie jabbed a finger into Vincent's chest. "Sadie cannot know about Jonas. Not now. It would destroy her. It's just too much."

"Agreed."

"So, we'll make nice with that rat-faced bastard. Iron it all out. Then get everyone in the same sandbox?"

Vincent nodded. "But before we make nice, I need to have a conversation with Galloway about actions and consequences."

CHAPTER 23

Galloway rubbed the bridge of his nose, sending his spectacles bobbing in and out of his auburn hair. "I didn't have time to tell you with everything going on. The hospital, DeBarre…but yes. There was an incident with Miss Malloy. It's what held me up reaching you."

An incident. And how convenient that this was suddenly the excuse for their not arriving to Harrisburg on time. Vincent was pretty sure the man's next words were going to include something about a misunderstanding, an overreaction.

Vincent forced a nonchalant expression onto his face. "Did they offer any explanation?"

"I've spoken to Millie and Douglas at length. It was simply a misunderstanding, an overreaction to what they perceived as an urgent threat. I did send Charley into the Charge to feed me information, that's true. And when Miss Malloy blindsided him at his meet with my people, they responded the way we've always responded."

"Murder?" Vincent struggled to maintain a calm demeanor as he said the word.

"You have to understand something, Vincent. We have eyes and ears inside several dangerous organizations. Mob families. Underground criminal rings. Even the government. When a spy is compromised, it almost invariably becomes a life-or-death scenario. In this case with Charley, it was different. But my people have a tendency to lean on old behaviors."

"So, you're saying they overreacted?" Vincent grumbled. "That this was just a misunderstanding?"

"In a nutshell."

Vincent folded his hands over his crossed legs, staring at the bandages from his wound. This was precisely the line of crap he was expecting from Galloway. At least he hadn't tried to spin a wilder tale.

"And what about Charley's daughters? He says you're holding them hostage."

Galloway removed his spectacles and tossed them onto the desktop hard enough for them to bounce. "Now, that's too much! And it sickens me to hear it. We've done nothing but show his family the utmost in hospitality. We feed them. Educate them. Protect them. No one in Zanesville is there against their will. I'm willing to drive you there. Today. I'll prove it to you. Won't phone ahead or anything of the sort. Would that satisfy you?"

Vincent lifted his hands to calm Galloway, who appeared ready to jump out of his seat. "Charley's under the impression that if he doesn't walk in lockstep with you and your people, his girls will pay with their lives."

"Absurd! And insulting!" Galloway looked away shaking his head. "But then, you have to take the man into account."

"How do you mean?"

"How long was he held at Ithaca?"

Vincent eyed the other man. "A year or so."

Galloway nodded somberly. "If I'd suffered that fate, perhaps I would suspect everyone in my life as well."

"You're telling me Charley made it up?"

Galloway turned back to Vincent. "I assure you, I hold nothing but the fondest sentiments for Charley. And I will own this much. I demonstrated poor judgment in sending him back to Sadie to spy for me. It was a greater burden than he was prepared to carry. Has he been spotted anywhere?"

"No," Vincent replied. "I'd be stunned if he showed his face to any of us any time soon."

"What can I do to make this better?"

"That's not for me to say. You admit to spying on the Charge."

Galloway's nose wrinkled. "And I won't apologize for that. This is war, Vincent. Wars are waged on intelligence. Sometimes you spy on your friends. That's brass tacks."

"Then Sadie's the one you have to make nice with about that." He leaned forward. "But about Miss Malloy...that's a personal matter for me. On that, you'll need to deal with me."

"What do you mean?" For a brief second Galloway appeared unnerved. "These are important assets. I can't throw them away. Perhaps if they were to apologize?"

Vincent gritted his teeth, forcing himself to remain calm. Apologize. Because somehow in this man's mind, that was adequate reparation for attempting to kill Hattie.

Leaning farther over the table, Vincent and held the other man's gaze.

"You will tell your people that Hattie Malloy is not to be attacked in any way. If someone so much as frowns at her, I will see them dead. And not just them." Vincent spread his hands out on top of the desk, never breaking eye contact with Galloway. "You will also pay with your life."

The other man's eye twitched, then he scowled. "Now

that is uncalled for! We're professionals here. I won't stand for you to threaten me or my people."

"I'm a gangster. I do a whole lot more than threaten people." Vincent smiled. "So if there are any more 'misunderstandings,' or 'overreactions' between your people and Miss Malloy, they'll be dead, and you'll be dead. You won't even see it coming. Do I make myself clear?"

For a brief second he felt as if something were pushing inside his head, calming him, easing him. It was so subtle that he almost missed it.

Galloway leaned back in his chair with a genial smile. "I assure you there is no need for this, Vincent. I will make sure everyone understands that Miss Malloy is to be considered a friend and supporter. You can trust me to ensure her safety."

Right. He could trust this man less than he could trust Vito Corbi. But he'd delivered his message, and if Galloway chose to ignore it, Vincent fully intended on seeing his threat happen.

"Which leaves you and Sadie." Vincent picked up Galloway's glasses and handed them to the man before returning to his chair. "Through Jonas, Masseria has delivered a devastating blow to Philly. He'll be hitting Baltimore next."

"So it seems."

"If he takes on Baltimore, it'll provoke a brutal defense from Vito. Corbi has more firepower than Sabella. Jonas won't be able to take out all their guns before he runs out of strength."

Galloway shrugged. "So. If Corbi wins, then he's weak and we can topple him without much effort. If Jonas wins, then we'll swoop in to pick up the pieces once he leaves."

Vincent shook his head. "That's not how things work among the families. If Corbi wins, he'll be primed and ready to take us on. This won't be like Richmond. It won't be easy.

It will actually be harder since he'll be armed to the teeth and prepared. And if Jonas wins? Well then you've got a bunch of New York heavy hitters with an army of their own descending down here to make sure there's a proper transition of power. If that happens, we're definitely in trouble. We need to take care of him."

Galloway frowned in thought.

"Jonas is going to endanger your plans to consolidate the territory from Philly to Richmond," Vincent told him.

Galloway nodded. "*Our* plans. You're a valuable partner in this organization, Vincent. Don't forget that."

Wormy. Yeah, Blake had been right. That was a good way to describe this man.

Galloway stood up and paced to the sole window in the cabin, staring out at the budding trees surrounding them. "The problem becomes if Jonas makes it to Baltimore. Correct?"

"Among other problems, yes."

"What happens, therefore, if Sadie finds out he's alive and where he is? She rushes off to try and save her husband."

Vincent stood. "You're suggesting throwing her to the sharks?"

"I'm suggesting that Jonas O'Donnell is a problem that won't go away on its own. Which means Sadie O'Donnell will be emotionally compromised. Which weakens the Charge. If she flies off to her dear husband, he brings his warpath to a halt. And the Charge will be left on a more solid foundation with stronger leadership."

"You?" Vincent guffawed.

"It is my brainchild, after all. As is this entire scheme. At the end of the day, we're back on track. We still need to take on this Arnoud in Philadelphia, but I'm already formulating a plan for that."

"I'm sure you are." Vincent shook his head. "I can't

condone this. We'd be sending Sadie off to her death. Or worse—Ithaca."

"I appreciate your sentiment, Vincent, but she's one person. How many more will benefit? It's a matter of weighing the cost versus the benefit."

"It's not a damned business account. And besides that, it will only buy us some time. I've been up close and personal with the man. Jonas isn't going to suddenly go all sunshine and daisies and skip off into the sunset with his long-lost wife. He'll deal with her as quickly and efficiently as possible, then he'll be back."

Galloway sighed. "Well, I can't force you to agree with me. I mean…I could." He chuckled. "But that's not something I would ever do."

"So you keep saying."

Galloway sneered. "Do you feel as if I've sway pinched you? Here you are telling me no. Listen, I don't require your trust."

"That's good, because you don't have it."

"Touché. But we're both intelligent men, capable of making complicated decisions. I want you to think about what I said about Sadie. Weigh the costs. Consider the benefits. That's all I ask."

A knock on the door captured Galloway's attention.

"Come."

Maria stepped inside holding a piece of paper. "Message from Baltimore."

Galloway glanced at Vincent, then took the paper. He reached for his spectacles to read the note. His eyes swept left-to-right several times as a smile lifted onto his face.

"Well, looks like you'll have to think on it quickly. Sadie O'Donnell has requested a summit."

* * *

VINCENT NODDED TO HATTIE, who stood behind Sadie at the wood table between her and Galloway. There was barely room for that table and six more people inside the dairy farmhouse kitchen they'd secured to hold this meeting. A brick fireplace crackled just behind Vincent, warming his back while gray clouds rolled past the tiny crooked window beside them. Floorboards creaked as everyone not seated at the table shifted on their feet. Cows raised a ruckus in the barn just outside the farmhouse as it was time for the evening milking.

Sadie sat rigid, eyes glaring forward. Hattie and Ghasawi stood behind her, Hattie with a hand on her shoulder.

Galloway, for his part, was filled with energy. He nodded to himself as he read over Sadie's proposal, written in print on a long sheet of paper like a legal document. To Vincent's left, Millie and Douglas huddled shoulder-to-shoulder, chastised, no doubt, by Galloway into top-shelf behavior, lest their presence ruin the tone of the summit.

Galloway removed his spectacles and smiled. "I'm happy to agree to these terms, with only a few minor amendments."

"No changes," Sadie said in a calm voice.

He nodded again, making easing gestures. "Perhaps I might make my case. Herein, you state that no one under my direct oversight will be allowed within the city or county of Baltimore. The major east-west arteries to Philadelphia and Wilmington run through Baltimore County. This would curtail our free movement, particularly as we'll be focusing on Vito Corbi's properties in Havre de Grace."

Sadie repeated, "No changes."

"Well, then…let's shelve that and move forward. Here, you claim free access to the B&O railway through western Maryland and West Virginia. This runs in contradiction to this proviso…" he pointed to a paragraph near the top of the document, "…which declares a five-mile buffer zone between all of our separate operations. The B&O runs directly through Cumberland, where we have already purchased property for a new safehouse. Clearly we cannot abide by this restriction without selling the property and moving the entire—"

"No. Changes." Sadie glared at Galloway, eyes alive with hatred.

Galloway snickered. "Sarah Jane, you really must try to meet me halfway. I'm being quite reasonable."

"Then we're done here."

She moved to stand, but Hattie leaned down to whisper something in her ear. Sadie released an impatient breath, then sat back down.

Galloway shook his head. "How can we expect to coexist if you won't listen to me?"

"I don't expect to coexist, Honor. I expect you to continue lying and lying. I expect you to push this hopeless war with the mob to its inevitable conclusion. And when you and your hotheads are dead, I expect to continue saving lives. All I'm asking here today is that you leave the dying to your own people and leave us out of your fight."

"It's your fight as well," Galloway informed her. "Whether or not you accept that fact. Our lives will continue to be reduced to that of cattle as long as we allow the masters to continue their reign. This isn't about me. It's about all of us."

Sadie slapped the table. "It's only ever been about you, Honor! It wasn't enough simply to escape Chicago, you had to strike back at him. Just as we had freedom in our hands, you were ready to throw it away."

"It failed because you left me to fight alone," he grumbled.

"We told you we weren't going to fight. You chose to go in anyway!"

Galloway folded his hands together. "Do you know why I called it the 'Charge' in the first place? Because I found the lives and destinies of pinchers across the world to be my personal charge. Responsibility." He leaned in. "I take responsibility for our plight. I won't duck and cover, hoping and praying that some higher power will come and even accounts. That will never happen."

A tense silence fell over the room.

Galloway lifted a hand. "We've come to this table as enemies, when we should be friends." He waved at the document. "This is not a treaty of cooperation, but of separation. What are we doing, here?"

Sadie did not respond, though her eyes were less hard, and more sober.

Galloway pushed away from the table. "Allow me to be the first to extend a gesture of goodwill. There is something you should know, Sarah Jane. Something that lesser minds might keep from you."

Vincent held a breath, then leaned down to Galloway's ear to whisper, "Don't."

Galloway lifted a hand. "This is no place for whispers, Vincent. Not anymore. We must be open and honest one with another."

Sadie shook her head. "What?"

Hattie stiffened as she caught up with what was about to happen.

Galloway stated, "Jonas is alive. And he's in Harrisburg."

Sadie sat still, slowly unfolding her arms.

Galloway nodded with mawkish contrition. "He is looking for you. I don't know why, but he seems highly motivated. I thought you should know."

Sadie leaned back in her seat. "More lies."

"No," Galloway asserted with a vigorous shake of his head. "He's with a party of soldiers from his keeper in New York and he's sweeping south. I believe he's trying to locate you personally."

Sadie shook her head with a dry laugh, then frowned. "You're unbelievable. Do you really think you can rattle me by invoking Jonas's name? How dare you?"

Vincent flexed his bandaged hand. He watched as Sadie gathered herself to leave. A wave of disgust swept through him. How dare Galloway? This was an outright ploy by him to send Sadie rushing off to save her husband from the influence of Ithaca. But he'd been straight with Vincent about this being his plan.

"It's true," Galloway said. "Tell her, Vincent. Tell her I'm not lying."

Vincent sucked in a breath as Sadie looked at him. Damn Galloway all to hell and back. "It's true," he grudgingly admitted. "I saw him. And I nearly died. One of my friends has died."

Sadie sneered at Vincent, then looked up to Hattie.

Hattie sighed, then nodded. "Aye. It seems so."

Sadie's face wilted. "And…no one felt the need to inform me of this fact?"

Galloway clucked soothingly. "There was concern for your well-being."

Another tense moment descended upon the room. And then, Sadie laughed. "That is so pathetic."

"I'm only being honest," Galloway told her.

"No, you're being stupid," Sadie replied. "Like my friends here, you've made a colossal error of judgment." Sadie reached up to grip Hattie's hand. "You all think I'm ready to throw everything away and rush off to Harrisburg to save Jonas. That's it, isn't it? Why you didn't tell me?"

Hattie nodded in misery.

"Well," Sadie declared, "I'm happy to inform you that I'm not quite that stupid. I know what those beasts did to Jonas. My husband is gone. What they've left inside his skin is just one more monster ready to kill our friends."

Sadie thrust a finger across the table at Galloway. "That's it, right? You figured I'd get caught up in some womanly vapor, rushing off to save my husband from the evil of this world? All while you wait for me to end up with a length of steel through head, or in the clutches of Ithaca? Please. You're not my equal, Honor. You never were. And this is exactly why. You continually underestimate the strength and moral quality of those you look down upon."

Vincent looked to Galloway. He simply sat rigid in his seat. Whether Galloway was willing to use his powers against other pinchers regardless of his assurances otherwise, or whether he was a genius at manipulating loyalties, he clearly wasn't a man he wanted to follow into battle, or anywhere.

But what choice did he really have?

Sadie pointed to the document on the table. "This was never a negotiation. These are my demands. I expect you to abide by them. If you don't, I'll consider it an act of war." She stood up, pushing her chair politely back under the table. "We are done here."

She turned with a nod to Hattie and Ghasawi.

Hattie glanced over at Vincent and he stepped around the table, refusing to look back at the others as he followed her out the door.

CHAPTER 24

*H*attie lifted her head to the unseasonably warm breeze flowing along Curtis Creek and watched as Vincent peeled off his jacket.

Raymond slung four lengths of framing lumber over his shoulder, pausing to kick aside a pile of offal as he nodded to the pair of them. "Almost like spring decided to show up?" he bellowed.

Vincent nodded. "Too soon for this, if you ask me. Gonna be a hot summer."

Raymond shrugged, lifting the lumber several inches beneath his muscular shoulder. "I can take the heat."

Vincent laughed. "Yeah, I'm well aware."

As Raymond carried the lumber to a brace of neighbors who were sawing the wood for the new buildings rising from the ashes of the shacks the Bianco Fiore had ruined, Hattie stepped up behind Vincent.

"Time for a break, boy-o."

Vincent grinned over at her. "Good. I'm trying to play it tough here, but I'm gonna have to sit down."

Hattie watched as Vincent tossed aside his jacket and sat,

catching her breath as her eyes drank in the view. This man had been at times a pain in her ass, and at times her best friend, but even when she was ready to slap him upside the head, she still thought he was the most gorgeous man she'd ever seen.

Better looking than Rudolph Valentino, in her opinion.

"I forgot to tell you," Vincent commented, obviously unaware of where her thoughts had drifted. "Lefty has a man who's willing to donate some plaster and lath. You got anyone who knows how to plaster?"

Hattie shrugged. "I don't even know what the hell lath is."

"It's a sort of wire mesh. You push the plaster into the lath so that it—"

She eased down onto Vincent's lap, grabbed him by the shirt and pulled his mouth to hers.

When they parted, she smirked. "And I couldn't give the first piss what lath is."

She went to get up, only to find herself held firmly on Vincent's lap.

"Oh, no. You're staying right here," he said with a grin.

She squirmed. "Am I now?"

"Yes." He hissed out a breath. "Stop moving around. That's not fair."

"It's totally fair." She pulled him in for another kiss, gasping against his mouth as he leaned back and pulled her down on top of him.

"That's better," he said, rearranging her weight across his chest and hips.

"Hey!" Her protest was half-hearted. Raymond was busy, as was Nadine. The others sawing wood and nailing boards were out of view and occupied with their work. There was no one to see them, no one to notice a little bit of indiscretion in the field. She kissed him again, losing herself in the taste of his mouth against hers, the feel of his hands cupping her rear. When they pulled apart, she wiggled a bit upright, checking to make sure no one was watching as she tried to turn herself to straddle him.

Vincent's browed screwed into a question. "What's wrong?"

"Just trying to…shift…"

He grabbed her hips and held her still. "Uh, no. Not here. Raymond sees us like that and he'll pound me to a pulp."

She scowled. "Raymond's over by the houses."

"And he could be back any second." He sat up, her still on his lap. "This really isn't proper, you know."

"Of course, it isn't." She shoved him with a playful push. "There's nothing proper about what I'm feeling."

He smirked. "Well then, let's not be proper." This time it was him kissing her. When they parted, she reached up to touch his face.

His dark eyes met hers. "I love you," he whispered.

What? She felt herself blush, heard herself stammering something unintelligible.

"Sorry." He turned his head to kiss her hand. "I didn't mean to lay that out there with no warning or anything. I do, though. I love you."

"I…I…" She stared at him.

"I'm being honest." He smiled. "And I've been a stupid sap to avoid saying it. Maybe I needed to grow up enough to say it out loud, but I've felt this way ever since…"

"When?" she asked, finally getting a coherent word out.

"That's a good question. I don't know. I mean, I knew before you busted me from Ithaca. Probably when you first slapped me on that boat." He laughed.

"What…what…"

He reached up to tangle his fingers in her hair. "I want a future with us together. Forever. With you. But I'm owned by the Crew and as long as they're here in Baltimore with a noose around my neck, I can't have what I want with you. That's why I was siding with Galloway. I thought if his army took out the Crew, then we could finally have a life together —a free life."

She leaned her forehead against his for a moment. "Vincent, you almost died up in Pennsylvania with DeBarre. Every time you leave, I worry you might not come back. I don't want to wait for all the stars to align. I don't want there to be any regrets if something happens. I want you now."

"Your mother would have a fit," he warned. "I'm not only a gangster, I'm owned by the mob, an owned pincher."

She leaned forward to kiss him again. "I've told you before, I don't give a damn what my mother thinks."

"Well I do. And I'm not about to have someone walk up on us rolling around in the grass," he teased.

"Oh, I'm sure you're more concerned about what rolling in the grass might do to your clothes," she teased back. Then she took a deep breath. "I love you, too."

There. She'd known it for months, but somehow saying the words out loud had been one of the most terrifying things she'd ever done.

"Good." He gave her a quick kiss. "Now that's settled, we need to think about how we're going to handle the bomb that's about to drop on us."

Hattie grimaced. "Which bomb? Galloway? Or Jonas O'Donnell?"

"Both, but I think the more immediate cause for concern is Jonas O'Donnell."

Hattie sighed. "Aye."

"I know everyone likes to talk about how plum a fellow he was before...but I can tell you from experience, the man he was is not the thing he is now. He's a walking nightmare. If he attacks Baltimore, I'm not sure we can handle him without Galloway's pinchers."

"I don't see that we have much choice. We can't trust Galloway."

Vincent nodded. "You know, I think he's been using his powers on me? Nothing as extreme as mind control, but just a subtle persuasion thing. It's unsettling."

"He's a known liar, boy-o."

"Right. But that doesn't change the fact that he has more manpower than we do. And the man is quick to adapt. If we're on the wrong side of his ledger, we might end up facing his people *and* O'Donnell at the same time from two fronts. And the only other force in the city is the Crew."

Hattie's scowled. "So, you're saying it's time to pick sides?"

"I know. I can't accept that it's come to this either. The Crew, or Galloway? Shall we flip a coin?"

"How about we pick neither?" Hattie asked. "Perhaps it's time we stopped looking at this in terms of choosing sides."

"What do you mean?"

She waved a hand around them. "We've taken all of this as it comes. You've already told me you're ready to work toward a future without Corbi and the Crew."

Vincent nodded.

"I'll admit, all this talk from Galloway about a state for free pinchers lit a candle inside me. Now, I'm with Sadie—I think Galloway's too quick to throw lives away. But perhaps Sadie's been too reluctant to act. I was tempted by her ways of keeping her head down and skulking in the shadows. It's how I've lived my life."

"And I was tempted by Galloway's 'shoot first' philosophy. It's how I've lived my life."

"What if the truth is somewhere in the middle?" Hattie asked. "And it's not up to either Sadie or Galloway to see it through? What if it's up to us?"

Vincent smiled. "I don't know, Malloy. Sounds like a lot of work."

She smiled back, realizing that this felt more right than anything had in the last week. "I'm up for it."

"Okay," he declared. "We take the best of both sides. Still leaves us with an army of rogue pinchers ready to kill anyone who stands in their way."

"Hearts and minds," Hattie said with a smirk. "We use Galloway's tricks against him."

"And the crack-skulled iron pincher storming south?"

Her smile thinned. "Aye. I'm still working on that."

"It's going to be more difficult without Philadelphia to back us up. We still have Arnoud, but he's Ithaca-minded. Loyal to the system, and Sabella. It'll probably shake their alliance with Baltimore."

"Think he'll side with New York and bring Philadelphia back into the fold?"

Vincent thought on it, and then looked up at the trees.

Hattie shifted as his face took that look he got when an idea grabbed him by the ears. "What?"

"That's how we do it."

"Do what?"

Vincent smiled at Hattie. "How we get Sadie and Galloway back at the table."

CHAPTER 25

Sadie stared at Hattie and Vincent from across her desk. "You're joking."

Hattie shrugged. "It'sa gamble, to be sure."

"The situation is essentially the same," Vincent told her. "Two halves of the Charge can't coexist with two leaders. And he has more manpower."

Hattie said, "We need everyone on the same side."

Sadie sneered. "He had a chance."

Vincent said with a lift of his finger, "What he lacked was motivation. He was focused so thoroughly on taking over the Charge and boosting you out, he's lost sight of his long view. Which was always taking out the mob structure on the East Coast."

Sadie shrugged. "So?"

"So," Hattie said, "your husband changes that."

Sadie closed her eyes and took a cleansing breath. "I know you two were eager to avoid mentioning him. And what I said at the farmhouse still holds. I'm under no delusions of saving him."

Hattie rolled her eyes. "That's not what I meant."

"I get it," Sadie said. "Common enemy. Galvanize Honor's forces against Jonas. But that doesn't put us on the same side. It only points us in the same direction."

Vincent said, "Not if Jonas strikes first, and we come to the rescue."

Sadie shook her head. "Why would I do that?"

"Because," Hattie said, "it won't be Jonas doing the attacking."

Sadie leaned back and took a sip of hooch.

"During the war, American airmen would paint German insignia on their aircraft to draw the enemy alongside," Vincent told her. "It's an old trick from the days of pirates, a false flag tactic." He leaned forward to tap his finger on the desktop. "Galloway is a planner. He has plans within plans. And he's a quick thinker. I say we use that against him. We drum up a party to attack the cabin. Hattie uses her illusions to make it look like Jonas' men."

Hattie nodded. "Then we swoop in and save the day."

Vincent concluded, "Galloway sees Jonas as a direct threat, and we become his best option. If we can't trust the man, we can trust his predictability."

Sadie rolled it over as her brow furrowed. "And where do we drum up this party to go waging war? We don't have any hands on deck, not that I would be willing to send them if we did."

Hattie smiled. "That's the beauty of it all. We won't be the ones doing the attacking. It'll be the third side of the coin."

Vincent said, "The Crew."

"Vincent can drop the right words in the right ears. They're ready for war with Masseria, anyhow. They're mobilized and armed. It'll only take a nudge."

Sadie squinted at Vincent. "You're willing to do that?"

"I am," Vincent replied.

"So, I'm not committing any lives to this pitch battle of yours?" Sadie smirked. "Is it a bad thing that I'm hoping the Crew and Galloway's people take each other out?"

Hattie shrugged. "I can't blame you for that. But if there must be fighting to do, might as well be the enemy doing the fighting."

Sadie tapped the top of the desk with a finger. "Here's where it can all go wrong. First, your illusions might not be convincing. What if Honor sees right through this scheme of yours?"

"It *is* a gamble," Hattie admitted.

"But waiting for Jonas to arrive is no gamble," Vincent said. "It'll happen, and it'll be lights out."

"Put your words in the right ears, Calendo. And welcome to the Charge," Sadie said with a smirk.

Hattie walked him to the front door. "Are you ready to betray your masters, boy-o?"

"I've been ready to betray my masters since Ithaca." He paused, a flicker of doubt rushing across his face. "But I'll have to be careful."

"That's a given."

They stood for a moment gazing into each other's eyes.

Finally, Vincent reached for the door. As he stepped through, he nearly bowled into a figure looming just outside.

Hattie reached to steady Vincent by the arm as she gasped.

Charley peered at Hattie with sunken eyes. His clothes were dusty and disheveled, face covered in grime.

Hattie eased Vincent aside. "Charley?" She patted Vincent's arm. "Go. I'll tend to this."

Vincent stepped away, leaving Charley standing outside the door in emotional turmoil.

"Well, then," Hattie said. "You're back."

The ragged man began to weep silently in front of Hattie, hands covering his face.

"Where'd you fly off to?" she asked.

Between breaths, he replied, "Zanesville."

"Oh?" She turned to check behind her. Blake filled the doorway, hand behind the door, likely with a rifle in it. "And?"

Charley sniffled and rubbed his sleeves over his face. "They…they're okay."

"Your girls?"

"I…watched. For a while. New clothes. They were playing with dolls."

A flood of relief swept through Hattie's chest. "That's good, Charley. I'm happy for you."

He blinked miserably up at the warehouse. "I know I don't deserve any respect. Not from you. Or from Sadie. And I don't expect forgiveness. But I thought you all should know our people are okay."

Hattie nodded. "And you think that excuses Galloway? Because he told the truth?"

Charley shook his head.

Hattie stepped forward, causing him to hop back. "Easy. I'm not the enemy."

"I almost got you killed. I thought I had. I didn't know. I just ran."

"Do you remember when we first met, Charley? You were running then, too. And I helped you out of that tight spot, didn't I?"

He nodded.

"Do you think I've changed so much since then? That I'd turn my back on someone who needs my help?"

"But I—"

"But nothing," she said, turning for the door.

She spotted Sadie watching the scene over Blake's shoulder. The woman gave her a cautious nod.

Hattie smiled, then patted Charley's arm. "Get inside, animal boy."

Blake gave Charley a wide berth as he stepped back into the warehouse. Sadie stood in the center of the anteroom, hands on her hips.

"Zanesville's no fraud?" Sadie asked.

Charley stood frozen in contrition for a moment, then nodded. "It's like he said it was. They all got food and beds. Windows. It's all out in the country and there's no one breathing down their necks."

Sadie sighed. "Alright, then. Get yourself cleaned up."

Charley cast a glance around the room. "Am... I should go."

"You should do no such thing," Sadie declared. "A lot's happened in the past couple days. It's more dangerous than ever, and we need your help."

Charley slumped a little, fresh tears flowing from his eyes.

Sadie gestured to Blake. "Help him out. I think the boiler's working again, so he can get a hot bath."

Blake escorted Charley into the rear of the building where they kept the washrooms.

Hattie leaned against the door, glancing at Sadie. "If Galloway was telling the truth about Zanesville, he might have done the same with Eden."

"We can't assume anything," Sadie said.

"You sent Orson a letter?"

"I did, but our arrangement out west makes it so that he gets our mail in dead drops. It could be weeks until we hear back."

"It'll be quicker if one of us just goes and checks for ourselves."

Sadie frowned. "Fat chance, with Honor circling the Charge like a buzzard."

"Unless our plan works."

"What are our odds, do you think?"

Hattie squinted toward the washrooms. "Actually, I think they've just improved."

CHAPTER 26

*L*efty sipped coffee from a tin cup, his collar pulled high over his neck as he stared over the top of his car down the forest path leading to Galloway's hunting cabin.

"I don't like it."

Vincent pulled his hat off his face, peering up at Lefty from inside the car. "What don't you like?"

"Masseria's men hit us in Morgantown, then on the Bay, then they hit the Philly boys up in Harrisburg. Now they're here outside of Waynesboro? There's no pattern here."

"Maybe that's the point?" Vincent offered. "Hit and fade. Keep us guessing."

"I guess. Maybe I'm just gun-shy after what went down at Winnow's Slip. They still got the same people, you think? The earth pincher and the man with the cannon arms?"

"And a couple more, I think," Vincent replied, trying to find the fine line to pilot this complicated gamble. "We were caught flatfooted last couple times. Now we have the drop on them."

Lefty tossed his empty cup back into the car. "I can't believe we got this much muscle outta Vito."

Vincent stepped out of the car, turning to face a line of six cars loaded with hardware and Crew men. "It'll be enough."

"You're confident today."

Vincent said with a shrug, "Because I know something you don't."

Lefty gave Vincent a hard stare. "Which is?"

"I have someone on the inside."

"And you're only now telling me?"

"I'm gonna check our forward eyes. Look for the signal."

Lefty rolled his eyes. "Remember when I used to be the one calling the shots?"

"Good times," Vincent said with a smirk as he trotted up the path and into the deeper forest.

The lane took two bends as it approached the cabin. He spotted two of the Crew gunmen hunkered behind wide tree trunks, one with a pair of field glasses. He crept up to them, shuffling lightly through the leaves on the forest floor.

"Any changes?" he asked.

The man with the field glasses replied, "Same sentry."

"The girl?"

"Yeah."

"Wait for the signal," he urged, slipping across the lane to dive into the thick of the brush. He slid between waist-high shrubs and trees, rounding the double-hillock on the west side of the cabin.

Two figures rested on the ground, looking up at Vincent as he huddled beside them.

"Millie's on patrol," Hattie whispered. "I know the wood pincher's inside. He's come out for a smoke once already."

"Is Galloway inside?"

"Most likely," she replied. "Haven't seen any faces at the window."

Vincent glanced over Hattie's back at Charley. "You know the scam?"

He nodded. "I never came back to the Charge. I saw Jones marching with his men this direction."

"Jonas," Vincent corrected. "And you shouldn't know his name. Just say the big guy who bends iron."

"Last time I did this sorta thing, they had someone hit me to make it look convincing."

Hattie scowled. "I think we can skip that bit."

"Alright," Charley said. "Is it time?"

Vincent checked his pocket watch, then the sky above. "As good a time as any."

Charley eyed Hattie.

"Break a leg," she whispered.

He nodded. His entire body popped and shriveled, clothes and everything, into a tiny bundle of fur. Vincent blinked rapidly as the mouse Charley had become scampered over the hillock and through the undergrowth toward the cabin.

"It'll be sunset before he reaches the cabin," he grumbled.

Hattie snickered. "Think it hurts when he does that?"

"I guess not. Doesn't hurt when I pinch time. Unless I do it too long."

"Wonder what hurts him, then?" she mused.

"I guess if he turns himself into a sperm whale, or something?"

She chuckle-snorted.

"I don't have to ask you if you know the scam," Vincent said.

"Charley gets inside, whips Galloway into a stiff peak. Then we signal your goons to come riding in."

"You don't have to pinch much. Pick a man and turn him into Jonas."

She sighed. "It'd help if I had more than one old photograph to go on."

Vincent nodded. Sadie had pulled a photograph from her keepsake box to show Hattie. The man was always large, but the eyes he saw in that photograph were markedly softer than the steel traps he saw in Harrisburg.

"Just give him a tight beard, and it'll be enough. They're gonna be in a panic, anyways."

"Then we let the fight run its course?" She glanced up at Vincent. "What about Lefty? Won't he be in harm's way?"

Vincent swallowed hard. "Don't worry about him. That's my job."

The Charley mouse slipped beneath the cabin door, and Vincent pulled his revolver.

"Ready?" he muttered.

"Give it a second," Hattie urged.

Millie turned to the cabin as voices raised inside. She reached for the door, opening it to check.

"Now," Hattie whispered.

Vincent lifted the gun into the air and fired two shots.

He pressed hard against the ground as a ray of bright light swept over the hillock searching for the source of the sound.

More voices from the cabin.

Motors roared up the lane.

Shouts from below.

The ray of light swept away from Vincent and Hattie's position.

Vincent rose to a crouch to survey the scene. The Crew hitmen were sweeping into the clearing in front of the cabin. Millie had hammered them with a burst of light, sending the first car fishtailing, blocking the path for the rest.

Douglas had stepped out of the cabin, his arms stretched out, hands gnarling into claws.

A series of popping sounds rifled through the forest as the trees on either side of the forest lane lurched to the side, sending boughs smashing into the approaching vehicles.

Gunfire erupted, spraying the front of the cabin as Millie tackled Douglas to take cover.

"Got your mark?" Vincent asked.

Hattie lifted a shushing finger as she concentrated on weaving her illusion, turning one of the hapless Crew men into the mirage of Jonas O'Donnell.

Millie and Douglas scrambled back for the cabin door. A figure leapt from inside the cabin, hurling a sofa into the fishtailed vehicle, smashing its windows as it landed.

"Ernie's home," Vincent grumbled.

More gunfire answered Ernie's attack.

Vincent spotted Lefty near the center of the motorcade, gesturing orders, sending gunmen into the forest to surround the cabin.

"Time I showed my face," Vincent said. "Good luck!"

She nodded briskly, face focused on her illusion.

Vincent rushed through the forest, pausing as Lefty's flankers lifted a gun to him.

"It's me!" he blurted.

They nodded and proceeded around him.

When Vincent reached Lefty, most of the Crew were busy reloading their weapons.

"Situation?" he shouted.

Lefty nodded to the cabin. "The limey's there. And the two you mentioned. No sight of the earth pincher, yet."

The ground rumbled, rattling the cars as a tremor shook the forest. Loud cracks filled the air as granite spikes shot up into the undercarriages of the front vehicles.

Vincent pinched time as Lefty's car pitched into the air. He reached for Lefty, guiding him back to the ground and restoring time as the car heaved with a spear of granite.

Lefty sucked in a breath, then nodded to Vincent. "Glad you're on my side."

The gangsters circling the cabin opened fire, pocking the

lumber siding and smashing the sole window. Ernie withdrew back into the cabin, head down.

"Looks like we got them pinned down," Lefty declared.

"Watch for more earthquakes. She doesn't need to see us coming to use that."

Lefty holstered his gun and lifted fingers to his mouth to let rip a loud whistle.

Two men from the rear truck slipped out and reached into the bed to pull a crate each. They looked like the same crates the Crew boosted illegal wine in. They lugged the crates up to the line. As they passed, Vincent spotted several bottles within each crate, jingling together with a clear liquid inside.

"What's this?" Vincent asked.

"Not taking chances," Lefty said.

"What's going on?"

The front line pulled several bottles, handing them down the line as men stuffed rags into the throats.

Vincent's stomach twisted. "You're burning them out?"

"Burning them down," Lefty said. "End of the threat, unless any of them are fireproof, which I doubt."

"You don't think that's overkill?"

Lefty squinted at Vincent. "You were there at Winnow's, right? We're ending this now."

Vincent shook his head as Lefty gave the signal to light the rags. This had moved faster than Vincent had figured. Galloway was being sluggish, barely organizing his people. Was this some ploy? Or had they truly gotten the drop on Galloway?

Still, though...he didn't intend for Galloway's group to perish from this. And Charley was inside. Had he just confirmed all of the bias Sadie and the others had saddled him with? Wiping out a group of talented pinchers with the mob just to preserve himself?

As the front line hoisted their flaming bottle bombs, a thump rattled the ground. Several of the front line lost their balance. Two or three bottles dropped from their hands, landing on the ground, spilling their contents in a flaming puddle.

As a Crew thug backpedaled away from the spreading fire, he slipped and smashed his bottle against one of the granite spikes that had impaled a vehicle.

Chaos unfurled as screams spread through the front line.

Two bottles, however, made it into the air. They sailed onto the cabin roof. One bounced and rolled off. The other, however, managed to spill its oil onto the roof, catching the eave aflame. It wouldn't be long for the entire structure to burn.

Lefty swore sharply and rushed forward to pull the men not set on fire away from the burning vehicle.

Vincent pinched time, the flickering blazes before him eerily reminiscent of his encounter with the demon over the winter. Something had to be done, or everyone inside that building would either emerge to the Crew's gunfire or burn alive.

He took his moment in the time bubble to think.

They'd expected this fight to last longer. It was always the plan to bring up the rear and act as cavalry once the Crew had softened up Galloway. But would Hattie know to trigger the next step of the plan this early?

Vincent bounded into the forest, legs churning to propel him forward as far as his powers could keep the time pinch alive. Every step he took in frozen time was a second he'd spare those inside the cabin.

He made it only a couple dozen yards before the pull of the time pinch chewed at his guts. He dropped the time pinch and the shouts from inside and outside the cabin rushed into his ears. Gunshots rang out from the motorcade.

Something large smashed through the front of the cabin tumbling into the burning gangsters. Vincent caught sight of it enough to recognize it was Galloway's desk, likely tossed by Ernie as a means to escape.

Vincent rounded the double hillock, gasping for air as his insides churned.

Hattie was already in a crouch position.

"Where the bloody hell is Galloway?" she spat.

"Think he's inside?"

"If he is, he's put his head in the sand."

Vincent nodded to the flames. "They're gonna get burned alive or chopped down if we don't do something. Bring the Feds."

"Already?" Hattie asked.

"No choice."

Hattie nodded. "Alright, but if the Crew don't bite, we're in trouble."

"Gotta risk it. Go."

Hattie closed her eyes and lifted her hands.

Vincent sat beside her, the illusions she conjured invisible to him. As he piqued his ears, the gunshots subsided.

New shouts, now. Not of pain, but of panic.

Motors kicked to life.

Vincent ventured a glance past the top of the hillock down to the line of cars. Three were ruined, one threatening to burn the forest down as it licked fire. The rest had turned three points, ready to retreat.

Lefty lingered at the rear, eyes working the forest in a panic.

Vincent swore under his breath. Lefty would have to choose to leave without him. That was unfair.

As Crew gunmen shouted back at Lefty, and the front car sped off, Lefty's face dropped. He jumped into the car and beat the side for the driver to go.

The cars rumbled up the lane and out of sight, leaving the sound of crackling flames and fatigued lumber.

Hattie trembled as sweat poured off her brow.

Vincent nudged her shoulder. "We're good."

She opened her eyes with a loud gasp, sucking in air as the toll of her illusion ravaged her body.

Vincent jumped up, rushing for the front of the cabin. The entire roof was aflame at this point. He trotted around the wrecked front of the building, where Ernie had thrown Galloway's desk. The roof framing had collapsed, spilling more flames into the interior.

Vincent tried pinching time, but he couldn't find a way into the building before his guts twisted too much for him to maintain the effect.

"Ernie!" he shouted, cupping his hands around his mouth. "Can you hear me?"

He didn't receive a response.

"Break out the north wall. No flames there."

A voice shouted from behind Vincent. "No, don't!"

Vincent spun around to find Sadie behind him.

"What are you—?"

Sadie ignored Vincent, shouting to the cabin, "The rest of the frame's already weakened. You'll bring the whole damn thing down on your heads!"

Vincent shook his head. She was right. Brute force would just kill them.

"Any thoughts?" Vincent whispered.

"Just one." She glanced to him. "This is gonna hurt like hell, so make sure I get all the credit."

Vincent cocked a brow at her as she lifted her hands in front of her.

A cloud of mist rushed out of Sadie's nostrils as she pursed her lips. It was a brisk spring day, but not cold enough for that.

Right.

Ice pincher.

Frost gathered on the tips of Sadie's fingers as her arms trembled. The mist rushing from her nose spilled over her arms, flowing into the air like a cognizant fog. As the fog thickened, pooling around the flames, Sadie released a pained scream. The woman sank to her knees, eyes bare slits as pellets of ice rushed from her hands. The flames dulled, the ice pellets sizzling against the burning lumber. The front of the cabin shimmered in a frosty rime, the fire on the roof subsiding enough to expose charred timbers.

With a grunt, Sadie pitched face-first onto the ground.

Vincent rushed to the frost-coated cabin wreckage, kicking aside some angled timbers.

"Calendo?" a voice called from inside.

"I'm here."

Ernie's voice replied, "Best step aside!"

Vincent complied as the snow-laden timbers shattered. An enormous figure bowled through the wreckage. Vincent squinted as that figure, a massive black bear, released a pained roar.

Ernie followed close behind, Douglas and Maria under each arm.

Millie staggered through the wreckage Charley had cleared for them, slipping on a slick of ice. Vincent reached to catch her, pulling her away from the cabin as the timber groaned and creaked. The embers on the rear of the building sprayed into the air as the north wall collapsed, the roof crumbling into the cabin.

Vincent checked Millie, who gave him a quick nod, then turned to find Charley face-down on the ground. He rushed forward to check on Charley. He was breathing, but unconscious. Same with Sadie.

Ernie took a knee beside Maria, who rubbed her head. A

long soot mark slashed across her face. "She took a beam to the nut. Nearly knocked her out."

Vincent pointed to Douglas. "And him?"

"Poor blighter overextended himself with the trees."

Vincent glanced back down the lane, now a nightmarish scene of cars speared on granite spikes and trees bent in half, their boughs slammed into the lane.

Ernie lay a gentle hand on Vincent's shoulder. "You couldn't have come at a more opportune moment. I thought we were fully nicked."

Vincent nodded to Sadie. "Thank her."

"Well, we're in your debt. That's for certain!"

"Where's Galloway?" Vincent asked, scanning the area.

"Off on a meet and greet, I'm afraid. Just like him to miss all the fun."

Hattie stumbled over the hillock, eyes wide. She rushed down the slope, sliding alongside Sadie to check on her.

Maria mumbled, "How…"

"Hmm?"

"How'd you chase Jonas off?"

Vincent shrugged. "Old trick, really. Same we used on you at Winnow's Slip."

Ernie chuckled. "The Feds? That was an illusion? Well played, old sport!"

They gathered the wounded and weak, pulling everyone clear of both fires. Before nightfall, Sadie had come to, as had Charley. Hattie gave Sadie a solid tongue-lashing while Vincent checked Charley's head.

"Gave yourself a good bump," Vincent said, running his fingers over Charley's scalp.

The fur pincher shrugged. "Just because I'm big, doesn't mean it won't smart like hell."

"You did good," Vincent whispered.

"We did," Charley corrected.

The sound of a motor pulled Vincent to his feet. He joined Ernie and Hattie as they walked past the ruined vehicles and tree limbs to greet a vehicle driven by Galloway.

He parked the car and stepped out, eyes wide. "What the hell has happened?"

Vincent waved generally around himself. "Jonas is what happened."

Ernie nodded. "He came storming the gates. Nearly had us all roasting on a spit until this lot showed up."

Galloway glanced past Vincent and Hattie at Sadie, huddled on the ground with knees to her chest.

"Jonas? He was here?" Galloway squinted. "How?"

Vincent shrugged. "What matters is he's gone, and everyone's alive."

Galloway surveyed the scene, mouth clamped shut, jaw tensed. He took in the ruined cars, the remains of his desk smoldering along with two corpses. He came to a halt in front of Sadie.

"Sarah Jane?"

"Honor."

"It appears I owe you."

He offered her a hand. She took it, getting to her feet.

"How did you know?" he asked as he escorted her to the others.

"You're not the only one with eyes and ears, Honor," she replied through a dry cough.

Handing her off to Hattie, Galloway addressed Vincent. "So, Jonas has made a target of us both."

"Looks that way," Vincent replied.

Galloway looked Vincent in the eye, his face twisting in thought.

"Listen, Galloway," Vincent said, "we can't afford this tug of war over the Charge. Not with that man hounding us both."

Galloway nodded slowly.

"Do you think we can call a truce? Work together...truly together?"

Galloway turned to Sadie. "What say you?"

Sadie nodded. "I know Jonas. He won't stop. He'll keep coming until none of us are left."

Galloway offered a thin smile, then shook Sadie's hand. "A truce it is. We work together."

Vincent stifled a sigh as the last piece of the plan fell into place.

Galloway withdrew with Ernie to gather his people to his car. Vincent stood beside Sadie, propping her up.

"Didn't trust the plan?" Vincent muttered with a smirk.

Sadie coughed. "I trusted it about as well as I should have."

"I didn't think you could use your powers outside of winter."

"It's a bad idea," she said. "Just cold enough today to pull it off. If I tried that on a warm summer day, it'd send me straight to the grave."

"Well, I'm glad you came."

She squeezed his shoulder. "Thank me when we've beaten Jonas."

Hattie called from behind, "I assume you drove here? Which means you have a car?"

"I do. And if you're nice to me, I'll even let you ride back to Baltimore in it!"

CHAPTER 27

Alton spooned some sugar onto his bowl of oatmeal, stirring it while avoiding eye contact with Hattie.

"That's quite enough sugar, Alton," Branna groused from the seat between them.

He nodded, sipped his coffee, then reached for the sugar again.

"Oy! What did I just say?" Branna snapped.

Alton pulled his hand away and stirred his oatmeal again.

Hattie watched from the under her lashes as she ate.

Alton slid his fingers along the table top haltingly until he touched the sugar dish again. Branna reached out and slid the sugar bowl to the center of the table and out of the old man's reach.

Alton raised his eyes to Hattie with a grin.

Hattie tried not to smile as she finished her oats.

A knock at the door jerked her out of her seat. She rushed to answer it, finding Vincent in the hallway in a fresh suit, holding a box.

Hattie whispered, "Any word?"

Vincent nodded. "Can I come in?"

Hattie stepped aside to allow him passage.

Vincent doffed his hat and bowed to Hattie's parents still seated at the table.

"Mr. and Mrs. Malloy."

Alton grinned. "Vincent, me boy! It's been an age."

Branna stared at the table without response.

"What brings you around on a Sunday morning?" Alton asked.

Vincent nodded to Hattie. "Your daughter and I have some business in the city. But," he added, slipping the box from underneath his arm, "I have something for Mrs. Malloy."

Branna looked up with a cautious lift of her brow. "Oh?"

Hattie stood behind Vincent, trying to keep her mother from seeing the smirk on her face, watching as he set the box onto the table, sliding it an inch toward Branna.

Hattie's mother blinked at the package, her lip lifting into something just shy of a sneer. "I truly don't require gifts, Mister Calendo. I've enough clutter in my life, as it is."

He nodded. "Very well. But I think you might enjoy this one."

She scowled. "What is it?"

Alton chuckled. "Open it, woman!"

She sighed and reached for the box to pull open the top flaps. Standing, she reached in and pulled a rectangular wooden shape from the container. It had gilt-edged mahogany-stained trim and a set of knobs and switches on the front.

"Crosley 5-50," Branna read the pamphlet that had come with it.

"It's a radio," Alton announced, exchanging an uneasy glance with Hattie.

"I see that," Branna snapped. "A waste of money. We don't need this frivolous thing."

"It's a waste of *my* money," Vincent told her. "So enjoy it."

She bit her lip. "Did you steal it? Threaten some shop-keeper into giving it to you?"

Vincent blinked in surprise. "No, I bought it."

"With ill-gotten money, no doubt."

Hattie saw Vincent turn his head and fight back a smile. "I get a regular salary, Mrs. Malloy. Although since it's from the Crew, you would probably consider that ill-gotten."

Hattie held her breath and watched as her mother ran a hand over the top of the radio.

"Does it run on batteries?" she asked.

Vincent nodded. "It does. There's an antenna in the box that you need to attach, and you'll need to run a wire out the window to ground it."

She nodded. "Edna's has that. Alton, can you hook that grounding wire up, or do I need to ask Edna's husband to come do it?"

"I'll do it, dear," he replied in a deceptively meek tone.

Hattie reached her arm around Vincent. "We have to be going, Ma. It'll be a late one."

Branna ran her fingers along the front of the radio, turning one of the knobs. "Be safe, then."

Alton lifted his coffee to toast the two.

As they turned for the door, Branna added, "You too, Mister Calendo."

He smiled to Branna with a nod, slipped his hat onto his head, then stepped into the hallway.

Hattie joined him. She closed the door behind her, shoved him against the wall and kissed him.

"What was that for?" he asked once she'd pulled away. "Not that I'm complaining or anything."

"For making my Ma happy."

He grinned. "See? You *do* care what she thinks."

"Maybe just a little bit." She said as they headed down the stairs. "So, what's the word from Galloway's people?"

"Word is Jonas is still in Harrisburg. Charley's flying there now to reconnoiter."

"And the Crew?"

Vincent held the door to Lefty's car open for her. "Well, there's good news and bad news. Good news is that having those pinchers at the cabin convinced Vito I was right, and it was Masseria's people. So, I'm still on the inside."

"And the bad news?"

"Too many losses. He's pulling back to the city."

Hattie groaned, "No gunmen, then?"

"Not from Baltimore. We can still tap Arnoud, see what he's willing to commit. Since Jonas actually *does* work for Masseria, he might throw in."

"Where are we going now?"

"Sadie's still walking it off, but Galloway's called everyone to Gettysburg. Something of a forward operation base."

"And Sadie's playing along?"

Vincent nodded. "We have no reason to trust the man, but his people are almost chummy. Even Maria, which by the way is about to put me off my feed."

They climbed into the car and Vincent headed out. The weather had improved, with a warm front bringing bright blue skies that offered a clear view of the still-barren orchards along the back slope of the Alleghenies. Vincent drove into town and spotted a clutch of familiar faces in the square outside of Gettysburg Hotel.

Ernie gave them a wave as they approached. "That was fast work, old chap."

"I have a lead foot," Vincent replied.

Ernie tipped his bowler to Hattie. "Miss."

Hattie nodded at the man, knowing full well he was all

spit-polish and cozy English charm until he threw a car at you.

"Is Charley back yet?" she asked.

"Not as such," Ernie replied. "He's still on the wing, if you take my meaning."

"And Galloway?" Vincent asked.

"The old boy's inside, holding court as usual." Ernie pointed to the hotel.

Hattie stepped through the front doors, turning to spot a clutch of hangers-on near Galloway. More than half wore uniforms, staff and servers looking to give the man whatever he wanted. No doubt, he'd uncorked his powers on these people.

Galloway waved the two into the crowd. "You've arrived! Excellent. Do you need some coffee or tea?"

Hattie shook her head, though Vincent did take a coffee from one of the nearby staff conveniently armed with a service trolley.

"What's the latest on Jonas?" Hattie asked, getting right to the point.

"Last spotted in Harrisburg. Seems he made quick time back from Waynesboro. Local heat pushed him north of town, but we think he'll sweep south soon."

"Through Gettysburg?" Vincent asked.

"Well, I'm not here for the history."

"So, it's an ambush then," Hattie mused.

"That's the notion, though it would be easier if we had some manpower from the Crew."

Vincent shrugged. "They're otherwise occupied. I put a call in to Philadelphia but couldn't get through to Arnoud."

Galloway nodded somberly. "We'll have to plan for pinchers only. We still outnumber him."

"Will it be enough?" Hattie wondered.

"I don't make plans that I intend on failing, Miss Malloy.

Since we're waiting for additional information, I've secured several rooms on the third floor. Find yourselves a corner to hole up in."

Vincent handed off his coffee. "I'm going to find a phone, give Arnoud another shot."

Hattie nodded as Vincent bustled over to the front desk. Galloway regarded her for a moment, eyes working hard beneath his spectacles.

"Can I help you?" she asked with a testy edge.

"I certainly hope so. For all our sakes."

"Ever the charmer."

He grinned. "I'm just deciding if I'm looking at you or an illusion of you. How would anyone tell?"

She smirked. "If I wanted you to be looking at an illusion of me, there'd be no way to tell."

"I suppose that's true. For a while. Then, as with all of our powers, you'd have to make a choice. Continue at the cost of your health or lose the effect. I wonder if there's ever been an illusion so important, you'd kill yourself for it?"

"There's been times I've been willing to go that far." Hattie frowned. "And what about you?"

He nodded. "It's a curious question. We all have our limits. I've found some people are more difficult to sway than others."

"I suppose it's why you surround yourself with the simpleminded?"

Galloway laughed. "Don't let Maria hear you say that. But, no. You have it backward. The more complicated the person, the easier it is for me to get my hands into them, so to speak. Conflicts of interest, ambiguity, self-doubt. These provide fresh loam for my shovel. It's those of singular purpose, that unflappable devotion to a cause, who require a pickaxe."

Hattie took a seat near Galloway. "True believers are your downfall, then?"

"They are the downfall of us all."

"Don't you ever wonder if anyone follows you of their own will?"

He squinted. "Do you ever pinch illusions without meaning to?"

Hattie shook her head. She hadn't, but she knew Vincent sometimes pinched time unconsciously.

"When I tell you that I never use my powers against other pinchers, it's not some pledge to morality. It's so that I know the people whose company I keep. Truly know them. I can never trust people whose loyalties were not truly given."

"Are my loyalties truly given, do you think?"

His lips lifted into a smile, but his eyes held a razor's edge. "My dear, I believe your loyalties are quite clear."

"I'll see if there's a room free," Hattie said, standing and gathering herself. She gave Vincent a nod as he appeared to be carrying on a heated conversation. It seemed he'd reached someone in Philadelphia after all.

The stairs were wide, her boots clopping against the wood planks as she reached the third floor. A run of closed doors provided a puzzle for Hattie. Which were Galloway's rooms? On a hunch, she tried the first door. Locked. Moving on, she opened the second, to find two figures writhing on the bed. Hattie pulled the door closed with a smirk. Now, there was a way to kill time!

The third door revealed a room with two beds. A figure stood at the window, back turned to the door.

"Sorry," Hattie muttered as she went to close the door again.

The figure peered over her shoulder with a lift of her brow. Maria, the earth pincher.

"It's fine," she said. "Come in."

Hattie nodded, stepping into the room. "Just looking for a place to wait."

Maria turned back to the window overlooking the square below.

Hattie lingered a bit, then sat on the edge of the bed to remove her boots which dropped with deep thuds onto the floor.

"If you listen, when it's quiet, you can almost imagine you hear the battle just over the ridge."

Hattie hopped up and joined Maria at the window. Three-story buildings ran along the compass points from the square. To the west a stately red-bricked building held vigil on a wooded hill.

"That's the seminary," Maria whispered. "Confederate cannons were on the hill just beyond." She swept a finger from the west to the south. "Firing over Seminary Ridge on the union soldiers."

"I'm afraid I don't know much about the war."

"My grandfather was killed at Antietam," Maria said.

"Was he for the States or the rebels?" Hattie asked.

"Burnside's Ninth Corps."

Hattie shook her head.

"Union," Maria added.

"I suppose you'll have your own battle to fight here, soon."

Maria stared dolefully out the window for a while before drawing herself away. "I'll give you the room so you can rest."

"No need for that."

"It's fine. I'll find some food."

She gathered a coat and hat, leaving Hattie alone in the room.

Leaning back on the bed, Hattie thought about the fight at hand until she drifted off to sleep.

Hattie awoke with a start, not because of the usual horrors that had filled her sleep as of late, but specifically from a lack of them. She sucked in a breath and sat upright in the bed, looking to the window which was now a dark square on the wall.

She shook her head, clearing the grogginess of the first solid sleep she'd had in a long time, laced up her boots, and went downstairs. The aroma of food from across the square drifted through the open windows of the lobby. There was no sign of Vincent or Galloway, so she wandered onto the street. Gas lamps flickered around the square. A warm night breeze washed over the town with the promise of the coming summer. She reached for her hair, realizing she hadn't bothered with a hat. Her red bangs flitted in the breeze, blowing into her eyes as she spotted Vincent watching her from across the square.

She strolled across the street to join him.

"Finally got some sleep?" he asked.

"Did you check in on me, then?"

"Yes, but I didn't want to disturb you. Figured sleep was a rare thing for you these days."

She nodded with a sigh. "Aye, true enough."

"Hungry?"

He held out an arm and guided her to a basement tucked in the corner of the square. They descended to the glass door and stepped inside. The evening crowd was thick. Hattie spotted Millie and Douglas sharing a table. Maria sat alone at the bar, nursing something sure to be inadequate as Pennsylvania remained under the enforcement of Prohibition. Ernie was entertaining a crowd of men at a long table, his voice booming with tales of battles.

Vincent guided them to a table near the corner and placed an order for stew.

Hattie regarded him in the low light of the flickering lamps on the wall, admiring his dark hair, his angular jaw, the way his shoulders filled out his suit jacket. "Do you have plans for after dinner, Mr. Calendo?" she asked with what she hoped was an enticing smile.

"Huh?" He gave her a puzzled frown.

"We have an evening away from your keeper and my parents. There's no Raymond, or people hammering nails thirty yards away. We have empty rooms in that hotel at our disposal. It's a beautiful, warm night. I'm suggesting we make use of those rooms."

He caught his breath. "Is that something you want to do now?"

"If not now, then when?"

He reached out a hand to take hers. "We have a fight coming. Maybe tonight, maybe tomorrow. One or both of us could end up…"

"More the reason to spend tonight in each other's arms." Hattie curled her fingers around his. "There's always a fight coming. There always will be, I suspect."

"I love you, Hattie. I like having you close," he said. "I like laughing with you. I like helping you. I even like bickering with you. The way you tease me. The way we can talk about things with each other that we can't share with anyone else."

"And you think if we share a bed, it'll change all that?"

"No, that's not it. I want you in *my* bed, not some hotel's. I want this to happen when there will be no worries we'll be interrupted by some blasted iron pincher, or one of Galloway's people, or the hotel staff. I don't want a hurried ten minutes with you because we're thinking we might die. I want more than that."

Hattie smiled. "That's about the best rejection I've ever heard."

"I'm not rejecting you. Far from that. And if I had to stand up from this chair and try to walk across the room right now, it would be very obvious to everyone in this room how much I want you."

"Teasing, boy-o." She smirked, running her thumb across the top of his knuckles. "Now that I know you like it, I promise to do it more often."

The door to the tavern-turned-bistro opened with a shove.

Hattie jerked her head up to spot Galloway striding into the room. He snapped his fingers, and each of his people hopped to, abandoning their private conversations.

"What's this about, then?" Hattie whispered.

"I'll lay money Charley's back," Vincent replied.

Galloway approached, his face taut. "Jonas is on the move."

CHAPTER 28

Vincent gazed north through his field glasses, past the rooftops of Gettysburg to the highway leading north to Harrisburg.

"How many cars?" Vincent asked.

"Just four," Charley replied, hugging the patch of ground next to Vincent.

The spot on Cemetery Hill afforded a clear view to the town, even with the spattering of budding trees running along the old battlement lines and fences preserved by the park.

"Is that fewer than before?" Hattie asked as she leaned against a concrete column.

"By a couple, yeah."

"Then that's good news."

"As long as Galloway's people hold off until Jonas and his goons are out of town. Otherwise this will get bloody."

Hattie reached for Vincent's glasses, taking a look to the north. "I've a queasy feeling about him."

"Did he say something?"

"Nothing specific," she said, handing back the glasses. "Just the way he was looking at me."

"I know what you mean," Vincent said. "Charley, you're on the inside with that gang. Any scuttlebutt from Galloway?"

"Nope," Charley replied. "Just talking about the iron pincher and battle plans."

Vincent turned to the west to check on Ernie's position. A single car sat beside a red barn, ready to pounce onto the road. Vincent could see Ernie's bowler through the car windscreen. Lots of stone walls and such to fling at Jonas's men. He had a good position.

"Looks like Ernie's ready."

"What about Maria?" Hattie asked.

"She's south of town," Vincent replied. "Charley, you said they were heading due south an hour ago."

"Yep," Charley chirped.

"They slowed up somewhere. Or else they've changed tack."

"There's more than one way to Baltimore from Harrisburg," Hattie suggested.

"Yeah, but they wasn't going east. Definitely south," Charley said.

Vincent took a knee, keeping an eye on the road. Another fifteen minutes passed before a glint caught his eye to the north. Four Dodges rolled down Harrisburg Road in tight formation. He lifted his field glasses to catch a closer look.

"I think we have a winner," Vincent muttered.

Hattie lifted a powder compact, angling its mirror to signal Ernie down below.

Vincent nodded to Charley. "You set for this?"

Charley nodded.

"You sure?"

"I'm not running from this fight."

"Okay. Let's displace."

They crept down the hill, trotting between paths and fences until they reached a stretch of stone wall running alongside Steinwehr Avenue.

Vincent glanced across the lane at the red barn. He ran his fingers along the stones in front of him. Not much metal to work with. All Jonas had to dismantle and throw at them was the steel he'd brought with him.

Plenty of materials for Galloway's people, though.

This might just work.

They waited behind the wall until they could hear the motors of Jonas's convoy approaching from the southern outskirts of town. He exchanged a meaningful glance with Hattie.

"Ernie's move. Once he blocks the road, find Jonas and lock him down with your full-immersion illusions."

Hattie nodded.

Vincent patted Charley's arm. "Your job is to keep her safe. Whatever skin or pelt you gotta wear."

"I will."

"And you, boy-o?" Hattie asked. "What'll you be doing this whole time?"

"I've got a little surprise for Jonas. Hey, think your Janissary friend's haunting us right now?"

She shrugged. "He wasn't invited, which means he's sure to be about somewhere."

"Good. This would be the perfect moment for a Hell pincher to make our lives difficult." He winced. "Did I just jinx the whole thing?"

Hattie jabbed his ribs. "Shut it."

Vincent pulled off his hat and peered over the wall. "They're about five hundred yards."

"When's that hammer-fisted Englishman going to move?"

"Right about...now."

Vincent ducked, bracing for a crash.

He opened his eyes when no crash came.

Venturing another peek over the stone wall, he swallowed hard. Two hundred yards.

Ernie's car remained behind the barn, its headlamps peeking at Vincent from around the corner.

"Now?" Hattie whispered.

"Come on, Ernie."

"What's he waiting for?"

One hundred yards.

Vincent grumbled, "Something's wrong."

The cars rumbled forward, gathering speed as they hit the open road.

"Hattie?"

"Got it," she grumbled, pinching an illusion onto the road.

The front car squealed to a halt just in front of their position. The rest stopped in a line on a flank directly in front of them.

"Shit," Vincent spat.

He pinched time.

Hattie blinked at him.

Vincent made a slashing motion indicating she should drop the illusion. With a mighty shove, he pulled himself up and over the wall, wading between the first and second cars to cross the road. He plodded across a length of tall grass toward the red barn and Ernie's car.

As Vincent rounded the corner of the barn, he stared through the windscreen to find the car was empty.

He pivoted, taking in the surroundings. No sign of Ernie.

Too much distance to make it back to the stone wall before his powers ran dry.

Vincent closed his eyes, nodded to himself, then pulled his gun and released the time bubble.

"Hattie!" he shouted. "Do it now!"

As Hattie rose from her cover behind the wall, Vincent raised his gun and fired shots over the tops of the convoy.

The passengers ducked to take cover, including the rear car whose door swung open. One of the doors peeled off the car, rolling flat in the fingers of Jonas O'Donnell, who brandished it like a shield. He strode toward the barn, peeling a length of iron from the car door. It sharpened to a savage point in his hand.

Jonas flipped the blade into the air.

Vincent ducked behind the corner of the barn.

The slice of metal thumped into the planks of the building, stabbing back out again just inches from Vincent's face.

"Hattie!"

Vincent dropped to the ground, crawling toward the corner of the barn. He swung his gun to take aim at Jonas.

The man stood rigid, his face contorted in confusion. He lifted his hands to the sides of his head, shaking it as if trying to knock loose cobwebs.

It was working!

Vincent spotted gunmen pouring out of the vehicles. He took aim and fired into the line. He spun one of the New York gangsters with a shoulder-strike. Two more dove back into their cars. However, the gangsters on Hattie's side of the road had spotted her standing on top of the wall, arms stretched out as she poured her light pinch into Jonas's eyes.

The gunmen raised their weapons at Hattie.

A blood-curdling scream filled the air—a scream that was most definitely not human.

A brown blur rushed from behind the stone wall.

Gunshots rang out as a cougar laid into the first of the gunmen. It slashed the gun from the man's hand, moving on with a lithe pounce to the next. The remaining stumbled over one another trying to escape the enormous cat.

Vincent checked on Jonas. He grimaced, nearly doubled over as Hattie flooded his brain with illusions.

"Not…much…longer…" she gasped.

Vincent got to his feet, setting his jaw and raising his weapon. He was only about ten yards away from Jonas. He stepped closer, as close as he dared as the enormous iron pincher swung at phantoms in the air in front of him.

Taking careful aim, he pulled the trigger.

Something hard pushed against his side. His shoulder struck the ground, and then he was in freefall.

Flailing, he tumbled head-over-heels into the tall grass several yards away, his head striking the ground hard enough to rattle his senses. The world swam, and he saw stars. As he struggled catch his bearings, Vincent found his way to his hands and knees.

A shriek from the road pulled his eyes back to Jonas. He blinked rapidly, shaking his face clear. Just beside him, at the corner of the barn where Vincent had stood, was a single pillar of stone jutting from the ground.

He checked on Hattie, who was doubled over, blood rushing from her nose as her powers reached their limit.

Vincent scrambled to his feet, swaying from the dizziness of his impact. Stone pillar where he stood. That meant…

Maria.

Gunfire renewed at the car line as Charley returned to his human form, reaching an arm around Hattie's midsection to pull her behind the cover of the stone wall.

Vincent shook his head, then lifted his gun to Jonas. Perhaps it wasn't too late.

He squeezed the trigger.

Jonas lifted a hand, the bullet spraying into pieces in his palm. The man swiveled his head slowly toward Vincent, an expression of deadly exasperation painted on his face.

"Shit," Vincent muttered.

Reaching for the car door lying at his feet, Jonas peeled a fresh strip of metal, molding it into a slender spear with several barbs. It was a horrifying thing, meant not only to kill but to punish. He tossed aside the rest of the door, advancing as Vincent lowered his gun, backing up and trying to decide the best course of action.

Jonas gripped his spear, lifting it to face level. As he reared back to thrust it through Vincent's chest, sparks sprayed off his face.

Echoes of gunfire sounded in the distance.

It was a welcome distraction. Vincent dove into the tall grass nearby as more gunshots sounded from the south. A line of cars swept up Steinwehr, tommy guns hosing down Jonas's men. The driver of the front car turned his car off the road, slicing across the field until it nearly collided with Jonas.

The iron pincher shook his head, bullets spraying against his face. Jumping to the side, he narrowly missed being hit by the car which careened into the barn yard.

As the driver's side door threw open, Lefty rushed out to offer Vincent a hand.

"You're a welcome sight," Vincent told him.

Grabbing Vincent, Lefty ran toward the barn. Just as they'd reached the building, the wooden sides creaked, the planks bowing out toward them.

"Down!" Vincent shouted, gripping Lefty by the collar to wrestle him to the ground before the entire southern face of the barn exploded into tiny jagged bits of shrapnel.

Vincent winced as blazing hot pain sliced across his back.

Lefty spun onto his back, lifting his revolver to fire off two shots at Douglas, who was emerging from the barn.

One bullet nicked the wood pincher in the arm. The second flew into pieces midair. Jonas marched forward, a flat hand stretched out between Vincent and the barn.

"Double-cross?" Lefty muttered.

"Of course," Vincent said.

"Guess you were right after all."

Jonas extended his left hand behind him, pulling the remnants of his car door off the ground, hauling it through the air until it rested in his hand.

"Iron pincher?" Lefty asked.

"That's him."

"Could've used him at Gallipoli."

As Jonas lifted the slab of iron, the door was smashed out of his hand, carried by the half-ton mass of a bull moose. Cradling the door in his antlers, Charley rushed around the side of the barn.

"Focus on the gunmen," Vincent told Lefty. "I've got O'Donnell."

Lefty rolled away to join the rest of the Crew gunmen he'd brought with him.

Jonas rushed Vincent, throwing a lazy haymaker at his face. Vincent dodged, landing a solid body blow into Jonas's ribs. The man grunted, staggering forward but keeping his feet.

Jonas sneered. "Your people won't win."

"I brought an army, my friend," Vincent countered.

A voice called from the barn. "You may have us outgunned, but we have the firepower."

Vincent glared at Galloway who emerged from inside, stepping past Douglas who pressed a hand against his wound.

"It was Waynesboro, wasn't it?" Vincent said. "Your meet and greet. It was with Jonesy here. You saw through our little false flag."

Galloway smiled. "We would have been a fantastic team. You and I both look ahead, plan the next step. And I applaud this little maneuver." He gestured to the Crew gunmen picking apart the New York thugs. "Inspired."

Vincent wiggled a finger from Galloway to O'Donnell. "What I don't get is how you two get on the same page. Isn't he what you're fighting against?"

Galloway extended his arms in a gesture of grace. "It's the same gambit you employed against me. Find the common enemy. Galvanize incompatible resources and set them in the same direction."

"The Crew and Philadelphia," Vincent muttered. "You both want them eliminated."

"I knew I had to eliminate the two families if I were to ever consolidate a proper free zone in the Mid-Atlantic. And Jonas here, well he's got his orders."

"Masseria," Jonas confirmed, "needs you gone."

One of Jonas's vehicles rose six feet into the air, lurching side to side as Ernie approached with it hoisted over his head.

"So this is how it ends, not with a bang but with a Ford on my head?" Vincent asked.

Ernie chuckled. "Sorry. But you were the one who—"

A tiny motion flickered from behind the stone wall. Ernie glanced up to his wrist, where two tiny balls connected by a length of copper wire wrapped around his arm. He grunted.

A wave of panic flooded his face just before the car dropped its full weight, smashing Ernie into the road with a wet crack.

Galloway flinched as his heave pincher perished under the weight of his own weapon.

As Vincent prepared to sprint for the line of Crew gunman, a searing hot stab of pain in his leg nearly knocked the wind out of him.

The noise of the conflict dropped into a muddy silence. He'd pinched time out of reflex. Reaching down, he found a nasty, sharpened plank of barn siding stabbing into his leg. Vincent eased it out, thankful that he'd stopped time before it had sunk too deep.

Yards away, Douglas stood with two more planks in his hand.

Lifting the wooden spear, Vincent strode forward, releasing time just as he hammered the plank into the bridge of Douglas' nose. The wood pincher yelped as blood sprayed from his nostrils. He fell backward, hand to his face.

Vincent brandished the spear, but before he could run the man through, a weight knocked him to the ground. Peering up, Vincent found Galloway snarling down at him. The sway pincher dropped on top of him, hammered a fist into Vincent's chin. Vincent lifted a knee into Galloway's backside, tilting him forward thrusting his forehead into Galloway's face.

Galloway rolled off Vincent who got to his feet, standing over the man on shaky legs.

A shadow fell over the field, as if a cloud had blotted the sun. Looking up Vincent found an inky tendril wrapping around the barn. The plume of shadow snaked into a circle, cutting Vincent off from the rest of the fight.

"Bolton," Vincent muttered. He looked down at Galloway again. "Of course, Bolton. Part of your arrangement with Jonas?"

Galloway blinked several times, then replied, "You can't win, Calendo."

"You're down a heave pincher and a wood pincher, Galloway."

"It won't be enough."

Screams from the opposite side of the shadow cloud filled the space between gunshots. Wet noises. Metal in flesh. While Vincent was occupied with Galloway, Jonas had torn into Lefty's people.

Vincent turned to sprint into the cloud, clamping his eyes shut as he rushed through the shadow pincher's tendril. Jonas was the real objective, here. Galloway only served as a distraction. The sensation of a cold mist peppered his face as he passed through the umbra. When the sensation ceased, he opened his eyes.

Millie stood directly in front of him, lifting her hand in a friendly wave.

"Hiya, handsome!" she said, just before a blinding flash of light filled Vincent's eyes with overwhelming brilliance.

He shouted and covered his eyes with his arm, but it was too late. As he blinked his watering eyes, he could see nothing but flickering darkness and stars.

A tiny fist smacked into his face. He staggered to the side swinging his hands to fend off the sun pincher. Another blow. Then a foot in his midsection.

Vincent fell, the ground nearly knocking the wind out of him. He scrambled onto hands and knees, feeling his way through the grass. His world shrank as gunfire and screams of pain filled his ears.

He heard Millie gasp, then approaching footsteps. Hands landed onto his shoulders and he thrashed out in defense before Ghasawi's thickly accented voice urged him to remain still.

Someone else approached, stopping just beside him.

"Is he hit?" Lefty asked.

Vincent waved a hand in front of his face. "Bitch blinded me. Don't worry about me. Get Jonas!"

"We're getting pounded," Lefty grumbled. "Come on. Help me get him out of here."

Ghasawi's arms reached underneath Vincent's shoulder, hauling him off the ground.

Lefty took Vincent's right side, and the two guided him

over the uneven terrain away from the barn. He heard a car door open.

"No!" Vincent shouted. "We can't run out now."

"Fight's over, son," Lefty informed him.

"We're not getting another shot at Jonas like this," Vincent protested.

Ghasawi gave him a deft shove, sending him onto the bench seat of one of the Crew cars. Vincent's face hit leather, and he squirmed to right himself.

"Where's Hattie?" he gasped. "I can't leave Hattie."

"I'm here," Hattie's voice answered just beside him. He felt her touch his face, both hands caressing his cheeks.

"You hurt?" he asked.

"I'll recover."

The motor started.

"This was our shot," Vincent grumbled.

"I know. And we missed," she said.

The car swerved into a tight turn.

"Down!" Lefty shouted.

Hattie pulled Vincent down as windows shattered, burying his face into her lap as she covered him.

"I really hate that iron pincher," Lefty grumbled.

"What's happening?" Vincent gasped.

Hattie shushed him, keeping her body folded on top of him. The motor whined as their car rambled over rough terrain before finding a road again. After a few minutes, Hattie eased off of Vincent, guiding him back upright.

"Anyone seen Charley?" Hattie asked.

Lefty replied, "Who's Charley?"

"Red beard. Looks like a hobo."

"Sorry," Lefty replied. "Didn't see no one like that."

Hattie sighed. "God, I hope he got out." Vincent felt her stroke the back of his head. "How're your eyes?"

He opened them but saw only darkness. "Not good."

"What is our destination?" Ghasawi asked.

Lefty grumbled, "Back to Baltimore."

Vincent shook his head. "No."

"What's on your mind?" Lefty asked.

"Arnoud. We have to go to Philadelphia."

CHAPTER 29

"We're gonna need fuel soon," Lefty urged from the front seat.

Ghasawi nodded at the wheel. "He is correct. We will not reach Philadelphia."

Lefty turned to glance at Vincent who was still staring blankly at the seat in front of him. "Why Philly?"

"Because," Vincent replied, "they're following us. Would you rather draw them to Baltimore where we're weak, or to Arnoud?"

"Hell of a gamble. You said Arnoud turned you down."

"Yeah, yeah. That was when I was asking him to send men to a fight. Now I'm bringing the fight to him."

Hattie grabbed Vincent's hand to give it a squeeze. "You have some explaining to do, boy-o." She gave Lefty a tap on the shoulder. "You, too. When were you two planning to let me in on this ruse?"

"Sorry about that," Vincent said. "I figured Galloway was onto us when he got to the cabin."

"Seems so. Clever plan telling everyone the Crew was occupied elsewhere and couldn't come."

Vincent squeezed her hand hard, and she realized she needed to be careful what she said. He'd protected the Charge from Lefty and the Crew once again, while giving up Galloway.

Lefty pointed to a clutch of buildings ahead. "There's a filling station."

Ghasawi guided the car to the side of the road. The three cars following behind made a line to the pumps.

The attendant stepped out with a smile which evaporated as the battered and bloody gangsters poured out of the vehicles. Before the attendant could backpedal into the building, Lefty lifted a handful of dollars.

"Okay, pal. This is enough for four fill-ups, a couple nights out on the town, and your absolute silence. You read me?"

The man's face paled as he took the cash with a nod.

Hattie helped Vincent out of the car, settling him aside one of the pumps to lean against.

"Any better?" she asked, peering into his eyes.

He frowned. "Maybe a little. Don't think this is permanent."

"That's good."

Vincent hammered the side of the pump with his fist. "Damn it, we almost had him." He shook his head. "Twice I've been so close to taking him down. Twice."

"Blame Galloway for our failure today, not yourself. We'd all be dead if you hadn't figured him out."

"And I'd be flatter than a pancake if our Janissary friend hadn't tagged along."

Hattie turned to Ghasawi with a smile. "His name is Assam."

Vincent scowled. "Yeah? Well, don't go getting too sweet on Assam now, okay?"

She laughed leaning forward to kiss him on the cheek. "You've got nothing to worry about there, boy-o."

The attendant worked quickly, eager to move them out of his business. As the last car wrapped up, Ghasawi peered to the east. He straightened and beckoned to Hattie.

"We are pursued."

Lefty made a whipping motion with his finger, marshalling his men to load up and hit the road. As they sped onto the road, Lefty turned to look behind them.

"They'll be on us all the whole way in. Is there anything you can do, Miss Malloy?"

"What?" she asked.

He nodded to a junction in the distance, a highway to Reading. "A pinch of light? Think you can get them moving north?"

Hattie nodded. "I'll try."

As their convoy approached the junction, Hattie pinched an illusion of duplicate cars slowing to a turn before rendering the real convoy invisible. It was a complex illusion, one which taxed her already low reserves of energy.

Vincent placed a hand on her leg.

The pull of magic eased, giving her confidence that she could hold the illusion from a distance as they sped straight past the junction.

Hattie sent her illusion north onto a state highway.

Lefty turned in his seat to watch. "It's working," he said. "They took the bait."

She held on to the illusion for as long as she could, but the increasing distance as they sped away, and the fact that she had no idea what the highway looked like past the junction, rendered the illusion inviable in short order.

Hattie opened her eyes. "That'll only buy us a few minutes."

Lefty nodded. "It's more than we had."

They continued into the outskirts of Philadelphia and on through downtown, crossing the Schuylkill River on their way to the cannery on the banks of the Delaware.

They pulled up as the sun began to set. Lefty bailed out of the car, rushing for the cannery doors, which were locked up for the day. He pounded on the large steel doors, looking back to the bedraggled men as they moved en masse for the building.

Hattie helped Vincent across the gravel pad as Lefty continued pounding on the door.

"Arnoud!" he shouted. "Open up, damn it!"

Hattie cast a dubious glance at the road. "They've had time to rest. If they get here before Arnoud, who will they have left?"

Vincent said, "Ernie's gone. I busted Douglas's nose and nicked him on the arm , but I don't think that'll stop him pinching. The real problems are Jonas and Maria."

Hattie nodded. "Lots of ground, here. And lots of metal."

"Sorry, I won't be much help."

Lefty hammered on the door again, then turned to the others. "What are the odds he's not even here?"

Hattie said, "It's possible. With DeBarre gone, he may be meeting with Sabella or the brewers."

Vincent scowled, staring at the ground. "Just as likely he's sitting on his ass refusing to answer."

"Heads up," Lefty said.

A line of cars rushed off the road and onto the gravel pad.

"Time's up," Hattie whispered.

The Crew men brandished their weapons, forming a half-circle in front of the cannery doors as the New York war party parked in a line. Gunmen spilled out of the cars, fewer in number than before but still more than Lefty had brought.

Galloway and Jonas stepped out of their vehicles. Galloway took in the cannery and the surroundings, nodding to himself with satisfaction. As the Crew chambered rounds and took aim, Jonas lifted two hands.

Each weapon jerked several feet away from the gunmen's grips, rattling against the ground. The Crew men gawked, now unarmed, retreating a step toward the door. The press of the men made Hattie squirm.

Jonas stepped forward, reaching for a gun with a contemptuous snatch. He ran a hand along the barrel of the rifle, extruding it into a fine spear point. As the stock warped the chambered round exploded in a puff beneath Jonas's hand. He stopped several feet away from the Crew, twirling his iron-pinched weapon in one hand.

"Where is the time pincher?"

"What is this, some vendetta now?" Vincent shouted.

"No," Jonas said as he pointed his spear to Vincent. "It's business."

"Go to Hell!" Hattie snapped.

Galloway shouted, "Stop wasting time! Just do it!"

Jonas turned to sneer at Galloway. He turned with his spear pointing at Vincent. "Make this easy. Hand over the time pincher. Do that, and I'll let the rest of you live."

The Crew men glanced back and forth, an unspoken conversation quickly turning against Vincent.

"Easy, boys," Lefty muttered. "He's one of us. And Vito would skin you alive if you handed him over."

The men braced themselves, turning back to Jonas in defiance.

"Very well," Jonas growled.

He hoisted the spear to shoulder level.

Then dropped it.

Jonas jumped at the clatter of his own weapon. He lifted his hands, shaking them and staring with disbelief as his fingers dangled limp.

Glass shattered overhead as each window in the cannery's

top floor smashed out, replaced with a tommy guns. Galloway's people bustled around the backs of their vehicles for cover as a burst of bullets rained down on them.

The steel doors behind Hattie rattled, sliding open to reveal Arnoud. He stepped up to the crowd, easing them apart with a lift of his hand, swimming through them until he reached the front to face Jonas.

Jonas squinted at Arnoud. "You."

"Yes," Arnoud replied. "Me."

"Been a long time."

"Not long enough. What are you doing in Philadelphia?"

Jonas scowled. "You made your bed with Corbi. Masseria can't allow that to stand."

"We're willing to have a conversation with Masseria, but not at gunpoint," Arnoud told him.

Jonas lifted his chin, then winced, shaking his hands and dropping to one knee.

"So in the meantime," Arnoud added, "get the hell out of my city."

Jonas tensed his shoulders, struggling to his feet. He glared, and a curl of metal screeched as it separated from one of the cars behind him.

Arnoud lifted his hands, fingers curled into claws and the iron pincher gasped, dropping to the gravel and writhing in agony. "I said to get the hell out of my city."

Jonas stood once more, staggering and breathing heavy. "Fine. You can have these idiots."

He returned to Galloway's people, and without looking back, got into his vehicle and waited for the driver to come out from hiding. One by one, the enemy returned to their vehicles, eyes on the guns trained on them from above.

Galloway stood alone, door held open. He glanced at Hattie and Vincent, a mysterious grin on his face. Then he slipped into the car and shut the door.

As they drove off, Arnoud turned to face the Crew.

"Are you okay?" he asked.

Hattie blinked in surprise to realize he was talking to her. "Yes. Thank you."

"Good. I would be very distraught if you were hurt, Miss Malloy." He turned to face Vincent. "I thought I was clear on the phone, Calendo."

Vincent shook his head, eyes staring into space. "You were. But I had no options."

Arnoud stepped forward, waving a hand in front of Vincent. "What's wrong with him?"

"Took a sun pincher to the face," Hattie said. "We're hoping it's temporary."

Arnoud nodded thoughtfully. "Might as well come inside."

Without another word, he strode into the cannery, leaving the rest loitering by the door.

Lefty shrugged. "It's weak, but we'll take it. One of these days, Vincent, you'll actually be wrong about something."

"Don't hold your breath," Vincent grumbled with a thin smile.

CHAPTER 30

Hattie lounged on one of the divans in the cannery's basement speakeasy, wiping dried blood off her face with a damp cloth. Vincent sat beside her, a warm rag to his eyes, head cocked back to the ceiling.

Arnoud stood behind the bar where DeBarre had always stood. His face was tight but calm. It was a new look for Arnoud, whom Hattie was used to watching pace with nervous energy while DeBarre stood at the center of the Philadelphia solar system.

"So, Galloway's cut a deal with Jonas," Hattie stated.

Lefty swiveled on his stool at the bar. "Who *is* this Galloway, anyhow? I mean, besides a rogue pincher."

Vincent replied, "That's about the long and short of it, Lefty. Think of him as a freedom fighter for free pinchers."

Lefty nodded, then turned back to focus on his drink.

"What is Jonas getting out of this, though?" Hattie asked. "Besides carrying out Masseria's orders, what's his goal? Is he thinking of teaming up long term with Galloway?"

"I doubt it," Vincent replied. "He'll probably turn on them in the end. I'm sure Galloway will probably attempt to kill him once he's taken out the Crew. And I'm sure Jonas will do the same. The man's unhinged. And I mean Ithaca-unhinged." Vincent added with a lift of his chin to the bar, "No offense, Arnoud."

"None taken," Arnoud replied. "The man is absolutely out of his mind. And dangerous. Thank you again for bringing him to my doorstep."

"Come on," Vincent said, moving the rag up and down on his face as he wagged his eyebrows. "You know you can't stay mad at me, Arnoud."

Arnoud scowled, then wound his way out from behind the bar. "Actually, I was meaning to contact the New York families. You've gave me the opportunity to provide a strong incentive for Masseria to come to the table. So, I forgive you."

"That man sure backed down from you in a hurry," Lefty commented.

Hattie chuckled. "That's because we brought him to a scarier pincher than he is."

Arnoud blushed. He dipped his head in a bow to Hattie, his eyes darting to hers, then down to look at his feet.

"He'll probably set up a line outside of the city," Lefty commented. "A snare for us to fall into once Arnoud kicks us out."

"No," Vincent said. "He won't."

"Where's he going, then?" Hattie asked.

"We were just a distraction," Vincent replied. "He's getting back on target."

Hattie shook her head. "So he's going to attack the Crew? But where? The Old Moravia?"

Lefty kicked back the last of his whisky. "Vito's gonna love that. How many times is he gonna have to rebuild that place?"

"Galloway and Jonas." Hattie let out a frustrated breath.

"Galloway's using Jonas to put every free pincher on the East Coast under his boot. And then there's Jonas who thinks he'll haul all of Galloway's people to New York in chains when this is said and done. They might as well be measuring manhoods."

"Galloway has the long view," Vincent reminded her. "I'll wager he has plans upon plans ready for Jonas. Plans that involve Boston."

"Or Maranzano," Arnoud suggested, taking a seat directly across from Hattie. "O'Donnell's absence from New York weakens Masseria on the home front."

Lefty hopped off his stool. "Yes, very interesting. But it changes nothing. If they're moving south already, then Vito's in for it. They'll have to refuel and regroup, but they still have the drop on us. Can't sit around here another minute chewing the fat."

Arnoud smiled. "Agreed. Although Miss Malloy is welcome to stay here where she'll be safe."

Hattie squirmed. "Thank you but no, Mr. Arnoud."

"Sure you don't want to help us out?" Vincent asked the touch pincher. "This whole alliance between our cities may have been stillborn, but there's substance to the idea."

"Not interested," Arnoud replied, sending an apologetic glance Hattie's way. "Sabella's ready to cooperate with Masseria against Maranzano. I'm not at liberty to violate his directives by an ill-advised foray into Baltimore."

Hattie scowled. "Of course, you're at liberty. You're no one's slave, Mr. Arnoud. You can make your own decisions."

"Sabella leaned on DeBarre for his advice as much as his magic," Vincent added.

Arnoud frowned. "I expect that sort of noise from a free pincher. But not from you, Calendo. Did you learn nothing from Ithaca?"

Vincent pulled the rag off his eyes, blinking furiously.

"Huh. I think it's coming back." He waved a hand in front of his eyes. "Dark and blurry, but I'm getting something."

"Yeah," Lefty grumbled. "Who knew sitting in a dark basement would be good for your eyes? Can we leave, now?"

"Where are we gonna go?" Vincent urged. "They've got a half-hour drop on us, minimum."

"They'll be watching," Lefty mused. "O'Donnell seems to want to take you out first, to make sure Corbi doesn't have any magical defense left. I'm thinking they'll wait for us to make a break south, then they'll follow us straight in."

"We tried a false flag," Vincent chuckled. "Might as well try a wild goose, while we're at it."

Hattie nodded. "I think Lefty's right. But lead them where?"

"We'll be outnumbered against their pinchers," Vincent warned. "Jonas and Galloway will blow the entire city, and they'll probably overtake us first."

Hattie sighed. "If only there were a way we could beat them to the city."

Arnoud released an exasperated huff. He stood up and straightened his jacket.

"If it'll get you people out of my city, I'll make a call." He marched toward the hallway. "Mancuso? If you'll join me?"

Lefty glanced around the room, then joined Arnoud with a shrug.

Hattie watched Vincent as he waved his hand in front of his face, lifting fingers in random orders. "Assam?" she said. "Might we have a moment?"

Ghasawi bowed and followed the others. Once they were alone, Hattie stood and crossed the room to sit beside Vincent.

"Got me all to yourself." He smiled. "You're making this a habit."

"I intend to. But I want to talk about something."

He nodded. "This again, huh? You want to go make love on the cannery floor? Or behind the bar over there? Have to be quick, so sorry in advance about that."

"No." She laughed as she slapped his arm.

"What? Rejection? I'm crushed, Hattie Malloy."

"Teasing and flirting later. This is time for grown-up talk, boy-o. You know what I'm carrying around."

Vincent stared in her direction. "You mean the soul trap?"

"Aye. And you know what I think is in that soul trap."

His sucked in a breath. "Deltaville."

"We've talked…or rather we've avoided talking about the implications of this soul twins thing."

"And?" Vincent urged her to continue.

"Soul twins. I love you, but sometimes I'm not sure if what I feel is love, or something more…mystical. Is it us, I mean really us? Or is it this bright soul thing?"

Vincent reached for her hand, grabbing it on the second try. "Hattie? I'm going to tell you this from a point of both friendship and detached reason. I do believe you're thinking way too much about all of this."

She smiled, nodding to herself. "Not everyone has to deal with Solomon's Crown, Hell pinchers, and Arab magic police."

"I guess they don't."

"But if we're to have a conversation about our future together, we have to think about this bloody Hell pincher."

Vincent pulled his hand away. "What are you saying?"

"I'm saying that putting our feelings for each other aside, it's either yes or no. We part ways and make it so hard for the Hell-pinching bastard to realize his ambitions that he gives up. Or we go all in. We work together. And we stick together, and we fight and maybe die if this Hell pincher finds us."

Vincent lunged forward, gripping her head, pressing his lips into hers with a desperate passion she hadn't felt from him before. By the time their lips parted, she was gasping for air.

"I choose the second one," he whispered. "I'm not leaving you. Ever. You understand that Hattie Malloy? It's you and me together. There's no other option."

She crawled into his lap, straddling him and wrapping her arms around his neck.

"Okay. You and me together." Her voice was soft and breathy. "Is that invitation to make love behind the bar still open? Because I changed my mind."

Someone cleared his throat from the hallway. Lefty rolled his eyes as Hattie glanced up. "Honestly," he grumbled. "It's like having teenagers."

Hattie scrambled off Vincent's lap, doing her best to collect her dignity.

Vincent turned his head toward Lefty. "Five more minutes?" he drawled. "You couldn't give me another five minutes?"

Hattie kicked his leg. "It'd better take longer than five minutes, boy-o!"

Lefty shook his head. "If you two are done, we have transportation. And a plan."

"Transportation?" Hattie asked.

"Well, yes. Our cars will move south to hopefully draw this iron pincher into the middle of the city, while we take something more direct to arrive ahead of them."

Vincent stood up, steadying himself as his eyes continued to focus. "More direct? What's more direct than a car?"

Lefty smiled. "I think Miss Malloy is gonna like this."

They headed outside the cannery together tending their wounds and resting their powers. Arnoud and Lefty lingered by the bank of the Delaware River, both in different states of quiet: Lefty in a smug sense of anticipation, and Arnoud in nervous annoyance.

Vincent nodded when he saw the lights of the riverboats. "Everything's got stars around it, but I think I'm almost back."

Hattie peered up and down the river. "Any clue what this pageantry's all about?"

Vincent shrugged. "We're hitching a ride, is my best guess."

After another quarter hour, Arnoud began to stir as a tiny vessel chugged up the river. Lefty sprinted to the Crew gunmen hovering near their vehicles to bark marching orders.

Hattie shook her head. "It looks like any other riverboat, to me."

Vincent watched the boat approach, then laughed out loud.

"What?" she urged.

"This is clever."

"What is?" Hattie repeated. "I'm in the cold, here."

The boat sidled up to the river bank. Two men splashed into the water, wading to the rocks to moor it up to a couple concrete pylons. A figure strolled out onto the deck, lighting a cigar with a broad grin.

"Well, lookie here," he bellowed. "A bunch of sad sacks in need of a boatman!"

Vincent marched up to the riverbank as the man strolled down the gangplank eased over the edge by his crew.

"Never thought I'd see you again," Vincent shouted.

The stranger nodded and shook Vincent's hand. "Twice in a week? You're just this side of famous, you know that?"

Hattie inspected the boat. Diesel engine. V-hull. Fairly new model, to boot. The craft ought to make solid time down the Delaware.

"Hold on," she said as the others conferred. "The

Delaware doesn't let out into the Bay. Where exactly are we going?"

The boatman turned to regard her, his face broad and friendly.

"True enough, miss." He turned back to Vincent. "Am I missing something, here?"

Vincent shook his head. "This isn't my clambake."

Lefty shouted from behind them, "We're not heading for the Bay."

"I thought we were trying to beat O'Donnell to Baltimore," Hattie said.

Arnoud replied, "There's no way to overtake them to Baltimore. However, Bill can get you to Wilmington. I've got transportation from there to the Elk River."

"And I put a call in to Tony. He should have a boat ready for us at the head of Elk River," Lefty added.

Hattie frowned in confusion. "Why can't we just take the canal?"

The boatman shook his head. "By the time you navigated the locks you'll lose any time you saved. Best to let in near Wilmington and hoof it across."

Hattie eyed the boatman. "I'm sorry, we haven't been introduced."

Vincent waved his hands. "Shit. Sorry! Hattie Malloy, this here is Bill McCoy."

Hattie recoiled. "Bollocks!"

McCoy laughed. "That's either the most or least flattering reaction I've seen yet!"

Arnoud sighed. "Yes, fine. He's the Real McCoy. Will you people please, for the love of God, leave my city now?"

CHAPTER 31

Vincent peered through the darkness of the balmy spring night. The car lights in front and behind were ringed in filmy halos, but his sight had mostly returned. The line of hired cars made top speed from Wilmington to Elk River, barreling single file down bumpy county roads.

Hattie sat silent beside him, eyes closed. She wasn't asleep, he was sure. Most likely trying to rest and restore her powers. Aside from a monstrous headache, Vincent felt able and ready. What weighed upon him most was the uncertainty of the fight ahead. Where it would be, what condition Galloway's people would be in. With any luck they'd pressed south on the road following the Crew's dummy convoy, which were instructed to lead them on as circuitous a route as wouldn't look suspicious.

"Penny for your thoughts," Hattie whispered.

"Just wondering if we have any hope of beating these people. We're hanging this all on the element of surprise."

"We need more weapons, you think?"

Vincent nodded. "More pinchers, anyways. Galloway has all the firepower."

"And then there's Jonas. The man's a devil."

"But he's not limitless. I've seen him reach his limit, or at least come close. Best strategy with him might be to let him use his powers until he's spent."

Hattie opened her eyes with a lift of her chin. "How many lives would that cost, I wonder?"

"Too many."

The cars swung off the highway, rumbling through unpaved paths and nearly getting caught in mud, until they reached the Elk River. Moonlight shimmered over the water, lapping against the hull of a brown-and-green painted excursion craft. Its cabin and engine house were angular and sharp, clearly a new vessel.

As Vincent stepped out of the car, Lefty pointed out the boat to Vincent. "Looks like Tony's got a new toy."

Hattie snickered.

Vincent turned to Hattie, whose smile shone in the moonlight.

"Hate to tell you boys, but that's not a mob boat."

She lifted a hand to wave to a figure on the deck.

"About time you slack-asses showed up," Lizzie Sadler shouted from the boat.

Tony stepped up from behind Lizzie. "We gotta move, people. Firefight's started."

They climbed onto the vessel, Ghasawi standing guard until all were loaded then nearly clearing the railing with a deft leap.

Lefty pulled Tony and Vincent aside. "Where's the fight?"

"They came straight through Elkton," Tony said. "We have them logjammed up by Havre de Grace."

Lefty scowled. "They didn't take the bait."

"I don't know where you thought they were going, but it's like they came straight for the vineyard."

"Galloway," Vincent said. "He's the one with the intelligence. He knew where to strike."

Tony shrugged. "Yeah, well they weren't expecting so many of us there to put up a fight. Got them pushed back. It's like the War out there."

"What about their pinchers?" Vincent said. "Surprised they haven't torn through you already."

Tony blinked. "What pinchers?"

"There's no pinchers?"

"Just mooks with choppers," Tony said.

Lefty nodded. "Main body of the excursion. Masseria sent more muscle down. They basically have two war parties."

"Which means," Vincent muttered, "it may not be too late. Jonas and Galloway might still be driving around rural Pennsylvania."

The boat's engine fired up, churning the river water as it pushed south along the bank of the Elk River. Vincent turned to look for Hattie, finding her in her own clutch of conversation with two others.

Vincent approached nodding to Lizzie. He froze, however, as Hattie stepped back to reveal Sadie O'Donnell.

"Calendo," she said. "I hear we're in for a hell of a fight."

"What are you doing here?" he whispered, peering casually over his shoulder to the gangsters.

Sadie pointed to the top of the cabin. Vincent turned to find Charley seated on the roof, legs pulled to his chest.

"You son of a bitch," Vincent chuckled. "You made it!"

Lizzie scowled "These two show up on my doorstep from outta nowhere, informing me they're Hattie's friends and that she's in trouble. I figured I'd either shoot them or let them tag along."

"Glad you didn't shoot," Hattie said.

Vincent nodded to Lefty and Tony across the deck. "Well, need I remind you who these men are? We appreciate the help, but this is putting you in a dangerous place. You do know where we're going, right?"

Sadie rolled her eyes. "I've been doing this longer than you, Calendo. Besides…" Her eyes darkened. "I have business with my husband."

Hattie ran a hand over the rail. "Nice vessel."

Lizzie beamed. "You like it? You oughta see the tanker. Got it shored up in Charleston now. Big son of a bitch."

Vincent nodded to Sadie, and the two withdrew to let the others talk boats. He turned to face the river.

"I need to know your intentions."

Sadie nodded. "I need to see him. See what's left."

"I can tell you, not much there that isn't hell-bent on murder."

"That may be, but I have to see for myself."

"And then?" Vincent asked.

"If it's as you say, then my husband's already dead."

Vincent nodded. "I've tried. I don't want him hauling you off to Ithaca."

They looked up as distant pops of gunfire rang over the drone of the engine.

"That's not going to happen." Her voice had a hard edge to it.

As the craft wound around the point of Elk Neck, everyone on the boat fell silent. Tony and Lefty double-checked their weapons. Hattie and Sadie moved next to each other as Lizzie returned to the cabin.

Leaving Vincent alone with Ghasawi.

Vincent peered over at the man. "Don't suppose you have any more of those null enchantments?"

Ghasawi shook his head. "Alas, no. They require a great deal of crafting and the proper moon cycle to charge."

"Sounds like work."

Ghasawi chuckled, then reached into his lapel pocket to remove a dark red pocket square. He handed it to Vincent.

"I can offer you this."

Vincent took the square. "What does this do?"

"It brings me luck."

Vincent tucked it into his pocket with a nod. "Didn't know you could enchant luck into a pocket square."

"You can't," Ghasawi replied. "It's more superstition than sorcery."

"I'll take whatever I can get," Vincent said.

As they drew closer, the sky over Havre de Grace flickered with muzzle fire.

"Think all this ruckus will attract a Hell pincher?" Vincent asked.

"Difficult to tell."

"You keep saying this bogeyman's about to pounce around every corner, but I haven't seen hide nor hair of this Hell pincher since you arrived."

Ghasawi nodded. "Which means I am doing my job. But you are right. This in-fighting between pinchers has provided the Hell pincher ample opportunity to strike. Perhaps we are fortunate he's chosen to bide his time."

"Assuming this isn't a load of hopped-up bushwa, I intend to take this Hell pincher head-on. Once this is all over."

"Then you will fail, and mankind will suffer at the hands of an omnipotent being."

Vincent turned to Ghasawi. "Is it really that bad?"

"You have tasted the power of the Solomon's Crown only once. And that is for the best. This sort of power is unimaginable in its capacity to destroy and corrupt."

Vincent thought of Galloway. Simple power was enough to corrupt the man into a backstabbing schemer. Absolute power the likes of which Ghasawi was describing? How could any human, regardless of their virtue, hope to survive that?

The vessel chugged across the estuary of the Northeast River, the village of Havre de Grace nestled on its shore. The glow of fires loomed over the tree line. As the engine shut down, the noises of warfare were that much louder. Each of the passengers disembarked, save for Lizzie.

Hattie stood on the pier to give Lizzie a wave farewell.

"You keep your head down," Lizzie shouted. "I'm gonna need you Tuesday."

"Don't you worry," Hattie replied. "I'll be there. I need the money!"

Tony trotted into the village, boosting a car left parked on the street. They squeezed into the stolen car, crammed tight three in the front and back with Tony at the tiller. Charley pinched himself into a raven and flew up to the nearest gable, croaking at them as they got the car moving. The drive to the vineyard brought them behind the enemy line, a length of cars and trucks almost twenty long blocking the main drive to Vito's villa.

Vincent asked, "Any thoughts on breaking through that line?"

Tony nodded. "Just one."

He hammered down on the accelerator.

They nearly reached the back of the firing line before the New York gunmen even noticed their arrival. They dove out of the way as Tony aimed for a gap between cars.

They all braced for impact.

The front fenders of their stolen car crumpled into the barricade, spinning the cars on their tires.

They pitched forward onto the circular drive, both front tires blown.

Guns poked from the corners and windows of the villa, preparing to open fire on them.

Vincent pinched time as the car swung sideways, about to roll. He glanced back at Hattie in the back seat, who offered a nod of acknowledgement. He opened Tony's driver side door, shoving him into the air outside with his foot before reaching back to drag Lefty after him. Hattie followed suit, hauling Sadie and Ghasawi free of the car. Together they eased their party back to the ground. As the tug on his powers grew more intense, Hattie reached out to press her palm against his chest. The strain eased and Vincent gave her a smile.

They pulled their time-frozen friends two-by-two behind a low wall branching off the porte cochere where one of Corbi's gunmen had taken cover. Once each of them was tucked away, clear of the flipping vehicle and Corbi's bullets, Vincent released the time pinch.

The car tumbled onto its side, smashing into the center fountain as bullets sprayed its undercarriage.

The others sucked in an alarmed breath as they got their bearings.

The gunman spun around.

Vincent held up his hands, stepping between him and his party.

"It's me!" he shouted.

"Oh!" The gunman smiled at Vincent. "Where the hell did you come from?"

"Philadelphia." He glanced back to the villa. "Where's the Capo?"

"Inside."

Vincent rushed for the tall oak double-doors leading to Vito's parlor room, jerking them open for the others to file inside. The parlor remained as he'd last seen it, a war room with an enormous map spangled with more ink-scratched notes. Curly stood near the center table losing an argument with a jammed tommy gun.

Vincent nodded to Curly. "Where's Vito?"

Curly pointed to the far door. "Holed up in the cellar."

Vincent turned to Tony. "Tell Vito we're here."

Tony swept around the table.

"Tell him," Vincent shouted, "Lefty and I are here."

Tony glanced at the others, nodded, then disappeared through the back door to the kitchens and the wine cellar.

Hattie said, "Looks like we beat the pinchers. But by how long?"

"Depends on the dummy," Lefty said.

"Galloway's too smart to take the bait for long," Vincent said. "We should get ready."

Sadie stepped up to the war map, lifting a hand to trace idle lines across its surface. She turned to take in the room, eyes narrow.

"The seat of evil," she whispered.

Vincent and Lefty exchanged glances, then Vincent said, "It's too warm for you to be of much use."

Sadie frowned, then marched over to Curly. She jerked the weapon from his hands to set it onto the table. Disengaging the butt and trigger grip assembly, she flipped it over to clear the spring which had cocked. After she reassembled the weapon, she slapped the magazine back into place and racked the cocking handle.

"I disagree," she said, handing the gun to Curly.

"Can you shoot as good as you can field strip?" Lefty asked.

"I'm from Chicago," she told him.

"Give her the gun, Curly."

He handed back the weapon. "We have some positions on the second floor."

Hattie nodded to Sadie, who followed Curly into the rear of the villa.

Vincent peered from one of the front windows, squinting

past the closed shutters. "I'd love to eliminate that firing line before Jonas gets here."

Lefty shrugged. "Wouldn't have a tank on you, would you?"

"If I had a heave pincher, I could throw a boulder at them. If I had an earth pincher, I could wall them off in stone."

"So, what *do* we have?"

"Not enough time, is what we have." He turned to Hattie and Charley. "We gotta conserve our strength for when the heavyweights get here."

"Agreed," Hattie said.

Lefty said, "They're not encircling the villa. Just sitting there, blocking the main road."

"They're waiting for the pinchers," Vincent said.

"They're trapping Vito here. He's the target."

Vincent nodded to Ghasawi who was haunting the corner of the room. "What about you? Got any Janissary tactics for us?"

Ghasawi approached the window, bending down to squint through the gap in the shutters. "A typical Ottoman charge would harass the forward guard with light fire until the enemy is drawn into a hopeless counter-attack. But we are the defenders, here. Therefore, we should identify the weak point of the line and concentrate fire."

"Then what?"

"Then we charge."

Vincent smirked. "We ain't on horseback, so I don't see that working."

Lefty lifted a finger. "Hang on." He rounded Vincent to point to the wreckage they'd created bursting through the back of the line. "There's your weak point."

"So?"

"He's right," Lefty said. "Turn up the heat there where

they're exposed. Soften the line. Then we ram them hard and pierce the line."

"Ram them with what?" Vincent asked.

"I got an idea." Lefty turned to Hattie. "Go tell your friend and the others upstairs concentrate fire at the wreckage. Tell them to go off full auto. Choose their shots. Especially Curly, that shiftless spray-and-pray moron."

Hattie looked to Vincent.

He gave her a nod, urging her to comply.

"Right," she said, taking the rear door Curly had used.

"Alright, you three," Lefty barked. "Follow me."

They ducked through the kitchen and into the courtyard at the center of the villa. The neatly manicured patio flickered in torchlight as they headed through to the rear of the property.

Reaching a broad building with wide barn doors, Lefty fired a shot from his revolver, knocking loose the padlock that chained it closed. Vincent and Charlie pulled the doors open to reveal several cargo trucks.

Lefty nodded to them. "Army surplus. Big and burly." He trotted between two of the trucks to nudge the first of a line of steel cans. "Grab two empties and split them fifty-fifty."

Vincent asked, "What's the play?"

Lefty snatched a can of motor oil and tossed it to Vincent. "Give each can a pint of this."

Ghasawi nodded. "I see."

"Someone want to fill me in?" Vincent urged as he popped a can and poured it into a half-filled canister of gasoline.

"Petrol for fire," Ghasawi explained. "Oil for smoke."

"Smoke screen?"

Lefty pulled open a truck door. "We ram the line, then toss these beauties right on top like bottle bombs. We'll cook the bastards right at the breach, and the rest lose visibility."

"When they see it coming, they're gonna give it everything they got," Vincent warned. "Whoever's driving will get pulped."

"We don't have time to armor this thing up," Lefty grumbled. "It's my best play."

Vincent grinned. "Not if they have two trucks barreling at them from the sides."

"We don't have enough trucks or manpower for that."

"No," Vincent said, "but we do have a light pincher."

Lefty sighed. "One day. You're gonna be wrong about something one day."

"Leave this to us," Vincent said. "Go find Hattie. Give her the skinny."

Lefty inched away toward the door, then paused to toss a box of rags to Vincent. "Be sure to get them down into the oil."

Vincent waved him off. "I got it."

Lefty nearly left the shed before pausing to add, "Fold them diagonal so you get more length."

"Would you go?"

Lefty rushed back to the house, leaving Ghasawi, Charley and Vincent to fill and wick four canisters of oil and petrol.

"Charley?" Vincent asked. "You drive?"

He shook his head.

"Yeah. Figured as much. What about you?"

Ghasawi nodded. "I am capable, but I believe my talents are better used lifting and throwing. Your talents are perhaps better found behind the wheel."

Vincent chuckled, shaking his head as they loaded the canisters into the back of the truck. "You're saying I got noodle arms?"

"That was...no..."

"Yanking your chain, Assam. Right, I'll get the wheel. Either of you got matches?"

Charley lifted a matchbox from his coat pocket.

"Okay. Let's get in position."

Vincent cranked up the engine and climbed into the truck. Once the others were in the back, he eased the truck out of the shed and around the corner of the villa's service drive. Gunfire from the villa sounded in individual pops. The firing line flared with automatic fire, muzzle flashes flickering at the ends more than the middle, where Masseria's men had hunkered down for cover.

He waited, one hand on the wheel, the other clamped onto the shift.

"Come on, girl," he whispered to himself. "Give 'em both barrels."

Vincent watched the firing line with shallow breaths. His foot nudged the clutch impatiently.

Shouts rang out.

Muzzle flares shifted wide, firing out into the vineyard. Vincent could only see the closer end of the firing line, but this had to be it.

"Here we go."

He hammered the gas as he engaged the clutch, sending the truck growling forward like an enraged grizzly. Vincent made it through two gears before the truck cleared the side of the villa. Its wheels thumped over the paving stones alongside the circular drive, shoving a bit of their ruined car to the side as he cleared the fountain.

A few wide eyes near the hole in the line caught sight of the truck as he approached.

Guns raised.

Vincent gritted his teeth and ducked to the side as the windscreen shattered.

He pulled his head back up and braced as the truck smashed into the firing line with a lurch.

The wheels spun as the undercarriage caught on a piece

of debris. Panic filled his chest as the truck rolled forward by inches.

The wheels hit the ground again, jolting the truck as it sped forward.

Flashes filled the side of Vincent's vision. He hit the brakes. The truck slid forward under its own weight, drifting to a stop several yards away.

Two more flashes.

All four canisters had been thrown, spilling a slick of gasoline and rolling flames across the nearest cars of the firing line.

Vincent hopped out of the car and drew his gun.

Charley was the first out the back of the truck. He gawked at the figures of men flailing as they rushed away from the black smoke belching into the night sky.

Vincent lifted his gun and fired, dropping one as Ghasawi emerged from the truck.

"You know your way around a gun?" Vincent shouted.

"The blade," Ghasawi replied, "is not the only weapon in my arsenal."

"I'll take that as a yes," Vincent said, tossing his revolver to Ghasawi.

Charley peered at Vincent. "You want me to go big?"

"Hold it," Vincent said. "Save it for Jonas."

Vincent glanced across the ground, then forward to the firing line in disarray. The illusion must have dissipated.

"Give me a sec," Vincent grumbled.

He rushed for the closest Masseria gunmen. Two spotted Vincent in his charge and raised their repeaters.

Vincent pinched time, pushing through the smoke that hung in the air like fabric. He reached out to grip one of the tommy guns, lifting it to take a wide swing against the side of the gunman's head. The gunman tilted a couple inches to the side with a heavy thump.

Vincent gripped the weapon by its barrel and rammed the butt into the nose of the second gunman before snatching his weapon. He released time and turned to walk back.

The gunmen hit the ground behind Vincent as he tossed one of the repeaters to Charley.

The fur pincher caught the weapon, staring at it blankly.

"Oh," Vincent groaned. "Don't tell me you're the one person in the group who's never fired a gun?"

"Never needed one before," Charley grumbled.

Vincent reached out to check the safety. "You're good to go. Just point and pull the trigger. Fire in three round bursts if you can, or else it'll start lifting on you."

Charley nodded, then turned to the opposite side of the line to test out the weapon.

His gun released roughly ten rounds before he'd managed to pull it back into control.

"Good enough," Vincent said.

They turned to the right and advanced. Vincent drilled two men with clean shots before rushing for cover. Bullets sprayed his cover as he held his breath. When there was a pause in the firing, he pinched time and stepped out from behind the cover to choose his targets.

Then he released time and plugged two more, a throb in his stomach warning him that he was already pushing his magic harder than he'd wanted.

Gunshots from the villa resumed, sending his half of the firing line diving for cover between vehicles. Three or four gunmen swung back out from between the cars as they got caught in the crossfire from the villa.

Vincent lifted his weapon and sprayed a long volley against the rear of the line. He pulled the trigger until the magazine was empty, then he tossed it aside and rushed for the weapon of one of the fallen Masseria men.

As he wrestled the weapon from the clutches of the dead

man, a lithe young thug rolled out from behind one of the vehicles. He lifted a gun directly at Vincent's head.

Before he could pinch time, the thug's head jerked back in a spray of red.

Vincent turned to find Ghasawi several yards away, still taking aim with the revolver. He gave the man a nod of acknowledgement, then jerked the repeater free of its owner's clutches.

Acrid smoke wafted over Vincent's shoulder, flying into the faces of his opponents. The New York gunmen who were caught in the crossfire from the villa began their retreat, rushing up the drive for the rows of vines nearby. Vincent let them go, focusing on those still trenched in.

A fresh salvo of gunfire sounded from the villa grounds. A clutch of Vito's men had rushed out of the villa and were advancing against the right flank. Sparks flew off the vehicle line, glass shattering as bullets slammed home to drop several New Yorkers.

Vincent turned to the left flank to check on Charley. As the smoke billowed past Vincent's face, he struggled to focus on the scene before him. Flames danced in and around an enormous black bear swatting gangsters aside as Ghasawi dropped to a crouch to take aim at those the bear missed.

"You better save some of that!" Vincent shouted with a grin.

The Crew's advance reached the firing line, sending the last of the left flank running for the vineyard. Vincent took a breath, coughing against the black smoke as he tucked his weapon under his arm.

The unearthly roars from behind him subsided as the Crew advance team split in half to mop up the right flank. Vincent cast a glance over his shoulder to find Ghasawi and Charley, in his human form, rushing to join him.

"Keep your head down, Charley," Vincent urged. "These

men are going to remember there was a hellbeast fighting alongside them tomorrow. There's gonna be questions."

Charley nodded to the villa. "But Sadie's inside."

"They don't know what she is," Vincent replied. "Too warm to use her powers. No one will realize she's a pincher."

"Where you want me?" Charley asked.

"Back at the villa," Vincent replied. "On foot, please. I told you to save your sauce for—"

The entire property erupted in brilliant white light.

Vincent shut his eyes, covering his face with his arm as his stomach dropped into his shoes.

"Go!" he shouted. "Now!"

He squinted over his elbow at the villa, gleaming as if in broad daylight.

The ground rumbled beneath Vincent's feet as he sprinted forward. One thump sent him staggering. He dropped his weapon, lifting his hands to absorb his fall. Then he rose to his feet and ran, not stopping to think or gather his weapon. He knew what was coming behind him.

Something sizzled through the air over his head. A slender length of iron pierced the paving stones of the fountain.

Vincent pinched time, shoving with all his might to close the distance to the villa. By the time he'd reached the side of the building and had released his time pinch he was gasping for air. He rolled around the low wall beside the service entrance, back against the ground, a wave of nausea rolling through his midsection.

A wall of brown rushed over his head.

Vincent lifted his hands defensively, peering down as hooves hammered against the gravel pad alongside the villa. A horse landed from a leap, staggering as its slender legs pinched back into human arms and legs.

Ghasawi, who had been riding on its back, tumbled to the

side in a graceful roll, landing in a crouch as Charley sputtered in the gravel.

The fur pincher glanced up to Vincent, a trickle of blood slipping from his nostril. "Sorry. Had to."

Vincent nodded. He'd be a hypocrite to call Charley out on using up too much energy. He'd done the same.

They were already close to tapped out, and now that Jonas was here with Galloway's pinchers, the fight would finally begin in earnest.

CHAPTER 32

*H*attie ducked behind the window as bright daylight flooded the courtyard.

"Shit!" she gasped.

Sadie winced beside her. "What *is* that?"

"It's their bloody sun pincher," Hattie grunted. "They're here!"

"How do we shoot at the sun?"

"We don't," Hattie grumbled. "Which is their point. Come on!"

Hattie grabbed Sadie's sleeve, jerking her off the floor to rush to the stairs. The two bustled back down to the first floor, slipping through a library before reaching the kitchen, and then the war room.

Loud collisions sounded against the side of the building. One of the windows shattered, the shutters splintering as a savage shard of steel sunk into the wall beside them.

Sadie gripped Hattie by the arm. "Is…?"

"It's Jonas," Hattie told her.

The far doors burst open.

The two women raised their weapons. Hattie relaxing as

she spotted Vincent plowing forward with Charley and Ghasawi in tow.

"That didn't take them long," she shouted.

"Yeah."

"You ready for this?"

Vincent eyed her with a weariness that conveyed one horrible fact.

"Oh God," she gasped. "You're not spent already, are you?"

Vincent leaned against the table, holding himself up with his fists as he sucked in air.

Charley staggered to a chair, wiping blood from his face.

"You too?" Hattie asked panic beginning to grip her.

Ghasawi lifted a hand. "This man saved my life."

Hattie shook her head. "That's temporary. We're about to face a truckload of pinchers out there."

Fresh screams sounded from the front lawn.

Lefty surged into the room from the kitchens. "Mary Mother of Jesus, that guy is a monster!"

Ghasawi asked, "Do we have adequate cover against this iron pincher?"

Hattie surveyed the room. "It's a solid building. Question is whether the wood pincher's still with them."

Vincent grunted, "I'd assume he is."

"You said you gave him a good lick," Lefty said.

Vincent nodded, still catching his breath. "Yeah, but he's had half a day to walk it off."

"We're not winning this on an even terrain," Sadie declared.

Lefty stepped up next to her. "Agreed."

"You said Corbi is this man's target. That's obvious, otherwise he'd have hit Baltimore first. Now, we know where Corbi is. We can either throw lives away trying to keep these pinchers away from the man, or we let them march in."

Lefty scowled. "You're kidding, right?"

Sadie shook her head. "No, listen. He's in the cellar. That creates a bottleneck. And we know that's where they're going to go. It's a known position."

Lefty replied, "But where's the exit strategy? Assuming we can't take advantage of the bottleneck, what's to stop him from reaching the cellar?" He shook his head. "If you'd spent a day in the trenches, you'd know you have to plan for failure."

Sadie jabbed a finger into Lefty's chest. "I've lived my entire life in a state of war. Sometimes there is no option for failure. Sometimes there is only win or die."

Lefty stepped away from the woman. "Win or die makes sense only when there *is* no other option. We're not there yet."

"But let's think this out," Hattie said. "What would we do with this bottleneck?"

"Eliminate the enemy asset by asset," Ghasawi answered.

All eyes turned to him.

He continued, "One man versus six? That is suicide. But one man versus one man? These are even odds. Even better if we possess the element of surprise."

Vincent straightened up with a vigorous clearing of his throat. "You're saying we take them down one at a time?"

Ghasawi nodded. "We have a path of access. If we provide obstacles to the goal—"

"I get it, I get it," Vincent snapped with a lift of his hand.

Hattie watched him with a worried frown. He was well and truly knackered. If he faced Jonas now, he'd die—either by Jonas's hand or from one pinch more than his body could handle. She turned to Sadie and Lefty, both of which seemed squared against one another as they argued strategy.

It was up to Hattie.

She clapped her hands several times and lifted her fingers

to count off.

"One, we have an earth pincher who's making it bloody well difficult to stand on our own two feet. Best choice is to take her off her feet. If there's anyone who can remove themselves from the ground, that's the best against Maria."

Hattie looked to Charley.

He eased away a step or two.

"Do you have enough left for another pinch?" she asked.

"Maybe," he muttered. "But not enough for a fight."

"We don't need a fight," she said. "All we need is time."

Charley thought it over. "I've pinched a golden eagle before. It's strong enough to lift a goat off the ground." He turned to Vincent. "How big is this earth pincher?"

"Bigger than a goat," Vincent told him.

"We don't need to pick her up. Just get her away from the rest," Hattie said.

Charley sighed, then nodded. "I'll try."

Hattie lifted a second finger. "Two, we have the damned sun pincher. Now, I can tell you from experience, I can deal with her myself."

"Sold," Lefty said. "What about the Splinter King?"

Ghasawi stepped across the parlor to the hearth, reaching above the mantel to regard Corbi's family crest mounted above. It was painted upon a bronze shield, with a fat blade sliding through the mount behind. Ghasawi slid the blade free of its mount, feeling its weight.

"Cinquedea," he proclaimed. "Close quarters combat weapon of the Italian renaissance." Ghasawi gave it a few test swings. "No wood on this weapon."

Hattie nodded. "You take Douglas, then. Next, we have the shadow pincher."

Lefty grumbled, "I have that one."

"Are you sure?" she asked.

"He's a distance asset. I have some experience moving

behind the enemy."

Vincent nodded to Lefty.

"Right then," Hattie said. "That leaves us with Galloway and Jonas."

Vincent and Sadie exchanged glances.

"Sadie?" Hattie muttered. "Are you sure you want to face him?"

She regarded her weapon. "I have to."

"With what?" Vincent asked.

"You leave Jonas to me, Calendo."

Vincent's eyebrows shot up. "More like I'm leaving you and Corbi to Jonas."

Sadie's eyes narrowed. "I suppose this is the moment, Calendo. You'll have to choose whose side you're really on."

Vincent looked down, then over his shoulder to Lefty.

Lefty avoided his glance, busying himself with his revolver.

Vincent replied, "I have Galloway. But listen…if any of you fail, it changes the math."

Hattie lifted her hands. "We don't have time to dicker over alternatives. They're coming."

The building rocked as another tremor raged underfoot.

"We're out of time," she concluded.

Hattie reached for Sadie, pulling her to the kitchen. "Go!"

"See you all later." Charley rushed across the room. He leapt, curling into a ball. As his frame smashed through the glass of the window and split open the shutters, a flourish of frenetic energy and feathers rose into the air.

"Give 'em Hell, gentlemen!" Hattie nodded to Lefty and Ghasawi then waited for Vincent to join her, before plunging through the back door into the kitchen.

Vincent pointed Sadie toward the slender door leading to the wine cellar. "That way. Best wait for me before you head down. I'll keep us from getting shot."

Sadie nodded once with a grim frown.

Vincent turned back to face Hattie. "This is your stand?"

"Assuming the rest of the boys do their part, aye."

"Just stick to the premise, okay? Take out that sun pincher, then get yourself outta here."

She balked at the notion of running out the back door to leave Sadie and Vincent in the hands of whoever was left to funnel into the dank bowels of this wretched place without her. She wanted to stay. Anything but leave.

Despite this, she nodded with a smirk. "You give that bastard hell for me, boy-o."

"Definitely." Vincent gripped her shoulders, pulling her in for a brief kiss, then he stepped back and held the door to the cellar open for Sadie as the two descended to join Vito Corbi.

Leaving Hattie alone.

The earth trembled, rattling the pans and dishes in the kitchen. Hattie steadied herself against a metal table. A chef's knife clattered on its surface threatening to drop off tip-first. Hattie reached to slide it to the center of the island, then gripped its handle. It made her feel stronger. She was armed.

She could do something besides wait.

Hattie shoved the door to the war room open, marching past the maps and table strewn with notes and plans as the building shook with some major impact. Standing in the doorway she peered into the drive.

As a gunman reached over the retaining wall to fire a few shots at their attackers a projectile plowed into his face at alarming speed. The man tumbled backward and Hattie held her breath, watching as his spasms subsided and the man released his final breath. She squinted at the ruin of his face.

Tree branch. This would be the wood pincher's work.

Leaving the doorway, she crawled along the ground behind the wall, peering around the corner at the apocalypse unfolding on the front lawn. The car they'd wrecked on their way in had been peeled apart like an orange, jagged shards of steel lifting from a plume of flames and smoke. Jonas presided over the scene from the edge of the fountain, his hands raised with a conductor's grace as he sent slices of iron flying into the remnants of Vito's people.

A chasm opened up from the drive to the front of the villa. Two of Masseria's vehicles had already slid into the rift, with a third teetering on the edge as one of the New York thugs screamed for help. The car tumbled over the edge, smashing somewhere far below.

Overtop the landscape of billowing smoke and dying gasps, a beam of blinding light swept back and forth to illuminate survivors. As the light lingered, a fresh salvo of iron spears cut short the life of whoever was found.

A keening cry sounded over the battlefield. The beams of light from the sun pincher lifted into the air, tracking an enormous dark figure as it swooped from the sky. Talons lashed out in the sun pincher's rays, smashing into the shoulders of the earth pincher.

Maria shrieked in pain as the eagle dragged her backward a few feet, dropping her onto the ground.

Jonas turned to survey the scene, reaching for a stray length of metal shorn from the car chassis before him. He brandished the metal at ear's height, waiting for the raptor to be illuminated once again.

The sun pincher broadened her beam, now shining as a cone into the sky. As it pivoted back and forth, Hattie watched Millie stagger, catching herself as her knees threatened to buckle. This was taxing her.

The eagle swept back to the ground, slipping into the light.

Jonas sent his spear flying.

The shard sliced through the air toward Charley.

His wings and feathers tumbled into a ball, morphing

back into the ragged clothes and beard of the man Hattie had first met only a few months ago. He dropped onto Maria's shoulders, jerking her to the ground as the metal spear sailed overhead. As they bowled forward, the earth pincher's head smacked the ground. Her shoulders sagged as she rolled to a limp halt.

Charley caught himself on hands and knees, blood rushing from his nose, eyes narrow with a wince of pain. He reached out to check Maria's pulse.

Jonas pulled two more strips of metal from nearby wreckage, brandishing them like spears.

With a titanic cry of pain, Charley roared to sky as he transformed into a black panther. The enormous cat gripped Maria by the back of her coat, hauling her behind the smoldering ruin of the New York firing line and out of sight.

One pincher down.

Hattie searched the field for the others. Millie stood beside Jonas, beaming her solar rays back and forth. Though the broad beam she'd employed to spot the Charley Eagle had taxed her, she still had some light left, now packed into tight spotlights.

Jonas pivoted with his steel shards, returning his attention to the villa.

Hattie rushed from behind the low wall, sprinting for cover behind a statue closer to the mayhem in the front drive.

Millie's beams snapped to her location, sweeping the ground Hattie had just covered.

Back pressed against the marble, Hattie closed her eyes and felt for Millie's beams. She could feel the edges of the light as the sun pincher swept for her. Holding a breath, Hattie opened her eyes and dove from behind the statue.

She lifted her hands and pinched the solar beams, bending them like a mirror to Jonas.

The iron pincher barked in alarm, clamping his eyes shut and staggering backward several steps.

Millie attempted to swing her light away, but Hattie locked onto her beams with her powers keeping the full brunt of the solar blast on Jonas.

A shadow crossed Jonas's face, easing the brightness.

Hattie frowned as she bent the light in circles, trying to restore the attack. But as she aimed toward Jonas, a plume of pitch-black fog snaked through the air to encircle the iron pincher in an inky wreath.

Hattie scowled, then angled the light straight back to Millie.

The sun pincher doused her light and balled her fists. With a war cry, Millie rushed at Hattie.

A fist smashed into Hattie's jaw before she could duck out of the way and Hattie's face swung to the side. As she lifted a hand to catch Millie's second blow, Hattie reached for Millie's coat, wrestling her to the ground.

Millie racked her fingers across Hattie's face and hot lines of pain sliced across Hattie's cheek. Then she pulled Hattie to the side, rolling on top of her with a grimace and clamping her hands around Hattie's neck.

Hattie reached between Millie's arms trying to land a blow to her chin, but the sun pincher's arms were just a bit longer than hers.

Blood choked Hattie's vision as her pulse pounded in her head. With a quick, artless pinch, she conjured a vision of horror onto her own face, a needle-toothed nightmare from a child's fever dream.

Millie shrieked, her grip loosening in reflex.

It was enough. Hattie swatted away one hand and threw the heel of her palm underneath the sun pincher's jaw landing the blow straight against the woman's throat.

Millie staggered off Hattie, gripping her throat as she

made gasping, choking noises.

Hattie pulled herself to her knees. As she planted a hand against the ground, she lifted a leg, swinging it at the hip to land against the side of the sun pincher's head. Millie spun backward, landing flat against the ground unconscious.

A tendril of the black smoke wafted across her vision and she sucked in a breath, back-pedaling away from the finger of shadow.

The cloud parted. Hattie stared up at Jonas O'Donnell, still gripping both jagged steel spears.

"Where is Corbi?" he asked.

Hattie clenched her jaw, crab-walking away from him as he continued to step forward.

He repeated, "Where's Corbi?"

"Go to hell," she snarled.

Jonas lifted the tip of his spear, stretching the point with his powers into a needle. The iron shrieked in a thin, tinny whine as it inched closer to Hattie's face.

"Last chance," he said.

A gunshot sounded, and a flash of sparks sprayed across Jonas's left cheek.

He shook his face, peering to his left. Hattie turned over, pushing off the ground and sprinting away, only making it a few feet before a tendril of shadow swept across her face. She blinked against the darkness, her shin ramming into some-thing hard. Hattie tumbled forward, splashing face-first into the fountain. She pulled herself out of the water, shaking her face with a gasp as her leg throbbed in pain.

"Dammit!" Jonas bellowed. "Give me a path! I can't see anything."

The darkness thinned slightly, and Hattie ducked low in the fountain.

"Now!" Jonas shouted. "I can't see anything you idiot."

The ball of shadow undulated, and the tendrils of darkness parted around them with a clear line of sight to his left.

Hattie dug deep, testing her reserves of magic. This would be simple. No form, no sound, no smell. She just wanted to make the tendrils snaking back to that dark sphere more obvious, like a giant arrow pointing to where the shadow pincher hid.

Pinching light, she sent moonlight streaming in a subtle outline across the vague outlines of the smoke, tracing a path back to the shadow pincher.

"Come on," she whispered.

Another gunshot.

The shadow trembled, then dissipated like fog in bright morning sunlight. At the center of the diminishing sphere of ink stood Bolton, eyes slack. He took one step forward, lifting a hand to his chest and pulled back bloody fingers before dropping to the ground.

Hattie grinned and muttered, "Fine shot, Mancuso."

Jonas spun around looking for the shooter, then looked back at Bolton's dead body, his face twisting in frustration.

A voice shouted from the open doors to the villa parlor, "They're inside! Move it!"

Hattie glanced back to the building to find Galloway holding the doors open.

"Bastard!" she hissed.

With a mighty heave, she cleared the coping of the fountain and rushed for the building, pinching light around her body to make herself invisible. As she closed the distance to Galloway, Jonas threw one of his spears. It sailed far to her right, sinking into the ground.

Hattie pressed onward, her boots slapping against the ground in wet splashes.

Galloway lifted a chin, eyes moving from the space above the ground to the ground itself. He threw a finger in Hattie's direction.

"There! The footprints!"

Something lashed against Hattie's ankles, pulling tight. She tripped forward as her ankles squeezed together. Hattie dropped hard against the gravel just in front of Galloway. Then, she slid inch by inch along the gravel as something pulled her away. Pawing against the ground, she pushed up high enough to find a thick rope of winter-browned vines encircling her legs.

At the end of the vines stood Douglas, smirking in satisfaction. With a flick of his finger, the vines snaked around Hattie's arms binding her tight as she came to a rest at his feet.

"Should've taken care of you long ago." Douglas gave the vines a twist.

They squeezed into Hattie, pressing her chest tight. She released a yelp of alarm.

Galloway called from the door, "Quit playing."

Jonas trotted up to Galloway, brandishing his last weapon. He cast a disinterested glance at Hattie, then stepped into the parlor. "In here?"

Galloway said as he followed Jonas inside, "I swayed one of Corbi's men inside. Said they were last seen heading for the cellar."

The doors closed behind them, leaving Hattie alone with the wood pincher.

"Let's see," he said as he crouched over her. "Shall we make this interesting?"

Pin pricks erupted all over Hattie's body as tiny thorns emerged from the vines. She shrieked in pain and anger, twisting her arms against the constricting vines.

With a lift of his hand, the vines arced in the air, pulling Hattie off the ground. She hung upside-down, staring into Douglas's face.

"This is for Millie," he said.

His fingers curled midair, and the vines pulled tighter. Hattie struggled for air as the wood began crushing her arms into her ribs.

A blur of motion parted the space between Hattie and Douglas.

The glimmer of steel.

The vines loosened, sending Hattie falling back to the ground. She landed on her shoulders, the wind knocked out of her. When air finally returned to her lungs, she looked up to find Ghasawi lurching forward with the fat dagger he'd pried loose from Vito's family crest.

Douglas reached for the oak doors, prying loose a slab of wood. It sailed several feet through the air, coming to rest in his hand just in time to parry Ghasawi's thrust. He warped the oak plank into an axe head, blade as sharp as the wood would allow and hacked at Ghasawi with a clumsy swing.

Ghasawi stepped to the side, spinning on a heel to bring the cinquedea into the axe. The wood split in half under the blow of the steel blade and Douglas snarled and retreated a step. Ghasawi spun again, swinging his foot in a wide hook, slamming it against Douglas' head.

The wood pincher dropped to the ground.

Ghasawi advanced, dagger pointed to Douglas's back. "Do you yield?"

Douglas reached for the vines nearby. They slithered into his grip, lashing up to wrap around Ghasawi's sword hand.

Ghasawi braced as Douglas attempted to jerk the sword free. The vines snapped taut between them.

Douglas grunted beginning to lose the battle of strength.

Ghasawi waved his sword arm in a circle, winding the vines around his forearm as he pulled Douglas off the ground and to his feet before giving the vines a solid jerk.

Douglas staggered forward into Ghasawi's sword.

The wood pincher's eyes widened in panic. Then

Ghasawi shoved him off the sword, slicing the blade across the man's throat.

Hattie sucked in several breaths, shaking off the vines.

Ghasawi approached to offer a hand. She took it and eased to her feet. "Are you injured?" he asked.

"Aye, in several—"

He yanked her aside, shielding her from a blur of motion off to the side. Millie sprinted toward the two of them, the spear Jonas had thrown at Hattie gripped in both hands. Ghasawi shoved Hattie behind him, his short blade held at the ready.

Millie shrieked as she hoisted the spear.

A gunshot sounded dropping the sun pincher face first onto the gravel in a widening pool of blood.

Hattie peered past Ghasawi's shoulder to find Lefty holding his smoking revolver on Millie. He stepped forward, nudging her with his shoe.

"Another fine shot, Mancuso," Hattie muttered.

Lefty nodded. "Where's the iron pincher?"

She pointed at the oak doors. "Moving for the cellar."

Lefty grunted, rushing for the doors. Hattie took a step, then nearly fell. Ghasawi caught her, holding her upright.

She gasped, looking over toward Lefty. "I don't think I can."

Lefty nodded to Ghasawi. "You got her?"

"I've got her," Ghasawi replied.

Lefty holstered his gun and pulled open the door, racing inside.

Hattie stood panting, Ghasawi's hand steadying her by the arm. Two dead pinchers were at her feet, and another shot dead by the wreckage.

Closing her eyes Hattie rested her forehead on her knuckles. She'd done everything she could for Vincent. Now the rest was up to him.

ootsteps pounded on the floorboards overhead.

"They're coming," Vito whispered.

Vincent nodded, eyeing the revolver in the Capo's hand. "Your gun won't do any good."

Corbi sneered. "I will not surrender to any man without a fight."

It was a brave sentiment, even if his opponent was liable to stab the Capo with his own gun. Looking over to Sadie, Vincent saw that she'd put down her firearm and was holding a jagged piece of glass from a broken snifter in one hand.

Outside of the guns, there wasn't much metal in the room. Wooden wine racks ran on both sides of the slender space, creating a corridor from the overturned tasting table to the cellar stairs. Gaslight flickered from sconces behind them, sending their long shadows dancing across the neatly chiseled stone floor.

The cellar door creaked open, spilling fresh light down the stairs. The sound of heavy footsteps echoed through the room.

Sadie sucked in a breath as Jonas stepped into view.

The iron pincher came to a halt, visibly jarred at the sight of his wife. His iron spear dipped as his grip slackened.

Galloway loomed in the stairway behind Jonas, eyes sharp and planted on Vincent.

Sadie stepped forward.

"Jonas?" she whispered.

The taut sneer eased. The man, for the first time, almost seemed human. A softness washed over his features as he beheld his wife.

"Sadie," he replied in a slightly higher register than Vincent had heard before.

"What've they done to you?" she asked.

He dropped the spear to the stone with a clatter.

Sadie took a step forward. "You were…so gentle. Before."

He moved toward her, hand lifting out to touch her arm.

"It's been so long," he replied. "So much pain."

Vincent held a breath. Never in a hundred years had he expected Sadie to actually break through the Ithaca indoctrination. And yet, here was the beast tamed by her presence.

"So much death," she said.

"I didn't… I couldn't…"

"I know," she whispered, reaching up to stroke the side of his beard. "They stole you from me."

Tears fell from Jonas's eyes.

Vincent glanced at Galloway, whose face betrayed no sense of panic or confusion. Only resolve.

No…

Concentration.

A tiny trickle of blood slipped from Galloway's nostril.

And a smirk lifted onto his lips.

"Sadie!" Vincent shouted.

Jonas' features snapped shut like a bear trap, his hand

reaching out as the spear broke into pieces and rose off the ground. The razor tip of the steel slid between Sadie's ribs. She cried out once. Then again as Jonas reached for her, holding her on her feet and pushing the blade deeper into her stomach.

"I'm so sorry," she whispered, slashing him with the piece of glass. It left a thin strip of welling blood across the man's arm.

He sneered. "Just die."

"I'm sorry," Sadie repeated. Then with a sob she reached out a finger to touch the wound on his hand.

The blood froze. Jonas gasped, his eyes widening as ice crystals formed around the cut then shot along his arm, skin bursting open as the liquid in his veins and cells turned to ice. The metal spear frosted over, and Sadie convulsed, blood pouring from her nose as well as the wound. Jonas went rigid, his skin becoming the color of mottled marble and Sadie screamed, her breath coming out in a cloud. She reached out to wrap her arms around her husband, slumping against him as the life left their eyes.

The pair fell to the ground, frost scattering across the floor as their frozen bodies landed with a thump.

Vincent stared in shock for a brief second, then glanced up to Galloway.

Vito lifted his gun, pulling back the hammer.

Vincent waved the gun down. "He's a pincher."

"He is also the enemy," Vito snarled. "And this is war."

Galloway glanced to Corbi, another trickle of blood from his nose. "How long, do you think? How long until your master realizes where your loyalties really lie?"

Corbi's face trembled.

Galloway continued, "That you're secretly plotting his downfall from within?"

Corbi's eyes shifted to Vincent.

"He's using you. His powers." Vincent backed a step away from Corbi, who began lifting his weapon.

"Vincenzo?" Vito scowled, pointing the gun at him.

Galloway smirked. "It's time we ended this. The Charge is mine. The Crew will be soon be a memory."

There was no mistaking it. The moment had come for Vincent to cross the line.

Pinching time, he reached out and plucked the revolver from Corbi's hand. Turning to face Galloway, he pulled the trigger.

The mechanism remained still, the hammer easing through time-frozen space. Vincent pulled in heavy breaths as the weapon lingered in his hand, mid-fire.

Vincent closed his eyes, and restored the flow of time.

The gun fired, the noise roaring through Vincent's ears as the report rattled the wine bottles surrounding him.

When he opened his eyes, he found Galloway slumped against the stairs, a red hole in his forehead, his spectacles split in half.

Corbi blubbered behind him.

As Vincent turned to face the Capo, he found the man rubbing his broad forehead.

Vincent emptied the revolver, spilling the bullets onto the ground before handing the gun back to Corbi.

"It was his power," Vincent said.

Corbi blinked several times and took his weapon.

"He could turn a man's heart against himself."

Vito glanced down to the bodies on the floor. "This…this was Masseria's man?"

"Yes."

"And the woman?"

Vincent sighed. "His wife."

Vito shook his head. "Such a waste."

"Agreed."

The cellar door opened, and footfalls pounded down the stairs, pausing at the bottom.

Lefty held a gun at Galloway's body, lowering it once he was satisfied the man was dead. He nudged Galloway aside as he continued into the cellar.

Vincent nodded to Lefty. "I'm here."

"The Capo?"

Vito cleared his throat. "I live to fight another day."

Lefty strode forward to inspect Vincent.

"I'm fine."

"What happened?" Lefty asked as nudged Jonas with his foot.

"The inevitable," Vincent replied. "Where's Hattie? Is she okay?"

He raced upstairs as Lefty pointed toward the door, heading outside to find a dozen Crew men policing bodies. The fires outside continued to smolder, sending choking smoke into the night sky. Vincent searched room-by-room for Hattie, starting to panic when he couldn't find her. Pushing his way through the double oak doors to the side drive, he finally saw her, arms covered in blood, a series of red scratches across her face.

He stood for a second, nearly passing out from relief. Then he ran, scooping her into his arms and holding her tight.

"What do you know," he muttered. "We survived after all."

"I was so afraid for you." She took his face in her hands. "Next time I'm taking you up on the nookie behind the bar boy-o."

It was a moment of levity before the realization of all they'd lost came crashing back. "Sadie is—"

"I know. I suspected that was the sort of thing she had in mind."

"They joined each other in the end." He shook his head. "I

think she'd gotten through to him. If it hadn't been for Galloway and his sway pinch..."

"Tell me that bastard is dead," she spat.

"He is," Vincent told her. "I only wish I'd killed him earlier. Maybe then Sadie wouldn't be dead."

Hattie's face crumpled and she wept into his chest. He held her close, tears flowed from his own eyes as he pressed his cheek against the top of her head. They'd lost so much in the past few days, lost friends. But they'd survived. It might seem selfish, but right now, that was the most important thing in Vincent's mind. They'd survived.

CHAPTER 34

Hattie dabbed powder onto her cheek, hiding the marks Millie had given her as best as she could. She fluffed her hair, then gave herself a little rouge, and a quick touch of color to her lips before regarding herself in the grimy mirror.

"Presentable enough," she muttered to herself.

Taking an envelope from the basin surface, she stepped out of the washroom and into the dark corridor of the Charge warehouse.

Blake stood at the far end of the hall, hands in his pockets.

"Are they downstairs?" Hattie asked.

"Yeah," Blake replied. "Everyone's waiting."

"See you down there, then."

Blake nodded, then blinked out of the corridor, popping into the center room downstairs.

Hattie trod down the stairs as several eyes rose to greet her. Vincent was sitting on the edge of a table near the front door, hat in his hands, a mysterious smile on his face. The Mullinses, the family of four from Nag's Head, gathered in a clutch near the sofas. Blake leaned against the far wall cross-armed. Just past the sofas stood Charley, beard trimmed and face washed. She glanced down to the final figure seated on the sofa.

Maria turned in her seat to watch as Hattie made her entrance.

Nodding to each of them, she made her way to stand in front of the blacked-out window of the main room before lifting the envelope.

"I have news from Utah. Orson has sent a response to Sadie's last dispatch." She opened the envelope, fingers reaching past the note to slide a few photographs free. "All is well in Eden."

The Mullinses smiled, the father releasing a held breath.

Hattie handed the photos to Blake. "He sent some photos as proof. Pass them around. You'll find clean, happy faces, nice tidy homes, and plenty of food on the table."

She waited for the photos to make their rounds before continuing.

"I know things seem uncertain right now. Sadie built the Charge up from the bones. And though there is no rite of succession, or whatever you'd call it, I feel as if her call—her charge—is also mine. I intend to continue Sadie's work here, to save free pinchers from falling into the hands of the mob. We know there is a safe place to send them, and we shall restore our arteries to the west."

Hattie glanced over to Maria. "This fight has cost us dearly. But it hasn't killed us. We persist. And we'll continue to do so as long as any of us draw breath." She looked around, making eye contact with each of them. "This is about life. Not just survival, but quality of life. Our bonds one to another are what give us that quality. We must treat one another as more than just allies. We are family, all pinchers. Like a family, we'll have our spats. We'll break each other's hearts. But our duty will be to one another, no matter what happens. That's my pledge to you. I hope you feel the same."

Hattie stepped toward Maria, extending a hand. "Are you with us?"

Maria peered up at Hattie, then nodded as she shook Hattie's hand.

Charley's decision to spare her made Maria the sole survivor out of Galloway's crew, and she seemed to appreciate what that meant to her.

"Right," Hattie said with a clap of her hands. "Blake and Charley. You two ready to hit the road?"

Blake nodded. "Got the Studey fueled up already."

"Good. Charley, you'll take the Mullinses to the B&O at Cumberland. Once they're off, you're free to go with Blake to Zanesville."

Charley gave Hattie a hug and turned to gather his things.

The Mullinses shuffled forward as Blake slipped out after Charley. They offered thanks in several variations. Hattie gave them as much assurance as she could that they'd have a safe and easy journey to Utah, knowing that she could only vouch for the destination. The dangers between the start and end remained, but at least there would be no band of rogue pinchers to grab them along the way.

When Charley, Blake and the Mullins family had departed, Vincent hopped off the table to join Hattie and Maria.

Maria stood up, straightening her clothing. "I suppose now's as good a time to apologize as any."

Vincent chuckled. "I think I liked you better when you were doom and gloom."

Maria smirked. "All I ever wanted was the right to live like anyone else. Galloway promised me that would happen."

Hattie said, "Perhaps it will, one day. But it's naïve to think it'll happen anytime soon."

"If he'd won, Galloway would never have trusted any of you," she muttered. "I don't know why you trust me now."

"Because we're not him," Hattie replied. "There are plenty of rooms upstairs. You're free to stay if you're willing to help us in our mission."

Maria nodded slowly and shuffled off up the stairs, leaving Hattie alone with Vincent.

"So, boy-o. Where do you stand now?" she asked.

"With you? You tell me."

"I know where you stand with me. I mean with the Crew."

"Ah." He nodded thoughtfully. "Galloway got into Vito's head. I'm not sure how much of that stuck. If any of it did, I might be in trouble."

"Will you have any warning?"

"I still have Lefty," he said. "And the Crew's been cut in half. There's rebuilding to do, and I think a good number of them trust me and are loyal to me at this point. Plus with New York still a threat, I don't think Vito would move against me now—even if he knows what I'm up to. He still needs me."

She traced a finger down his shirt. "He's not the only one."

Vincent smiled, then slipped his hat back onto his head. "You gonna be okay running this operation?"

"Time will tell, I suppose. Which reminds me. I have an appointment to make."

"What sort of appointment?"

"Old business. New business. A little of both."

Vincent shrugged. "I'll leave you to it, then."

She kissed him, then grinned as she wiped her lipstick from his mouth. "Fontainebleau? Tomorrow night?"

"I'm buying the first round," he said with a wink. "You can pick up the next, big shot.

* * *

Morning sunlight bathed Locust Point in a brilliant yellow glow. A light fog rose off the water, drifting between buildings and rolling over the street before it boiled off into the warming spring weather. A lone car chugged up the street, sweeping into the parking pad in front of Lizzie Sadler's warehouse. A finely-decked woman stepped out, garbed in a conservative dark brown dress and fur-lined coat. A matching mink cap covered dark brunette curls spilling over the coat collar.

As the woman approached the warehouse, the door slid open to reveal Lizzie Sadler. She offered the woman a stiff-lipped grin.

"Ms. O'Toole?"

The woman extended a gloved hand to shake. "Call me Brigid."

As Lizzie beckoned her to step into the warehouse, Hattie searched the emptied space for Raymond. She spotted him lingering in Lizzie's office, peering in confusion at this stranger marching into the building.

Lizzie had a series of papers spread out over two barrel heads, leftovers from the last run of hooch that had left the warehouse two days ago.

"Would you like to take a look around?" Lizzie offered. "Before we look over the paperwork."

Hattie waved off the comment. "No need." She rounded her Americanized brogue into something more similar to her mother's Old World accent. "It's the land I'm interested in more than the building."

With a nod, Lizzie led her to the barrels.

"Deed to the property is filled out with a bill of sale. Here's last year's tax assessment. There's a littoral easement to the city, but I've never used the property's waterfront for anything other than fishing."

Hattie gave Lizzie a stiff, formal smile through her illusion-draped face. "I don't care much for fishing."

She reviewed the documents of sale, taking her time so that Lizzie felt confident this Brigid O'Toole was a disinterested businesswoman. After sufficient perusal, Hattie reached into her clutch to produce a bank check. She handed the check over to Lizzie, who received it with a conflicted expression.

"Employees?" Hattie asked as if an afterthought.

"Hmm?"

"Are there employees I must retain?"

Lizzie nodded to the office. "I have two. I've spoken to each privately about this transaction. Both are willing to stay on with you…what was your business again?"

"Imports," Hattie replied.

Lizzie leaned in. "Well, I have a man who owns a boat. Between you and me, he's one you definitely want to keep." She added with a lift of her hand to cup her face. "He is black. I hope that's not a problem?"

"Not for me," Hattie replied. "May I meet him?"

Lizzie gathered the paperwork and led Hattie back to the office. "The other employee isn't here at the moment, but I'm sure you'll be able to speak to her in the next day or two. Her address is in the file if you want to send her a message to come in."

Hattie made a noncommittal noise in response.

Raymond held the door open for them and the pair strode into the office.

"Raymond Bowles, you'll be pleased to meet Ms. Brigid O'Toole."

Raymond nodded, hands behind his back. "Miss."

Lizzie sat behind her desk, pulling her stamp and notary book from the desk drawer. "Ms. O'Toole has offered to keep you on, Raymond. I didn't speak on your behalf, so you two should probably discuss that between you."

Raymond's face betrayed a moment's relief. "That'll be fine, miss."

"Very well, then," Hattie replied. "Will forty cents per hour suffice, Mr. Bowles?"

Raymond's eyes widened, and his posture straightened. "Uh…that's just, ah. That'll be fine."

Hattie nodded once, glad he couldn't see her smirk behind the illusion. She'd just nearly doubled his pay with one off-hand comment.

Lizzie finalized the paperwork and gathered her things, emptying the last drawer.

Hattie waved a hand. "Oh, no need to vacate this very moment."

"Nonsense," Lizzie said. "I've been moving out for a week, now."

The two women stepped back into the warehouse. Lizzie took a moment to look around, eyes filled with memories. "My husband bought this place almost ten years ago," she said. "It's treated me well."

Hattie smiled. "I hope for the same luck, then."

Lizzie chuckled. "Aim higher, Ms. O'Toole. My luck hasn't been what I'd call top-shelf."

Raymond stepped out of the office.

Lizzie approached, tapping him on the arm. "So, here we are."

"Ms. Sadler, I sure do hate to see you go."

"Oh, I'll be around. Spending most of my time down in warmer climes, but I'm keeping the house in the city."

"Well, alright then."

Lizzie nodded. "I'm probably going to catch a train south tomorrow morning. If I don't see Hattie before then, tell her

I'm sorry I didn't get to say goodbye. Then tell her it's her own damn fault for not showing up to work this morning."

Raymond sighed. "I will."

"Well, time to get a wiggle on. You take care of that baby, Raymond."

Lizzie tucked her paperwork under her arm and gave Hattie one more handshake.

"Best of luck," Lizzie said before marching for the open warehouse door and taking her final exit.

Once her car had cranked up and had driven away, Hattie turned to Raymond.

"So, Mr. Bowles," she said, maintaining the illusion that had begun to eat away at her guts. "I don't suppose you know a good place to get a drink?"

He shifted uncomfortably on his feet. "Well, uh, miss… I don't know much about the city."

Hattie laughed, and released the illusion.

Raymond's eyes widened in alarm, then narrowed in anger. "Well, what now? What're ya doin'?"

Hattie shrugged off a shiver as the light pinch dissipated. She hoisted the deed to the Locust Point warehouse into the air. "I'm buying Lizzie out, is what I'm doing."

Raymond shook his head. "What was all that? I…you had me thinkin'…"

"I know. It was for Lizzie's sake. I can't very well march in here with a big fat check without her getting complicated about all of't."

Finally, a smile broke out across Raymond's face. "You really bought this place?"

"With Lizzie moving into oil and hot-footing it to the Gulf of Mexico, I got the place for a song."

He released a thunderous laugh, then abruptly stopped as his eyebrows lifted. "Wait, now. That business about forty-cents an hour…"

"I meant it," Hattie replied. "And listen. We're keeping the boat-legging business. That won't change. But I'm going to need to fill you in on some modifications I'll be making."

He nodded and took a seat atop one of the barrel heads as Hattie laid it out for him. He'd be in charge of the booze runs, with an extra pair of hands around to lug the crates and barrels now that Hattie had the Charge to take care of. And with Charley coming on board, the warehouse would become a front for the Charge's pipeline of free pinchers. Moving people over the water would help keep the Crew's eyes elsewhere.

Raymond took the news well, eyes still calculating the changes his increased income would provide for his family. Once he'd signed on to help the Charge, he reached up behind the ceiling partition of the office to pull out a bottle of pear brandy he'd squirreled away. Pulling the cork from the bottle, he lifted it to Hattie.

"Here's a toast, baby girl. To you bein' the boss, and me bein' in charge."

He took a swig and handed it to Hattie.

She swallowed a belt of brandy, the hooch warming her gut, and a sense of irrepressible hope spreading through her chest.

CHAPTER 35

A seven-piece band belted out a bouncy West Coast tune as a handful of young people danced along in the lounge of the Old Moravia Hotel. Cigarette smoke wafted to the high ceiling, spilling out into the lobby as Vincent and Lefty strolled with clacking footsteps against the terrazzo floor.

"The Capo all settled in?" Vincent asked.

"Penthouse suite. His usual."

"How long you think until they rebuild the vineyard?"

Lefty shrugged. "If he does. I don't see him moving out of the hotel. I'd lay short dollars he'll cotton to the city beat."

They took a seat at the bar. Tony approached from the windows, sipping his club soda and lime. "You partaking this evening, gentlemen?"

Lefty lifted a finger. "Sangiovese."

Vincent shook his head. "Got a date tonight. Not getting greased up beforehand."

Tony snickered. "You and that Malloy girl make a couple."

"Coupla misfits," Lefty muttered.

"Thanks, and go to hell," Vincent told the pair of them.

Tony stepped behind the bar to pour Lefty a glass of red wine, then set the bottle on the bar top. As the bartender rushed to collect it, Tony tossed a couple dollars onto the bar.

"Leave it. For my friend."

Lefty saluted Tony. "You're a gentleman and a scholar."

"Yeah, yeah," Tony grumbled. "Anyways, you two gonna be here for the meet tomorrow?"

"What meet?" Vincent asked.

"Sabella's riding in to talk shop with the Capo. Bringing that creep with him. I forget his name."

"Arnoud," Vincent replied. "Gotta be Arnoud you're describing."

"Yeah, him."

"Can we get a preview?" Lefty asked. "What's the conversation?"

Tony leaned in to lower his voice. "Word around the campfire is that Masseria's plan backfired big time. He wasted his best pincher and a good dozen men playing us. In the meantime, Maranzano smells blood in the water. He's got himself a new pincher about as bad as O'Donnell. Some glass pincher who's tearing his men into ribbons."

Vincent and Lefty exchanged glances.

"Yeah," Vincent muttered, "I can vouch for that."

Lefty asked, "You think Vito and Sabella are game for a unified front?"

Tony shrugged. "Our boys play nice out on the beat. We got no problems to the south. Why not? With the New York war winding down, we're gonna want friends close by."

"Thanks, Tony," Lefty said, taking a sip of wine.

Tony nodded and slapped their backs, wandering back to the lounge and a lithe young woman with bobbed blonde hair who was giving him an interested smile. Vincent watched as Tony sidled up next to her. The two were on the dance floor within minutes.

"Looks like Tony's bounced back quick," Vincent said.

"His old flame outta the picture?" Lefty asked.

"Yeah. She's sold off and blown town."

"Wasn't she one of our freelancers? The one Miss Malloy worked for?"

Vincent nodded. "Looks like she's moving into oil, now."

"Malloy?"

"No, Sadler."

Lefty eyed Vincent. "And what about Miss Malloy, then? Is she looking for work?"

Vincent smirked. "Not with the Crew she's not."

Lefty shrugged. "Maybe that's for the best." He contemplated his wine, swirling it in the goblet with deliberation. "We talked not long ago about shooting straight, you and I."

"Yeah?"

"I'm not here to say it's so or it isn't, but I just wonder how it is you had all these pinchers suddenly at your beck and call. It's not an accusation. Just an observation."

Vincent looked away. "They were rogues. All working for this Galloway."

Lefty leaned in to whisper, "I ain't blind, you mook. I know O'Donnell's wife wasn't no part of Galloway's crew. And I know she and Miss Malloy were familiar. Which made you and her familiar. Then there's that man-animal thing I saw fighting along with all of you."

Vincent's jaw tightened.

Lefty concluded, "You got secrets. You kept them from me, and from the Capo. Some secrets I get. Who you're sleeping with, who's buying your booze. That's none of mine. But when you start talking about free pinchers in Baltimore, that becomes Vito's business in a big damn hurry."

Vincent turned to face the other man. "Listen…people will get hurt if Vito catches wise."

"You think I don't know that? I put enough of this together on my own. What we were marching into over in Waynesboro? Your complete lack of surprise in Gettysburg? You had a plan all the way." Lefty jabbed a finger into Vincent's arm. "And you made me a part of that plan. Not a partner. A piece on the board. I don't like being your pawn, Vincent."

"I was in a tight spot."

Lefty shook his head. "So, I'm guessing the days of shooting straight are over?"

"I don't see it that way."

"How do you see it, then? You get to lie to me, but I gotta show all my cards to you? So that you can keep your pincher friends free and clear from the Crew? That involves me. What's worse? It's *using* me." He finished his wine. "I didn't sign up for that."

Vincent turned to face Lefty fully, looking into the man's eyes. "I'm not trying to use you, Lefty. I think maybe you're my one true friend in the whole world outside of Hattie. And you protect me all the time. I guess I'm doing the same, too. There's things out there that are bigger than the Crew and the Capo and all this."

"You're protecting me, huh?"

"Yeah. And I got others I'm trying to protect, too. I guess the truth's getting in the way of all that. So, I have to choose who I talk to about what."

Lefty frowned. "It don't bother me so much that maybe you're not on my side, anymore. What bothers me is that you don't trust me."

"I do!"

"Do you?"

Vincent closed his mouth and lowered his eyes. It was a

good question. Lefty was Crew. He could never truly trust Lefty with the full truth of the Charge, or of Hattie and the Hell pincher. It would only lead to one or all of them dead.

Vincent turned away and they sat in silence for a while.

"Maranzano's not coming away as clean as Tony thinks," Lefty finally said.

"How's that?"

"Lucky Luciano's been in the wings, waiting for something like this."

Vincent nodded. "I guess we'll see if Betty Sharp or Floresta ends up on top."

"As long as they don't end up on the same team."

Vincent winced at the thought, then checked his watch and slid off his seat. "I gotta make my date."

"Send my regards to Miss Malloy," Lefty said.

Vincent nodded and walked off.

Before he made it out of the lounge, Lefty called, "Vincent?"

The other man stood and buttoned his jacket. "If can't be straight with me, then there might come a time when I'm not there for you. Do you understand?"

A wave of dread flooded Vincent's chest. He nodded once, then turned to leave.

As Vincent walked across the downtown toward the Fontainebleau a knot twisted in his chest. He'd come to rely on Lefty being there for so long. Lefty was his security. His one friendly face in the Crew. Though times had changed, with Vito sniffing out Vincent's true loyalties he'd need more friends than ever before.

And now Lefty had just put him on notice. When it came down to it, would Lefty choose the Crew over him?

A storm cloud filled Vincent's thoughts even as he pushed his way into the Fontainebleau. The old piano jangled as a husky voice lifted over the crowd, the tune and the singer bringing him out of his funk just a little.

He searched the room for Hattie, table by table, peering over the young faces sipping gin and nodding to the music.

Finally, he found her.

Hattie stood beside the piano, decked in that gold dress with the crystals, the one that stopped short of her knees. Her eyes were done in smoky tones. Gloves rose up her arms, her fingertips brushing the piano as she sang.

A smile danced in the corners of her lips as she spotted him.

And he stood there, unable to look away.

* * *

**Don't miss book 5, Trouble Boys. Sign up for new release alerts at https://debradunbar.com/white-lightning/

ACKNOWLEDGMENTS

A huge thanks to our copyeditor Kimberly Cannon whose eagle eyes catch all the typos and keep Debra's comma problem in line, and to Damonza for cover design.

Special thanks to all our readers who have individually followed us to Hel and back, and enthusiastically cheered us on during our first collaborative project. May there be many more ahead!

Debra and J.P

ABOUT THE AUTHORS

Debra lives in a little house in the woods of Maryland with her sons and two slobbery bloodhounds. On a good day, she jogs and horseback rides, hopefully managing to keep the horse between herself and the ground. Her only known super power is 'Identify Roadkill'.

A Louisiana native, J.P. relocated to the vineyards and cow pastures of Central Maryland after Hurricane Katrina, where he lives with his wife and son. During the day he commutes to the city of Baltimore, a setting which inspires much of his writing.

For more information:
www.debradunbar.com/white-lightning or
J.P. Sloan's Author page
Debra Dunbar's Author page

Imp Forsaken
Angel of Chaos
Kingdom of Lies
Exodus
Queen of the Damned
The Morning Star

* * *

<u>Half-breed Series</u>
Demons of Desire
Sins of the Flesh
Cornucopia
Unholy Pleasures
City of Lust

* * *

<u>Imp World Novels</u>
No Man's Land
Stolen Souls
Three Wishes
Northern Lights
Far From Center
Penance

* * *

<u>Northern Wolves</u>
Juneau to Kenai
Rogue

Winter Fae

Bad Seed